Guardian

A Guardian's World Book

Steve Allanson

The Devil hath power to assume a pleasing shape.

William Shakespeare

Chapter 1 – Beginnings.

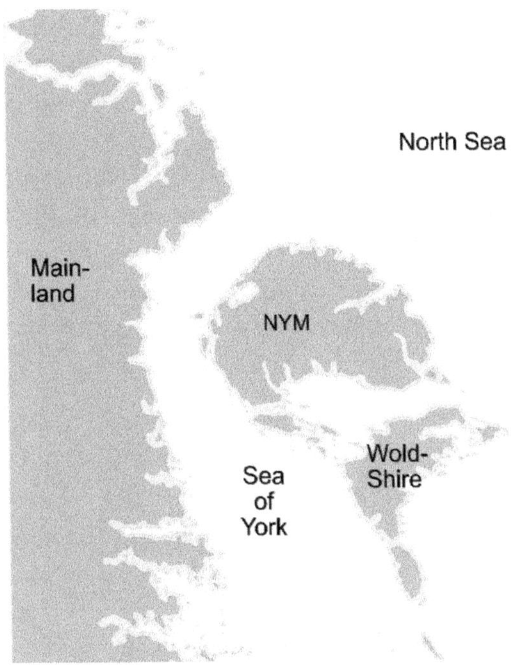

Nadya pulled her knees up close under her chin, folding her arms around them as if to pull herself into the smallest ball possible. The sunset coloured the evening sky with russet hues, which, just for one single moment, matched exactly the colour of her hair as she gazed across the inland sea. The sound of the gentle lapping of the waves on the rocky foreshore, and the low voice of the nearby sheep, was punctuated by the tap-tapping of her friend Layna as she hammered home the last few nails of the fence they had just repaired.

The two of them had toiled all day to replace the ancient timbers, which had rotted and finally given way in the recent storm. They had been lucky to spot the break before the sheep took advantage and gained access to the carrot field beyond the fence. Good food was not plentiful enough to have it wasted, and, after all, waste was one of the many things they needed to minimise to remain free of The Guardian. Nadya and Layna had been careful to straighten the rusted, used nails and reuse them to fix the replacement timbers. Nadya knew they had a small store of bright new ones and that more, from the foundries and workshops in Nym, could be traded for food, but that could, in a bad year, mean less food for the family and workers, so reusing the old ones made a deal of sense.

Now, with only the last few nails to hammer, she had left Layna to it and had come to sit in one of her favourite places, looking down the steep slope to the rocky shore below. She loved this spot, especially at the end of the day. Soon the light of the sun would fade entirely, and then she would be able to make out the lights from the mainland far away as they were reflected in the clouds above She could not imagine how many candles or lamps it must take to create the glow that could reach all the way to the sky and, indeed, to reach her as she sat on the fallen trunk of an old beech and wondered. She knew that most of her family and friends would give an involuntary shudder and make the sign of the crossed fingers to ward off misfortune when they saw those lights, but for Nadya, the fear of the mainland and The Guardian was tempered slightly by a curiosity which nagged at her like the itch from a horsefly bite.

Away to the other side of this field, the road curved sharply before dropping down onto the shore and beyond. There were still remnants of the road to be found on the short beach itself and, if she looked carefully, she knew she could make out its traces as the road disappeared into the depths. What must it have been like, she thought, to have travelled down that hill and away across the old, submerged vale towards the cities of the mainland? Now, the vale was deep under the Sea of York, and the mainland was a place of mystery and dread that grandmas used to frighten children who would not go to bed.

"If you don't climb into bed now and turn out the lamp, the mainlanders will see your light, and The Guardian will come to take you," they would intone, coaxing their charges into their beds.

Of course, the children wouldn't have the knowledge or wit to question why the lights of the adults in the farmhouse kitchen or the common room wouldn't attract the mainlanders, the servants of The Guardian, as they were called.

Nadya turned back towards where her friend was finishing off and called to her.

"Layna, have you ever wondered what powers the lights over the sea there?" she asked, but there was no reply.

"Layna, can you hear me?" she called more loudly, but still there was no reply.

She stood and walked the short distance to where she could see Layna was bending over and peering at something in the undergrowth below the post she had been working on.

"This post is loose somehow," said Layna as Nadya approached. "I can't work out why. It seems as if the post hasn't been sunk properly and is only a few inches into the ground."

"Let's have a look," Nadya replied, and knelt down beside Layna.

She could see what Layna meant; the post was clearly loose in the damp ground and moved at its base with only the slightest of shoves.

"Well, it's going to be dark soon, so there's nowt we can do about it tonight," she said after a brief inspection. "I'll come back tomorrow morning with a spade and see what I can do."

"For now, though, we should be going; it's a fair walk for both of us over the fields."

With that, the two friends picked up the well-worn tools they had been using and set off across the field and up the hill. At the top, after passing through a creaking field gate, they parted ways, Layna down the lane towards the row of workers' cottages by the old road, and Nadya in the other direction towards the main farmhouse. Woldshire was an agricultural country organised around age-old land wardenship, with farm owners who had been in possession of the land for many generations. The relationship between farm owner and worker, though, was one of cooperation and sharing of the produce of their combined labours rather than exploitation. There were differences in wealth amongst the population, but these differences were small. Although, nominally, Nadya was in charge, the pair rarely thought of this distinction between them. Nadya's father had raised her to understand that they, the Knowles, were privileged to be in the position of farm owner but that they were in no way superior to those who worked with them to produce the food they all needed to live.

One of the things they had been taught in school was the effects of the "Great Melt", as it was known. Nadya knew that whilst the world's climate had changed dramatically and, indeed, some places had become much hotter, even uninhabitable, here in the UK and its islands, the warming had been countered by a cooling effect. This, she had learned, was because a tremendous sea current, which used to carry warm water and air from the south, had faltered when the ice caps melted, and as a result, when the climate had finally settled into the new stable regime, this part of the world was largely unchanged in terms of temperature. Winter was still winter and could be bitterly cold, although snow was uncommon throughout the region. She was aware that millions of people had died of starvation, storms and floods, or fighting during the transition and the mass migrations, but that the people here were lucky, in the end, to live in a climate still compatible with human life and society. During the transition, there had been a great number of storms which had done considerable damage to life and property but, again, although the warmer climate did make for more storms, these were now largely located in other areas. There were still periods of severe weather around Woldshire, and some could be very destructive. Life, though, could largely continue as it had for centuries before the warming.

Nadya walked briskly in the growing gloom and chill. This late in the year, the evenings were short and the nights increasingly cool and damp. She thought with pleasure of the warm fires and lamplight waiting for her in the farmhouse. She also anticipated the filling evening meal; her mother was a good cook and made the most of the seasonal foods available. Maybe this evening she would have made a rich and tasty lamb stew with some of her speciality herb dumplings - simple fare but tasty and satisfying after a long day's work. Nadya's mouth watered as she thought of this, and she smiled with pleasure as she visualised the chatter and banter that would entertain the family at the table. Her brothers would tell of their day's work with the stock, and her father would no doubt have an anecdote or two from the market, where he had taken a couple of young heifers to sell. Nadya would also tell of the work she had done that day, but something made her want to keep the story of the loose fence post to herself. She felt there was some small mystery to be discovered there, and she wanted to own it for a while at least.

To go with the talk and the meal, there would be beer from the cellar, and perhaps her mother would take a glass of the deep purple damson wine she so enjoyed. As a young lady of the house, Nadya knew she should follow her mother's lead, but she was more drawn to a good mug of the rich brown ale.

As she came over the last rise of the chalk hills before the lane down to the farmyard, she saw the lights burning brightly in the house, and she thought again of the lights across the sea. She wondered, once more, what lamps could burn so brightly that they shone all the way to the clouds, and what lives the people must lead who could master such things. Would they gather around the table and share tales of the day, or did they have other wonders to entertain them? There was that itch again, but even for Nadya, the thought of crossing the Sea of York to find out such things filled her with fear, although that fear also brought a shiver of excitement. She knew that, in the far past, Woldshire and Nym had been part of a single country with the land over the sea, but that the Great Melt had caused the sea to engulf the land in between, and that this had provided her people with a barrier between themselves and the dominance of The Guardian. She had been taught that the people of the mainland were slaves to whatever The Guardian was, and that the people of Woldshire and Nym had been lucky to escape and live free these last five hundred years. She had once asked her father why they couldn't sail over the sea, but he had been reluctant to talk of it, only muttering vague hints of impassable currents and dangers from things sunk beneath the waves. Woldshire folk didn't venture more than a few hundred metres from shore, just enough to catch a few fish or octopus for the table and even that was only in the east, so Nadya had no personal experience of boats. The only vessel of any consequence, and of which Nadya had knowledge, was the ferry which wound its way between the islands from the northwest town of North Grimston, past Westow and Whitwell islands, and on to Howard's Mull on Nym.

These musings had occupied Nadya for the length of time it took to walk down the lane, and she now crossed the muddy yard, took off her boots, and pushed open the heavy green door which led into the farm kitchen. Immediately, all thoughts of boats and other lands were swept from her mind by the happy call of welcome from her mother and the deeply tempting scent of herbs and meat simmering on the stove.

Nadya's mother, Meena, was still a beautiful woman in her mid-forties, slim, with long, wavy, flaming red hair which was, as usual, tied in a ponytail that hung nearly to her waist down her slender back. Her eyes were bright and green and shone with intelligence and warmth. She wore a simple outfit of a brown skirt with a white short-sleeved blouse. Clothes in Woldshire were functional first and attractive second, but her mother was a skilled needlewoman and made most of the clothes the family wore, helped, of course, by the women of the workers' families. Such endeavours tended to be communal ones, and the clothes the Knowles wore were not much different from those of their workers. Maybe they had a few pieces of lace or a small area of embroidery, but the similarities far outweighed the differences.

Just as she did on her return every day, Nadya gave her mum a huge hug before heading off to the wet room to wash away the dirt of toiling on the farm. She liked to get there before the men returned so that she could be out of their way and changed into her evening wear - not dissimilar from that worn by her mother - before they were all called to the table. This also gave her a short time on her own in her room to read or just to daydream. Weekdays, especially at this time of year with its relatively short days, tended not to yield much time for leisure, so that just a half hour of her own company was precious to Nadya. Once dinner was finished and the things washed and cleared away, there might be a family conference about some aspect of their lives, or Nadya might chat briefly to her father, brothers, or mother, but she would be asleep well before ten p.m. worn out by the day's work.

On this particular evening, after they had all eaten their fill of a delicious stew and freshly baked bread, the talk was all of the storm and the damage it had caused. John, Nadya's father, was pleased she had spotted the broken fence and had repaired it before any harm was done. Nadya climbed into her bed still with a faint glow of pride that she had been praised in front of her mother and brothers. She thought again briefly of the lights over the sea and of the post she would investigate in the morning, before being joined by Layna for another day of scouring the boundaries for further damage. Within minutes, though, she was asleep and snoring gently.

At just 19 years old, Nadya was the youngest of the family and was the second of the two natural children of John and Meena. The eldest was Nat, a strong, handsome man, now in his late twenties. Nat was a natural farmer, he seemed almost to be born of the land, especially with his ruddy red mop of hair - darker than the bright red of Nadya's — which so closely resembled the colour of the rich clay soil. The second son, only a few months younger than Nat, was Jeff. He had been adopted by John and Meena as a boy after his parents died in a terrible blaze which destroyed their house one night. Jeff and Nat were great friends, and he had been staying over at the farm on that dreadful night. Although there was no blood relationship between the two families and, as there didn't seem to be any close relatives remaining to look after the boy, they had readily agreed to take on the responsibility and had raised him as one of their own. Jeff was dark haired and much slighter than Nat, he was blest with a sharp and ready wit and would often have the whole family laughing until they cried. Nadya loved them all deeply, her family seemed to her like a favourite blanket wrapped around her, keeping her warm and safe.

She woke as the first light began to creep in through the sides of the thick, dark curtains covering her window. The sun would be up in an hour or so, and Nadya wanted to be on her way back to the loose fence post by then. She washed and dressed quickly in her work clothes: stout leather trousers and a stiff but thick and warm chequered overshirt over her workaday blouse. Apart from the sturdy but comfortable working boots she would don only as she left the house, thick brown socks completed the outfit. Thus attired, she went down into the kitchen, where her mother was already preparing the breakfast meal. Her brother, stepbrother, and father would have porridge and then a plate of bacon, black pudding, and eggs with bread, but Nadya was satisfied with a large bowl of the creamy, unctuous porridge with a good spoonful of damson jam to further sweeten it. A large mug of hot, sweet hop tea accompanied this and, before the sun had climbed over the eastern hills, she was striding along the lane, back towards the spot where she had finished work with Layna the day before. The walk didn't take long, and just after sunrise, Nadya was once again standing by the loose post.

She moved it to one side, managing to flex the rails so that she could get the bottom of the post clear of the hole and give herself room to explore. After clearing a small amount of the rich brown earth from the hole, she could see that the problem was a rock in the bottom. Thinking that the loose post may well have caused the partially rotted rail timbers to come adrift, she wanted to get it much more firmly secured. She didn't want to be back here again after the next storm, or the next, replacing rails again or, worse, retrieving the sheep from a denuded carrot field. She took the spade and widened the hole until she found the edges of the rock. It was about half a metre across, but when she dug down around it, she found it was almost flat and only a few centimetres deep. Having cleared away all the earth, she was easily able to prise it loose with the spade and remove it entirely.

In everyone's life, there are moments when, looking back later, they will wonder, "What if?". The next few seconds were just such a moment for Nadya. Throughout her later life, she would often ponder what would have happened if she had acted differently. If she could have seen all that was to flow from what she did next, would she have done the same?

Under the rock, she was surprised to find a large, bluish container, around twenty centimetres by thirty centimetres and fifteen deep. This appeared to be made of the old oilplas which was so common in the days before the flood and the self-imposed isolation of the people of Woldshire. There were still pieces of this, large and small, to be found, but they were mostly useless fragments. This container appeared to be intact, although the 'plas had become a little brittle with age. Nadya could feel that it was filled with something, but not something heavy enough to be wet soil or water. She could lift it easily, and removing it from the hole, she decided to hide it in the undergrowth to be examined more closely later. She knew all such things should be reported to the council, but surely it would be ok to explore the container first before handing it over. With a frisson of excitement tinged with guilt, she set about hiding the box.

She had just covered her discovery with loose bracken when Layna appeared, walking briskly across the field to join her. Quickly loosening the earth in the bottom of the hole to conceal where the box had been, she set about removing the rails from the post to replace it with a longer one they could set more deeply into the earth and make it more secure.

"Good morning, Layna," shouted Nadya to her friend, "You're just in time to help me put a new post in here. I found what the problem was, just look at the size of that lump of rock there."

Layna looked at the rock with surprise. Pieces of chalk were all too common in Woldshire, regularly unearthed as they ploughed in the late autumn for the winter wheat or in the spring. This was something different, almost like a piece of flagstone often found in cottage floors. Why would such a thing be found in the open fields, she wondered. But being practical, she simply said, "So now we can put a deeper post on, and the fence will be much stronger here. I wonder why they didn't just get the stone out when they first put up the fence?"

Nadya thought she knew why - the whole thing, rock and short post, had been put in place to hide the oilplas box. What she didn't know was what had been concealed in the box, but she intended to find out later.

"I don't know, but let's put it right now, shall we? Go and fetch a new post from the stack we made in the field corner while I deepen the hole," she said. "We'll get this done and get on with the rest of the fence around this field before lunch, then we'll move on to the top field. Dad says there's a few damaged rails there too."

The two young women soon completed this task and spent the rest of that day repairing gaps in the other field and making it fit to put the sheep in again. Early in the afternoon, Nadya announced that they could finish early today, and Layna didn't wait to be told twice, hurrying off home to enjoy a few hours of unexpected freedom. She was going to heat some water and have a long soak in the tub before her own family got back from the day's work. There was a dance coming up at the weekend, and a chance of a bit of pampering beforehand would help her look her best.

Nadya waved farewell to her and hurried back to her find. With luck, she would be able to sneak it into the house and up to her room while her mother was out feeding the hens. She retrieved the box from the undergrowth and set off towards the farmhouse, climbing quickly back to the lane and along to where she could see the farmyard. Here she paused, looking to see if her mother was out of the house. Seeing that indeed, as expected, she was tending to the hens, Nadya hurried down, through the gate, across the yard, and into the house. Once inside, she quickly climbed the stairs to her room and hid the box amongst her clothes in the wardrobe, then went back downstairs to the kitchen.

Just as she did so, Meena pushed open the heavy farmhouse door and, taking off her muddy boots, entered the room. She looked at Nadya, startled for a moment to find her here already.

"You're home early today," she said to the girl. "Something wrong?"

"Layna wanted to have some time to get herself ready for the dance on Saturday," Nadya replied, not entirely truthfully but not entirely untruthfully either. Even so, a small voice in her head ticked off another deception and tried to remind her that what she was doing was dangerous, not just for herself. The fear of The Guardian was ever-present in their lives.

"So, we decided to work through midday and take an early finish today. We'll work extra hard next week to make up for it."

Sensing her guilt, Meena reassured her daughter.

"You work hard enough, young Nadya, and I can't remember the last time you had a day off, so you don't need to excuse yourself to me, love."

She went on, "There's hot water, as I've had the stove on all day. Why don't you have a soak and get yourself ready for the dance too? It's about time that boyfriend of yours took you more seriously."

Nadya blushed. Although she was aware her mum knew all about Milo, and had indeed known they were a couple for many years, it still sometimes embarrassed her to talk about it. Blowing her a thank you kiss, she ran up the stairs and set about filling the bath with hot water. In her mind, she knew she wouldn't soak for long; she was itching to explore the box. She did wonder just for a moment why she had become so obsessed with her find, but nevertheless, she spent only a short time soaking in the bath. If her mum had known this, she would have frowned, as normally whenever Nadya got the chance, which was rare, she would soak for hours, often topping up the bath several times with fresh hot water if she could. Meena, however, was busy preparing the Friday evening meal, always something a little special as a celebration of the start of the weekend. Not that the weekend on a farm was entirely work-free, but they did tend to do only the essentials for the two days. Besides, as Nadya had said, there was the dance this weekend.

Once Nadya was dried and dressed, she closed the door to her room and took out the blue box and, sitting cross-legged on the floor, gazed at it for several minutes, pondering what it might contain. She was almost reluctant to open it. In a way, the mystery had been what this was all about, and opening the box would end that. She wondered to herself why she felt that way. It was true that she led a somewhat privileged life. She was the daughter of a landowner and would undoubtedly marry the son of another one day and become, like her mother, the matriarch of a family and a wider community of support workers. It had been a long time since there was a serious food shortage in Woldshire, and the weather patterns had long since settled since the Great Melt that brought about the rise of the seas and the flooding of the land. Altogether, she lived in relative comfort. For some time, though, she had felt a rebellious streak rising inside her against the certainty of her future, against the inevitability of becoming a wife, a mother to her allotted two children, and then living out her life as that person. There was something in her that niggled at her mind, wanting something more, something unexpected, even something a little dangerous.

She examined the box slowly and could see that the lid was sealed in place by two levers, one at each end. Now that she could look closely, she observed that the sides were not completely opaque but allowed her to see a little of what was inside. This confirmed that the box was not filled with muddy water, as she might have expected after so long buried in the damp earth. There appeared to be several papers or books and some objects she did not recognise. Would the papers be readable? Would they crumble to dust when the air was allowed inside the box? There was really only one way to find out and, after checking that she still had time before being called down to the Friday meal, she slowly lifted first one lever, then the other. The levers themselves were made of a metal which had not rusted in however long the box had been in the earth, they lifted easily and without breaking. Someone had taken a great deal of trouble to make sure this box survived intact. That it was made of oilplast in itself made it at least five hundred years old, and its survival all that time seemed like a miracle to Nadya, whose daily struggles with the constant degradation of metal and wood were such a major feature of agricultural life in today's Woldshire.

After carefully examining the seal around the lid, she very tentatively lifted one corner. There was an audible hiss as air rushed out of the box. Nadya sniffed carefully but could detect no odour at all in the escaped gas. Inside, she could now see that there was something between the lid and the box which had kept a perfect seal all this time. She lifted the lid the rest of the way and placed it carefully on the floor beside the box itself. Now she could see inside properly. It was clear that the box was divided into three compartments. One comprised a full half of the length, and the other half was divided again across the width to make two smaller, equal-sized compartments. The larger of the three contained papers, two books, two magazines similar to the monthly council magazines but much thicker, slicker, and glossier, and one was filled with bright images. Finally, there was also a folder with more papers inside.

One of the two smaller compartments contained a number of objects, most of which were unfamiliar to Nadya, all made of oilplas. Amongst these were some small models of animals and birds, some of which were easily recognisable as farm animals. Others, Nadya had only seen in the few picture books which showed animals from before the catastrophic change of climate; one she remembered was a tiger, a kind of large striped cat, and one was a white bear. The final compartment contained small booklets of more photographs and some jewellery and other personal items, presumably of the person who put together the box.

Nadya carefully lifted out the two books and opened each one in turn. They were, startlingly, as pristine as if they had been placed in the container only yesterday. The covers were both similar, brown, glossy, and with just the word "Journal" in the centre. The paper of the pages was crisp and white, lined and covered with writing which, although English, contained many words and spellings unfamiliar to Nadya. Each section was headed with a day name and a date. Nadya was familiar with the idea of a journal, but books to write in were a luxury few could afford in her time. Indeed, the time to write down one's daily "doings" was something she felt she could only dream of. The first page was headed with a number, "2080" and, flicking through the book, Nadya could see that there were numerous sections, each headed with a date, and that the dates progressed through several years. The entries weren't daily or even at regular intervals. Maybe they were only made when something important had happened. She would not know until she had time to read through it all.

The voice in Nadya's head was more insistent now. She knew that this was important and should be handed over to the council immediately. Maybe it contained information which would continue to keep Woldshire free from The Guardian and its servants. It might even contain something which would, in the wrong hands, endanger the island. The council, as protectors of Woldshire's continued freedom, kept tight control of all information from before the flood. Nadya ignored the voice. She would, of course, hand in the box, but not yet.

She put the journals carefully aside and looked next at the magazines. One appeared to be densely filled with text with a few illustrations, but the other, much more to her liking, was full of bright images and many fewer words. As she turned the pages of this one, her astonishment grew. Each page was covered with clear, glossy pictures. Many were of young women wearing clothes, the variety and quality of which Nadya had never seen. There were bright dresses of all sorts of styles and an amazing variety of colours, all of which were brighter than anything the weavers made in her time. There were suits of trousers and tops, again in a startling variety of colours and shapes, and there were also pages showing women in underwear, the likes of which she had never imagined would be possible (and which did not look very warm or comfortable). And shoes! Shoes with huge, thin heels and which barely covered the feet of the flawlessly, staggeringly beautiful women wearing them. Shoes with amazing colours and shapes, some even covered with dazzling jewels. Most of them did not look as if they would last an hour in the fields, and many looked decidedly uncomfortable.

Then there were pictures of the insides of houses, each filled with such a multitude of what Nadya assumed were machines, with bright lights and sharp, clean edges and brightly reflective surfaces. Rooms with chairs, sofas, or beds, all of which looked as if they had just been made and had never been sat or laid on. And there were pictures of cars. She knew what cars were from the rusting heaps still to be found scattered around the country, which were a source of highly valued and useful metals, nuts, bolts and screws. In the pictures, though, the cars were all brand new, and, again, dazzlingly bright and often shown running on beautifully smooth black roads, most unlike the tracks and rutted roads which linked the farmsteads and villages of Woldshire.

Nadya was engrossed and did not notice the passing of time as she gazed at page after page of luxuries and beauty she had never imagined, let alone seen with her own eyes. With each passing page, the past took on a more and more glamorous, dazzling aura, and the present seemed less exciting and more rustic.

Her reverie was interrupted by her mother's call, "Nadya, are you coming down for the meal? Can you come and help me set the table, please?"

Nadya quickly packed everything, except the first journal, back into the box and hid it at the back of her wardrobe, behind her hanging clothes. She then covered it with an old blanket, which she carefully arranged to look as if she had casually thrown it in there out of the way. Satisfied that only a careful search would uncover her treasure, she put the journal into the top drawer of her bedside cabinet, under her letters from Milo. She knew no one would disturb those, as everyone knew they were private.

She descended the stairs two at a time, trying to forget what she had seen, and to focus on the Friday evening meal, after which there would be songs. Her father might even regale them with one of his humorous renditions of the goings-on at the last council meeting.

Beneath his serious demeanour, "Da", as she called him, was quite the comedian, in a small way, a performer. He loved being the centre of attention at these Friday gatherings and would have them in stitches for hours as he made jokes about his fellow council members and their discussions. She loved him dearly, and there he was as she entered the kitchen. She threw her arms around his neck and kissed his stubbly cheek as she always did. She could see by the glint in his eyes that she was still his favourite of the family. As usual, he smelled of horse, soil, woodland and meadow. Nadya felt that his presence was one of the most solid, most constant things in her life.

Meena looked across the room at the pair and rolled her eyes.

"Come on, you two, put each other down," she laughed.

She knew that, although John still loved her passionately and unstintingly, she had long ago been usurped from the top position by her daughter, and this was just as it should be. Of course, eventually, Nadya would set up home with Milo and they would have a family of their own. Both parents liked him and approved of their daughter's choice, even if John still maintained a stiff formality towards him at times.

Nadya laughed and let go of her da, moving to help her mother get the table ready for the meal. At that moment, her two brothers returned. Now the whole family were present, and when the men were washed and changed, the evening could begin. As always, the smell from the food, carefully prepared by Meena, was mouth-watering, and Nadya was, for a time, distracted from her guilty secret.

The fire burned brightly in the hearth, and the dark brown beer flowed generously as the evening wore on. The family were fed, and laughter rang out around the room as John told of his last meeting of the council.

"So, Robert walks in with a cow in tow and proceeds to milk the damn thing whilst the meeting is going on, says this one got missed at milking time.

"As usual, he was getting fired up and annoyed at the proceedings, and the more he did, the more the cow got agitated 'til eventually it kicked him clean off his stool, sending the milk all over the floor. The whole place was in uproar, with the cow mooing frantically, Robert cursing and frothing, and Ted banging his gavel and shouting 'Order, order!'"

"A real old-fashioned farce, we should put it on as a play for the midwinter festival."

With that, the whole family dissolved into raucous laughter, and that, it would seem, was the signal for the evening's entertainment to come to an end. The boys headed for their room, John went out to check the animals in the pens, and Meena and Nadya set about clearing the table. Nadya yawned widely as she cleared the plates and cutlery and filled the deep granite basin with water from the faucet. She yawned again as she started to wash, so Meena took pity on her.

"Get yourself off to bed, young Nadya," she said, putting her arm around her shoulder.

"You've had a long day after your early start."

Nadya kissed her mother and gratefully accepted the encouragement to retire, though not entirely because she was tired. She was eager to take a look at that first journal. She climbed the stairs two at a time, quickly undressed, closed her door, and climbed into her bed with the journal. She opened the book and began reading in the soft, warm light of the lamp on her bedside table.

Chapter 2 - Harry. January 1st, 2080.

There was no scream, no cry of despair, no yell of anger, just a dull thud behind me. Immediately, I felt a warm, wet, and sticky substance strike the bare back of my calves and then a piece of cloth attached to a string fell gently over my shoulder. Looking round I was horrified to see the crumpled body of a young man in the centre of a wide splattering of blood and brains. Two things happened in quick succession: first, I felt my stomach heave so that I could not help but add my partly digested breakfast to the mess on the ground, and second, I realised how close the falling body had been to landing on me. My knees buckled, and I slumped to the floor, shaking uncontrollably. I later learned that the cloth, along with several others, had been attached to the man's ankles with strings, the purpose of which was to create drag, ensuring that the body fell headfirst, leaving no chance for the authorities to salvage the brain for experimentation.

That was this morning, just a few short hours ago. It was not the first suicide amongst my close neighbours - such acts of distress are all too common these days - but it was the first time I had witnessed such a thing first-hand.

Whilst I am sure the jottings of just another ordinary man will have no importance in what I perceive to be the slow-motion collapse of our society, I have, nevertheless, decided to keep a record of current events as they unfold. It is hard to be optimistic when one looks back over the last eighty years, but I hope there may be some distant time when the mass of humanity can once again dream of a better future and not be driven in such large numbers to the dreadful end I witnessed today.

Way back in 2020, the encouraging start to the twenty-first century came to an abrupt halt. Sure, there had been crises before this, but, as in the example of the so-called financial crash of 2008, they were largely man-made and not existential in the same way as what followed.

The slow climate change disaster had begun to gather pace, but it had seemed to many that it was still possible that at least the worst effects might be averted. Of course, the politicians talked and talked and did little. The rich saw it as a further opportunity to become even richer, and society split over the issue. However, even with all of that, clean energy generation seemed to be increasing, and there were commitments made by most countries, even the US, to reduce greenhouse gas emissions.

In 2016, Britain voted to leave the EU. This was later discovered to have been partly orchestrated by Russia and was soon followed by their invasion of Ukraine. Putin, the Russian leader, had correctly calculated that the EU was considerably weakened by the departure of the UK, which was itself beginning a downward spiral of reduced importance and influence in the world.

And then, in 2020, the world experienced a respiratory virus pandemic, and this triggered further polarisation in society and a distrust of science. There seemed to be an alignment between climate change denial and those who saw the pandemic as a global conspiracy. Societies across the globe were split, and there was a general move to the right in the politics of most democracies.

There had been ongoing wars and conflicts throughout the twentieth century, and the twenty-first had already seen major outbreaks in Afghanistan, Iraq, Syria, and parts of Africa, but the "western" nations had been largely free of conflict since 1945. This all ended in 2022 when Russia invaded Ukraine, and the ensuing conflict dragged on for ten years. Many people believe the final tipping point came in 2023 when the Israel-Palestine conflict erupted, and the Israeli armed forces set about eradicating Hamas. The cost in innocent lives, though, was huge so that many, particularly on the political left, quickly turned against Israel. Eventually, with more and more countries of the world, even their long stand ally the US, expressing deep concern at the level of casualties, the Israeli Prime Minister and his party were ousted and a difficult and tenuous ceasefire brought about. The EU and US, along with Arab nations, began the long job of rebuilding Gaza and Lebanon.

But it was not to last. Many Palestinians had been radicalised by the scale of destruction so that, with a sense of inevitability, violence erupted again in 2032. This time, in a result long feared by governments and people around the world, a short but deadly exchange of nuclear missiles was unleashed, with massive casualties throughout the region. It is thought that North Korea then saw the world's focus on the middle east conflict, as well as the crossing of the nuclear line, as an opportunity to deal with their South Korean neighbours in a similar way. This, though, was a serious miscalculation and the US retaliated by targeting several North Korean military and nuclear facilities with their own tactical warheads.

The final step in this initial cascade of nuclear exchanges saw Russia, aware that the nuclear threshold had been crossed, use tactical weapons in Ukraine, targeting not just the battlefields, which had remained deadlocked for years, but also Kyiv and Odessa. Only frantic diplomatic activity, led by China, prevented an all-out nuclear war between the US and its allies, and Russia. That war was, thankfully, averted, and peace talks finally began in Ukraine.

The world now held a fragile stalemate for several months, but the nuclear monster had one last blow to deal the world: a significant exchange between India and their old enemy, Pakistan.

The planet now had several major contaminated zones and more than a billion dead. The injured and dying grew, eventually, to nearly two billion, and a mass migration of often seriously ill and contaminated people in desperate need of medical assistance began. Countries across the globe closed their borders and repelled all refugees, seeking to protect their own health resources. In all countries, life expectancy fell sharply, with a major rise in cancers and other diseases. Suicides reached epidemic proportions, and societal cohesion nearly collapsed throughout the world. A further huge shift to the right followed as people voted for more protection against the rising tide of violent crime. In less democratic regions, there were military coups, many of which were welcomed by a tired population, again seeking safety in discipline. The democracies of the US and Europe were eventually effectively suspended, so that by the start of the 2040s, virtually the whole world was under tight authoritarian control. Social media was closed down across the world, something many saw as a benefit, with news and views being strictly controlled by governments.

A clear majority of the population were happy, or at least content, to sacrifice their freedoms and democracy for safety and protection from crime, mass migrations, and war. However, the breaching of the nuclear threshold and its aftereffects was not finished with us yet. I now use the word "us" as I was born in the Northeast of England in 2042 and have seen first-hand much of what came after that.

Initially, the world seemed to have at least settled, and the spasm of destruction ceased, but two things had not been foreseen. Firstly, the right-wing had always been tightly associated with climate change scepticism, and this became the political norm. This was further popularised by the cooling of the atmosphere which followed the nuclear blasts and associated increase in atmospheric dust. All climate change mitigation was effectively halted and reversed. People needed power, and they needed it cheaply, and coal, oil (what remained of it), and gas became, once again, the dominant fuels. For a decade, it seemed that the sceptics were right, and the heating of the atmosphere had stopped and been reversed. But the insidious effects of CO2 levels increasing ever more rapidly and to unprecedented levels were only being masked by the short-term effects of the nuclear dusts. These began to settle in the late 2040s, and, with the atmosphere starting to clear, greenhouse gas-driven global warming returned with a vengeance. Temperatures soared, the climate ran hot, with massive increases in storms, droughts, floods, and wildfires. The Amazon burned to nothing, along with much of southern Europe and large parts of Canada and Australia, and this further increased CO2 levels. Eventually, the ongoing disaster was accelerated by two events scientists had long predicted: the release of large quantities of, even more damaging, methane from Arctic tundra and from methane hydrates under the surface of the deep North Atlantic and elsewhere.

This was the final straw for the environment. The ice sheets of Antarctica and Greenland, as well as all glaciers, were now doomed. The complete melting would now not take thousands of years as had been expected, but a mere few hundred years. The sea level was set to rise by some seventy metres in just those few hundred years. In one final, bizarre, but long-predicted twist for the UK and northern Europe, the inpouring of trillions of litres of fresh water into the North Atlantic Ocean turned off the flow of the North Atlantic Oscillation, commonly known as the Gulf Stream. In consequence, for many decades, northern Europe suffered dramatic cooling, especially in winter, resulting in major food shortages. This was the background to my early life.

As I write this first entry of my journal, the signs of sea level rise are now clear, and coastal areas, towns, and villages have already begun to be periodically overwhelmed. New York, London, Sydney, Wellington, Paris, Oslo, and many others will disappear in just a few decades.

Items of recent news include:

Life expectancy in the refugee camps in Egypt, housing the descendants of refugees from Israel, Iraq, Jordan, Lebanon, and Iran (the few survivors of the short nuclear war of 2032) has fallen to less than forty years. Although aid has increased gradually, after several decades of minimal support, there is still almost no provision for cancer treatment nor for the treatment of birth deformities. Suicide rates are reported as high as thirty percent of those in their thirties.

Researchers report that the Netherlands will cease to be a viable state within fifty years, as flooding events become so frequent that recovery is no longer possible. The Dutch government has responded that it will build more and higher sea defences, with plans for the creation of a range of artificial hills up to two hundred metres high and two kilometres wide. It has asked for international help to source the trillions of tonnes of rock needed for this enterprise.

The Island Nation of the Maldives has been officially abandoned, with the final few inhabitants rescued and relocated to India, after the latest storm surge overwhelmed every island, leaving dozens missing.

Chapter 3 – Milo.

Nadya awoke, as usual, to the sound of the cockerel crowing in the yard outside her window. She had heard this sound every morning of her entire life, and to her, it said "Home" and, more importantly at this time of morning, "Breakfast".

On weekdays, she would quickly wash and put on her work clothes before heading down to eat something in the farmhouse kitchen, but as today was Saturday, she could afford to linger a little longer. Putting on her well-worn but warm and comfortable dressing gown, she brushed her teeth and then went down to the kitchen. Her mother was already there with the kettle boiling on the hearth, tending to a pan from which the wonderful, mouth-watering aroma of frying bacon wafted across the room. Nadya helped herself to two thick slices of fresh brown bread and spread creamy, pale-yellow butter on both, before standing next to Meena and receiving two generous slices of bacon placed on top of one of the slices of bread.

She helped herself to a mug of milk and sat in her customary place to eat and drink. It was normal for her and her mother to be the first to breakfast on Saturdays. During the week, her father and brothers might well be up and long gone before daybreak, but on Saturdays, they too could afford to rise more leisurely. On this day, and Sunday, the only farmwork was to milk the cows and tend the other animals. Even so, they still awoke early. It was now barely seven a.m. but cows didn't wait until late morning and would be hollering loudly if not milked before another hour had gone by. But the cows were men's work, and Nadya could afford to take a few moments to savour the salty meatiness of the bacon "sarnie", which oozed with both the fat from the meat and the melted butter.

Today, she had much to think about from her reading the previous night. She had not understood all of what she had read, but she had got the gist of a world in turmoil, which culminated in the Great Melt that transformed the land and isolated Woldshire and Nym from the rest of Britain.

"Are you seeing Milo tonight?" her mother asked. The two of them often said little during breakfast, each content with the other's quiet company.

Nadya swallowed and replied, "Yes, at the dance. It should be a good one tonight, I think."

After a few more bites, she finished her breakfast, wiped her mouth on a cloth, and got up to go back upstairs.

"I'll go and get dressed and do the hens and pigs, Mum. Will the boys and Da do the sheep and cows, do you think?"

"Aye, I think so, Nadie," Meena replied with a smile. "You can get yourself ready this afternoon."

After a short pause, she continued. "Will you two be making any sort of announcement soon?"

"I can't think what you mean, Mum," said Nadya, laughing. "But seriously, we're happy just being friends at the moment. There's time enough for anything else."

As she spoke, Nadya was pondering whether to share her secret with Milo. He was a good friend, but he was also much more settled with his future in the community than she. He had asked her to marry him several times already, but Nadya felt there was something - or some things - she needed to do before she settled for married life, her two children, and all that would follow. She wasn't at all sure how he would react to her discovery, and particularly to her keeping it secret. She wasn't exactly breaking any laws, as far as she knew, but she knew that her keeping it secret and not handing it on to the council would be viewed badly by most of their neighbours. The fear of the mainlanders and their overlord, The Guardian, remained strong, following the unrest that preceded the isolation of the people of the two islands.

Livestock chores and a quick lunch over, Nadya went back to her room and, telling Meena she was going to do some sewing and get ready for the evening, she reread the first journal entry. She knew about the flooding and how it had changed the world, but she knew little about wars and had no idea what "nuclear weapons" were. She assumed from the narrative that they were something extremely bad, and it seemed clear that they killed a lot of people. She simply could not imagine what two billion people looked like, let alone what could kill that many. She had to search in her schoolbooks to even know what a billion was. Trying to imagine such a number, she thought of blades of grass in the big top field - that must be a huge number. Were there that many people in the world? Where were they? How many animals and how many fields of corn would you need to feed that many?

Still mulling over what she had learned, she washed her hair and bathed to remove the smell of the pigs. Personally, she liked the musky, ripe smell and would often rub her hands over her favourite sow and then, putting her hands together over her nose, breathe deeply of the scent. She chuckled internally though when she thought of how her friends would react to such a thing, and Milo - he would be utterly horrified. Milo was the son of the local miller and had little to do with livestock. She still remembered the time she had met with him without scrupulously removing the scent of pig - he had kept a good distance between them all evening.

Satisfied that she smelled of young woman rather than pig, she looked in her wardrobe to decide what to wear. She quickly chose a long green woollen dress with a design of three intertwined circles in yellow thread. She would complete her outfit with her best green coat and her long winter boots. It was still autumn, but she felt the boots lent her an air of sophistication that she was sure would impress her friends, and Milo in particular. The boots were black leather, a bit worn after several years of use, but they were very comfortable. As she looked at them, she thought again of the shoes she had seen in the magazine - what wouldn't she give to own a pair of those. She would certainly be the envy of everyone. What an entrance she would make, she thought, in some red, jewel-encrusted shoes with a thin, high heel. It was no use though - although they were well clothed in Woldshire, the clothes they did wear were largely functional rather than decorative. There was no-one who could make such shoes as she was imagining, even if they had the materials.

"Ah well," she said quietly to herself. "I'll still wow them all."

Making sure the journal was safely tucked into her drawer, she pulled on her boots and, grabbing her coat, headed down the stairs. She had quite a walk to the village hall unless… unless she found that her Da was downstairs and she could convince him to give her a lift in the buggy.

"Da, Da, are you there?" she called as she reached the bottom of the stairs and walked into the kitchen. And there he was. "Da, can you hitch up the buggy and give me a lift, please?" She gazed at him with her best pleading eyes, which she knew he wouldn't be able to resist, and, indeed, he smiled back and asked, "What time do you need to be there, lovely girl?"

"In about an hour," replied Nadya, smiling inwardly at her little win. Now she could sit by the fire while John got the buggy ready and would arrive like a queen of old, in style.

And indeed, just an hour later, she stepped down from the buggy, feeling very special indeed. The hall, an age-old building of white limestone with thick walls and a great wooden door set in an arched doorway, provided an imposing setting for the various functions that provided the chief entertainment for the locals. There was already a good crowd of youngsters there, and the atmosphere was livening up nicely. Nadya turned to her Da and blew him a kiss.

"Want picking up, lovely lass?" John called.

"No thanks," she called back, "Milo will walk me back, don't worry. Thank you for bringing me."

John turned the buggy and drove away towards home, and Nadya set about finding Milo or Layna. Quickly spotting both of them chatting together near the bar, Nadya joined them, got herself a beer, and immediately felt the glow of being amongst people she loved.

As usual at such gatherings, the girls were much quicker to begin dancing than the lads, who spent the early part of the evening hovering around the edges of the hall, laughing and joking. Soon, though, Nadya pulled Milo into the midst of the dancers, and this seemed to signal all but the shyest of the young men to attach themselves to a young lass or, at least, for the dancing groups to become mixed gender.

Music was provided by a group of local musicians who knew their trade, beginning with lively numbers that had everyone whirling and jiving merrily. As the evening wore on, they gradually inserted slower songs to allow the youngsters to form into couples and settle into relaxed and mellow happiness before being disgorged into the coolness of a late autumn evening.

Unlike in the darker, older times they had all heard tales of, there was no fear of violence or of girls being assaulted. They simply could not conceive of anyone attacking or harming another, and so they would make their various ways home alone, as couples, or in small groups.

———

Nadya slipped her small hand into Milo's, entwining her fingers with his, as they walked along the track back to Nadya's home. The sky was moonless, and the stars shone with a brightness and intensity that both of them took for granted. The Milky Way was a clear, sparkling band across the sky, ablaze with light and colour like a huge, diamond-encrusted sash around the world. Their eyes had adjusted to the dark so that they had no trouble staying on the path. They had, earlier, sat on a fallen log in the gateway of one of the fields and listened to the sounds of the night - owls hunting and calling, the fluttering of bats, and the rustling of roosting birds, amongst many other sounds. Of course, they had kissed, passionately, Nadya's tongue playing gently across Milo's. She had satisfied his boyish urges without difficulty. A simple shrugging of her shoulders to let her dress fall and expose her youthful breasts to his mouth and hands, and her practised ministrations of his eager erection, had soon provided the stimulation to bring him to orgasm. He had tried to return the favour but, as yet, his clumsy caresses were unable to do the same for her, he would learn, she would teach him. And when they were married, if they were married, she would happily, willingly, fervently consummate their sex life. There was no moral reason for her decision to hold back at this point, merely the practicality that if she became pregnant with him then she would be bound to marry him as, of course, neither would be able to conceive children with anyone else. This was simple biology.

The two had been friends for as long as Nadya could remember. They had gone to the local school together from the age of five and had progressed through all its stages in the same class group. The transition to lovers and expected life partners had been a gradual one from the age of around fourteen. Neither had experimented with other partners, and it now seemed settled that they would marry eventually. Nadya had no desire to be with anyone else, and yet... And yet, something held her back. Milo had asked her several times to agree a date for their marriage, but she had always replied,

"Soon, Milo, when the time is right." Now she had found another distraction and wondered if maybe, when she had finished exploring the box and the questions and possibilities it opened, she would be ready to settle. Milo knew nothing about the box, and Nadya was undecided whether she should share this with him. She had sensed, in the last year or so, a slow-growing impatience on his part. She knew he wanted to marry young and have their two children, so they would have the energy and youth to enjoy, in turn, their approach to adulthood.

Nadya's parents had done exactly that, and she knew they were very different from Milo's, who were much older and had little in common with their son, nor indeed with their daughter, who was a few years younger than Milo. She urged him to be patient with her, and so far, he had been, but he was a handsome boy and would inherit his father's mill, so he would make a great catch for someone like Layna, for example. Maybe this one last thing would be her final rebellious act as a teenager and, as she turned twenty early next year, she would settle. "Settle" - didn't the very fact she thought of it that way mean she still was not ready?

All of this she pondered as she walked with him under the stars, relishing the warmth of his friendship and the intimacy of their relationship. As they came over the brow of the hill at the top of the long sloping track to her house, she saw again, in the distance, the glow of the lights from the other land over the sea.

"Milo, have you ever wondered what life must be like under The Guardian?" she said softly.

Milo gently put his hands at the sides of her head, turned her face to his, and whispered, "Nadya, I only ever want to be where you are. Nowhere else matters."

She pulled a face at him and stuck out her tongue, laughing. "Don't attempt that romantic pish-tosh with me," she said. "It might have worked with the girls when we were twelve, to get you a quick feel, but it won't work with me.

"Besides, I'm being serious. We see the lights all the time, but we know nothing of what or why they are, or how people live their lives over there. Are you not curious at all?"

Now Milo looked at her singularly, as if he couldn't understand what she was saying at all - as if she were babbling nonsense.

"Of course not," he replied. "We know that we are the only ones not under the control of The Guardian, and that's enough for us, isn't it? Weren't we taught in school that the servants of The Guardian were our enemies, and that they nearly wiped us out at the end of the war? We know, don't we, that the people over there, the people all over the world, have their minds and bodies controlled. That after the insurrections, The Guardian gradually gained control over the whole of mankind, so that by the time the flooding was finished, we were the only free ones. We only stay that way by never having any machinery that The Guardian could use to control us or even know we are here. So, what interest can it be how those others live?"

"But that was hundreds of years ago now," replied Nadya, somewhat frustrated by his total lack of curiosity. "Things might have changed by now, mightn't they?"

"Why?" said Milo. "And if they had, why wouldn't they have come across the sea to see what was here? We know that we only stay free of The Guardian by staying - how did the teacher put it? - 'technologically silent.' That way, they have no interest in us."

Nadya could hear real fear in his voice, and she was a little sorry she had brought it up and spoiled the evening.

"Ah well, never mind," she whispered in his ear. "It's been such a lovely evening, thank you. And thank you for walking me home. Don't worry, just me being silly again, I guess."

"It's time you had something to keep your mind full," Milo laughed. "Children, maybe." With that, he winked at her, and she knew the conversation was over. She was disappointed that she could not share her curiosity with him but saw little point in continuing. Besides, she was tired now and wanted to climb into her bed.

"Well, I hope it takes us a while to make babies," she winked at him in her turn. "I want you to have to try many, many times."

With that, she kissed him again and then turned and ran down the lane, only pausing to call back to him.

"Bye, my love. See you soon."

"Tomorrow," he called back. "And don't forget, we're going swimming after lunch at mine. Love you."

Nadya waved once more and then turned for home. She could see the lights in the kitchen, and she was hungry as well as tired.

She wondered if Meena might have been baking this evening. One of her favourite shortbread biscuits would make a nice treat to take to bed with a mug of warm milk.

She opened the door and was delighted to smell the wonderful aroma of her mum's baking. There was the scent of apple cake and, yes, the warm buttery smell of shortbread. Nadya smiled and entered, seeing her mum and da sitting by the fire. Da was drinking ale and reading aloud from the latest council magazine, and Mum was knitting whilst listening to his deep, calm voice. Nadya knew she had little interest in the actual council business and often just liked to hear her father's voice. Would she ever be content just to listen to Milo talking about milling, she wondered? And, with that, she kissed both her parents, told them she'd had a lovely time, and, yawning widely, said she was going up.

She poured some milk into a pan and set it on the stove to warm, while she gathered two biscuits onto a plate, pulled off her boots, and gave them a wipe before putting them in the porch for cleaning in the morning.

Finally, she gathered up her supper and, with a wave to her parents, climbed the stairs, threw off her dress, and climbed into bed. She was going to read a little more of the journal before she slept.

Chapter 4 - Selected entries from Harry's Journals.
January 2nd, 2080.

In the news as I write this today:

Storm Wendy has brought major flooding to the east of
England. At least a thousand were killed in Kingston upon Hull
as the flood barrier, at the confluence of the River Hull and the
Humber, failed. Several other major towns along the Humber
Estuary were also overwhelmed, including Goole and Selby,
and many minor communities were totally destroyed. Decades
ago, when the naming of major storms began in Europe, it was
normal for midwinter to be reached with storm names still
beginning with the first few letters of the alphabet, for
example, Storm Charlie or Delilah. Today, only two days into
the new year, we are already at the end of the alphabet and have
seen twenty three devastating storms this season. Each has
brought flooding across swathes of England, with hundreds
killed each time by the destructive winds and tidal surges.

Meanwhile, the US government has designated large areas of
Texas and the Midwest as uninhabitable, signalling that no
further building will take place there. Current inhabitants will
be given federal assistance to relocate further north.

Wildfires once again swept across Australia and Indonesia,
destroying billions of hectares of forest, with deaths reported
in the tens of thousands.

King penguins have been declared extinct in the wild. These
birds have been struggling to successfully breed for years due
to a combination of retreating ice making their feeding

journeys, to the sea, no longer feasible, and to wet conditions at nesting sites leading to chicks becoming waterlogged and freezing to death. No king penguin has been seen in the wild for five years.

————

Thoughts about the development of AI and the control of the ordinary people:

I guess it began around 2020 with the advent of the first publicly accessible, so called, AI models. These were primarily used to generate written content or images, although video and deepfake videos and audio were already available to some. At around this time, there began to be the first mutterings about security and the danger of unfettered development, but the usefulness of the models meant that little was done.

Of course, the various security, military, intelligence, and counterintelligence services around the world also had no interest in stopping or curtailing the rapid developments. As ever, soldiers only saw the need for more weapons, more means of destruction. They always called it "defence", but most people knew what they meant was being better at attacking than "the enemy", whoever that might be.

Then there were the criminals, the hackers, and the criminal gangs interested in extortion, cyberattacks, and ransomware attacks. To these people, the growing sophistication of AI meant both an opportunity and a threat. Again, they wanted to stay ahead of the rest and were intent on continuing the rapid development of more and more powerful models.

There were a few who objected, initially the artists and writers whose livelihoods were threatened, and at one point the actors who realised that the studios no longer had need of them, their likenesses could so easily be replicated by the AI systems. Some scientists also spoke out, warning about disruption to society from massive job losses as well as the criminal activities. Some also warned about the potential for AI to replace or dominate mankind. None were listened to with any seriousness. The wars only hastened things along, including the reckless development of AI-controlled weaponry and surveillance systems. At this time, humans were still in control, or so they imagined.

In the aftermath of the nuclear exchanges and the shift to the right of most governments, the use of technology to control populations began in earnest. Facial recognition, tracking, surveillance, and control became the norm, and people accepted it as the price of safety. The mass migrations that followed the conflicts only added to this, as governments sought to know who was where and which people were supposed to be in each country. It wasn't long before someone came up with the idea that all people should be tagged - "chipped" as it was known - and it was suggested that the presence of a tag could be linked to easier financial transactions and to access to social and medical services and, especially to the receipt of any state benefits. And so, people (apart from a few) acquiesced. There were protests in some countries, notably the UK and Europe, but governments quickly passed laws requiring all those arrested on any charge to be automatically fitted with a tag. Many thousands of protesters were arrested and therefore tagged.

There was a rise in illegal tag-removal or "tag silencing" services; it was an offence to remove tags, and many people were arrested and charged, and of course re-tagged. So the "detaggers", as they became known, grew more sophisticated, offering to plug removed tags into machines which fed them fake geophysical and, as tags became more sophisticated, false biometric information. This battle has raged ever since, and now some seventy five percent of people are tagged. Tagging at birth became mandatory about twenty years ago.

The first rumours of a new type of electronic chip began to circulate about ten years ago. These new chips were reputedly not only able to convey information about the bearer but also to control some aspects of their emotional and physical functions, driving or inhibiting the secretion of certain hormones or even stimulating the autonomic nervous system. This level of control would not have been possible without the sophisticated AI systems that had been quietly developed over the years. The response to these rumours was almost universal horror; for the first time, people began, in large numbers, to move against the right-wing governments that had dominated the political landscape for so long. Where democracy still clung on, there were huge defeats at the polls for the right-wing, and where not, there was increasing unrest and street protests. This uneasy standoff has persisted to this day, except in a few isolated countries. Only a few countries with highly controlled populations have managed to get these new chips into a significant number of people.

Despite the ousting of the right-wing Keep Britain Safe party and its replacement with the first Labour administration since 2030, the UK government, in June last year, passed a new law allowing trials of new chips on a small number of prisoners and on all new asylum seekers as a condition of being granted asylum. There have been numerous legal challenges to this, but these have recently been overcome by the use of an act of parliament, similar to that used by Conservatives in the 2020s in an attempt to prop up plans to send so-called illegal migrants to Rwanda. There has also been widespread unrest and street protests, along with a huge surge in the illegal removal of previous, old-style chips. As I write this journal, the government is about to embark upon a new effort to begin these trials and to ban street protests as well as legal challenges from prisoners' representatives. In essence, new legislation coming before parliament in the next session will mean that all those convicted of a crime which carries a custodial sentence will be stripped of their rights as citizens and even of the much-weakened human rights protections. It is clear that the Labour Party is controlled just as effectively by the technos and their mega-corporations as was the previous right-wing regime. I cannot see how these trials will not go ahead as planned.

For decades, a small number of people have warned against allowing AI systems to control any aspect of human behaviour and against allowing them access to weapons systems. It now appears that the first of these red lines is about to be breached, and I, among many thousands of people, am extremely worried about what this means for the future of humanity.

Chapter 5 – Sunday.

Nadya didn't sleep well after reading more of the journal. There was so much she did not understand, even when she could decipher the words themselves. Harry, the journal writer, seemed to be describing a totally alien, and deeply disturbing, world. She woke later than usual with a headache and took a mouthful of the bitter-tasting willow essence before she cleaned her teeth. Hopefully, that would help shift the dull pain behind her eyes before she set off for lunch at Milo's house. Breakfast was mostly finished when she had dressed and made her way down to the kitchen, where Meena was already clearing away.

"Late night last night, dear?" she asked as Nadya munched on a slice of buttered bread. "I saw light under your door when John and I went up. Were you reading?"

"Yes, for too long, I think, Mum," Nadya replied. "I'm trying to understand a bit more about history, so I've borrowed a book about life before the flood."

Meena looked at her daughter with a worried frown; such books were rare and such research frowned upon by the council.

"Where did you get such a thing?" she asked. "You know the council doesn't like such things." Nadya did indeed know this, the official explanation was that there was a danger of Guardian propaganda being rained down from above – although no-one had ever seen such a thing. She hesitated slightly before answering. "Just from one of the girls at the dance, Mum. Don't worry, nothing out of the ordinary. Do the animals still need feeding and cleaning this morning?"

"No, you're too late, love. They're all done today. I'm sure you'll do more than your share later in the week. Why don't you take a walk, clear your head?"

"Good idea," Nadya replied, and, pulling on her boots and a coat, she opened the door and breathed deeply of the cool, moist autumn air.

"Don't be too long though," she heard Meena call as she walked briskly away. "You'll need to be ready by eleven if you want a lift to Milo's."

Nadya thought briefly about where to walk and then set off through the lower fields to the woods by the sea. She would take the short path through the wood and then along the clifftop overlooking the shore. The sea air would do her good, and she wanted to look over towards the mainland as she tried to piece together what she had read the previous evening. The journal was certainly not the light-hearted reminiscence she had imagined, but by now she was hooked and wanted to know more. She also knew that the council would certainly not approve of this book and would confiscate it if they knew she had found it. So far, there had been no mention of The Guardian, but there were dark hints of its origins which created a certain level of anxiety even in Nadya. The indoctrination against allowing The Guardian to find and control their lives was extremely powerful.

The path through the fields was still muddy from the last rains, and the sticky clay soon clogged her boots. She would be glad to reach the woods, where she could wipe them on the longer grass under the edge of the trees. In the distance, the haunting cry of a curlew seemed to mirror her melancholic state of mind. As she neared the wood, though, it was replaced by the harsh croaks of the rooks she knew nested there. As they became aware of her approach, the large, black birds took to the air, swirling around the tops of the trees and swooping towards her with their warning calls. They didn't approach closely and presented no real threat to her, and, as usual, she laughed to herself at their fuss. In the days of her childhood, she might well have tried to climb the trees to steal an egg or to see if there were chicks in the nests. She held no fear of these birds, nor of any of the wildlife of Woldshire. Coming, at last, under the trees, she cleaned her boots of as much of the mud as she could and headed towards the clifftops. The path here, in front of the woods, was one she knew well, although each year it would change slightly as the sea ate away slowly at the soft chalk cliffs. Where there had been a clear path beyond and on top of the cliff, she might need to re-enter the wood itself and clamber over dense and tangled undergrowth to continue on her way. Maybe one day such erosion would threaten their own farmhouse, which lay only two hundred metres away.

On this day, though, she found the path clear of most deviations, and the ground dry and free from mud and puddles. This close to the edge of the cliffs, the path was free-draining, and the covering soil thin and sparse. Indeed, for much of the time, she walked on the exposed chalk. To her right, the ground fell away in a mix of steep slope and sheer cliffs, some metres high above the waves. At low tide, a short stretch of white stony beach was exposed, but at high tide, the sea broke directly on the cliff face. There were few easy routes down to that beach on this side of the little bay where Ridings Beck flowed down from the higher ground and into the sea.

She looked out over the sea towards the mainland and allowed her thoughts to drift back to what she had read. Was life still as seemingly tumultuous and threatening as the world she had read about in the journal? Everything there seemed to be in turmoil and existence so fragile. The idea of having something implanted, which enabled someone else to know where you were and what you were doing, or even to control your body, was utterly repugnant to her. She knew about The Guardian, the entity which had seized power over all of the people on Earth using the machines of war, and of the domination it wielded. She knew that, even before the rise of the sea was complete, Woldshire had been cut off from the mainland, as the intervening land was turned into a swampy and impassable no-man's land. This had allowed the people to destroy all the machines, terminals, and other things that were linked to The Guardian, and that only once they had done so were they sure they could evade control and escape slavery. She also knew that to remain free they had to live without the machines and to stay hidden from the mainlanders. Her teachers had told her that, in the early days of the formation of the inland sea, passage had been impossible due to the dangerous tidal currents which could sweep even a powerful boat away, never to be seen again. There were many obstacles just under the surface - the remains of old, tall buildings and giant machines - against which a boat could be dashed to pieces in an instant. The currents could still be seen sweeping around the coastline, often still carrying floating debris from some old, submerged structure which had finally broken apart and cast its remains into the waves. It was still the case, she had been taught, that passage between the mainland and Woldshire was so treacherous that only a fool would attempt it.

By now she had reached the road where it ran down from the farm into the valley and crossed the small, gurgling stream they knew as "the beck", before leading on to Milltown, the village where Milo lived. This was the one place nearby where anyone could easily get onto the beach and follow it north under the cliffs. Years ago, she had gone that way with Milo as the tide went out, and they had followed it all the way round to Wilton, where the old village ran right down to the sea. She remembered how her da had been horrified when he found out and had grounded her for days, threatening not to let her see Milo again.

"What if you'd fallen or twisted your ankle?" he had said more sternly than at any time before or since. "There are no places you could have climbed up, and you would have been drowned by the incoming tide."

After that, Milo had been unwilling to take part in any more of Nadya's adventures and had become much more cautious. She guessed he had been severely punished by his father. That seemed to Nadya to be the beginning of a process leading to Milo being as he was now - sensible, unadventurous, solid. And obedient, she thought, immediately feeling a little guilty but also a bit rebellious. Was this the life she was destined to settle for? Was this why she kept hesitating? But what was expected of her - if not with Milo, then with some other farmer's son, blacksmith's son, or something similar - was clear: to become a mother, and oversee the household and the raising of the two children. A life of cooking and baking, a life built around the family and the home. Would she ever be ready for that, she wondered?

Suddenly, Nadya stopped in her tracks. It was as if the shutters on a window had opened in her mind, instantly letting the bright sunlight stream in and reveal something hidden and unnoticed in the shadows.

She quickly climbed the short hill along the road and ran down the lane to the house, arriving a little out of breath and warm but feeling less headachy and brighter. She was now looking forward to her swim. It was a good day after the cool start, warm and dry with only a slight breeze to ruffle her long hair. She had already seen that the sea was calm with few waves, and she knew that in the bay there would be no current to concern them. But first, she wanted to look at something, to see if the memory revealed by the light in her mind was correct. Excitedly, she climbed the stairs, giving only a quick wave to her mum, who was busy cooking their own family meal. Once in her room, she quietly closed the door, and then retrieved the oilplas box from her wardrobe, opening it carefully. She took out the magazines and started to turn the pages eagerly, looking quickly through the first. She then returned it to the box and set about searching through the second. About twenty pages in, she stopped and stared at the page. There it was, in black and white, as a title to an article:

"Two, three or four: What is the optimum number of children?"

Nadya blinked several times and continued to stare at the words, not knowing what to make of it. Three or four children? How could that be possible? She knew that some women were unable to have any babies, and occasionally there might be a third child if the second pregnancy resulted in twins. She had even heard a tale of a woman many years ago who had triplets in the second pregnancy and so had four children in total. But that story had concluded that two of the three triplets had died soon after birth, leaving the family with the expected two. The idea that more than two children could be a deliberate choice was entirely beyond her understanding. Her basic biology lessons had taught her that, hundreds of years ago, a mutation in human genes had limited pregnancies to two. In addition, that once a woman had become pregnant by one man, it was not possible to become pregnant by another. Indeed, the same was true of a man. Once he had impregnated one woman, something in his reproductive makeup locked on to that woman, meaning that he could not do so with another. These were fundamental facts of reproductive biology and were integral to maintaining a steady human population which did not outstrip the capability of the Earth to sustain life.

So how could it be that a mere five hundred years ago women were debating how many children was the right number? She quickly read through the short article, and it confirmed that women were routinely having more than two children back then, and even having children with multiple fathers. She sat back on her bed, her head spinning with this barely believable information. She was brought back to the present by her mother calling.

"Are you nearly ready, Nadya? Da will need to go soon if you are wanting a ride."

Nadya quickly put the magazine back in the box and once again concealed the box in her wardrobe. Grabbing her swimming bag, which was already packed with her costume and towel, she looked around the room to make sure she had hidden everything and, closing her door behind her, ran down the stairs, reaching the kitchen just in time as her da was making for the door.

"Come on then, love," he chuckled. "Let's get you over to Milo's. You'll have to make your own way back, I'm afraid. I'm off to see Ron over at Home Farm about sharing the ploughing teams this coming spring."

"Coming now!" replied Nadya as she kissed her mum and picked her coat from the pegs above the old priest's bench just inside the door.

The two climbed onto the trap and, with a cheery "Gee-up," her da urged the horse into motion.

"Swimming after lunch, is it?" he asked as they rode up the short slope to the main track down to the ford at Givenbrook and Milltown beyond.

"Yes," replied Nadya distractedly, still half in a dream, trying to absorb what she had read. "After lunch at Milo's. I'll be home in time for supper this evening and an early night. Layna and I need to continue with the fence checking and fixing tomorrow, so I'll need to be up early."

They now rode in silence for the short journey to Milo's home, content and familiar with each other's company. The track down to the ford was well kept and they were soon splashing through the shallow water and out onto the road to Milltown. The late October sun was still warm and, as there was still just a gentle breeze from the east, it would be a delightful afternoon for swimming in the Milltown inlet. She was a strong swimmer and could outpace Milo in their customary race across the inlet and back, around three hundred metres in all. When there was a strong wind from the west, though, the waves could build up significantly even in the short crossing from the mainland, and then the inlet could be dangerous. If one were to be washed out beyond the headlands at the wrong time, the tides, sweeping up or down through the Sea of York, could carry you away from land very quickly.

Entering the village with the familiar smells, sounds and sights of Woldshire life all around them, Nadya wondered again what life on the mainland was like. She loved her home and her family, loved the life they all had, but somehow a curiosity had been sparked within her. She had always been a wonderer and an enquirer, but her find had triggered an almost overwhelming desire to know more. To understand how the world was, and what other possibilities there were, beyond the rural life of Woldshire. Her da nodded and waved to all those they passed, going about their Sunday business, calling to each one by name and exchanging pleasantries or jocular banter. He was well liked and well regarded in the village and, indeed, in Woldshire itself.

Beyond the square and the inn, the main street bent sharply to the north, and the road to Milltown Hall branched off to the right. Taking this road for a short way, they then turned right again into a narrow, hawthorn-lined and rutted lane. The white chalk of the land showed clearly through where generations of wheels had passed, taking loads of wheat, barley, and oats to be milled, and then taking back the resulting flour or meal. Only in the centre of the track was there green grass and small, hardy plants. At this time of year, there were still some berries on the hawthorn hedge, but these would soon disappear now as the thrushes, blackbirds and others feasted to survive the cooler, wetter and darker winter days.

After around seventy metres, they came to the mill yard and da brought the buggy to a halt in front of the bright green door of the house. They could clearly hear the rush of water over the wheel of the mill, a constant background to life in Mill House. That water was channelled from a pond higher up the valley beyond the Milltown pastures and provided the main power for the milling of all of the locally grown grains. Milo's family were not wealthy landowners but were nevertheless quite well off, as they took a small percentage of all the flour and meal they produced. This was their payment for the milling service, and they either kept the produce for themselves or sold it to those who had no land of their own. Milo's mum also ran a small bakery on the main village street and used the flour levy from the mill to bake a variety of breads and sweets that were sold both to locals and to any travelling artisans passing through the village.

Jumping down from the trap, Nadya ran to the door, knocked once and entered. She was treated as part of the family here, and even her brief knock on the door was not really needed, but she felt it was polite to do so. She waved back to her da as she passed through the doorway and into the relative gloom of the hallway, making first for the kitchen to say hello to Mr and Mrs Meggison, Milo's parents, but then heading for Milo's room.

"Lunch in thirty minutes, Naddie love," called Mrs Meggison in her high, bright voice as Nadya made for the short staircase leading to Milo's room, in the annex just off from the main house.

"Thanks, Mrs Meggison. I can't wait. I do love your cooking," she called back and pushed open the door to find Milo standing in only a shirt and underwear in the centre of the room. She could have knocked before entering, but she was sure Milo would have heard, if not seen, her arrival and, besides, they were so familiar with each other after all the years they had been close, that such niceties weren't needed.

Milo laughed and put his hands over his groin in mock shock and shame. Nadya ignored him and, shoving him backwards onto the bed, she climbed on top and kissed him, pressing herself teasingly against him and bringing him quickly to a state of arousal.

"Well, that's enough of that," she laughed, climbing off again, "You're insatiable, young Milo."

Milo winked at her and replied back, laughing himself, "you just wait 'til you're Mrs Meggison, Nadya and we'll see what's enough".

Nadya threw his pants at him and sat down in the window looking at him appraisingly.

"What's that look for?" asked Milo.

"Just deciding whether you're up to the job of being my husband," she laughed again, enjoying the deep affection that existed between them. "Now hurry up and get dressed, I'm hungry. I've had a long morning of walking and thinking already this morning."

"Thinking about agreeing a date for the wedding I hope," Milo fired back at her, only half in jest.

Now, throwing a cushion straight at his head, she responded, "When the dish and the spoon dance a jig and your dad's cow has kittens, that'll be soon enough."

Milo knew better than to start to spoil the day by showing his frustration at her delays or, indeed, by sulking, so pulling on his pants, he grabbed her around the waist and kissed her hard once more.

"Got your swimming stuff, I hope," he said, with joking emphasis on the word "hope", clearly indicating that he really half hoped she hadn't and would need to swim naked.

Nadya simply responded with a toss of her bright red hair and by sticking out her tongue, dangling the bag with her kit in front of her.

"And you'd better remember yours," she threw at him. "Otherwise, you'll be sitting on the bank and watching."

"Besides, you know I'm going to beat you across the inlet and back again today. So, it wouldn't surprise me if you deliberately forgot your gear to avoid the humiliation."

That statement earned Nadya the cushion landing squarely in her face, knocking her back in the chair. Greeting ceremonies complete, the two of them sat together on the chair and looked out at the yard and the small flower garden Milo's mother grew just in front of the house. Nadya sighed. She really did love her life and probably Milo too. In a way, she wished she could cast off the feeling she had - that there was something she had to discover - and settle down to enjoy raising a family with him.

Nadya stripped off her clothes and pulled on her swimming costume in the warm afternoon sun. She had no shyness or modesty about shedding her clothes in public or in close proximity to Milo; nudity just wasn't an issue in Woldshire. All such nonsense had been cast away, along with organised religion, in the aftermath of the wars and disasters of the twenty-first century. Some people still believed in one deity or another, but all such beliefs, and any rituals and rules, were kept private. The "state", such as it was in Woldshire, was entirely secular and had been for centuries. The only reason they wore swimming costumes at all was tradition, and certainly, there were many who simply didn't bother.

Their favourite swimming spot was just along the shore from where the Clay Farm stream tumbled down the small cliff and into Milltown inlet. The clear chalk stream was often dry in summer, but at this time of year, the clear bubbling water made a small waterfall onto the narrow beach. The stream only emerged from the chalk a hundred metres or so further up the slope and so was fresh and clean to drink whenever it was flowing freely. Nadya and Milo, and indeed others who swam or bathed from this place, would regularly quench their thirst from the stream. When in full flow, it also provided a somewhat cool way to rinse salty bodies after being in the sea. The grassy field sloped gently down to the shore, with only a small drop just above the flat chalk shelf from which it was easy to enter the water. It was not unusual to find several couples, and even a family or two, picnicking on the grass in the summer, but this late in the year, Milo and Nadya had the place to themselves.

The sea was slightly chilly and the first few steps into the water would result in sharp intakes of breath or even a few shrill shrieks, but once fully immersed, it was refreshing rather than cold.

"Come on, slowcoach," Nadya teased Milo, who, as usual, was still neatly folding his clothes and stacking them in a tidy bundle before stepping down onto the shelf. Nadya, by comparison, had thrown her clothes in a heap and was still pulling on her costume as she ran, laughing, into the water.

"Some of us like to look after our things," he said in return. A conversation that had taken place many times before and both had no doubt would take place many times again. It was all part of the ritual of swimming.

By the time he had gingerly immersed himself, Nadya was through the small breakers and thirty metres or more from the shore. The tide was high today, almost full, so the chalk shelf was only a few metres wide. On days when the tide was low, the place where Nadya had reached could be almost dry, only reached by the final wash of a few larger waves. She waited now for Milo before they set out together to swim across the one hundred and fifty metres or so to the other side. Nadya would stay with Milo until the last fifty metres or so, when she would usually say, "and go," before racing ahead of him to emerge triumphant on the far shore. There was a time Milo would have been twenty metres or more behind, but as they had grown beyond teenage years, his strength had increased, so that her advantage of technique was lessened. These days, he would only be a short distance behind, and indeed, on some days, he pressed very close.

They climbed onto the somewhat steeper but still grassy bank of the south shore and lay on the grass breathing deeply after their exertion. The sky was a brilliant blue with just a few white, wispy clouds and the grass beneath her, regularly grazed by sheep, was soft and warm. There was not another person in sight. Nadya leaned over and kissed Milo on his mouth, her lips parting to allow his tongue to press against hers. He responded passionately, returning the kiss, and then, rolling her over on to her back, lay on top of her. He moved from her mouth to kiss her on her neck and behind her ear and then run his tongue gently over her ear, probing into the opening itself. He knew this would arouse her instantly. She groaned quietly in response and did not resist as he pulled the straps of her costume from her shoulders to free her breasts. Moving his attention to these he ran his tongue over first one nipple and then the other and then gently bit each nipple between his teeth, causing Nadya to gasp with pleasure and involuntarily thrust her hips forward to press her sex against his groin. He continued in this fashion, at the same time caressing, and squeezing, each firm young breast with his work roughened hands. Nadya cupped his scrotum in her hand and squeezed, causing Milo in turn to groan with pent up passion. She pushed his swimming pants down his legs and freed his hard penis, and grasping this, she squeezed gently along its length.

Lifting himself from on top of her, Milo now removed her costume entirely and, beginning at her ankles, kissed the whole length of each leg in turn to the top of each inner thigh. Once more she groaned, more loudly this time and writhed and thrust herself at him with increasing passion.

He again lifted himself from her and this time, parting her legs with his body he placed himself in a position ready to penetrate her and looked down at her, questioningly. She desperately wanted to feel him enter her and to make him climax inside her and she could sense that he was as desperate as she for this. His look made it clear that nothing less would do this time, and he was pleading with her to let him push into her. Nadya groaned and almost relented but then at the last moment something made her stop, and she pulled away slightly and shook her head, tears now brimming in her eyes.

"Please, no Milo" she begged. "I am so sorry, but I can't."

Milo looked again deep into her eyes, his whole being pleading with her in the height of his lust, but she again shook her head gently and closed her eyes. She could not bear to look at him.

He rolled away from her with a moan and lay on his back breathing heavily. She knew that he was confused, angry and frustrated but he would never have taken her without her willing consent. He did not say anything, but after a few moments, he pulled on his swimming pants once more and, running back down to the shore, he threw himself into the water and began to swim away to return to the north side. Nadya brushed away her tears, angry with herself for causing the situation and for not being able to make this final commitment, but, as usual, something had held her back. She knew that once they began to make love completely, it would not be long before she became pregnant and that they would then be tied irrevocably together, certainly if either wanted another child. It was simple biology that once a couple initiated a pregnancy, neither could do so again with any other partner, and, as much as she loved Milo, she was just not ready for this ultimate step.

She pulled on her costume and followed Milo into the water. He was swimming strongly, and she only managed to catch him as he was emerging onto the chalk shelf where they had first started to swim. He climbed the bank in silence and, towelling himself briefly, changed back into his clothes before sitting on the grass with his head on his knees and his eyes closed. Nadya knew from long friendship that she should leave him a while before sitting next to him and, putting her arms around his shoulders, offer comfort for her unwillingness. They had been through similar experiences before, although never had she wanted him so badly and come so close to pulling him inside her. She was also sure he had never before wanted so badly to consummate their lovemaking with the final act, and she shared his confusion at her unwillingness.

Nearly half an hour elapsed before she sensed the time was right and she moved next to him, now fully clothed herself, and, whispering "sorry" in his ear, laid her head on his shoulder. She really did love him, and she did not want to keep on hurting and confusing him, how could she explain why she held back when she wasn't even sure herself?

Finally, she lifted his head, kissed him gently and sat facing him.

"Milo," she began tentatively. "Why do you think it is that we can only have two children and only with the same partner?"

Milo looked at her blankly, not understanding what she was saying.

"Do you think it's always been like this? Or is it something that began when we separated from the mainlanders?"

Milo's eyes now lit with the anger which he had subsumed only moments ago.

"Nadya, just stop it," he said in a soft, flat tone. "Just stop with the nonsense about the mainlanders, you know we're not supposed to talk about such things. We keep ourselves separate to avoid being overrun by The Guardian, in order to keep our freedom and independence."

"But suppose some of the things we have learned aren't true?" she pleaded. "Suppose that in the past people could have more children and more partners?"

"Ah, so that's what it's about, is it?" Milo now answered sharply, eyes really beginning to blaze with anger and his face flushing red. "I'm not enough for you and you want to have me but be free to have others too. In case I'm not good enough for the lady landowner I suppose?" he hissed.

Nadya did not know how to reply as she didn't understand her own reaction. Instead, she murmured, "But I've read that things were different in the past."

"What!" Milo now stood and glared at her. "What can you possibly have read, Nadya? Why are you lying to me in this way. Please can't you at least just be honest and tell me I'm not enough, instead of inventing this nonsense about some link with the mainlanders and the past."

Nadya had no reply, she had already let slip something she had not meant to, so she simply stood and, tears once again falling down her cheeks, looked at him pleadingly. Finally, Milo spoke again in a calmer but bitter voice.

"I've had enough, Nadie love. If you don't want me then it's time we stopped this, and you let me find someone who does."

He picked up his bundle and shaking his head at her he muttered quietly but firmly.

"It's still early, I assume you can find your way home safely. I'm going home. Let me know when you come to a decision." And then finally and with the full force of the bitterness of the afternoon. "Don't leave it too long, I've waited long enough for you already." With that he turned from her and walked away with his head low, clearly crying softly to himself. Nadya too was sobbing uncontrollably. How could this have happened, how had such a lovely day turned into such a disaster? Watching Milo retreating slowly she wanted to call out to him that she was wrong, that she was sorry and that they should wed as soon as possible and that she loved him and only him. Instead, she turned away and began to wander along the path to the cliffs, she was not ready to return home. She did not look back again and so did not see Milo turn once more and wave slowly, before he disappeared into the wood at the edge of the pasture.

Chapter 6 - Selected entries from Harry's Journals. January 5th, 2080.

Some items in the news today:

An uprising in India has been brutally put down by the Indian government. There has been unrest in the mid-regions of the country for decades, as the monsoon rains have continued to bring radioactive contamination from the north. Every year this has caused deaths from radiation sickness in any who drank contaminated water, and has continued to drive the huge rates of cancer deaths, exacerbated by the collapse of the healthcare systems. Those in the south have resisted the migration of people from further north, and over the last week, a major surge in illegal migrations had put increasing pressure on the border fence. Yesterday, the fence was breached in several places, and the desperate migrants killed several border guards and some civilians in a nearby town. Government forces responded by clearing a region some three kilometres wide north of the fence, killing all who refused to leave. The actions of the migrants have been condemned by the UN and independently by the US, EU, and China.

The death toll from Storm Wendy has been put at eighty thousand across Europe as storm surges and flooding overwhelmed much of the low-lying regions of the Netherlands and France. In the UK alone, fifteen thousand are reported dead or missing after a major tidal surge swept along the Humber Estuary, submerging Kingston upon Hull, Goole, Selby, and all villages and outlying settlements in its path. Waters were reported as deep as eight metres in Goole.

The last African elephant, surviving in a refuge in Kenya, was killed yesterday by starving locals, who reportedly held a feast with the carcass.

In my last entry, I wrote about the role of AI in the development of implanted microchips which are now almost ubiquitous in the population, and of the new chips being tested which are capable of controlling aspects of human biology. It is worth clarifying that these chips, and the architecture which monitors and potentially controls them, fall under the common definition of Artificial Intelligence. However, recent advances in thinking have now clarified that this designation will in the future only be applied to a system that demonstrates what has been termed "Autonomous and Unprompted Origination of Thought and Action" (AUOTA for short). It would seem that, even after decades of research and advancement of AI systems, this point has not yet been reached. The systems have become ever more powerful and far-reaching, but to date, none has reached a level of sophistication whereby it acts independently of human input.

There has been much discussion in the media, and across social media, in the last few days regarding whether this line is likely to be crossed in the next few years. Most systems scientists believe not and point to the one thing that has not been achieved in the field yet, namely the mimicking of the ability of the human mind to reconfigure all of its architecture, sometimes in just a few seconds. It is thought that this ability is what drives true independent intelligence or consciousness. An AUOTA system would need to be conscious to pass the more recently developed tests for this state.

Mankind has long feared the rise of conscious machines capable of self-replication, but for myself, I wonder if this is merely a distraction from the ongoing loss of independence and freedom of ordinary individuals, facilitated by sophisticated machines but controlled by other humans. If the first trials of the new "Track and Calm" chips in convicted criminals are approved, then for the first time the authorities will have the ability not only to know where someone is, but to monitor their physical and emotional state, and intervene to change the individual's behaviour, or even remotely render them unconscious. Several deaths have been reported in countries where the chips are already in use, but these have been put down to teething troubles.

Could the authorities actually use the chips to stop someone's heart or to drive a catastrophic autonomic reaction leading to heart failure? This has been strenuously denied by the UK government, but questions continue to be asked, and the topic is driving a wave of protest and unrest. Next week the first implant of one of the new chips is scheduled to take place in a "volunteer" who is serving a life sentence for violent affray. It is reported that he has been told he may be eligible for parole (something not normally possible for those convicted of violent crime) if the implant is successful. Major protests have been taking place outside Wandsworth Prison, where the operation is to take place, and these are likely to increase dramatically as the day of the implant approaches.

———

On a more personal note:

I may become eligible for a workplace this year. Unemployment in the UK runs at around ninety three percent and the few jobs that exist are allocated using a points-based system, with points accrued by things such as volunteer work, demonstrable skills, and positive social scores. My own accumulation is middling to good, and I received a message today to inform me that there may be work opportunities for those in my band later this year. I have no idea what the work might involve, but it is likely to be in the manufacturing, construction, or societal maintenance sectors, tending the machines which actually do the manufacturing, construction, or maintenance. This will provide me with the opportunity to acquire additional credits, which I could use to improve the home, in one of the housing estates on the edge of Leeds, where I live in with my wife, or I could exchange them for improved tech items or furniture. It is unlikely, though, that I would earn enough to fund an overseas travel permit unless the placement were to last at least three years. It has long been a dream of mine to visit France, but this is something rarely achieved these days, partly due to the expense and partly due to the hugely complex application process. I can, at least, still afford to dream.

Chapter 7 - The Council.

It had been six long, sad days since Nadya and Milo had parted company with bitter words, and she could still not stop thinking about their argument. She felt so very alone with her secret; she had only wanted to share it with Milo, who was closer to her than anyone. It seemed to Nadya that no one else in the whole of Woldshire had any imagination or curiosity. They were content to continue with their lives as ordained by the council, cut off from the mainland and the rest of the world. Cut off indeed from learning anything new.

Now, she felt that her very foundations had been shaken. Even what she had thought was simple biology might not be true, although she could not imagine what might have happened to change such a thing to the current reality. She didn't particularly want to have more than two children, and she had never thought of marrying anyone but Milo, but she needed - yes, she thought, needed was a good word - she needed to understand. Ever since she could remember, she had been curious, had wanted to know how things worked, where they came from, what made them what they were. As a young girl, she had collected the shells of hatched birds' eggs, discarded snail shells, and suchlike. She had gathered worms and insects, put them in glass tanks, and watched how they grew and changed, observing what they ate. She had read every book she could find, which wasn't many, and had pestered her mother and father with endless questions about how things worked, why things were the way they were, and more, until they had grown weary of answering her.

For a time, when she left school and began to work on the land, she had been content learning the whole range of new skills needed to run the farm. But still, she had looked at the stars and wondered.

And then there had come a day when, for the first time, she had looked across the Sea of York and seen the lights in the far distance as day turned to night. She had been entranced, caught in a swirl of imagination about what kind of life could provide such powerful lights that they could be seen from way across the sea. Why didn't her people travel to the mainland? Why did they hide from the world? She even dared to question, if only in her own unspoken thoughts, whether The Guardian was real and really did threaten to enslave them if it became conscious of them.

She had asked some of these questions of her mother and father, and they had given such answers as they could, but eventually they had run out of knowledge. Her father had warned her not to ask such questions outside the home and cautioned that there were many, even the majority, who would be threatened and frightened by such curiosity. The council itself, in the name of maintaining the peace, security, and tranquillity of their lives, would not allow such threats. They had few sanctions for such things, but they could isolate a family from the community in order to contain the threat. If the family itself was unable to control the individual causing the disturbance, then the whole family would be shunned, excluded from society. Nadya knew of only a few people who had been sent away by their families to prevent their family's isolation, and just one family who had removed themselves entirely to another area to avoid the punishment. A shunned family was not going to gain approval for any member to marry, and marriage without the approval of the council was unheard of. They did not normally withhold such consent in any other circumstance, unless the couple were too closely related or there was any hint of coercion. If the long-ingrained threat of The Guardian was not sufficient, in itself, to maintain adherence to the quiet isolation of the island people, then the threat of shunning certainly was.

Given Milo's reaction to her questions, it was clear that he did not, and never would, share her curiosity and questioning spirit. She realised now that she had known this all along and that this was the reason she continued to hesitate to take the plunge and marry him, even though she loved him dearly. Whether there was anyone in Woldshire, or even Nym, who would be as inquisitive and questioning as herself, she did not know.

Now, it was Sunday again, and for the first time since she could remember, she had no plans to see Milo. She had not been out of the house, except to work, all week, and it was obvious that her mum and da knew something was amiss, but they hadn't yet asked her about it, preferring to wait until she was ready to talk. Today, she was going to take a long walk and read some more of the journal she had found. She packed a small rucksack and put both books in there before heading down into the kitchen for some breakfast.

"I'm going for a walk up the coast today," she announced casually as she entered the room. "Can I take some bread and cheese for lunch, Mum?"

"Of course, love," her mum replied with a concerned look. "Are you OK, dear?"

"Yes, I'm fine," she lied, barely holding back the tears that threatened to brim in her eyes. "I just need a bit of time to sort out some things in my head. I'll be OK once I do, I promise. I can see you and da are worried, but you needn't be. I'll be fine."

Meena guessed it was something to do with Milo, but she had no idea of all the other things Nadya was discovering and thinking about. She had always known she was a strange one, apt to question everything, but had put it down to youthful curiosity. She was certain that, in time, Nadya would settle with Milo and the two would make a good life. Nadya ate her breakfast in silence, then cut a hunk of the loaf her mum had baked yesterday, along with a piece of the homemade cheese from the pantry and a small piece of butter, which she wrapped in some greased cloth. She packed the whole bundle in another piece of cloth, which she placed carefully in her rucksack. As she headed out of the door, she turned and smiled at her mother, saying, "I'll be back in time to help get the evening meal ready."

She turned west out of the farmyard and headed towards the coastal woods, just as she had done a week ago. This time, though, she didn't push through the woods towards the cliffs but turned north on the landward side to skirt the trees, which creaked and groaned in the wind. After a time, the woods turned inland, cutting off further progress unless she went under the trees, but she soon found the old path which led down to a small woodland stream, easily crossed. She was heading, first of all, for the old, abandoned village of Wilton.

She planned to sit and eat some lunch on the beach, a place littered with the ruins of the old houses, still crumbling more than two hundred years since the village was abandoned to the rising sea.

There was a cool wind from the east as she trudged along, trying not to think about anything other than the advancing autumn and its effects on the land around her. The leaves of the trees were turning a golden brown, with occasional flashes of red or orange from a mature sycamore. The ground was damp and smelled of musty, rotting fallen bracken and of many different types of fungi - the bright red with crusty spots of the agaric and the greys and browns of innumerable other species. Climbing back out of the wood into the open, Nadya was pleased to feel the heat of the sun on her back as she continued to walk north through the family's own fields. She crossed the old Given Lane and on through more open fields, fields she had recently inspected with Layna for the security of the fences. She soon topped a small hill where she began the descent into Wiltondale. She could now clearly see the remains of the old village.

Once she entered the abandoned village, her surroundings changed dramatically, from open, fertile fields to rough scrub between the tumbledown wrecks of the old houses. The roads had long since decayed and crumbled but could still be traced by the lines of relatively sparse vegetation. Crossing one such line, she passed between ruins until she reached a place where two parallel tracks ran on both sides of a small stream, which tumbled down onto the short, rubble-strewn beach. From here, rumour had it, that many years ago, it was possible to see the old tower of York rising above the waves. How long ago the old Minster had succumbed to the erosion of its always-uncertain foundations, sending the tower to finally crash under the sea, no one knew. Certainly, many decades before Nadya was born, maybe even more than two centuries ago. Now, all that could be seen was a distant smudge of rising hills more than forty kilometres away on the mainland.

Nadya found herself a perch and ate her homely lunch. Checking that there was no one else around, she pulled out the first journal and opened it to the section she had read the previous night. This had contained many ideas alien to her, so she read it again, trying to fathom what it all meant. What was a "tag", and how could it trace where a person was? And how could it be possible for something to stop someone's heart? And the idea that not everyone worked? She tried to imagine how life could be possible without everyone working at something. How could they have provided enough food for everyone? Every time Nadya read another part of the journal, she was left with more questions than answers. She wondered if she would reach a point where suddenly it all fell into place and the things she had yearned, all her life, to understand would become clear.

Gathering up her empty wrappers, she continued north once more, climbing away from the old village. She crossed two fields which, this far north, no longer belonged to her family and soon came to a wood that reached all the way to the clifftop, with no path on her side that she knew of. There was a path that wound through the trees, and she had walked it many times, so she was not afraid of losing her way. Under the trees, it was cool and pleasant, sheltered from the hot afternoon sun, and she enjoyed the muffled sounds found in the dark interior of the wood. These trees were ancient and large, mainly oaks, crowding out the sun with their broad crowns and still thick leafy dressing. The leaves of the oaks were some of the last to fall and carpet the floor of the wood. They were now dark green, if not already turning brown, but she could picture the bright new green leaves that would provide the trees with their brand-new clothes once the weeks of full winter passed.

After more than an hour under the trees, she emerged at the side of a large road, which led from Fridaytown away east down to the sea. At this point the road was known as Garrow Hill, and it climbed steeply from the sea as it headed east before descending again into Fridaytown. Beyond that, Nadya had never been. She did not intend to go beyond the road today, so she turned around and headed back the way she had come.

She had not been walking quickly, and the afternoon was wearing away. She thought it might already be dark before she reached home, but again this held no fear for her as she was very familiar with the paths through the fields. She decided, however, to track slightly east to eventually pick up the main road, which would bring her to the top of the lane leading to the farm above Wilton. Once she was on this road, she quickened her pace and soon reached the lane to the farmyard.

Halfway down, she stopped in surprise at the sight of several horses in the yard, and wondered how and why so many visitors had appeared - her mother had said nothing about a gathering this evening. Something triggered caution in her mind, and she quickly wrapped the two journals in the cloths from her lunch and hid them under a tree in the copse just to the north of the lane. She felt foolish doing so, but she didn't want anyone prying into her discovery should someone decide to empty her pack when she arrived home. Covering the package with the dried leaves that had already fallen, she returned to the lane and walked slowly down to her home.

The horses in the yard snorted and shuffled uneasily as she passed but did not make any noise likely to be heard inside the farmhouse. When she opened the door and walked into the warm kitchen, the company gathered there were taken by surprise at her entrance, and all turned to look at her as she closed the door behind her. They continued to stare at her as she removed her coat and boots, giving her an uneasy feeling that something was indeed amiss, and that she was either disturbing a discussion she was not meant to hear or, indeed, that she was the subject of the unexpected meeting.

Finally, her father broke the silence.

"Come in and sit down, please, Nadya," he said quietly, with a distinct sound of sadness in his voice. As she approached, she saw for the first time the box she had hidden in her wardrobe, sitting open on the table. Her mind raced as she looked quickly around the room, looking to see who was here and for some support in the faces of those present. Even her beloved mother could not hold her gaze and lowered her eyes to look at her hands, which were folded in her lap.

"Can you tell us about this box, please?" her father asked gently. One of the others, who Nadya now recognised as members of the council, tried to say something more, but her father waved him to silence. He would ask these questions in his own way and would not let his own daughter be interrogated by others in his house.

"What do you want to know?" Nadya replied, frantically trying to construct a story that would be credible and not damn her. She knew, of course, that she should have handed the box, unopened, over to the council immediately she found it. Although there was, in theory, no censorship in Woldshire, the reality, as everyone knew, was that the council kept tight control over what was openly discussed about the past. They certainly did not allow the free flow of such information as could be found in the items in the box.

"Well, where does it come from, why have you got it, and why haven't you handed it over, for a start?" the man she knew as Ted asked loudly and bluntly, pushing himself up from his chair with his hands on the table and looking squarely at Nadya.

"I'll ask the questions if you don't mind, Ted," her father said, waving again for the others to remain seated and be quiet.

"But - " interjected Ted.

"No buts, Ted. This is my house, and you're here as my guests. I'll ask any questions that need asking." Nadya could see that her da would not let her be intimidated or bullied, but it was also clear that he wanted to know the answers too. She decided that there was no avoiding telling the truth, or at least most of it. She had no idea how the box had come to be sitting on the table in front of her and would want to ask questions about that later, but now was not the time.

"Well," she began haltingly, "I found it a few days ago, buried under a rock as I was replacing a fence post in one of the fields. I had to take the rock out to get a new post in, and it was under there. I was going to hand it in, I really was, but I wanted to take a look for myself first. I've always been curious about the way things are, and about the past, and I didn't think it would do any harm if I looked first for myself."

"Was Layna with you when you found it? Does she know about it?" her father asked.

"No, she didn't see it, and I've never told her about it," Nadya said truthfully. She knew that the more truth she told, the better it would be. "I dug it up early one morning and brought it straight back here and hid it in my room."

"Why did you hide it, Nadya? You know you should have handed it over straight away, don't you?" The question was gently asked but she knew that her answer could damn her.

"I, I, I didn't know what was in it," she stammered, struggling. "I had to get on with my work, so I just hid it in my room to deal with later." She knew immediately she shouldn't have used the word "hid", but it was too late to take it back, so she just ploughed on. "I've only glanced at it once and was going to hand it in, but then Milo and I fell out, and I haven't been myself since, and it just went out of my mind." Tears welled up in her eyes as she was reminded of her falling out with Milo, and she wiped them angrily away; she did not want these men to see her as a silly, tearful girl.

"And what did you see when you looked at what was in the box?" her father asked.

"I saw lots of bright pictures of clothes and houses and machines and things," she burst out.

"And you wanted…" Ted shouted again, but John looked at him sharply and silenced him. Nadya never knew her own father had such authority over the council. He had always made a joke of it, but now she could tell that, even though Ted was supposedly the chairman, the real leader of the men was John.

"And what else did you see?" He now asked, "Did you read any of the things in there?"

"Erm," she hesitated again. "I only read a little bit, something about babies. I was more entranced by the pictures. I had no idea such things could exist."

"I see," John said. "And the article about babies was where you got the idea that people used to have any number of children and with any number of people?"

Nadya was stunned into silence. She now knew exactly why this was happening. She was immediately both heartbroken and furious with Milo. At the same time, though, a new resolve arose in her: she would not be cowed by these people. She had a right, surely, to know such things. What right had these men to keep knowledge to themselves? She looked around the room at the men sitting in judgement on her, and her face flushed with anger.

She spoke now with a determined calm. "Yes, and I don't understand how that could be. I would like to, but I don't think the answer is in that box, so I now do hand it over to you. The rest of what is in there is frippery."

With that, she folded her arms in front of her and looked defiantly from one to the next, making it clear she was finished and would not be answering any further questions. Yes, she had broken a convention, but not really any law that she knew of, and she certainly hadn't done anyone any harm.

Ted rose again and was about to speak, but her da stopped him.

Right, I think that's all we can do now, gentlemen," he said firmly. "Thank you for bringing this to my attention before any further damage could be done. We'll discuss at the next meeting what to do about it."

Ted was about to speak again, but once more her da spoke across him. "It's getting late now, gents; I suggest we are all in need of our dinners and to settle down in our own homes."

With that, he moved to the door, started to take the coats and hats of the company from the pegs, and hold them out. Meena took his lead and went to stand beside him to hand the coats to each of the men as they left. One by one they all stood and shuffled obediently towards the door. Only Ted tried to speak again, but this time he was cut off by one of the others.

"OK, Ted. Enough for now, she's only a lass, we can take this up properly at the next meeting."

With that, even Ted moved towards the door but couldn't resist a nasty look in Nadya's direction as he collected his coat and hat. He was the last out of the door.

As John ushered the men out of the house and onto their horses, Meena motioned to Nadya to take herself off to her room.

"Best to let your father settle a bit before you two talk." She spoke quietly but firmly, and Nadya knew she was making sense. Although her da had prevented the questioning from turning into a witch hunt, she knew he would be angry and disappointed with her.

"Go and get yourself cleaned up after your walk, dear. Supper will be about an hour. It won't be much I'm afraid as we've been entertaining the gentlemen of the council since mid-afternoon."

She finished by saying, again in a low but firm voice as Nadya left the room through the door leading to the stairs, "I suggest you have a think about some better answers than you have given just now, Nadya love. Your father won't be satisfied with your scant explanation so far."

————

Supper, a simple affair of cold meat, preserves, thick slabs of Meena's delicious bread, and fresh, creamy butter, was eaten in silence. Nadya's father avoided looking at his beloved daughter, and she could see he was struggling to control his emotions. She had only once in her life roused him to real anger, and on that occasion, he had shouted at her, and his eyes had blazed with fury. She had been terrified, even safe in the knowledge that he would never hurt her, and had also felt keenly a sense of having let him down. She could see he was both angry and disappointed now, and she dreaded the end of supper when she knew he would begin again to ask her questions. He would be less ready to treat her so gently now that they were alone as a family.

Once the table was cleared, the three of them sat down at the table, the boys having been asked to take themselves off to the inn in Milltown for a few hours. They knew something was amiss but not the details. It was highly likely they would return from the inn fully informed, although only from the perspective of the council. Nadya decided to pre-empt the discussion and, looking her father straight in the eye, said, "Can I tell you everything as I remember it, da?"

He looked at her, grim-faced, but she also detected a hint of pride in his eyes, pride that his daughter was not cowed and also prepared to face up to what she had done.

"Go on then girl," he said plainly. "But not the sorry tale you tried to spin the others."

She nodded and, beginning with the discovery of something preventing her and Layna from putting in the new fence post, she told the whole thing in as much detail as she could recall, leaving out only any reference to the journal. She was not ready to part with that yet and was even prepared to deceive her mother and father in order to hang on to the two books. She told them of her wonder at the pictures of the old life, at the dazzling display of clothes and things in the houses, and of her excitement as she had seen the shoes they wore. Then, she told of reading the article about babies and how she had been shocked to learn that what she knew of human biology appeared not to have been true a mere few hundred years ago. She had planned this carefully whilst waiting for supper, and she was careful not to speak of anything she had read in the journal, but only those things she had seen in the magazines. Finally, she told them about how she had asked Milo how he thought the limit of two children worked, and how he had been furious, not just with that, but even more when she had added the bit about being able to have children with more than one father. At this point, tears began to flow freely, and she sobbed as she told them she thought that he would never now want to marry her, and their relationship, which had gone on for so many years, was over forever. She stopped and sat with her head in her hands, crying freely. Her mother now came to sit beside her and, putting her arms around her daughter's shoulders, tried to comfort her.

John sat in silence for a time, staring at the fire, which was by now beginning to die away, leaving only the glowing embers in the grate. The steady click-click of the cooling ironwork punctuated Nadya's sobs. After many long minutes, he spoke without looking up.

"Nadie love," he began haltingly. "I love you more than anything, and you must know you have hurt me with this deceit and have brought shame and pain to the family which will not heal quickly."

Again, he stopped for several minutes before continuing.

"I still think there's something you're not saying, Nadya, but I suppose you must have a good reason for not doing so. I'd like to know what is so important that you would hide it from your family, but we'll leave it for now."

Now he looked at her across the table and continued with a sadness in his voice.

"I think you may be right about Milo. Certainly, what has passed between you will not heal for many years. You must have guessed, of course, that it was he who brought the council to our door. Whether deliberately or without meaning to, I don't know, but it's not something we can easily raise with him. In any case, the council would certainly not approve of you marrying anyone right now. We need to find a way to put this to rest and prevent any further damage to the family. There is a very real danger that we could be shunned. We have certainly lost a great deal of reputation, and I may have used up much of my influence with the council this evening."

He now stood and walked over to Nadya. Sitting down on the opposite side to Meena, he took hold of both her hands and pulled her gaze towards him.

"I think you need to go away for some time, Nadie love. I'm thinking of your aunt Annie and uncle Cliff in Nym. You could go and stay with them and learn the craft of metalworking and smithing."

Nadya drew in a sharp breath and let out a small moan. She had not at any time thought that such an outcome might be possible. She had never spent even one night away from the farm, nor away from her parents. She could barely comprehend the idea of moving so far away and not seeing her family for many, many months. She sobbed quietly to herself, feeling utterly wretched.

"I'm sorry," was all she could think to say.

Chapter 8 - Selected entries from Harry's Journals.
January 15th, 2080.

In today's news:

The USA and Canada have seen ten days of temperatures below minus twenty centigrade as far south as Florida, with Toronto at minus sixty. Hundreds of deaths from hypothermia are reported to have occurred in Ontario, where many electric cars failed, leaving people stranded in the desolate temperatures.

Meanwhile, the island of Bali has raging wildfires which have destroyed much of the main city. People are being rescued from the beaches by ship, but many are reported to have burned to death before help could reach them.

In Europe, large parts of France and most of the Netherlands continue to be underwater following record rainfall coupled with record high spring tides.

Police were called to control riots in Paris, as large-scale demonstrations took place against the government's move to implement trials of the new metabolic control chips on long-term prisoners. In the UK, demonstrations continued outside Wandsworth Prison, where the procedure to implant a metabolic control chip in the volunteer prisoner went ahead. The Supreme Court had ruled that the chips did not contravene the individual's rights as he volunteered. The procedure was carried out by the EMEA region of the newly named Z Corporation, which recently took control of all UK prisons, adding to their existing control of all police services in the country.

The last known wild polar bear was found dead several days ago near Toronto. Ecologists are hopeful that there may remain a small number of individuals in the far north, but they warn that there are probably insufficient numbers to bring about a population recovery, especially as there has been almost zero sea ice cover except in the depths of winter. Perversely, this year has seen the largest extent of cover for decades, although, even after the current prolonged freeze, still not of sufficient depth to remain stable for more than a few weeks once the weather changes. It is thought this bear had trekked the huge distance south from it's normal range in search of food, it had died eventually of starvation.

Thoughts on the end of democracy in the western world:

In 2024 Professor Yanis Varoufakis published a book called "Technofeudalism: What Killed Capitalism". In this, he described how the capitalist system was finally undermined by the rise of a new power, those who had essentially privatised the internet and had begun to extract wealth from all others who would use it. He coined the term technofeudalist to describe those who had "fenced off" large parts of what used to be the commonly owned internet and, as the feudal lords of the Middle Ages did with land ownership, forced all those who wished to do business on their platforms must pay a tithe or rent. As these tech platforms increasingly replaced the high street stores and entertainment centres as well as the old mainstream media so the power and wealth of the technofeudalists grew exponentially.

Human civilisation has always been characterised by the gradual concentration of wealth, and therefore power, into the hands of fewer and fewer individuals. This trend is punctuated by periods of rapid change, where the newly wealthy emerged due to their exploitation of new technology. For example, the largely feudal societies of the Middle Ages and Renaissance, where wealth and power remained in the hands of historic landowning overlords, were somewhat replaced by the owners of industrial developments. This change continued into the twentieth century with multinational industrial businesses, and the associated financial establishments that financed them, dominating late twentieth century economies throughout the world. Then, in the early twenty-first century, the emergence of the technofeudalists took place, and the few hugely wealthy individuals and their corporations gradually brought even the largest industrial businesses within their empires. After the financial crisis of 2008 the central banks pumped out huge volumes of newly printed cash in an attempt to stabilise economies. Sadly, the vast majority of this new cash simply landed in the hands of these new feudal overlords, the already rich, the tech billionaires. The injections of new cash were repeated on an even bigger scale during the pandemic of the early 2020's and for the first time we saw individuals with wealth exceeding that of most countries. The financial institutions were not slow to follow the money and the gap between ultra rich and poor grew apace. In 2010 foodbanks were unheard of in the UK, by 2024 there were thousands. Over the same time period, the number of billionaires tripled and by 2024 the amount of wealth held by the richest 1% exceeded that held by the poorest 55%.

In the mid-2020s one individual from the tech world held personal wealth which exceeded the Gross Domestic Product of more than ninety percent of countries, and one investment group managed assets worth more than all but two of the largest economies of the world. Political donations from a few corporations or individuals could now exceed all other donations and essentially "buy" the election of their chosen candidate or party. Democracy was in grave danger, but nothing was done. The world had other issues, and the vast majority of people simply did not care.

During the years from 2020 to 2040, the technofeudalists (or technos as they had come to be known) began to take on ownership of more and more governmental functions and societal service provision. By 2040, following the war years, control of almost all aspects of service provision, including transport, water, and power, as well as services such as health and increasingly law and order (police and even courts), were provided by just five large multinational techno entities. These five dominated service provision across Europe, the US, and Canada. The years of right-wing dominated governments, with the low-tax and small-government dogma, contributed to these shifts, so that these years saw the emergence of a huge underclass of workless and desperately poor people. This mass of people had little hope of any possibility of improving their circumstances. They survived in minimal quality housing, were fed largely from food banks, and could not afford either healthcare for themselves or education for their children. Uprisings were brutally suppressed, leaving thousands of dead.

The collapse of international law, following the middle eastern wars of 2023–2027, and the withdrawal of countries such as the UK from European courts, and eventually even the UN, left little ability for anyone to challenge these mass exterminations.

In the 2050s, the continued collapse of work opportunities, as AI and robotics dominated sector after sector, led to a realisation, by the technos, that unless something changed, their markets would also collapse, as fewer and fewer people had any disposable income. This realisation instigated the widescale introduction of minimum income provision for the masses, with only occasional work opportunities for a few. These fortunate few gained, temporarily at least, a somewhat higher than average level of income. But even these lucky individuals had no chance of ever moving into the spheres of the ultra-rich and their descendants.

A very few in various entertainment sectors, such as sport, social media, and music/cinema, might look as if they had reached those high echelons of society and were apparently accepted into the society of the wealthy. Even those individuals, though, did not achieve a multigenerational hold on their status as rich, indeed, just like the few remaining independent industrial giants, they were subject to the tithes or rents of the technofeudalists and entirely reliant on continued access to the social media platforms where they earned their money. The overlords could, at a whim, remove their access and destroy them. Human civilisation had finally settled into two distinct societies: the ultra-wealthy and the rest. Democracy, or at least the pretence of it, clung on in a few countries, but the reality was that all meaningful governmental functionality sat with the tech corporations.

This state has continued to this day, and when we talk of government, we really mean the democratic veneer covering the reality of a return to feudal rule over the vast majority of humankind. The long-held fear that AI systems would take over from humanity has failed to materialise, and instead we have both corporations and an elite class of people who use AI and robotics to control humanity.

Personal Notes:

My own scheduled work period is due to begin in April; I hope to continue in work long enough to secure a long-term lease on a small apartment in the region of the Yorkshire Wolds. There is no hope, though, of buying a home, as house prices are now measured not in years of income but rather in several lifetimes of minimum income levels. Most people live in the minimal state (in reality, corporate) housing provision, with only a few able to afford private leaseholds. I continue to try to capture a flavour of the events which have led us from the relative prosperity of the late twentieth century to today, and to document the changes which I am sure are unavoidable. All hope of avoiding catastrophic climate change is gone, and we must try to survive what is surely coming; we are in the unknown. The climatologists tell us that eventually the Earth will settle into a new steady state once all the melting has occurred, but until that time the only certainty appears to be uncertainty. We do know that the storms, floods, droughts, and freezes will continue, but with a huge level of unpredictability.

I have been assigned to a care facility for my work detail. This is one of the last areas where humans continue to have advantages over the robotics which have decimated other physical work. It seems we still value the human touch when we are at our most vulnerable. In the early parts of the twenty-first century, there were concerns over the ability to have enough younger people to both pay for and supply the labour for the care of an increasingly elderly population. Since those days, though, so much other work has been removed from the human sphere that the provision of labour is not a problem. The whole economic model has also changed since then, with almost total ownership of societal service provision now in the hands of the technos, so that cost is a somewhat outmoded concern. All services are now provided in return for power and the continued ability of new feudal overlords to live their privileged lives entirely separate from the bulk of humanity. In many ways, the majority of humans are becoming irrelevant to them, as they need us less and less. There are regular rumours that "they" have worked out how to finally eliminate the masses without dangerously shrinking their gene pool. Is that our true role now, I wonder? To provide regular injections of fresh genetic material so that the elite can maintain a healthy population. Certainly, we have little to offer in terms of provision of life's necessities, as modern robotics can now do all of this. Little did human society of the 2020s realise where driverless cars, robotic factories and farms, and then robotic education would lead. The ultra-rich technos do not now even share the living spaces with the rest of us; they have long removed themselves to remote and isolated regions, supposedly safe from the ravages of climate change. It is rumoured they no longer even have human servants, preferring to maintain complete isolation and so relying on robotic help.

A very lucky few people do manage to make a living out of creative entertainment, but even there it is impossible to tell which work is human-derived and which is AI. I suspect that only a tiny amount is truly human-generated; after all, we never really meet the supposedly human creators. Again, I wonder if the people of the 2020s would have been quite so keen on the large language models, the various AI image and video generators, etc., if they had thought properly about the future. I have read that some in the entertainment industry refused to work at some point in 2022, demanding that the film studios would not replace them using AI. The resulting victory was short-lived, and by the 2030s most of the video content used only AI-generated characters. The studios may not have used AI video of the previous stars, but this did not prevent them creating new "stars" who were wholly AI-generated. The same was true of the music industry, and the gaming industry had been computer-generated from its outset. The film and music studios were soon absorbed into the tech giants' empires and became some of the very first industries to disappear as sources of human employment.

Chapter 9 - Partings.

Over the next two weeks, messages were sent to Uncle Cliff and Aunt Annie, explaining that Nadya needed some time away from home and asking if Cliff would take her on as an apprentice to teach her metalwork and smithing. Both were valuable trades and extremely useful on a farm. No mention was made of the trouble that had led to this situation; John hoped that his brother was far enough away that any rumours would not have reached his ears. After some days, a reply was received confirming that Cliff would be delighted to take on Nadya and teach her his craft. Cliff and Annie had been one of the very few couples who were not blessed with children, and so there was no heir to his smithing business and no natural candidate for apprentice. They explained that Nadya would be more than welcome in their home and would be treated just like she was their own daughter.

And so, far too quickly for Nadya, the day of departure came around. John himself would take her in the cart. He had not seen his brother for several years, and so this would give him a chance to catch up with family business and reacquaint himself with both Cliff and Annie, to whom he had always been close. Cliff, being the younger brother was not destined to inherit, unless the farm was divided. Luckily, this had not been a problem, as he was more inclined towards smithing anyway and enjoyed both the practical side - horseshoeing, repairing various farm and other implements - as well as having a talent for creating intricate and detailed works of art in metal. His gates, garden ornaments, and sculptures were renowned throughout Woldshire and Nym. Sadly, there had already been an established family smithing business around Milltown, but their father had secured him an apprenticeship in Nym, near Rosedale with its ancient metalworking connections. In time, Cliff had proved both his metalworking skills and business acumen and had taken over the business when the owner died.

Nadya had just one thing she had to do before she left, and so she took the cart into Milltown first thing in the morning while everyone else ate breakfast. They knew where she was going, and although they were concerned for her, they knew that this was something she had to do before leaving for what could be many months. The sun was still low in the misty sky as she drove the cart the few miles into the town. The hedgerows were bedecked with a thousand glistening, dew-laden cobwebs, each like a sparkling silver midwinter festival decoration. The autumn berries each carried a hanging drop of water, some small and some larger and ready to drop. Down in the Milltown valley, the mist hung low and the air was still chilly, so Nadya pulled her coat tighter around her as she descended into the moisture-laden air. Visibility was low, and even sound was muffled; she didn't hear the burbling of Milltown stream until she was almost upon it. Splashing through the shallow water, she was soon into the village which, this early in the morning, was nearly deserted. She quickly made for Milo's home and pulled up in the yard, the horses snorting and stamping in the haze. She wasn't sure what sort of welcome she would receive, but she had been determined that things between her and Milo should not be left hanging. She wanted, above all, to know why he had felt the need to report her to the council.

She crossed the yard and knocked on the large wooden door. In previous times, she would then have walked straight in, but she was not sure where she now stood with regard to Milo or his family. She heard footsteps approaching the door from the inside, not heavy ones but more the light step of Milo's mother. The door was pulled tentatively open. Clearly, they were surprised to be having visitors this early, and Mrs Meggison looked at Nadya with a frown and pursed lips.

"Hello, Nadya," she said coolly. "What brings you here so early?"

"I would like to speak to Milo, please," Nadya replied, straining to keep any emotion out of her voice or tears from rising in her eyes.

"He's eating breakfast; wait here, and I'll see if he wants to speak to you." With that, the woman whom Nadya had come to regard as a second mother closed the door and retreated.

Clearly, Nadya was no longer welcome and certainly no longer "like one of the family". She was filled with sadness and almost turned to go, but at that moment the door opened once again, and Milo stood on the doorstep looking at her.

"Can we walk?" asked Nadya, not wanting to have a conversation in this manner.

"I suppose. Let me get a coat," said Milo, retreating and closing the door once again. He emerged in just a few moments and stepped down. He didn't offer a hug or even to take Nadya's hand, so that, in a sense, she already knew what the outcome of the conversation was going to be. She had intended to begin by explaining that she was going away and asking whether they could remain friends, perhaps write, but now she simply, and perhaps too bluntly, said:

"Why did you feel the need to report me to the council?"

Milo took hold of her arm and pulled her around to face him.

"Is that what you think?" She could hear the hurt as well as anger in his voice.

She snapped back, "Well, someone did. They repeated back to me the question I had asked you, and only you, that Sunday."

This wasn't going well at all, and Nadya felt she had to do something or just leave, so she spoke again quickly and more calmly.

"Look, Milo, I didn't come to have a row with you. I'm going away, possibly for a long time, maybe even forever, and I would like us to remain friends and perhaps write to each other."

The anger drained from Milo's face, and he let go of her arm.

"I'm sorry about what has happened," he said quietly. "I didn't report you. I made the mistake of talking to my sister after our row. I was hurt and angry and hoped that she would help me understand you women. I wasn't to know she would go straight off to Ma, and the two of them would chitter about you to Ted."

Nadya now understood what had happened. Marta, Milo's sister, had always been jealous of her closeness to him and had clearly taken the opportunity to drive a wedge between them and remove her as a threat.

"Oh," was all she could say, close to tears again now.

They walked on in silence for several minutes before she went on.

"Well, what's done is done, I suppose. I think we had reached something of a crossroads anyway. I did love you; I do love you, but I have some things I want to do before I marry, and I know this doesn't fit with your plans and desires."

She went on, with a formality she felt was called for by the occasion.

"In the circumstances, I don't expect you to wait for me; I don't know how long I need to stay away. So, I release you from any promise you might feel exists between us. You can go and find yourself a bride who matches your own ambitions."

Milo looked at his former lover and friend of many years.

"Thank you," he said. "I need some time before I decide anything."

After a pause, he went on, "I would like to write. I would like to understand more about these strange questions you have, and maybe we can talk about things better with the remoteness of writing."

Nadya looked at him for a long time before saying, "You will need to promise me anything I write will never be revealed to anyone else. I have got my family into enough trouble as it is. I'm sorry, but you are going to need to prove to me that I can trust you again."

With that, she turned to him and kissed him briefly on the lips, as if to show that she, at least, had forgiven him. Finally, she pulled away, and turning back towards the house, she spoke decisively.

"I need to go, Milo. Thank you for this and for everything. Thank your mother for all that she has meant to me over the years, and please tell her I'm sorry for any hurt I've caused."

Milo looked as if he was going to say something more, but she silenced him with another kiss and then turned and ran for the cart. She climbed aboard, turned once more to him, and waved with a cheeriness that was a million miles from how she felt. She urged the horses into a trot and pulled quickly out of the yard, turning at the last moment and shouting, "I'll write and let you know where to write back. Goodbye, Milo. I love you."

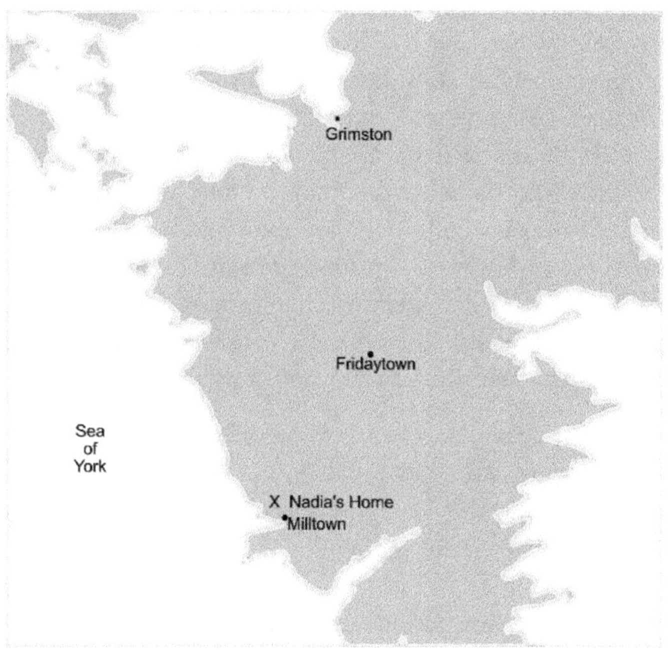

Nadya climbed aboard the cart to sit next to her da. The two had reconciled since the acrimonious meeting with the council. He still did not fully understand her need to be curious about things that were forbidden, or at least frowned upon, but he was prepared to accept that she was genuinely sorry for the trouble she had caused. He also knew that she had been the victim of a jealous and vindictive sister. They had a long journey ahead of them; it would take most of a day to reach the ferry at Grimston and then another full day to make the crossing to Terrington Ferry. Uncle Cliff was to meet them there and take them on to Rosedale. The cart and horses would have to be left at Grimston, and John would collect them on his return a week later. He had arranged the stabling and the ferry crossing, all at considerable expense, but at least this way Nadya would be placed out of reach of the council and, hopefully, the whole thing would blow over in time. For Nadya to become fully trained in smithing and metalwork would take at least five years, and John hoped she could then return to the farm and to Milltown to resume her life. Of course, it was perfectly possible she might decide to make her life in Nym, something which, John knew, caused Meena more consternation than she was showing at the moment.

He also knew that, despite the show of bravado from Nadya, this was a devastating upheaval for her. She would be able to visit her family as often as she wished, but it was a long journey and, in taking on the apprenticeship, she was committing herself to living away from her home for several years. Her future had for years been assumed to be with Milo, setting up home in Milltown. Now she needed to find a different future for herself and amidst the sorrow of leaving her family there was a tiny spark of excitement at this prospect.

"Did you settle things with Milo?" John asked as they left the farmyard.

"Yes, I think so," replied Nadya. She had already explained how his sister had been the one to cause the trouble but had not gone into what had passed between her and Milo. "We have parted friends at least, I think," she went on. "I know everyone, including the two of us, has always thought we were destined for each other, but now I think we both accept that we have grown to be different, too different for a marriage ever to work between us."

"That's probably for the best, given the way things have turned out," John said sympathetically.

They had turned south on leaving the farm, crossing the small stream at the bottom of Grimthorpe Hill before turning northeast on the road to Fridaytown. They would stop there to water the horses and get themselves some lunch at the inn in the village. In other circumstances, this would be quite an adventure, but neither was in the mood for enjoying the journey for its own sake. At least, thought Nadya, they would soon be out of the local area where she had spent all her life so far. Every turning, every stream, every hill, and even every tree seemed so familiar to her, and it felt as if she were leaving everything behind forever. In her head, she knew this was not true and she would be able to return several times a year to spend time with the family, but her heart wrenched every time they passed a familiar landmark. They had agreed that she would not return for the midwinter festival this year, as that was only a few weeks away. Everyone hoped she would make the journey for the spring equinox, but to Nadya, that seemed like an eternity away. She had met Uncle Cliff and Aunt Annie only infrequently, and she was leaving behind all of her friends. She especially felt sad that she would no longer spend days working with Layna.

She had retrieved the journals after a few days, when she was sure that no one was watching her, and she had packed them away carefully in her trunk. If nothing else, she had learned a valuable lesson about trusting anyone. She would not be sharing with anyone what she learned as she continued to read, at least not until she was absolutely sure of them. She felt that would be many years away, if at all; in the meantime, she was content to keep everything to herself. There was a small voice in her mind which told her she should have handed everything over and forgotten it, but then her rebellious and stubborn nature fought back, strengthening her resolve to keep this for herself. In any case, it was too late to change her mind now, as admitting that she had not immediately submitted fully to the wishes of Milltown council would have meant even more severe trouble for her family. Of one thing she was very sure: she would not be saying, or doing, anything which might make her aunt and uncle regret taking her in.

She had not had the chance to read any more since the day of the council questions; indeed, given the frantic preparations for her departure, she had barely had time to even think about what she had already read. It was unlikely that she would have any time in the next few weeks either, as she would need to settle into her new home and begin her apprenticeship. In return for her new home, she would be expected to work hard and learn quickly so that she could be of use to Uncle Cliff. There had been no mention of pay, but her da had assured her that, once she was useful, Cliff would treat her fairly and she would have cash of her own to save or spend as she wanted. As she thought of all these things, she found they had covered many kilometres and were already on the main road to Fridaytown. Her da seemed content to pass the journey mostly in silence, only whistling to himself as they passed through the autumnal countryside.

The fields were all harvested now, and most were ploughed and ready for the early spring crops, if not already sown with winter wheat or barley. The hedgerows and the trees were largely bare of leaves, but the autumn berries brought a welcome touch of colour to the otherwise drab, brown landscape. It was now late autumn, but there had, as yet, been no frosts; indeed, the year had brought a prolonged warm spell after the summer. Nadya and Milo had made the most of this with their swimming, but soon it was likely that the weather normally expected during winter would take hold; another reason why Nadya would not be returning home for the midwinter festival. She wondered what midwinter would be like at her uncle's house; would they enjoy the good food and feasting she had come to know since her childhood?

After a long ride, the two travellers pulled up outside the Friday Inn, which overlooked the old town green and pond. The pond was quite low, due to the recent dry spell, and the water was surrounded by a broad expanse of dried mud, pocked with footprints of ducks, geese, and others. The birds themselves were sitting on the grass on the far side of the pond, heads tucked under their wings, as they basked in what remained of the warmth of the sun this late in the year. In the distant past, these birds would have been purely decorative, but these days they were a useful source of additional protein for the people who lived adjacent to the green. Ownership of the pond and its resources lay with a small cooperative, with each share belonging not to an individual but to a dwelling, and whoever happened to reside in it at the time.

As Nadya and John entered the inn, the loud background chatter ceased immediately, and all eyes were turned to the newcomers. John motioned Nadya to a table by a window and walked over to the bar, where a stout, balding man with a red face and glittering eyes had looked up from a deep conversation with a customer who was nursing a half-litre glass, with just a covering of dark brown liquid in the bottom. As John approached, the man took the tiniest of sips from the glass so that the level of liquid was not noticeably altered. "Ey up," the barman greeted John amiably. "What can a get thi'".

"Soup?" asked John.

"Aye," came the reply. "Bacon and tattie, for two?"

"Please, and two glasses of your bitter."

"Large or small?" asked the barman, referring, John assumed, to the ales.

"Large please," was John's answer.

"Grand, that'll be twelve stirls. T'lass will bring it over."

John handed over twelve stirls, a stirl being the main denomination of the island's currency, and took a seat next to Nadya, who was still the centre of attention of the other men in the room. Her long, bright red hair and youthful beauty were clearly something not seen often in the inn. The two travellers sat in silence while they waited for their food and drink, and soon enough the gazes of the others turned elsewhere, and they returned to their conversations, satisfied that John and Nadya were not about to burst into song or do anything else untoward. "T'lass" turned out to be a short, stocky blonde girl with short hair and a plump but cheery face and the same glittering eyes as the barman. Clearly, they were related. She set down two dishes of a thick and aromatic soup, two chunks of fresh brown, thickly buttered bread, and two glasses of crystal-clear, pale brown ale, each topped with a good two centimetres of white froth. Apparently, the innkeeper knew how to keep his ale.

Without a word, the girl withdrew, and Nadya and John tucked into the welcome meal.

"This is good," offered John. "We could do with this innkeeper taking over the pub in Milltown."

The establishment in Milltown was widely known for its average ale and the frugality of its food offering. Nadya laughed, for the first time in weeks, John thought. It was good to see some cheer in her face again. This small exchange released the slight remaining tension that had existed between the two all morning, and soon they were chatting easily about what John could remember of Uncle Cliff and Aunt Annie.

"They're good folk, and I'm sure you'll settle in," he reassured Nadya. "You'll need to be careful not to be causing any more trouble, mind you."

"You don't need to worry on that score at all," said Nadya forcefully. "I've learned to keep my thoughts to myself, especially if they are ones others are unlikely to share."

John looked at his daughter sadly. "Well, it's a shame you hadn't learned that lesson earlier, love. Still, I think it may all turn out for the best in the end. I'm sure you'll make a good smith, and that will open up whole new avenues for you, either back at the farm or wherever you decide to make your life."

He reached out and took his daughter's hand over the table. "You know the farm will always be your home; we just need to let the dust settle on this nonsense. I'm sure, soon enough, there will be some new scandal to capture people's attention."

"I know, Da," said Nadya quietly. "I really am sorry for the mess I've made."

John did not reply but simply gave her hand a squeeze before returning his attention to his meal. Their talk now turned to less weighty matters, John telling Nadya what he could remember of the countryside around Rosedale. He told how it was hillier than around Milltown, with steep-sided dales and moorland rather than farmland on the heights. Down in the valleys, where most of the villages nestled, the land was rich, and they were able to grow good-quality vegetables and fruit. There was little dairy farming, apart from one or two cows kept to provide milk to the locals, the main farm animals being sheep and some pigs.

"Like everywhere, the folk can be wary of strangers," he stated plainly. "But as a relative of Cliff and Annie, you'll soon be made welcome and will make new friends. You might even meet a young man who takes your fancy and bring back some fresh blood to Milltown in a few years."

Nadya looked at him with raised eyebrows and replied, "Oh, I think I've had my fill of men for the foreseeable future. I'm not sure any of them are worth the trouble and grief they bring."

"Haha, well you're a beauty like your mum, young Nadya. That flaming hair of yours will turn heads, and, again like Meena, you've a figure which men find it hard to ignore. Still, you've her temperament as well, so I'm sure you'll soon gain the upper hand and control the admirers like a good shepherd does his flock."

Nadya laughed again, colour returning to her face and her eyes regaining the shine of inner confidence that had been missing these last weeks. John breathed a sigh of relief; his daughter would be OK, more than OK.

———

After completing their meal, John and Nadya once more climbed aboard the cart and set off on the last leg of the first part of their journey to Nym; they should easily reach Grimston before dark. John made a mental note to call again at the Friday Inn on his return journey to sample once more the food and ale. There were two ways from Fridaytown to Grimston: one required them to continue past the pond before taking the small road which wound through the dales to rejoin the main road at Wharram Street just south of their destination. The other, longer but probably quicker route, took the main road west out of Fridaytown before turning more northerly to Fimber and down to the crossroads before Sledmere, where they would take the north road direct to Grimston. John decided to take this quicker route as the afternoon was already passing. Although crime was almost unheard of in Woldshire, he didn't want to risk being caught out in the winding and narrow dales after dark. Fimber was a delightful village set on a hill with its own pond and inn. It sat at the top of the long, straight, descending road to the crossroads. Once past the village, John let the two horses have their heads a little, and the cart sped rapidly down the excellent road. Just before the crossroads, he reined them in once more and took the smaller road which climbed again, heading north. They now had only eight or nine kilometres to go, although it would still take another two hours or more as the road was steep in several places. The crossroads was surrounded by deep woodland but, as they climbed north, they soon emerged again to pastureland and into the late afternoon sun. Since the lunch stop, they had been much more relaxed with each other and with the journey. John sensed that Nadya had turned a corner and was much more her optimistic, positive self. Nadya found she was looking forward to something of an adventure and a new start. She would desperately miss her parents and brothers as well as the farm and her friends, but for the first time since her break-up with Milo, she could see a future as something which held the promise of happiness. She moved closer to her da on the bench seat and, linking her arm through his, she rested her head on his shoulder, breathing in his scent, wanting to capture it in her mind and hold on to it through the coming months until she could see him and the rest of the family again.

They came at last to Grimston and sought out the stabling for the horses; they would also look after the cart until John returned in a week. He satisfied himself that they would look after the valuable horses well. Even though they had come by recommendation from one of the few members of the council who, at this point, were still positively disposed towards the Knowles family, he would only be fully satisfied once he had inspected for himself. The owner, a tall, wiry man called Ron, was more than happy to show John around while Nadya unhitched the cart and lifted most of the luggage down. She would need a hand with her trunk as it was quite heavy, but her overnight bag and John's case she could manage easily. That done, she stroked the noses of the two horses, muttering her goodbyes to them, and by that time John had returned, happy with the arrangements. Together, they lifted down the trunk and loaded all onto a trolley that Ron had kindly lent them for the short walk to the harbour inn, where they were to spend the night. Nadya took the trolley back to Ron, while John checked them in and ensured their rooms were satisfactory.

Nadya's room was small but comfortable, with a good soft mattress and a small dressing table and chair. The walls were covered with pictures of the sea and of the ferry, and she was surprised to see that it appeared to be powered by some sort of engine. This would be the first engine she had seen in her life, and she was intrigued. She had expected only a small craft with oars or, at most, sails. With the image of the small but sturdy-looking craft, smoke pouring from a chimney at its centre, still in her mind, she took control of the shared bathroom and ran herself a hot bath to soak away the dirt and grime of the road. Some forty minutes later she emerged, glowing, having run several hot top-ups, and knocked on her father's door.

"Shall I leave the water in, Da?" she shouted through the door. "Do you want a bath?"

She heard the simple and mumbled response as though he was just waking from sleep.

"Aye, lass, why not."

Nadya returned to her room to dress, and from there heard her father plod along the hallway and into the bathroom. Unlike her extended soak, she heard him as he came out again a mere ten minutes later, washed and fresh.

"See you downstairs in half an hour?" John asked as he passed her door, knowing that his daughter would take at least that long to be ready to present herself to the company in the inn for the evening. In the meantime, he would take the time to exchange news with the locals over a glass of ale. He wasn't normally a great drinker, but he was a gregarious individual and would enjoy the change of company.

———

In the end, the evening was a quiet one; there weren't many customers at the inn, and those who were there weren't particularly talkative. Chatting to the innkeeper, John discovered that this was normal for this part of Woldshire. He explained that, being on the coast and within striking distance of Nym, folks tended to be a little wary of strangers and to keep to their homes after dark. Seemingly, even people from Nym were viewed with suspicion amongst the locals. They were "others", and the lack of trust of anyone or anything different was deeply ingrained in the psyche of all Woldshire folks. He explained that most of his evening trade came from people, just like John and Nadya, who were heading for the ferry. There were one or two locals who called in for a beer or to meet with a friend but, although not particularly unfriendly, they mainly kept themselves to themselves. That night, there were no others staying at the inn whilst waiting for the morning ferry, so Nadya and John ate alone, enjoying a good solid meat pie and local autumn vegetables. Altogether very satisfactory, and they retired early to their rooms and both slept soundly.

Breakfast was similarly hearty, and the two found themselves on the dock, awaiting the arrival of the ferry, not long after sunrise. Not uncommonly on this northern coast, the morning was misty and distinctly chilly. The swell in the harbour was low and the sound of the waves muffled by the mist. They heard the ferry long before they saw it, the sound of its steam engine a deep throbbing that was almost felt in the damp air as much as heard. As the sound increased, they finally saw the boat, slicing through the fog and sending it swirling away from its prow. As soon as it was within the harbour, the boatman spun the wheel hard to the left and then threw a lever, which sent the propeller into reverse, so that the dull grey metallic vessel swung round in a sharp half-circle. He completed the manoeuvre by deftly swinging on the wheel so that the rudder turned again, while shifting smartly back to forward thrust for a brief moment before shutting off all power. This brought the stocky little ship perfectly up against the dock, enabling the sole other crewman to step quickly ashore and secure the rope, bringing the craft finally to a halt, perfectly positioned. The whole thing was executed without a word, obviously something the two had managed so many times they could probably do it whilst both were blindfolded. Nodding briefly to John and Nadya, they then placed a rope across the entryway to the boat and left the dock, heading in the direction of the inn.

There was a young farmer on the dock who proceeded to herd several short, fat sheep into a pen next to the boat, and, seeing that the two passengers were looking somewhat bemused, he explained.

"Don't worry, me ducks, they warn't be long. They've gone for their breakfasts. They'll be back along shortly."

John nodded his thanks, and he and Nadya sat down on her trunk, pulling their coats tightly around them against the chill of the now resettled mist.

Just half an hour later, the two crewmen returned, took the twenty stirls fare from John and helped them aboard with their luggage. As they settled into the warmth of the not particularly clean passenger "lounge" and huddled around the wood-burning stove in the corner, the farmer moved a few bits of portable fence and guided his charges onto the boat forward of the cabin, then paid the crew before departing. Clearly, the sheep would be collected at the other end by someone else and would make the crossing unaccompanied. After another ten minutes and at eight thirty sharp, Nadya heard the quickening of the steam engine, followed by a loud clunk as the gearing was thrown into place to provide power to the propeller. The younger crewman threw the two securing ropes aboard, leaped across the rapidly widening gap between the boat and the dock, and they were underway, leaving behind the island which had been Nadya's home for her whole life. She felt a tightening in her throat and turned away from her father so that he wouldn't see the tears welling up in her eyes. John, though, was more sensitive to her mood than she gave him credit for. He put his arm around her shoulders and squeezed. He didn't say a word, but she felt immediately comforted and leaned back into his embrace.

The little boat steamed along the coast for a while before crossing a wide bay to the southwest and then hugging the flat coastal plain to their left once more. After an hour, they finally left the coast and headed out into open water, although by now the mist had cleared and they could already discern the blue-grey shape of steeper shores in front of them. Two islands loomed ahead of the boat, and Nadya could see that they were headed directly between them. The higher of the two lay to the southwest and the other, a low, flat green expanse, to the northeast. Neither seemed to have any habitation until, as the boat navigated the passage between, she finally saw a small settlement on the north coast of the larger of the two islands. They now passed into a wide area surrounded on all sides by land masses and with two tiny, low-lying islands just to the right of what appeared to be their course. Both were mere rocky outcrops, with wheeling, soaring gulls flying over them, and with large numbers of seals basking along the shore.

"Seal islands," shouted the older boatman above the din of the steam engine. "Good hunting here in the season, but we are approaching pupping time in the next few months, so we leave 'em alone right now."

As he had broken the silence, Nadya felt she could ask a question.

"Can I ask how it is that you have the only steam engine I've ever seen?" she asked as politely as she could muster, not wanting to cause any offence.

"Aye, lass, ye can ask," he replied, smiling broadly. He winked at the younger boatman before going on, "Over there in Woldshire, we know that there are no engines of any sort, but here in Nym we are not quite so obsessive in our adherence to the rules about mechanisms. We take the view that simple engines are not likely to be infiltrated by The Guardian, and so we use them, both for transport and other things."

He looked over at the younger crewman and laughed. "Ain't that right, Will? And without the steam engines we wouldn't be able to provide Woldshire folks with some of the tools and stuff that are needed for farming."

Will nodded and smiled. "You're reet, Tom, we wouldn't be able to make this trip so easily in a sailing boat or a rowing boat, not to carry passengers and goods anyway."

Nadya was not quite sure what to say. It seemed that much of what she had grown up thinking of as hard and fast rules was not quite so. She nodded her thanks and added, "I don't think we even have any boats in Woldshire."

At this, John spoke up, somewhat defensively. "Ah, we do, you know, Nadie love. Over on the east coast there are a few fishing boats. All using sail rather than any engines, I'll grant you, but we do have some boats."

Nadya looked at her da with astonishment, her mouth open and her green eyes wide. Before today, she had only ever seen boats in pictures.

"We don't use them on the west coast at all," John continued, "for fear of someone being carried over to the mainland as much as anything. We do get reports of the occasional craft, presumably from the mainland, stumbling over towards our island, but none have landed in living memory."

Nadya continued to stare open-mouthed at her father until Tom piped up, "You'll catch flies if you stay like that, lovey."

He laughed loudly, his rich, deep voice seeming to echo all around the islands. She closed her mouth but continued to look inquisitively at her da. Clearly, she had a lot to learn. No wonder the council didn't like questions being asked, if simple things like this were hidden. She set a mental reminder to quiz her father more about things later when they were more private.

By now, they were nearing a small harbour in a south-facing bay. Behind the harbour, the land rose, green and bedecked with sheep, to a large manor house which sat on the top of the hill. This commanded a sweeping view of the bay and the wider seascape all the way out to the two large islands they had passed between. There was a small gathering of people on the harbour, presumably some waiting for the next journey to Grimston. There must also be someone waiting to collect the sheep, she thought, and, of course, Uncle Cliff should be there as well. Both Nadya and her father now left the cabin, and, leaning against the steamer's rail, John peered at the people on the harbour until, eventually, he caught sight of his brother and waved over his head with his hat in his hand. Almost immediately, there came a returning wave from the shore, and Uncle Cliff pushed his way to the front of the small gathering, ready to meet them.

Tom and Will executed a docking as slick and quick as that at Grimston, the tightly packed sheep swaying from side to side, and John and Nadya being forced to hold tightly to the handrail to avoid being tossed overboard. Once tied up, Will lofted a small gangplank into place, as the tide had now retreated, leaving the deck of the boat somewhat lower than the harbour. The passengers for the return leg were corralled behind a barrier, so that the two could disembark and the sheep could be offloaded behind them. The whole operation was as well executed as they remembered at the other end of the short trip, so that, within minutes of docking, John and Cliff were embracing and patting each other vigorously on the back. Both grinned widely and said, almost together, "It's been too long." Clearly, they were extremely fond of each other, and Nadya could see that they would enjoy this week of catching up with each other's lives. After a few moments, the two disentangled themselves, and Cliff threw his arms around Nadya, almost squeezing the breath from her lungs with the strength of his embrace.

"By 'eck, lass. You've grown into a beauty beyond even your ma," he said, pulling back and looking at her admiringly. Nadya could feel the heat of a deep flush of red rising up from her neck all the way to the top of her head, and she kissed him on both cheeks, partly to hide her embarrassment.

"I mean it, lass," he continued. "I'll have to lay in extra ale for all the gentlemen callers we're going to have in the next few weeks."

Nadya felt herself blush even more deeply as she laughed. "Nonsense, Uncle Cliff, I'm sure there are many young women in Rosedale who will outshine me."

"Besides," she went on, "I'm off men for the foreseeable future; you won't have any trouble on that score from me."

Cliff looked at her again and shook his head. "We'll see about that, young Nadya," was all he replied.

He now led the two of them away from the dockside to a smart-looking buggy, painted in bright red and yellow and pulled by two fine-looking white horses. "We have a long ride ahead of us, I'm afraid," announced Cliff. "Make yourselves as comfortable as you can; I've put blankets under the seats as it will get cold before we arrive. Ann has sent some vittles - in the basket there. We'll stop once we get across the Ampleforth Bridge."

Cliff helped Nadya into the buggy, and, whilst John loaded the luggage, jumped aboard himself. Once all three were in, he set the horses to climb the steep, winding road away from the harbour. They snorted and strained into the harness, perhaps surprised at the increased weight in the buggy, but nevertheless climbed steadily up the hill. Once at the top, the vista to the north and south opened up, the road following a ridge with steep sides robed with deep beds of pale brown bracken leading down to the sea. Nadya noticed that the vegetation was very different from that around Milltown; there was less cultivated land and more rough pasture as well as large swathes of bracken. Every so often, the road passed through thick woodland, much of which was made up of plantations of pine rather than a natural mix of trees. The road under these was dark and gloomy, and the air thick with an aromatic scent. The ground under the trees was thickly covered with fallen needles, with frequent large mounds which Cliff explained were anthills. Nadya thought that walking in such woods would be unpleasant, to say the least, and hoped that there were more natural woods around Rosedale. She was already missing the dappled sunlight, flowers, and constant trilling birdsong of the woods she had known all her life. An unexpected memory of lying with Milo on a warm grassy knoll, covered with the sunny faces of daisies and the bright yellow of dandelions, came into her mind. She shook her head to wipe away the vision. Maybe one day she would be able to remember such times with a smile but, for now, they brought a lump to her throat and the hot sting of imminent tears to her eyes.

After something like two hours, the woodland faded and was replaced by extensive stretches of moorland, with occasional enclosed fields of sheep. They began to descend a long sloping road to a narrow ribbon of grey sea, crossed by a sturdy-looking iron bridge.

"Ampleforth Bridge," announced Cliff. "We'll stop just at the other side for some lunch; there's a nice spot looking down over the water and sheltered from the wind."

As they came to the brown iron bridge, Nadya asked to be let down to stretch her legs walking over the short crossing. Looking over the side, she could see that the tide was out, and the rocky bed of the channel was strewn with green and brown weed, which lay flat, clearly pointing out the direction of the retreat of the water. Hopping amongst the weeds were numerous seagulls and several varieties of wading birds, none of which Nadya knew by name. She was no bird expert. Looking more closely at the structure of the bridge, she could see that it was brown from decades of rust, and, in some parts, there were jagged holes in the beams. Some were even fully rotted through or connected only by a narrow thread of remaining iron. "It won't be long before this thing collapses entirely," she thought.

"Aye, lass," Cliff spoke, surprising her both by the fact he had joined her on the bridge and that she had spoken her thought aloud.

"We have the skill to rebuild it; whether we do so in wood or again in iron, I don't know. It will cost a pretty penny either way. There has been talk of just building a stone causeway instead but that would mean we could only cross at low tide, or the ferry from Woldshire would have to make a much longer trip to dock on t'other side at New Helmsley, Sproxton, or the like. The council here has talked about it for many a year; one day the bridge will become unusable, and they'll have to decide."

They had been walking as they talked and were now at the northern end of the bridge. They crossed onto firm land and, passing the buggy, which was parked at the side of the road, they descended a short path through thick banks of gorse with rattling brown seed cases. Earlier in the year, the bank had been a sea of sweet-smelling yellow flowers. John had laid a blanket on the grassy slope below the bank of gorse and had set out the food that Ann had prepared for them - a veritable feast akin to that described in the children's book The Wind in the Willows. Nadya made a mental note that she would need to be careful she didn't fill out too much if this was typical of the fare she was likely to be fed at her aunt and uncle's home. After eating their fill, the three lay back in the warm, late autumn sun. Nadya drifted into a half-doze, hearing only faint birdsong and the calling of gulls. She half-imagined she was still lying on the grassy slope above the Milltown inlet with Milo lying next to her. If only she could turn the clock back and unsay the words which had resulted in the chaos of the last few weeks. She came back to full awareness with a start.

"'Reet, we'd best be off, or it'll be dark before we get 'ome. The road isn't as straight as it was afore the flood," called Cliff, jumping up smartly.

Everything was soon packed away, and the journey resumed, first climbing the steep northern slope from the channel, and then across the long plain before picking up the new coast road at Old Abbey. This road wound in and out of the southerly entrance to the valleys, sometimes the "new" road made after the flooding was over, and sometimes running along the ancient road of pre-flood years. The sun was already hidden in the western sky, somewhere behind the eastern slope of the Rosedale valley. The sky and the jumble of clouds had turned a startling array of pinks and reds as they pulled around the last bend of the road and saw Rosedale village spread before them. The cottages lit up, one by one, as the evening grew gradually darker, until the whole village glowed with warm and inviting light. Finally, they stopped in front of Smithy Cottage, and the door was immediately flung wide. Light streamed from within, blocked only by the outline of a female figure standing in the doorway.

Annie, a plump, round faced woman with rosy red cheeks and glistening eyes, stepped out of the doorway and threw her arms around a slightly startled Nadya. "Ee lass, let me hug you," she chuckled. "I've been so looking forward to you getting here." After a moments hesitation Nadya returned the embrace and knew immediately this woman would be someone she would take to her heart. After several minutes Annie released Nadya and turned to John, she opened her arms and he stepped forward to be similarly hugged.

Once the immediate greetings were over John and Nadya unloaded the luggage and carried it into the brightly lit kitchen, while Cliff unhitched the horses and led them into their stable. Only after wiping them down, and feeding and watering them, did he appear in the cottage to be embraced and kissed by his wife.

Later, the four of them sat around the smoothly worn, pale wooden kitchen table and enjoyed a meal of steaming, rich, and delicious lamb stew with heavy but satisfying suet dumplings. Nadya once again thought she was going to need to be careful not to fill out until she was huge, but she was glad of the meal after a long day's travel. There were also large tumblers of brown, malty ale. After they had eaten, Cliff raised his ale and spoke to his guests.

"Welcome, John, for your visit, and more than welcome, Nadya. We hope you will be happy here with us in your new life."

Chapter 11 - Selected entries from Harry's Journals. January 25th, 2080.

In today's news – snow has fallen in the Austrian, Swiss, Italian, and French Alps for the first time in eleven years. A significant fall of more than fifty centimetres in places has meant that artificial snow may not be required for this season's skiing. However, authorities warn that the risk of avalanche is extreme, as the snow is falling on bare rock and earth and not on other snow. Off-piste skiing has been banned in all resorts, and a high alert exists in all localities. All flights are reported as full, as people flock to see the phenomenon of natural snow.

A prisoner, Raymond Torres, has been released on parole in the UK after being fitted with an emotional control chip. He had previously been serving a life sentence with no possibility of early release after murdering fourteen people over a period of ten years. He has been given a new identity, and the location of his release is being kept secret in order to avoid adverse public reaction. The response to the release among the general public has been largely muted, but there have been protests outside the prison where he was previously located. Police broke up the protests with tear gas and live fire, killing seventeen protesters.

Due to a prolonged drought throughout the last growing season, citrus crop yields across the Mediterranean are reported as the lowest since records began. Italy has banned exports of all lemons, oranges, clementines, and other citrus fruits. Greece, France, Albania, and Spain are expected to follow suit in the next few days.

In the UK, a new variant of coronavirus related to the original pandemic, which was known as Covid-19, has been reported. So-called Covid-79 seems to have evaded all previous immune responses in those individuals infected, and numerous fatalities have been reported. Travel to and from the UK has been restricted to essential, diplomatic, and government personnel for the foreseeable future. The UK government is reported to be considering movement restrictions across the country.

———————

I have secured a housing unit near to my allotted work detail for myself and my wife, Rosa, and we have begun the process of packing our belongings for the transfer. The flat is in a block of three hundred, with outside areas for recreation and data access included in the monthly rental costs. We will have two rooms, a living space and a bedroom, plus a kitchen area and a balcony. We are on the ninth floor of thirty, with elevator access guaranteed. There is a transport unit rental facility, which is shared between our block and two others; we have been told we should be able to obtain a rental unit once per month for up to two days. I am to start work at the beginning of April, and my contract is initially for nine months, taking me to the end of 2080. The care unit where I am to work is approximately ninety minutes' travel by fast transit from the housing unit. It houses two hundred elderly people, who range from being confined permanently to bed, to those who are still moderately mobile.

Last weekend, Rosa and I took a trip to the Yorkshire Wolds, where we searched for a likely spot to deposit our time capsule in a few months, or years, time. Obviously, we wanted somewhere above the predicted seventy metre sea level rise, but also somewhere unlikely to be dug up or built on. Ultimately, though, the site does need to be rediscovered in order for our package to bring the climactic events, we are currently living through, to the future, a future I fear may be very different from the one we have enjoyed. I think the higher Wolds might offer what we are looking for: high-level mixed woodland and farmland, a low likelihood of large-scale development, and, of course, well above the predicted seventy metre sea level. We have plenty of time, as I want to capture several months, if not years, of what is happening around us.

There is, I believe, a developing battle between the leaders of the giant tech companies, with their development of chip technology to control humans, and the population, who are beginning to feel threatened by these developments. For the first time since the 2020s and '30s, I think people are starting to believe that less power should be in the hands of the few who rule over us, and more in the hands of the common people. The fear that followed the war years seems, at long last, to be dissipating, and people are becoming less accepting of authoritarian rule.

The oligarchs, though, are not going to relinquish their wealth and power easily, but even after the population declines following the nuclear exchanges and mass migrations, there are still around five billion people. If they could come together to resist, then things might start to take a different turn.

There are rapidly deteriorating climate conditions and further imminent mass migrations as large parts of the world become uninhabitable due to heat, storms, or floods. Neither will help the overall sociopolitical situation, and it may be that people will return to meekly accepting control in return for safety. Personally, I hope not, but I cannot speak out about these things. If the contents of this journal were to become known, I would certainly lose my work placement and probably end up incarcerated, or worse.

Thank God for Rosa; she keeps me sane. We met ten years ago now and married a year later. As soon as I saw her for the first time, I was immediately entranced by her beautiful eyes and fair, freckled complexion. I soon learned that she was also possessed of an extremely keen intelligence, far beyond mine. She studied computer science and robotics at university but has not been able to find work in her field and has joined the ranks of the "not currently working." The waste of an intelligence such as hers is one of the great tragedies of our age. She has been offered work within the central AI research and development units, but she refuses to be part of the current programmes.

Ah, my Rosa, what would I do without her? When I am at my lowest, she is the one I turn to; she shares my ambitions and my fears, and I hers. We both share a desire to leave something of these times for the future, the future beyond the climate chaos and the floods. I wonder what life will be like then. Will we be controlled by AI? Will AI save us from the disasters that seem almost inevitable as the climate changes? I have no answers to any of these questions, and, it would seem, neither does anyone else.

These questions are even more important to both of us now that we have decided to have a child. For a long time, we felt it was not a good idea to bring a child into the world as it is, but once it was confirmed that I have a work detail, we thought that it was now or never. We will only have one child. Some people believe we need to bring the population back to pre-war levels and, consequently, are promoting large families of three, four, or even five children. However, we are certain this is a retrograde step, and that the future world - certainly beyond the now inevitable sea-level rise - will not support anything close to nine billion people. I hope our child, girl or boy, inherits Rosa's intelligence as well as her beauty.

Chapter 12 – Rosedale.

There it is again, thought Nadya as she finished reading the latest instalment of Harry's journal and settled down in the soft, warm bed of her new room. The idea that people just five hundred years ago could choose how many children they had. This was the puzzle that had brought about the move to Nym and the collapse of everything she had thought was certain about her life. She was determined to find answers but would certainly not be having a discussion on the matter with anyone else, not until she was absolutely sure they would share her open-minded approach to such things. She was unsure such a person existed anywhere in Nym or Woldshire.

She turned her thoughts to her place in Rosedale. She supposed she should start to think of it as her home now, as it would be where she would live for the foreseeable future. Her room was on the first floor, at the end of a hall lined with paintings of the Nym countryside. It seemed that Ann was a talented artist, and her works were in great demand in Nym and even in Woldshire. She had been at her aunt and uncle's for three days and three nights and was already growing very fond of Cliff and Ann, as they had insisted she call them. They had welcomed her with open arms, completely opening their home to her and her da. So far, they had treated Nadya and John as visitors, showing them all around Rosedale and introducing them to as many of the locals as they could. For John, the local inn was a particular favourite with its varied selection of ales, all brewed on the premises. He had sampled several of them in one evening, accompanied by a superb dinner of local lamb pie and vegetables. His favourite, so far, was the rich dark brown "Home Ale." Nadya had not realised, until now, that her father was something of a beer "expert" and certainly a great fan. She was not sure what her mother would think, but she was sure that, now John and Cliff had become reacquainted, there would be more visits to Rosedale in the future, especially as the boys at home were now grown and perfectly capable of looking after the farm while John and Meena took some time to enjoy life.

Nadya knew that her life here would not continue as a holiday, that she would soon start work as apprentice to her uncle and would need to apply herself to the task of learning the arts and science of smithing. She was enjoying her time off but at the same time she was eager to start her new life, to put behind her the life she had known until now, especially the events of the last few weeks. She was now sure that her relationship with Milo, long though it had continued, was not right for her, nor indeed for him. She knew now that they were too different; they had come together in childhood but had grown in different ways and now wanted different things. Nadya wanted desperately to learn as much as she could, about smithing, about Woldshire, about the wider world in which they lived, and about how that world had come about. So far, that desire had led only to trouble for herself and her family, so she knew she needed to be much more circumspect in her endeavours. However, the realisation that there were questions she was not supposed to ask had only served to firm her determination. She would learn, and she would find answers!

Right at this moment, though, it was time for her to climb out of her warm bed and get ready for another day. For now, she needed to focus on finding out about her new situation, her surroundings, and her neighbours. She had decided to spend the day walking the ancient trail around the rim of the Rosedale valley - a day of walking, discovery, and time to think. This would be the first time she had ventured out on her own here. She had asked permission, of course, and had been surprised and pleased by the response of her uncle.

"Hey, Nadya, this is your new home and on your free days you are free to please yourself. You need no one's permission to spend the day by yourself."

And so, having selected robust walking trousers, a thick, deep-brown woollen jumper over a bright green, soft, and warm blouse, knee-length green wool socks, and her favourite brown knee-length leather boots, she wandered down to breakfast. Breakfasts here were hearty and filling: eggs with deep yellow yolks, thick-sliced aromatic fatty bacon, rich dark black pudding made from the blood of slaughtered pigs, and thick slices of soft, delicious brown bread spread generously with homemade creamy butter. Her aunt and uncle seemed to have what Nadya considered huge portions, and her da followed suit while a guest. To be fair, they tended not to eat again - other than maybe an apple from the store in the barn - until the main meal, known here as supper, in the evening.

Nadya still preferred to eat a smaller portion at breakfast: one egg, one slice of bacon or black pudding but rarely both, and a small piece of bread. Today, she asked for a second egg, cooked on both sides so the yolk didn't break, and an extra slice of bacon, which she placed between two slices of buttered bread. Along with an apple, this would be her lunch as she walked high on the hillside.

In the olden days, the moorland above the valley would often have been deeply covered with snow at this time of year, but these days, such an event was quite rare. She was more likely to get wet from one of the frequent downpours sweeping in on the westerly wind, so she tied the waxed, waterproof coat her uncle had given her to her pack. She would be warm climbing the slope that ascended out of the valley, but it might be chilly on the top. Those less used to walking might have put on the coat straight away and arrived at the top of the slope sweaty and clammy, but Nadya knew better.

"Remember it's dark around six," her uncle advised as she pulled on her boots. "You should aim to be back well before then. It shouldn't be a problem but don't linger too much amongst the ruins up there and get caught out."

"Sound advice," Nadya acknowledged. In all but the thickest cloud or mist, she would be able to estimate the time to sunset using the finger width method taught to her by her da. By holding up her hand at arm's length with her palm facing her, each finger width between the horizon and the sun indicated approximately fifteen minutes of daylight remaining. She was confident this would give her enough warning that it was time to head back down. Looking at the map Cliff had shown her, however, she thought she would be back well before then anyway, even with a long lunch stop.

She gave everyone a cheery wave as she closed the door behind her. She breathed a sigh of satisfaction to be heading out on her own once more into the open air. Turning right from the door of the cottage, she passed through the village and then veered west, immediately starting to climb as she crossed two fields, each stocked with sheep. Once across the second field, she entered a rough track which she knew led to a farm on the hillside. She couldn't remember the name of the farmer but gave him a wave as she saw him further down the lane. He waved back and continued on his way, clearly unconcerned, either because he recognised her, or because he was used to people walking that track. Once past the farm, the track ended abruptly, but she quickly picked up a steep, rough path which climbed diagonally up the bank, passing through a high-sided gully which cut her off from the low winter sun. The air in the depths of the gully was damp and chilly; Nadya pulled her jumper up around her neck against the chill and pressed on. Soon, though, she emerged onto the rougher pasture of the top reaches of the bank and, striding through dense patches of heather, she quickly reached the top track. This had been a railway in the dim past, centuries even before the events in Harry's journal had taken place. The area here had been something of a boomtown, with the development of ironstone and iron ore mining in the nineteenth century. The railway had been used to transport the ore away to be processed or used in the construction of other train tracks. All that was left was a rugged area of slightly flatter land, cut into the steeply sloping bank some thirty metres below the top. It wound its way around the head of the valley, providing perfect walking terrain and an interesting set of ruined mine and railway buildings along the way.

Walking along the track, Nadya was entirely alone with her thoughts, not seeing anyone for kilometre after kilometre. She heard only the seemingly piteous and lonely calls of curlews, or the harsh croaking of the crows. The desolation and wild nature of the high moor struck a chord with Nadya, and she immediately fell in love with her new home. She would be happy here, she realised, roaming the high moors on her free days and working with the iron and other metals on other days.

Passing the farthest extent of the valley, the path turned back southwards to return, eventually, to the village. It was still only just past noon, though, so Nadya decided she would climb through the heather to the very top, where, by her reckoning, she would be near the very centre of the island of Nym, and the farthest she had ever been from the sea. The heather was a range of dull browns and greens, its flowering season long past. Its tangled, resistant branches made the going tough, but Nadya pressed on, gradually gaining height until she saw that the terrain, in front and to the north of her, dropped away rather than continuing to climb. She gazed out over the wide expanse of moorland, tinted blueish at this season of the year. The air was strikingly fresh and sharp as she drew breath after breath, regaining her wind. With her long golden red hair streaming in front of her face, as the breeze freshened from the southwest, she stood out against the sky, standing proud of the rolling folds of the land. Absorbed by the view, the immensity of the landscape, and her own thoughts, she did not see the figure approaching from behind her. Only when he called out, "Hello!" did she turn and see the tall young man, taking great strides with his long legs across the moor towards her.

"Hallooo," he called again, now only twenty or thirty metres distant. "Can I help? Are you lost?"

She waited until he had come up beside her, all the time watching him closely and working out whether to feel threatened or simply put out that he had disturbed her solitude.

"No, I'm not lost, thank you. I've come up out of Rosedale and was just taking in the view."

"Breathtaking, isn't it?" the young man stated simply, but with the love of the land resonating in his voice.

"Yes, I'm new around here, and this is my first time up here. Do you come here often?" She was conscious of the cliché in her words and blushed slightly, turning her face back to the north to hide her embarrassment.

"As often as I can, yes. My name's Rob. I live at Low Gill Farm just up the valley from the village. This is my place to blow away the cobwebs or the stress of the day, or sometimes to come and try again to capture the beauty of the place in a painting."

"Ah, my aunt paints too. I've just moved here to be apprentice smith with my uncle."

"Aye, that'll be Ann and Cliff. Ann sometimes paints up here too. Cliff has told the whole valley how his beautiful young niece would be coming to live with them for a time. He wasn't wrong then."

"No, indeed. It's been something of a whirlwind, but yes, I'm here for a good while, I think, several years I expect," Nadya looked him squarely in the face, secretly wishing he would go away and leave her to her explorations.

"Well yes," he said. "But I didn't really mean the bit about you coming." Rob's face lit up with a broad grin as he stood up to her gaze without flinching.

Puzzled at first, Nadya played back the brief conversation in her mind and then blushed even more deeply when she realised what he was saying. Then she laughed at the audacity and cheek of this tall stranger, and the laugh broke through her reluctance. She held out her hand to him, saying, "Nadya, very pleased to meet you, Rob."

"And me you, Nadya," he said, experimenting with the sound of her name.

"And now I'm going to sit and eat my pack-up, if that's ok. You're welcome to join me unless you want to get on your way and back to your walk."

With that, he plonked - that was the only word for it - straight back into the deep heather and, pulling himself into a slightly more sitting position, opened his rucksack and pulled out a huge, buttered, cheese-smelling scone. Without saying a word, Nadya just laughed again and mimicked his plonking motion, almost falling over backwards, but stopping herself just in time to save her dignity. She pulled out her own lunch, and, spreading out the paper she had wrapped it in, set down her cold breakfast sandwich.

"Shares?" she smiled at him, already tearing the sandwich in two and extending one half towards him. He took it and, breaking the scone where it had been sliced and buttered, replied, "Top or bottom?"

"Oooh, bottom for me if you don't mind." And so Nadya took the bottom half of the scone from him and, leaning back against the yielding heather, looked up at the bright blue sky and sighed happily. It was going to be OK, more than OK.

The two ate in silence for some time, until Nadya tasted the scone. The taste and texture were so similar to those her mother made, it almost brought a tear to her eye. "Who made this?" she asked, expecting him to reply that it was his mother. She almost choked when he said quietly, "I did. Do you like it?"

"Yes!" was all she could say, emphatically. "A man of many talents, clearly."

His reply of, "Thank you, fair maiden," set her laughing again, and Rob soon joined in, both laughing and leaning back in the soft heather.

Lunch finished, they stood, and Rob asked if she wanted to complete her walk alone, or if she would be ok if he accompanied her on the return leg, on the east side of the valley. An hour ago, Nadya was sure she would have said that she would go alone, but now she didn't want to leave the company of this funny and charming new friend, so the two walked on together. After they had gone a few hundred metres, Rob pointed out a spring, bubbling from a sandy dip beside the path, and the two of them quenched their thirst with the crisp, clean water. They chatted amiably as they walked along, Rob telling her all about his life here on the farm, admitting that he was something of an anomaly, being the one who did most of the cooking and baking for his family.

"In the old days, chefs, as they were called, were predominantly men, you know, and I'm better at it than my ma."

Nadya nodded, saying that, if the scones were anything to go by, she would have to be something special to be better than him. Mentally, she noted his casual reference to the "old days" but said nothing. She had learned a hard lesson and would not very easily be letting her guard down on that front. The path now started to descend steadily back towards the valley bottom. When they were about halfway down the height of the eastern bank, Rob pointed southwest, across the valley, to a smart, white-painted farmhouse and a tidy-looking set of buildings.

"That's Gill Farm," he said. "I'll leave you shortly, but I wanted to show you something, just around this next bend in the path."

As they rounded the bend, Nadya caught sight of a long series of arched tunnels set into the hillside, mostly in ruins but still obvious.

"They used to heat the iron ore in those tunnels. The process was called calcining, and after it, the ore was much drier and lighter, so it could be carried away much more easily. The wagons would pull in here, drop a load of unprocessed ore, and then move forward to be loaded again with the processed stuff, which they then used to take down the valley to a place called Pickering, now drowned under the sea."

Nadya looked again at her new friend and pondered his knowledge of, and curiosity about, the deep past. She said nothing about her own inquisitiveness but smiled and congratulated him on knowing so much.

She asked, "You seem very knowledgeable about metalworking, Rob. Are you a smith as well as an accomplished baker?"

Now it was his turn to redden with embarrassment. "I'm no expert, although I can manage the stuff needed for the farm."

"I bet you can," quipped Nadya. "Just like you can 'manage a bit of baking.'"

Rob just smiled and a short distance further on, he pointed to a track that led off across the valley.

"This is the way I go. Will you be ok finding your way back from here? It's just straight on down this path until you get to the road, which will lead you right back into the village. Should only take you half an hour or so."

"Yes, I'll be fine, thanks, and thank you for your company - and for making me laugh," Nadya replied, happier than she had been for weeks. "I'm sure we'll bump into each other again soon, Rob. It's really nice to have found a new friend."

As he turned to go, Rob stopped and waved back, "You don't know how good it is to meet someone who appears to have the ability to use their mind. Would you mind if I knocked on your door some evening and invited you for a drink at the inn?"

Not at all, not at all, Nadya thought. "Please do, any evening you like." And with that, she turned back to the path and hummed to herself merrily as she almost skipped the last couple of miles to the village and her new home. Yes, everything was going to be OK.

Chapter 13 - Selected entries from Harry's Journals – March 25th, 2080

Raymond Torres is dead!

It is widely reported in the news that the body of Raymond Torres has been found, outside the flat of a relative of one of his victims. Apparently, there are no injuries on the body, and the circumstances of his death are unclear at this stage. The relative, who wishes to remain anonymous, told reporters she had no idea the dead man was there until she saw the lights of police and ambulances flashing through her curtains at approximately ten p.m..

Police are not looking for anyone else in connection with his death.

———

In other recent news –

The Mediterranean citrus and olive crops are officially recorded as the worst in living memory, with intercountry transfer all but completely banned. In Italy, there were riots when the government seized all crops and issued ration cards with extremely limited quantities per person per week. Governments in Spain, Italy and Greece report that many trees have died completely, as there has still been no significant rain across the whole region for more than twelve months.

"Whole olive-growing areas are lying dead. We haven't seen anything like this since the Xylella plague of the 2020s. This time there does not seem to be the option to breed a resistant variety, as trees basically need water. This is a national and international catastrophe."

Olive oil prices, where it can even be found in non-growing countries, have risen tenfold.

———

Governments in Europe continue to struggle to contain the outbreak of Covid-79. A vaccine is expected to be months away. Research was delayed at several of the major pharmaceutical companies due to sabotage and blockades from the antivax lobby. "Never again," they chant, referring to the vaccination programmes of the early 2020's which they still claim caused a range of fatalities from heart failure to cancer. No evidence has ever been found to link the vaccines of the 2020's to large scale deaths.

The UK prime minister said on TV news, "This time at least we don't face damaging economic impacts as employment levels are so low that movement restriction orders have little impact on commerce." Cold comfort, of course, to the tens of thousands once again dying from the virus. The other "This time" which he didn't mention was that – this time hospital admission is prioritised based on the ability to pay. Since the provision of social programmes, including health, became the responsibility of the Technos it has become a wholly two tier system with those of us in the lower echelons of society receiving only basic provision. Who knows what the death toll will be.

All travel out of the UK, France and Germany - the main focus of the outbreaks - is banned. Neighbouring countries have instigated shoot to kill policies on illegal migration from these countries.

In the US, the city of New Orleans has been declared unviable within the next ten years. Since the major flood in the early years of this century, caused by Hurricane Katrina, New Orleans has experienced several major floods, and the frequency has increased dramatically in the past twenty years. State government now says that, due to a combination of sea level rise and the continued sinking of the area, the city cannot now be defended from the rising sea. This is the first major city in the US to be declared unviable, and it will be effectively abandoned within the ten year time period. Plans to relocate the one million people who still live in and around the city have yet to be finalised. Insurance companies argue that the abandonment is a deliberate act on the part of state and national government, and they are refusing to honour any policies currently in place.

A number of residents are lobbying the government to build a new New Orleans further inland on the Mississippi Delta, but government sources say that this would just create a problem in future decades, and that all new construction should now only take place above a seventy five metre elevation.

Senator John Haslip of Florida has called for the construction of a ninety-metre-high wall around the Gulf of Mexico to repel the sea, pointing out that without such a bold move, a full one hundred and ten kilometre width of land and the entire state of Florida would be lost within two hundred years. He was heckled by groups of people claiming the whole thing was a hoax and a plan to steal their homes from the coastal region after forcibly relocating them.

"We have as much right to live by the sea as the corrupt legions of politicians and oligarchs," stated one resident of Miami. "We will defend our homes against this barbarity being foisted on us using the climate change hoax."

———————

March 26th, 2080

Today, Rosa and I move to our new home on the edge of Driffield. We have been packed and ready since early morning and are currently waiting for the transport unit assigned to take us to our new apartment. We have been told that we have only one truckload allowed, with a maximum volume of forty-five cubic metres and no more than twelve tonnes. It is difficult to know what this means until the truck arrives, but we imagine that our fairly frugal possessions will easily fit within this limit. We have boxed everything except major furniture - our bed, sofa, table and chairs, two storage units, and two sets of bookshelves. All is currently stacked, on the pavement outside our old block, awaiting the truck. We have been told that we will need to stand clear and allow the robotics to do the loading, as any attempted interference could result in injury to ourselves. I hope the rain holds off a little longer.

———————

The truck arrived just a few moments after my last entry, and we have now arrived at our new block near the small town of Driffield. The robotics unloaded our stuff and piled it neatly at the side of the road, and we are now moving it up to our apartment on the second floor. The locals all seem very friendly, and several have come out to help, a godsend, as without them, it would have taken myself and Rosa all night. Frankly, and I know this is very non-PC, I would rather Rosa weren't lifting, as we found out just last week that she is indeed pregnant with a baby girl. I wonder if she will inherit Rosa's flaming red hair and freckles. I hope so, rather than my bland brown hair and pale, slightly olive skin.

I start work in one week and have a preliminary visit next Wednesday to meet the other staff. At the weekend, Rosa and I plan to revisit the area around Millington to continue our search for a place to put the time capsule when it is complete, possibly after the birth of the child. We will walk the ninety-metre contour line along the western edge of the Wolds and see if we can find a likely spot. Trying to predict what is going to happen in five hundred or one thousand years is tricky, so rather than risk destruction and total loss, we might seek out several sites - perhaps another one right over on the coast above Scarborough. I plan to record grid references and a description of the location of each at the back of the final journal so that if one is found, it should lead to the others. Apart from copies of the journals, the contents of each capsule will be somewhat different.

———

March 27th, 2080

Day two in our new home, and we're both exhausted. We worked until nearly midnight, getting stuff in the right place and putting things away. Rosa insisted we thoroughly clean every room before moving anything in, even though it will have been professionally cleaned when the last tenants moved out. This morning, we went out to explore the local area and meet some more of our new neighbours. They all seem very friendly and open. Most of them are living on the Basic Minimum Salary with little hope of permanent employment. Like most places, this area also has its problems with drug use and the petty crime that accompanies it. Hopelessness makes that inevitable. The draconian law enforcement and severe punishments you can expect, particularly for violent crime, do keep something of a lid on it, and as long as you are prepared to be a good citizen and not step out of line, then life can be at least tolerable. Many people tend to live their aspirational life through the movies and the everlasting TV dramas.

Drug use itself also tends to be behind closed doors and not a street issue, again due to the severe penalties for misuse in public, which were introduced following the synthetic opioid crisis of the mid-to-late 2020s. Personal use in your own home, while still technically a crime, is mostly ignored, and the supply is now carried out via "official" routes and not via the drug cartels. It has been said, though, that all that happened was that the drug- supply criminals became the official supply chain, merely losing the illegality that fuelled much drug-related crime.

Maybe it will be no bad thing for humanity if the ongoing climate-driven catastrophe brings about a significant reset. Somehow, I doubt that will happen, however – the current domination of the Technos seems wholly entrenched. It would certainly seem that, for the moment at least, the long-held fear that AI would somehow take over and destroy humanity has failed to materialise. All that has happened is that the tools of AI and robotics have been used by the ultra-rich corporate entities to consolidate power in their own hands and facilitate their relegation of democratic or other political entities to a supporting role in the drama of humanity.

————

April 1st, 2080 – Late evening.

Well, that was an interesting first day. The job is to provide one-on-one care and support to the elderly residents where required. It is physically and mentally quite taxing, but not impossibly onerous. I now see why this sort of role has survived the move to AI and robotics. There are robots in the facility, and they are of the latest generations and in many ways very humanlike. But - they are not human, and this is very obvious.

I remember reading some time ago about a phenomenon known earlier this century as the "uncanny valley" effect. This was where almost-human robots triggered a negative emotional response in humans that were much stronger than robots that were obviously not human. No-one ever got spooked by an industrial robot assembling machinery, but a near-human robot gets more and more spooky the closer they get to real humans. This is still very real. The robots in the care facility are very humanlike but there is just something in the way they look at you, something in the way they speak to you, that sends shivers up the spines of most of us.

It's not so bad for the staff who work alongside them, but it's plain to see that most of the residents, particularly those who have lost some mental as well as physical capacity, are terrified of the robots. It would seem that, as with very young children in the general population, the more significant the level of dementia, the greater the fear of the robots.

There have been great strides made in the detection and treatment of all forms of dementia in the last fifty years, but it still occurs and, in some people, still progresses, before something else kills them, to the point of disability. We have yet to reach a point in the development of these AI robots where we begin the climb out of the uncanny valley. Indeed, at the moment, and for some people, we seem to get deeper into the depths of the ravine of fear, suspicion and loathing with every advance.

Don't get me wrong, the robots don't do anything wrong. When they do interact with residents, they are courteous, caring, and gentle, but still they instil terror in some and, at the least, discomfort in most.

We have allowed, or rather the corporates have required, robots and AI to replace humans in almost every sphere of employment: in manufacturing, in almost every area of administration and finance, in medicine, and in large parts of the arts. It's ironic that, at the end of our lives, we come to rely on human contact again.

And, of course, this situation has given me the chance of climbing out of the drab normality of everyday life for most and to get ahead just a little.

Chapter 14 – Apprentice.

Nadya woke to late winter sunlight streaming in through her small window. She shivered in the early morning chill of the house as she climbed, still bleary-eyed from sleep, out of bed and made her way along the narrow, low hall to the bathroom. The house would not get warm until Ann lit the stove to begin preparing breakfast, and that was at least an hour away yet. Since her da's departure weeks ago, Nadya had settled into a routine of rising to take the dogs for an early morning walk before the household, and indeed most of the village, awoke. She loved the early morning, it gave her time to think, often about the latest instalment of Harry's Journals she had read the previous evening. The extent of her nightly reading had been somewhat reduced since she began her work in earnest as Cliff's apprentice. By the time she had eaten supper and perhaps chatted with her aunt and uncle or taken a walk to the village inn for a quick drink and a catch-up with her new friends, she was exhausted and would flop into her bed and be asleep within minutes. Only rarely did she have the capacity, during the week at least, to open the journal. This also meant, however, that she had had no time to lament her lost life in Milltown, nor to mope about missing her family.

There were a few young people of her age in the village and surrounding areas, and Rob had taken the trouble to introduce her into the main group, where she had easily established herself as someone who could spin a yarn or make everyone laugh with her ready, if sharp, wit. Even the older residents had quickly come to regard the young lass with the fiery red hair as a valued addition to village life. Those few who were up and about during her early morning walks through the village, as she headed for the steep path up the west bank, would wave and shout, "Mornin', Nadie!"

"Mornin'," she would call back, already feeling the warmth of village life surrounding her.

Uncle Cliff had been proven right too, tales of "the gorgeous redhead" seemed to have spread rapidly into the surrounding countryside, so that it was not unusual for some young farmer's son, who had not been seen in The Coach before, to appear on a Saturday evening and ask Alun, the landlord, if "the redhead" would be in that evening. Only her apparent disdain for all the attention and dismissal of all invitations to "come outside for a stroll" had prevented the local girls from taking against her out of jealousy. Instead, she had been accepted into their intrigues and gossip. It probably also helped that she was often seen at the inn and walking the surrounding hills with Rob and few of the lads were brave enough to approach Nadya when she was in his company. He seemed indifferent to the attentions she attracted; indeed, he appeared amused by it. A sharp look from the tall and confident farmer was all it took to see off any who were persistent enough to disturb them.

All in all, she felt she had dealt with the upheaval well and had even come to see the change as an adventure. Secretly, she quite liked the attention, although she was sure the novelty would soon wear off - being mainly, she thought, because she seemed to be the only redhead in these parts, and of course because of the allure of the new and slightly "furrin". She and Rob had become firm friends and were often seen, on Sundays, climbing the paths out of the valley, making for the high moors, reappearing near dark after trekking here, there and everywhere over the heather-clad heights. Rob had walked there all his life and was enjoying showing someone new his favourite haunts amongst the wild places filled with ancient history.

Nadya had grown to love the deep green of the heather, the clear blue of the sky, and the melancholy whistle of the wind as it swept across the moors. On occasion, they would hear the high piping call of the curlew or the "pee-wit" of the plovers, and several times they had witnessed the jinking, dodging flight of a short-eared owl as it hunted for small mammals amongst the heather. Nadya had shouted with excitement the first time they saw one spot something and plunge in an instant, to emerge after a short pause with its unfortunate victim held firmly in its claws. She had never seen these around Milltown, and Rob explained that they preferred wild places rather than the well-tended farmland of Woldshire, so it was no surprise they were new to her. Another frequent visitor to the skies above the moors was the gull, with its high piercing "caaw caaw caw caw caw" calls. These reminded Nadya of one of the things she missed about her old home. She missed the sight of the sea with its constant movement and the hiss and crash of waves against the cliffs. She promised herself and Rob that one Sunday, when the days were longer, they would set out early and hike down to the coast beyond Lastingham, or even, if she could convince Cliff to let her take a Saturday off, take a two-day hike over to Robin Hood's Bay. They would need to find an inn to stay the night before the long walk back, but that shouldn't be too difficult. She was sure Alun would be able to get a message to a fellow landlord and reserve a couple of rooms for them.

Saturdays were usually at least partly workdays for Nadya, as the local farmers would come in on that day with tools to mend, horses to shoe, or requests for Cliff to fashion some new implement or piece of ironwork. Even if the day was quiet, Nadya would have to set to and clean the tools and the smithy until midday. The work didn't bother her; she was learning fast, and her quick mind, ready hands, and the strength which had come from years on the farm lent themselves to the new craft very readily. She also had a ready way with animals and could hold a huge shire horse calm as her uncle fashioned a shoe to fit and then pressed it into place with a hiss and the familiar smell of burning hoof, ready to receive the nails that would hold it firmly in place for many weeks.

As she mused on these things, she found herself at the top of the bank. Here, she let the dogs loose and ran down the hill alongside them, often leaping from rock to rock or over the streams that broke through the bank's side as bubbling springs. Coming at last to the bottom, she slowed and gathered the two animals back to her before walking back along the road to the cottage and smithy. Her aunt and uncle would be up by now, and breakfast would be ready on the stove. As usual, her walk had whetted her appetite, and she would hungrily devour steaming eggs and bacon, or eggs and a slice of the highly fragrant black pudding, wiping her plate with a chunk of the wonderful soft and flavoursome bread her aunt had baked the day before. She was pleased to note that, even though she now ate much more than she had at the farm, the physical nature of her new work meant she was not putting on weight. She wasn't yet ready to welcome any sign of middle-aged plumpness, although she had noticed that neither her mother nor father had any such tendency, and Uncle Cliff was as fit as a fiddle and a tower of strength. The smithy was hot, uncomfortable, hard, physical work, but Nadya loved it when they created something out of metal. Some of Cliff's more elaborate creations - gates, ornate hinges, and door handles - were things of great beauty.

After finishing her breakfast, she walked the few steps to the workshop and donned her sturdy leather apron, gloves and boots, along with the scarf she used to keep her long hair out of the way of the dirt and grime, and the flames of the forge. This morning, Cliff was going to teach her how to create a metal scrollwork, but first, there was a horse to shoe, practicality always before ornament. These were the realities of agricultural life in the year 2580 and, so far, the things Nadya had learned were from this practical, but essential, side of the business. She was excited to be about to take her first steps in the more intricate and challenging part of the work of a smith.

The horse completed, they set about creating the scroll, first heating the metal bar in the fire, and then carefully fashioning the end by curling it tightly on itself. Nadya worked diligently under her uncle's instructions and soon could see the final shape emerging. The scrollwork was to be part of a gate for one of the village gardens. The garden itself was the very essence of practicality and productiveness, but this new gate was to hold pride of place at its entrance. It was an important and expensive commission, and Nadya knew it would be judged critically by the owner. There were four scrolls to do, and after Cliff closely inspected the workmanship of the first, which Nadya had made under close supervision, he left her to make the other three.

Several long and tiring hours later, she was satisfied enough with her work to ask Cliff to come and inspect. She had taken much longer than he would have done, but he had been clear that he was more interested in the quality of the work than speed at this stage. He held each of the pieces of cooled metalwork in turn, turning them over and over and peering closely, looking for any imperfections or roughness in the work. Nadya held her breath, not daring to believe that he wouldn't want at least one of them remade, but after what seemed an age, and after some second looks, several occasions of running his fingers over the work repeatedly, and a few intakes of breath, he handed the scrolls back to Nadya.

"Well, lass," she could hardly breathe, so tense was she, tha's done a real crackin' job o' those. I doubt I coulda' done better meself. Well done, Nadya, lass. Tha'll make a fine smith one day if you have a mind."

Nadya let go her breath in a whoosh and almost fell backwards onto the rough wooden bench behind her. Then she grinned, the grin spread to her eyes and, according to Cliff later at supper, her whole face lit up with such relief and pride he was sure she was going to burst.

"Tomorrow you can do the frame and the vertical bars, Nadie love," he said, picking up the scrolls and looking at them again, this time admiringly. "You know how to make a frame, and you've seen me do bars with a twist. Do you think you can read the spec. and the drawing I got Jim to approve?"

"I'll do my best, boss," she replied, still beaming.

"Good. Now get tha'self off and clean up. I'll tidy up here. See if you can persuade Ann to come out to the inn tonight for a celebration drink. You deserve it, lass."

With the beginnings of a tear of pride and relief in her eyes, Nadya gave her uncle, her boss, a hug and ran out of the smithy back to the cottage. She burst into the kitchen, surprising Ann, almost causing her to drop a tray of scones, and gave her a huge hug too.

"Whatever's come over you, Nadie?" asked the startled woman, so Nadya explained how she had been so filled with relief and joy at having satisfied her uncle with her work. "Well now," her aunt said quietly. "You must have done a good job indeed; Cliff is a perfectionist and hard to please in the smithing. Well done, young Nadya, and yes, I'll come out with the two of you this evening for a bit of a celebration at The Coach. Will your chap be there, do you think?"

"Chap?" Nadya asked, surprised, as she wasn't aware she had a "chap."

"Yes, young Rob," her aunt replied, taking Nadya aback.

"Oooh no," she retorted, perhaps just a little too emphatically, as she didn't want even rumours of such a thing to start. There was no way she was ready to be "Courtin", as it was known in this part of the islands. "Rob and I are just friends, that's all."

"Aye, alright, love," her aunt said, returning to the oven to remove a second tray of scones. "Well, he's a lovely lad; it'll be good to see him again if he is there."

Nadya tilted her head quizzically, peering at Ann's back, before giving her head a shake, an action that sent her hair, newly released from the scarf, cascading down her back.

"I'm going to have a bath. Is there hot water?" she asked as she retreated from the room, a little flustered.

"Aye, lass, there's plenty." But Nadya had already gone, climbing the stairs to start running the bath. This was the first early finish she had been given on a weekday, and she intended to make the most of it with a nice hot soak and then an hour's reading before they headed out to the inn. She grinned again as she shed her work clothes in her room. How she would love to share her happiness with her mum and da! Perhaps it was time to write to them. She had been meaning to do so for a few days, she didn't want to lose the close connection she had with her family. She knew that to keep it strong, she would need to make an effort.

A few hours later, the little family of three opened the door to the inn, letting the warm light from within stream out into the darkness of the village road. As soon as Nadya walked through the door, there was a huge cheer from the small crowd inside. Clearly, Cliff had not been idle or merely "tidying up" whilst Nadya had been relaxing in the hot, soapy water and then in her room. Above the bar, Alun had strung a banner reading,

"Nadya, Smithing Apprentice Class 1," and someone had roused many of her friends from in and around the village. She felt her pale, freckled complexion rapidly turning to the colour of her hair as she looked around the room. Rob was standing by the bar, holding out a glass of Nadya's favourite ale for her, and beckoning the three of them over, he showed them to a table set for four at one end of the long bar.

"Hope you don't mind if I join your little celebration, Nadya? Cliff seemed to think it would be OK."

"Ah, but of course, Rob," Nadya beamed at him and her uncle. Then, remembering Ann's words earlier, she turned to her aunt and whispered, "And you behave, Auntie, dear. We're just the best of friends."

With that, Cliff and Ann took a seat while Rob and Nadya returned to the bar to spend a few moments in the company of their mutual friends. Nadya continued to blush as she was made to feel like a queen from the old days, being hugged and patted on the back by everyone before leaving them to their revels to return to Cliff and Ann. She threw her arms around her uncle's neck and kissed him on his rough cheek.

"Thank you, Uncle," she whispered in his ear. "Thank you for everything. You've made what could have been a sad exile from home into a welcome to a second home. And you've inspired a new calling in me, I love working in the smithy."

Cliff just smiled broadly. Now at last, he had an heir to his business.

Several hours later, Cliff and Ann took their leave, Cliff reminding Nadya that tomorrow she needed to complete the work on the gate and so shouldn't stay out too late. A few of the younger ones, who had farm work to attend to in the morning, had already made their way home, leaving just half a dozen of Nadya's closer friends to enjoy a last glass or two before Alun cheerfully shooed them all off home. Rarely did a winter Monday bring in such a crowd, bringing a not unwelcome boost to his profits.

Rob and Nadya walked along the village road towards what she now really did think of it as home, before he left her to make his own way back to his farm. As he was about to turn off, he turned back and said cheerfully,

"Well, that was an unexpected evening out. Well done, Nadya; I'm proud to have you as a friend."

After a moment he continued, "I'm planning a long walk on Sunday if you fancy it. There's somewhere I've been meaning to get to for some time - it'll be a good eight hour trek, maybe nine with a stop at the far end of the walk for something to eat."

"Sounds wonderful," Nadya replied enthusiastically.

"Ok, I'll call at yours at eight am. Pack some lunch and plenty to drink. Oh, and a waterproof. I'm not sure the weather will stay dry all day."

"It's a date," replied Nadya, before reaching up and kissing him on the cheek as she had her uncle. "And thank you for everything too - you've helped make me feel at home here. I hadn't thought to find such a close friend so soon."

With that, she turned towards home and ran the short distance to the cottage, turning only once more to wave. "Goodnight, dear Rob," she said softly to herself.

Chapter 15 - Selected entries from Harry's Journals – January 14th, 2082.

The news today is dominated by Canada's closure of the border with the US to stem the flow of refugees from that country seeking a life in the more liveable north. Much of the southern US is now wholly uninhabitable due to the combination of heat (a record temperature of fifty three degrees centigrade was recorded in Houston last July), the increasing frequency and ferocity of hurricanes, rising sea levels, and storm-driven tidal surges around the coast. Alaska is also rumoured to be actively considering seceding from the US to halt the seemingly unstoppable levels of migration from the south.

The report of the public inquiry into the death of Raymond Torres has been published and has exonerated the prison service of all responsibility, acknowledging that he himself accepted the risks inherent in the still-experimental insertion of behaviour controlling microchips. The first insertion of a microchip into the human brain took place way back in 2024, at the time suggested as a mechanism to allow paralysed people to communicate with external devices through Wi-Fi. It seems ridiculous now to think that it was widely ignored that, of course, communication by Wi-Fi is a two-way thing, meaning that if the individual could control external devices, then it was not such a great step for an external agency to control things inside the mind or body of the person. It is reported that Torres' death was caused by a malfunction which caused a cascade reaction in his body, resulting in instant and total heart stoppage. Reports are emerging of other, similar deaths in countries where these chips have been in use for several years.

The same issue seems to be a common factor - something triggers an exponential and unstoppable cascade of autonomic nerve activity and hormonal release, which overwhelms the heart's control leading to complete cessation of heart muscle activity. Rumours that AI owners have been investigating such a reaction as the "ultimate control" for human behaviour have been dismissed but persist.

Several other UK prisoners have been granted release after being fitted with the chips, and no further deaths have been reported. An extension of the trials to include the most dangerous of criminals, including serial murderers and rapists, will be debated in parliament this month, with ministers suggesting that this may finally be a solution to the decades-long crisis in the UK's justice system. It is widely expected that a bill allowing this will be introduced and passed within months, few now expect parliament to do anything significant to oppose the technos. Democracy is merely a convenient and comforting label these days, and everyone knows it.

The UK has instigated a panel of inquiry to determine the extent of habitable territory after the now-anticipated seventy metre rise in sea levels. The scope of the inquiry includes determining when, and where, new towns will be built to replace those that are expected to be lost. It will also include the more difficult task of predicting the location and output of farmland, which will be required to feed a population that currently stands at some sixty million people, even after the population reductions of the last fifty years.

In an earlier entry I spoke about the outbreak of Covid-79 and wondered what the death toll would be. We were never told, officially of course but we all know people who died. It would have been many more were it not for the compulsory testing, isolation and vaccination programmes which came into force very quickly. Many people we knew in Leeds became ill and several died but, luckily, the outbreak was largely confined to major population centres and our new location here on the edge of the small town of Pocklington was largely spared.

Tomorrow will be my last day at the care home facility, where I have enjoyed employment for the last two years. Having this job has transformed the lives of Rosa and myself, enabling us to enrich our lives in so many ways. I can't say I have enjoyed every minute of it; the work can be hard, and sometimes the clients can be rude and frustrating, although I recognise that this is most often because of their own frustrations and struggles. Most of the time, though, it is demanding but also rewarding, knowing you are helping a fellow human being, and the rewards of being amongst the minority of employed persons brings huge benefits. Rosa and I have even managed two short holidays to the coast in the last two years - something beyond the reach of the vast majority who exist on the Basic Minimum Salary. We also managed to upgrade our apartment to one with a balcony and even a view over the open Wolds - well, at least if one leans out as far as possible and looks to the left.

The other great change in our life has been the birth of our daughter, Samantha, or Sam, as she seems to want to be called, now over a year old and walking and talking. She is as beautiful as Rosa, as well as having her fiery temperament and a way of looking at me after a disagreement that assigns me to some lower level of intellect, albeit with compassion and pity. I can see that life with these two ladies is going to be a challenge that will keep me on my toes for many a year.

So why am I leaving this job?

About three weeks ago, we had a temporary resident from the nearby village of Millington, a middle-aged artist called John. John was paralysed from the waist down in an accident some years ago, and his wife needed some respite from the full-time job of caring for him. I was assigned to John's care, and we got on extremely well - he is relentlessly cheerful despite his disability. He chose a career as an artist long ago, even though this offers little in the way of income in these days when most commercial art is created using AI. He has sold a few pieces, but he and his family live on the Basic Income, with some help from his brother, James, whose circumstances are very different.

A week ago, John was scheduled to return home to the care of his family. His wife visited and had some news. James, who apparently harbours some sense of guilt over John's accident, has offered to pay for a private carer and provide accommodation for them in the village. As with many others who needed care, John preferred a human over a robot carer. In many ways a robot could be more efficient and unlike a human it never tired or needed time off for illness or family issues. Nevertheless most people preferred a personal relationship with those who were called upon to provide personal, often intimate, care.

John immediately asked if I would be interested. After talking it through with Rosa, visiting Millington to look at the small cottage that comes with the job, and meeting with John's wife

166

and his two small boys, we have decided to make the leap. Life in a small rural village must be an improvement on our suburban existence, and it should be a much better place to bring up our Sam.

So, in just a few days, we embark upon a new phase of our lives.

Chapter 16 – Secrets Shared.

On Sunday morning, Nadya woke, as had become the norm, before the rest of the household. Relishing the clear, crisp air, she took the dogs on her usual route up the side of the valley and back. She didn't linger this morning, as she was looking forward to the long walk with Rob to wherever he had in mind. The path up the hill was somewhat muddy after recent rain, but that same rain had brought the first of the spring flowers, providing the promise of hedgerows full of the gently nodding heads of yellow daffodils. Set amongst these early blooms, and spreading more widely into the open fields, there were still a number of late-blooming snowdrops. With the first of the year's lambs having been born, the whole valley seemed to buzz with the primes of new life, beckoning in a new season of growth and renewal. This was one of Nadya's favourite times of the year, one she yearned for through the dark, endlessly wet, and dreary days of winter. Since the warming, even the possibility of frost or snow transforming the landscape and covering the mud with clean whiteness was remote. There had been only one severe frost this winter and no snow for many years now.

Nadya had missed the Winter Festival at the farm, and there had been a few days when she was tearful and not her usual cheerful self, but on the morning of the festival Annie had presented her with a long letter and some gifts from her parents and brothers. She had exchanged several letters over the weeks and months but this one was special and contained pages of news from everyone, including two pages from Layna The gifts were small things she missed, a jar of her mum's blackberry jam, a well wrapped pat of butter and some apples from the farm orchard, all of which she shared with her aunt and uncle – and Rob, of course.

And now winter was almost behind them, spring was imminent if not already upon them raising everyone's spirits. Nadya also hoped to visit home soon, once she could be spared for a few days, altogether it felt like a time of promise and of new beginnings.

Returning the dogs to the cottage, she left them in the small front garden rather than let them, wet and muddy, into the house. She knew that Cliff would take them to the smithy once he had eaten breakfast, where they would spend the morning curled near to the warmth of the furnace, allowing the mud to dry and be more easily brushed from their short-haired coats. Even though it was Sunday, Cliff would spend most of the day in the smithy. Metalwork was his life's passion, much more than his work, so for him a Sunday spent on his own in the smithy was his way of relaxing. Perhaps working on one of his own designs or just pottering about the workshop, cleaning tools or mending something that had not worked quite perfectly during the week. Ann had grown used to this over the years. She might join him for periods during the day, bringing him some lunch or a mug of dandelion tea and sit with him in the dark homeliness of his workshop. The rest of the time, she would busy herself with her small garden or, if the day was warm enough and the sun shining, might just sit on the bench - fashioned lovingly by Cliff many years ago - by the front door. She would chat to other villagers who passed by on their Sunday promenade along the streets of the village, a common pastime and a way to catch up with the latest gossip and goings-on of others. There were few things that remained a secret for long in the small, tightly knit community.

Nadya grabbed the backpack that she had packed, with a waxed and waterproof jacket, hat, scarf, and things to eat and drink, the previous evening. Rob had introduced her to the concept of "Scoggins", small snacks of broken biscuits, sweets or dried fruits and nuts to eat along the way, and ever since she was sure to have a good selection of these energy-giving treats in her pack. They were particularly useful if the weather turned foul so that a stop to eat anything more substantial was uninviting. She had arranged to meet Rob partway along the same track she had returned down on the day they first met, seemingly ages ago now. There was a place where another, smaller path branched off to ascend the eastern flank of the valley, and this was to be their rendezvous. He was already there when she arrived, looking, she couldn't help thinking, quite handsome in a rugged, outdoorsy sort of way, perched as he was on a large rock, chewing a piece of straw which almost perfectly matched his fair hair. He was taller and fairer than most of the other inhabitants of the valley, and this always lent him something of the air of a traveller, wanderer or visitor, set slightly apart from his friends and neighbours.

"Good morning, my lady," he greeted her, doffing his cap with a cheeky grin and a wink.

Falling into the play, she retorted, "Never mind winking, you cheeky young scamp. Be more respectful of your betters."

"Very well, your ladyship. Shall we start? Would you like me to lead the way or walk along behind - at a respectful distance, of course?"

And with that, they both burst into laughter. The day was off
to a good start. The two of them seemed to get along so easily,
Nadya did wonder if this was, in some way, because just as he
appeared slightly apart, so she too was a newcomer. This did
seem strange in a way, as Rob had lived in the village all his life
- or so Nadya had assumed.

They set off along the ascending track, and for a time, neither
said much as Rob set a stiff pace and the way was steep. A
short way from the top, they stopped to catch their breath and
turned to look back down into the valley. The night had been
cool, and an inversion had formed so that smoke from the early
morning fires in the houses mingled with a faint mist to
produce a line of pale grey cloud below them. There were
several rising, curling plumes of smoke which penetrated this
layer, punching higher into the clearer air above. Up here, at
the rim of the valley, the air was sparklingly clear and fresh. Just
breathing was like drinking water from a clear, cool stream.
They said nothing but, after a few moments, both turned to
stride the last few dozen steps to the point where the slope
would give way to the flat, open moorland above the valley. As
they passed this point, the country to the east opened suddenly
and breathtakingly before them as a sea of brown heather, just
beginning to show the new green shoots which would, later in
the year, turn brilliantly purple with blossom.

Nadya, who was more accustomed to the tamer and more
managed countryside around Milltown, had fallen in love with
the wildness and openness of the moors and couldn't wait to
see the heather "put on its indigo overcoat," as Rob had
described it to her. She smiled and sighed audibly at the sight
and slipped her hand, without thinking, into Rob's, who, falling

into the familiarity of the close friendship between them, gave her hand a small squeeze in return. He pointed, with his free hand, to a faint path in the almost knee-deep heather.

"That's our path, made mainly by the sheep, I believe. It should cross this section of the moor and skirt to the north before turning southeast towards the Wheeldale valley, which we'll cross to bring us to our destination."

"Where are we going?" asked Nadya, not really caring that much about the destination, being content to simply enjoy the hike.

"Ah now, that would spoil the surprise," he replied, without offering any clues.

"OK," she laughed. "Then, as we walk, will you tell me more about yourself and your family?" She had been curious for some time, but their growing familiarity now made it seem OK to ask. "You're a three, aren't you?" she asked, referring to the fact that Rob, unusually, had two brothers. "My own family is a three too; one of my brothers was adopted from a family in our local village, where the parents had both died in an accident. How did your family become a three?"

Between two people who were less close, this might have been an impolite question, but Rob answered her directly.

"Our situation is a bit more unusual." He spoke quietly and, thought Nadya, somewhat tentatively.

"In our family, I am the one who is adopted. Would you like the real story or the one we tell folks around here?"

Nadya looked at him quizzically, but before she could say anything, he went on. "Of course, you'd like the true story, I think, but please bear in mind that few people know this, so it shouldn't be spoken of, not even to your aunt and uncle. As far as I know, they have only heard what we call the 'dead relative' story."

He said nothing more for several minutes as they walked on through the heather, only the doleful call of a distant curlew breaking the silence. Nadya, though, knew better than to prompt - he would tell his tale in his own time.

"Some twenty-five years ago now," he began, "my father had to take a trip to the north of the island to visit his sister, who was ill at the time. She lived with her family in a little coastal town called Nunport. As a south islander, it might surprise you to learn that up on the coast there, they still fish the North Sea, and Nunport is a thriving fishing port. My uncle himself is a fisherman who owns his own boat as well as a part share of a fish and chip shop. I'm guessing you've never tasted fresh fried fish in batter with fried chips. One day, we should take a trip up there, and I will buy you some. I would dearly love to see the look on your face as you bite through the crunchy golden batter and into the sweet, juicy flesh of the fish."

He looked across at Nadya but could tell from her expression that she wasn't convinced; it was well known that the south islanders, particularly those in the west, were more fearful of The Guardian and being discovered by the mainlanders and so had more or less abandoned sea fishing, apart from by rod from the shore. She said nothing, however, so he continued with his story.

"My aunt had suffered a nasty cut while gutting a fish, and the wound had become badly infected. For a time, it was thought she might die, and so my father had been sent for to settle the matter of the inheritance of the farm here in Rosedale. There was no dispute, as her sons were set to inherit the fishing business and wanted no part of the farm, but my grandfather's will had made it clear that the farm was jointly owned by his son and daughter unless one of them formally relinquished ownership. This had never been addressed, and it was felt that her injury and illness brought things to a head. Anyway, my dad had made the trip to sort this out, as well as to see his sister."

For the first time, Nadya interrupted to ask a question. "Were they close?"

"I think so, yes," Rob answered, before continuing. "They still are. In the end, she survived with only some bad scarring on her right hand and arm. They write regularly still. So, my father was staying with them in Nunport when one day there was something of a local commotion - it dominated the news around there for quite some time. A strange boat had been found on a local beach about a week after one of the worst storms for years. In it was a dead woman and a small baby, wrapped tightly against the cold but half-starved and very dehydrated. The boat had no sail and no oars but whether these had been lost overboard in the storm, or the woman and child had been deliberately cast adrift into the storm, was never discovered."

"And you're that baby?" interjected Nadya, not realising she was speaking aloud.

"Yes, Nadie, but patience, love, while I finish." Rob replied, not looking at her and clearly finding it emotionally quite difficult to tell the tale.

"It was the two young sons of my aunt and uncle who had found the boat; they brought the baby home as soon as they realised it was alive. The body of the woman was retrieved and buried, and the boat destroyed. You must realise that even up there on the north coast of Nym, where fear of the mainlanders and The Guardian is less, people are still extremely wary of strangers or of strange goings on. There have always been rumours of landings from the mainland, and they are always alert to reports of the unexpected or unusual. My aunt and uncle were ready to take me in and raise me as their own, but given the commotion, it was felt that it would be better if I was brought up somewhere where the circumstances of my being found were not known. This was reinforced when, in the weeks following my discovery, rumours of strange craft landing on remote beaches at night became quite common. It was feared mainlanders were looking for the woman and child. Some locals even suggested I should be put back on a remote beach and left to be found or to die as chance decided.

"My aunt, uncle, and my dad would have none of this, though. So, once it was clear that his sister was on the road to recovery, and the inheritance business was settled, Dad left, taking me with him, and brought me home to a very surprised Mum back at the farm. She knows the truth, of course, as do my brothers now. But the story put about, and one which has been kept up to this day, is that my mother died giving birth to me and my father would not have been able to cope with a newborn, so I was adopted into the family here."

He stopped talking at that, and the two walked on in silence for a while, Nadya digesting the story and Rob wondering how she would react to the news that he was a mainlander.

"Thank you for telling me the true story, Rob," she said after a short time. "It means a lot to me that you feel you can trust me, and of course your secret is totally safe with me."

She put her arm through his and rested her head briefly on his shoulder before going on.

"I wonder if all mainlanders are tall, fair, and devastatingly handsome?"

Rob laughed. Clearly, he had been right to assume that Nadya would not be disconcerted by the news that she was friends with a mainlander.

They walked on for several kilometres, the heather occasionally giving way to rocky outcrops as they skirted the northern end of the Hartoft valley. At one point, they stopped to admire a pair of buzzards wheeling and crying in the sky above them, flying around and around each other in ever-shrinking circles as they danced together in their pre-mating ritual. Their single, steady, almost whistling cry echoed across the moor, providing the background sound to some dramatic aerial displays. Several times, they climbed high, locked claws, and plummeted towards the earth in a swirling spiral, as if they were caught in a downward whirlwind that seemed certain to end in catastrophe. At the last moment, they would release each other, to whirl around, and climb once more into the high blue sky before repeating the performance. The two friends chattered excitedly at the display, both admiring the skill and daring of the buzzards.

After some time they left the displaying birds behind, turning southeast to start a long trek across open moorland, Rob spoke again, without looking at Nadya, simply staring straight ahead as if he needed to keep her from seeing his face.

"How much do you know about the mainland and mainlanders, Nadie, and how much about how we came to be isolated and fearful of The Guardian?"

Nadya swallowed hard and, for a moment, said nothing, remembering how the last time she had said anything on this subject, it had landed her in so much trouble. Finally, she plucked up enough courage to say, "It's my turn to tell you my own story, Rob."

She told him everything, from when she used to sit and gaze at the lights across the sea from Milltown, wondering what they meant, to her discovery of the time capsule and its contents. She told him of the pictures she had seen in the magazines and how she had read about people being able to choose to have any number of children with multiple partners if they wished. She explained how she had been engaged to Milo, but how she had always hesitated to set a date. She looked down at the ground, feeling the heat as her neck and face turned bright red while she spoke about how she had never felt able to give herself fully to Milo because of a nagging doubt in her mind about whether they were truly suited. Despite everyone assuming they would be a couple forever, the thought of committing to having children only with him always caused her to shrink back from that final step.

She explained how reading the article which described how the current biological constraint was not, as Nadya and everyone else assumed, the historic norm had triggered something in her mind. How she had tried to discuss it with Milo, there being no-one else she could think of who might understand. Describing how Milo had unwittingly betrayed her, leading to the dramatic meeting with the council, brought a tightening of her throat and caused unwelcome tears to well up in her eyes. She related to her newfound confident of how steadfastly her father had defended her but how the time capsule had been taken away, and her future torn apart, as she was forced to move to Nym.

Finally, wiping away the tears and tugging on Rob's arm to pull him around to look her straight in the face, she told him about the two journals she had managed to keep hold of, containing the story of the late twentieth-century chaos, which led to the wars that killed so many, and to the warming and unstoppable melting of the ice which triggered the rise of sea levels.

"So, you see, dear Rob," she said, looking into his bright blue eyes. "I know more than most, I think, about the history part, although I confess to knowing next to nothing about the mainland and mainlanders today. I am sure, though, that the journals will lead to an understanding of the sundering of our two islands from the rest of the world. I think it will explain why we fear The Guardian, believing as we do that it controls the rest of the world, and that we had to rid ourselves of all technology to remain free."

Nadya was amazed that in a few short weeks, she had gone from betrayal and a vow to herself never to speak of any of this to anyone again, to such a complete and unexpected opening up of her knowledge, thoughts and fears. It amazed her that in such a short time, she had come to trust this handsome, endlessly jovial man so completely. How, despite the fact that he was still a relative stranger, she could share her deepest secrets with him.

Holding on to both his hands, she now looked up into his face - he was a good fifteen centimetres taller than she was - and said, "So we've both let out quite a secret today, Rob. I wasn't expecting anything of the sort, but I'm glad you felt you could share with me, and somehow, I feel totally at ease knowing my own secrets are safe with you."

"They are," he replied simply, and, leaning down, kissed first her freckled nose and then, tentatively at first but, as she didn't pull away or object, with more passion, her soft, warm, and slightly trembling lips.

As if fate had decreed what happened next, they had come to a space where the heather gave way to a small patch of soft green grass. Nadya pulled Rob into the middle of this and then removed his coat, shirt, and then the rest of his clothes, leaving him naked in the warm sun. She looked at his body admiringly and could feel lust rising in her. Slowly, she peeled off her own garments so that the two of them stood with their bodies completely open to each other. Rob put his hands on either side of her face, pushed back her flaming red hair, and bent to kiss her once again, this time without holding back the passion he felt.

She lowered herself first onto her knees, then lay back on the grass, shivering slightly at the feel of its coolness on her back.

She in turn had put her hands on his face and pulled him down with her, so that now he lay on top of her. Without hesitation, she opened her strong legs and moved slightly to position his erection at the entrance to her own sex. With the slightest of pushes, he entered her gently. She felt a slight tear as her maidenhood yielded to him, and then only delight as he penetrated more deeply.

Their lovemaking was slow and gentle. Several times, he stopped to prolong the delight they were both feeling, but finally, he could hold back no longer and moaned softly as his orgasm flooded her with his semen. He kissed her again and again, holding their young bodies together as they lay glowing with passion and the warmth of the spring sunshine on their bodies. The grassy space was surrounded by half-metre-high banks of heather, so they were completely alone in their own world. A brief thought passed through Nadya's mind before she surrendered fully to the pleasure of the moment. "So, Aunt Ann, you were right after all."

Chapter 17 – Selected entries from Harry's Journals.
January 28th, 2082.

On this day in 2024, the Neuralink Corporation implanted the first chip into a human brain, allowing the individual to control external devices by thought alone. Today, the first non-prisoner in the UK was fitted with a controlling chip in his brain. John McAndrew, a serving soldier with the Special Services, volunteered to be fitted with the chip to allow his actions on the battlefield to be controlled through a computer at HQ. Orders will be issued via satellite to him anywhere in the world, and he will be unable to disobey those orders. As a safeguard against any infiltration of the controlling mechanism by a foreign entity, there is a separate device that must remain in constant contact with the base computer. In the event of loss of contact or detection of hacking of the main chip, the unit (meaning John himself) will be terminated.

John will be able to control many of the AI-managed weapons at the disposal of UK armed forces, and this has caused major controversy in NATO and the UN. It is thought it may breach the rules which have been in force for many years, preventing an AI computer from controlling such weapons. The UK has argued that John is a human being and that it is he who controls the weapons. However, many commentators have pointed out that if John is controlled by a computer, then, through him, that computer can directly control the weapons. The UK government has denied this, stating that there are unspecified safeguards in place to prevent such a control route.

In the last few days, the Humber estuary has flooded again due to exceptionally high spring tides, reinforced by the largest storm surge in decades. The city of Kingston upon Hull, along with the towns of Goole and Selby, dozens of surrounding villages, and hundreds of isolated farms, were evacuated. The Drax nuclear power plant remained protected, thanks to its surrounding ten-metre-high perimeter wall. This was the second time in two years that the entire estuary had flooded, and it is now doubtful whether any of the towns, villages, or other settlements will be rebuilt.

In the cities of York and Leeds, there have been widespread protests by the evacuated residents, with many claiming that, unless their homes are rebuilt, their whole culture and identity will be erased. Many claim this amounts to ethnic cleansing. The waters reached five metres deep in some areas, and thousands of homes have been destroyed. The refugees are calling for the resurrection of plans to build a protective barrier between Hessle and Barton at the site of the long-abandoned Humber Bridge. However, the Prime Minister has stated that we must adapt to the coming sea level rise, meaning that large-scale relocation is inevitable.

———

Two weeks into our new life in Millington, and it's hard to believe the transformation in our lives. We live in a delightful little cottage on the outskirts of the village, surrounded by fields and woods in which we are free to roam as we like, when work allows. John and I have become close friends, and having me around to care for him has returned to his wife, Lily, her independence. She still provides care for John when I'm not there, but with my help during the day, she is able to have a life of her own - something she hasn't had for some time. Evenings and nights are her responsibility, but we are only a short distance away, so I can assist at any time if needed. And Rosa, my lovely Rosa, is happier than I have ever seen her, seeming to glow with contentment and delight. Village life suits her. She has integrated so easily and already has a number of firm friends. This is helped by being one mum amongst several who have small children, including Lily. Indeed, Rosa and Lily already seem to have struck up a firm friendship.

Life can be strange at times; opportunities drop out of a seemingly empty blue sky to change things utterly. It's only a few short years since we lived the usual, seemingly hopeless life which is the lot of the majority, and now we count ourselves amongst the most privileged. Without doubt, we are still amongst the masses of ordinary people, so far removed from the remote and unimaginable lives of the technos, but we live in a way we could never have dreamed of in those earlier days.

We have not yet discussed our plans to bury a time capsule with John and Lily, but I have found what I think is the perfect place: under a large flat rock near a young oak tree in the corner of a field on one of the local farms. The field apparently alternates between pasture for sheep and arable, but in all events the corner I have in mind is secure against disturbance due to its proximity to the oak. Oak trees typically live for hundreds of years, so this should carry our messages well into the future. Who knows? Maybe our own children's children's children - or beyond - will still live somewhere nearby and might get to see whatever we, in the end, seal in our capsule.

What will the world be like then, I wonder? What will happen after the flood that is now inevitable? Will the long-held fears of AI coming to dominate humanity come to fruition, or will we merely continue the slide into separation between those who have and those who have not? I am reminded of a book I read as a boy, "The Time Machine" by H.G. Wells, in which, in the distant future, mankind has evolved into two distinct species: the Eloi, an indolent people who seem to live lives of plenty and want for nothing, and the Morlocks, who maintain the machinery of the civilisation, and yet who turn out to use the Eloi as mere cattle to feed themselves. The separation between the ultra-wealthy, in their isolated paradises, and the rest of us, who continue to toil or merely to exist, is already incredibly stark. And yet, there appears to be little chance of any major change or revolution due to the control the ultra-wealthy have over the state and military. Will the continued advancement of AI and the interface with the human mind reinforce this situation, or will something, such as the development of AUOTA, come along and shatter everything? It is questions such as this that prompted me to want to bury a time capsule so that those who live in the distant future might be reminded of where, and who, they came from.

In the meantime, the beautiful Rosa and I have so much to be thankful for. And now, I must put away this journal and sleep. I can already hear Rosa snoring gently in our bed. I have a busy day tomorrow - John and I are going to take a trip into one of the wonderful U-shaped chalk valleys that lead out of the village. He has an all-terrain mobility scooter but has not used it often in the past, as Lily was worried in case anything happened.

Chapter 18 – News from the North.

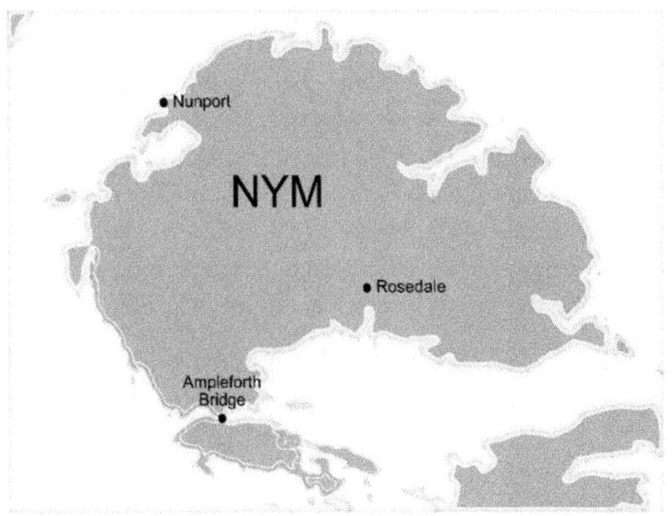

Three years passed. Nadya completed her apprenticeship and was now a fully-fledged smith in her uncle's business. Her work was much in demand in the village and beyond, but the mundane day-to-day tasks of shoeing horses and repairing farm implements dominated the workload of the smithy. Time, and money, for more artistic endeavours were limited.

She and Rob lived together in a small but cosy cottage on the farm, and they had their two children: Rosa and a boy they had named Sam. Nadya had chosen the names to honour the woman in the journals and her firstborn, even though, in Sam's case, the name was short for Samantha and not originally a boy's name at all. From their earliest days, the two children had been raised within and around the smithy, with Cliff having created a warm and safe corner for them so they could be close to their mother while she continued learning metalworking skills. Rob's mother had initially been horrified at the idea of the children being in the smithy, which she regarded as akin to the fires of hell. Ann had also been a little concerned, but Nadya had refused the idea that the babies should be taken from her while they were still dependent on her milk. Once Rosa had turned twelve months old and become more inquisitive and mobile, Nadya had relented, allowing the toddler to spend large parts of each day with Ann or, on some days, on the farm in the care of Rob's mother, Julia.

Rosa had been born exactly nine months to the day after Nadya and Rob had first made love in the heather, and her middle name (a rarity in Nym in the twenty-fifth century) was a remembrance of that occasion. Rosa Heather had inherited her mother's startling green eyes and bright red hair, but her's was distinctly curly rather than gently wavy like her mother's, something they assumed came from Rob's side of the family. Sam, on the other hand, as far as anyone could tell at the ripe old age of fifteen months, appeared to be fair-haired but brown-eyed like his father. He had also reached the walking stage and had therefore passed into the daily care of his grandmothers.

The whole family had visited Nadya's home several times, and her da had assured her that the kerfuffle surrounding her finding of the time capsule had long ceased to be anything but an old story, an old storm in a teacup. For the moment, though, both she and Rob were content to remain in Rosedale. The Knowles' farm would eventually pass to one of Nadya's older brothers, whereas Cliff had promised her a place in the smithy for as long as he lived and beyond if she wanted it. Rob, easy-going and already a competent metalworker and general mechanic, would fit well into such a future, either as a full partner in the smithy or splitting his time between it and the farm.

She was delighted to learn that Milo had married her old friend and workmate, Layna. The two couples had bumped into each other one evening during a visit to Milltown, and Nadya was genuinely pleased with that outcome. She knew that Milo could never have given her the sense of fulfilment and wholeness that she had found with Rob, whereas he and Layna seemed a perfectly matched couple.

The late spring evening still had some light as Nadya returned to their home with the two children, finding Rob already there and preparing the evening meal for the two adults. The children had eaten at Nanny Ann's, and Nadya busied herself with bathing them and storytelling while Rob finished the cooking. The pair worked well together and had created a smoothly functioning family unit. The children, as always, loved Nadya's tale of Tip the dog, who sailed off in a boat and had adventures all over the wide world.

Nanny Ann and Julia were less approving, often telling Nadya that she shouldn't fill the children's heads with tales of a wider world when their safety from The Guardian lay in remaining hidden in Nym and Woldshire, but Rob backed her up. He had begun to read from Harry's journals, though neither of them had found much time in the past three years, with their whirlwind romance (as the locals put it) and then the trials of parenthood.

Rob seemed a little distracted this evening, not humming and whistling endlessly (and, as Nadya often pointed out, relatively tunelessly). She knew him well enough by now to understand that, whatever was bothering him, he would speak of it when he was good and ready. No amount of prodding or poking from her would yield a faster result. So, she left him to the final preparations and poured them both a glass of their favourite malty red ale. Sure enough, as they sat down to eat, he immediately opened the conversation.

"I heard something today, Nadie, love," he began, hardly lessening the intrigue Nadya felt.

"Oh, yes?"

"There has been another landing near Nunport," he continued. "This time, some poor chap who seems to have suffered a mishap at sea and nearly bled to death. From what I heard, he has lost an arm but is beginning to recover very slowly."

He looked at Nadya in a way that told her exactly what he was going to say next. They had both long talked about the mainland and how Rob, quite naturally, had been curious about what it was like and, more importantly, what his people were like.

"I'd like to go and talk to him; do you think that would be possible?"

"Well, it's been nearly a year since our last trip, and well over two years since you and I went anywhere with just the two of us," Nadya had commented.

"Oh, I didn't really mean both of us," said Rob, a little startled, at least for a second.

"Well, dear, if you think I'm going to miss out on something like this, you've got another think coming. It's quiet in the smithy at the moment, and I'm sure your aunt and uncle in Nunport could put us all up for a day or two." Nadya gave him a look that he knew meant she wouldn't be budging on this.

"Or," she continued pensively, "Ann would be delighted to look after Rosa and Sam for a few days, with the help, I'm sure, of your mum."

"We would need to be careful that only close family knew the reason for the trip," Rob said pensively. "As far as everyone else is concerned we must simply be going to see family up there."

"Yes, of course," agreed Nadya, recollecting the furore that had erupted in Milltown over her questions about fertility. "But, all the same, it would be nice to have you to myself for a few days."

"Yes, that would be delightful," Rob replied with a grin. "I wonder if they have any walks in the heather up there."

Nadya flashed him a mock severe look with her startling green eyes, but couldn't help herself and burst into laughter, completing the discussion with a wink and a grin that promised erotic delights as well as an adventure. Just the thought seemed to arouse them both, and, without even finishing their evening meal, they found themselves in each other's arms on the large rug in front of the log fire. Rob simply couldn't resist the red-headed beauty he had found all those years ago, and he couldn't believe his luck that she seemed to feel the same about him. He adored it when, in the warm summer months, and if she knew he was working alone in a field somewhere, she would sneak away from the smithy and surprise him by emerging, naked and glowing with passion, from a nearby hedgerow. At such times he thought she was like a woodland nymph or goddess, distracting him from his work with an hour or more of lustful pleasures.

It was therefore much later, that they agreed that she would speak to Cliff and Ann in the morning, and that they would aim to leave as soon as the weekend if everyone agreed. He, in turn, planned to speak to his parents to be excused from farm work for a few days. Neither of them were at all sure of the reception their plan would receive.

The next day, Nadya explained to Cliff what had happened and asked if she could be spared. They had already talked about Rob's history, so she was hopeful he would understand. She also hoped he would understand her own desire to speak to the stranger, as he knew all about her time capsule and the journals, though he had made it clear at the time that she shouldn't speak openly about them, not even to Ann.

Long days working together in the forge had built a closeness and trust between the two of them, one that encouraged openness, knowing the other wouldn't leap to judgement. Cliff had no desire himself to read the journals and remained distrustful of anything to do with the mainland, but he had been prepared to indulge this young woman who had come to be just like a daughter to him.

In the event, he was more sceptical than she had expected and took some persuading. He knew and liked Rob, but Rob had been brought up from a baby in the ways of the islands, and an adult stranger from the mainland was a very different prospect. One that, in his view, should be treated with the utmost caution. Yes, he had indulged Nadya with respect to the journals, but he admitted to her that he had always suspected they were fakes. Besides, curiosity about the past wasn't the same as risking the isolation of the islands from The Guardian in the present.

In the end, he agreed she could be released, but only on the understanding that, apart from Rob's parents, no one else must ever know of their real reason for the trip. He suggested that, as far as Ann or anyone else was concerned, they should simply say Rob had some family business in the north. That this necessitated a visit and that they wanted to take a delayed honeymoon now that the children had reached an age where they could be left in the care of their grandparents. He was sure Rob's parents would feel the same, not having shared anything about Rob's connection with the mainland with local people, even after all these years.

"Be careful, Nadya," he concluded. "This curiosity and non-conforming streak of yours has gotten you into bother already, I don't want to lose you over it, but nor will I let it bring danger to my own doorstep."

Nadya accepted the admonishment, hoping she had not damaged her relationship with this man she had come to regard as a second father. She hugged him and kissed him on the cheek whilst uttering a subdued "Thank you."

On the day of their departure, a watery sun poked its face above the southeastern flank of the valley into a pale sky with thin, high, but all-covering clouds. There was a chill in the air and a feeling of rain to come later in the day, so that Nadya and Rob double-checked that they had stowed waterproofs in their packs. They had decided, for speed, against using the buggy and would, instead, ride two of the farm horses. For Nadya they chose a young chestnut gelding she had ridden often before and for Rob his favourite white stallion. Both were accomplished riders and would enjoy the journey, although Nadya suspected that after a full day in the saddle she would have a good deal of aches and pains needing a hot bath and Rob's attentions with massaging her tired muscles.

The two children waved, a little tearfully, as their parents rode away, down the track to pick up the road up to Blakey Ridge, which they would follow to Castletown. From there they would head east, after, Rob insisted, refreshments at the Dunne Arms. They would then follow the line of the old railway before turning north towards the peak of Roseberry Top and finally to Nunport by mid-evening. A long ride, but one that would see them at their destination in just one day. Using the buggy would have taken at least two days and required an overnight stop somewhere, at an inn or at worst sheltering in the back of the cart itself.

As they reached the high point of Blakey Ridge, they could see gathering dark clouds in the southwest. Before an hour had passed, the rain started, so they stopped to pull on their ponchos, which covered not only their upper bodies but extended over their legs and feet. They also served to cover the backs of the horses, at least behind the riders, although there was little they could do to keep the horses heads dry. Their own heads were covered with sturdy, wide-brimmed waxed hats, held firmly in place against the wind by straps under the chin. "We look like a pair of travellers," Rob commented, referring to the folk who lived life on the roads, making a living by providing entertainment or doing odd jobs at places they stopped for a few days, and receiving only a forlorn look from Nadya. She did not like the rain, especially not a cold rain of late spring.

The road was well made though, so that they made good progress despite the weather. They saw few other travellers on the road, which was not unusual for these times. Nadya recalled something she had read in one of the journals about traffic and something called commuting where people would drive their old polluting cars for hours to get to and from work. She had tried hard to visualise a world with so many people and with the air choked with fumes and dust so that people coughed and sometimes even died from just breathing the bad air. She shuddered, and Rob turned to her, concerned that she might be getting chilled, but she assured him that she was ok and that it was just thoughts of the old mechanised technological world that had caused her to shiver.

After a few minutes more of silent riding, Rob asked her, "Do you think the mainland is still like that, with polluted air and lots of people, cars, and the like?"

Nadya considered before she answered. "Well, if the air was polluted, wouldn't it come to us as well? The wind is from the west or southwest most of the time, so surely, we would sense pollution."

She went on, thinking of the times she had sat and watched the lights in the west from her favourite seat on the cliffs near Milltown: "I never saw any evidence of smoke or pollution over in the west when I used to look at the lights. Maybe we will be able to ask the man who landed from the mainland, if he will speak to us."

After another pause, she wondered aloud, "I wonder if we'll be able to speak to him at all, do they speak the same language as us after all these years?" Rob had no answer, even though he himself had been born on the mainland. He had been far too young to have any memory of it and had learnt his first words here in Nym.

After an hour or so, the road began to descend sharply into the Esk valley, and the rising ground to their left and right provided a little protection from the driving rain. They spurred their horses to a faster trot as they descended, both now looking forward to finding shelter, some warm broth, and a beer at the Dunne Arms. It was another hour, though, before they caught sight of the town, and by the time they arrived, they were both damp and cold and in need of a rest. Rob took the horses to find the inn's stables, dry them down, and make sure they had some food and water, while Nadya pushed open the door to the inn, braving the usual stares of the locals, and asked about food.

"Well, my lovely," the innkeeper replied, "I'm sure we can find some broth and a glass of ale for a beautiful traveller such as yourself. What brings you here all alone on such a foul day, me duck?"

Nadya laughed, being more than used to such compliments by now. "My husband is just seeing to our horses and will be in shortly, so soup for two and two glasses of your best ale would be wonderful. I'll take that table over in the window if that's ok."

She laughed again at the disappointed look, not just on the face of the innkeeper but several of the other men sitting near the bar. "I'm sure your welcome will be just as warm for a married mum and her man as it would have been for a lone woman," she said, so that all would hear, but with a conspiratorial wink to the innkeeper. She shook her long red hair over her shoulders and, putting on her best haughty air, walked over to the window table and took a seat. After a few moments, Rob entered and made his way over to her, just as the innkeeper arrived with the ales.

"Welcome, stranger," he grinned at Rob. "Your wife here has already caused quite a stir with her looks, you had better keep a close eye on her or she'll have all the eligible men of the town following you as you leave. Rob laughed in turn; he also was used to his young wife turning heads wherever she went.

As they ate and drank, both travellers regularly looked out of the window and saw the raindrops bouncing on the road outside or splashing in the rapidly deepening puddles. In both of their minds, doubt was forming as to the wisdom of continuing their journey today. The thought of putting on the ponchos, which, although they were steaming by the fire, they knew would still be damp and would rapidly chill once they stepped outside, did not fill them with enthusiasm. On the other hand, the thought of sitting warm and cosy in the bar and then retiring to a room, before spending the evening enjoying the company of the locals of Castletown, was very appealing. Neither spoke of these thoughts though, assuming the other would want to press on. Then, just as Nadya was about to say something, a single shaft of sunlight pierced the clouds to illuminate the pretty little house on the opposite side of the road. In just a few moments, the rain lessened and then ceased altogether, and the road outside began to steam in the growing spring sunshine.

And so, with not a little regret, they both finished their meal and stood to don the mostly dry outer garments, and to pull on their riding boots. Rob paid for the meal, and for the food and short stabling of the horses, and they strode out of the door of the inn and into a pleasant afternoon. They resaddled the horses, who also seemed to regret having to leave the warm, dry stable, remounted, and set off along the road, out of the small town, to pick up the trail, which led initially to the north. The old road continued north, up a steep bank onto Kildale Moor, but they soon came to a turn that led onto the old rail track. Since the demise of rail transport in the wake of the removal of advanced technology from Nym and Woldshire, the tracks had been removed. The old railbed had been turned into an excellent new road, one that avoided the rise and fall of the old road, instead taking a slightly longer, but almost level, path along the valley bottom.

As the afternoon wore on, they made steady progress, eventually turning north to cross the open moors towards Roseberry Top, before finally descending onto the coastal plain leading to Nunport. The small town was originally a suburb of the old industrial conurbation of Middlesborough. For decades after the flood, the waters of the coast here were extremely polluted with little life. Several hundred years, though, had served to clean the sea, and the fishing was now excellent, especially further out to the east, in the deeper waters of the original North Sea. The town was now a busy fishing port, something new to Nadya, and she was fascinated by the sights, sounds and smells as they weaved their way through the narrow, and rapidly darkening, streets towards the port itself and the home of Rob's aunt and uncle. Their knock on the bright green door of the cottage home was quickly answered, and they were swept inside by a plump, white-haired lady in her mid-sixties.

"Welcome, welcome, welcome. Do come in, my dears." She cried, throwing her arms first around Rob and then, with the merest hint of hesitation, around Nadya.

"Oooh, pet, you are a pretty one," she said, holding Nadya at arm's length and looking her up and down and running a wrinkled but strong and healthy hand over her hair. "Very pretty indeed, I'm very glad you weren't around forty years ago when I met my Will." She laughed in a loud and high voice before finally releasing Nadya and beckoning the two arrivals into a warm and brightly painted kitchen.

"You must call me Sal, and may I call you Nadya?"

"Nadie," would be perfect answered Nadya, swept up by the enthusiastic friendliness of this delightful woman.

"Aye, pet, that'll be grand." With that she turned her attention to Rob, who received a stern look but a grinning rebuke.

"And, as for you, young Rob, we don't see nearly enough of you, we still think of you as 'our lad' you know."

"I guess it's been a good few years indeed," he laughed back. "I can't remember the last time I tasted one of your fish and chip suppers; I've told Nadie many times how wonderful they are."

Sal bustled around with an energy that belied her plumpness, throwing on a coat, she almost ran out of the door, calling back over her shoulder.

"Make yourselves right at home, my dears. Rob, you know where your room is, we've made it up ready for the two of you. There's hot water for you to wash up, and there's ale in the pantry too. I'll be back in two shakes of a duck's tail. I'll bring Will, and some supper; the boys can finish up in the shop tonight."

With that, she was gone, and it seemed to Nadya as if a whirlwind had passed by, leaving a contrasting stillness and sudden silence in its wake.

"Wow," was all she could say, as Rob ushered her up the narrow staircase and into the small, but simply and beautifully furnished, room. She spotted the bathroom and, throwing off her still damp riding clothes, pushed her way in before Rob had even brought up the bags.

He knocked on the closed door when he had brought the last ones up, but received only a muffled answer, faintly heard above the sound of running water.

"Go away, this is mine for the next half hour, I'll leave the water in for you."

Rob sighed, clearly washing the grime of the long ride from himself would have to wait. He consoled himself by going back to the kitchen and pouring himself a large glass of ale.

Chapter 19 - Selected entries from Harry's Journals. July 21st, 2085.

Today, the UK government suspended the requirement for general elections, citing the continued fall in voter turnout. Prime Minister Richard Cesare said "There is no longer a need for this outmoded form of democracy. With the support of the six largest global tech-corps, the population of the UK is safe in the hands of this government. People can now concentrate on enjoying their lives, freed from the burden of both work and of participating in the onerous task of governing this great country and the world."

The mandatory implantation of location and control microchips in anyone taken into police custody for any reason has been justified on the grounds of security and societal well-being by Home Affairs Minister Justin van de Rouse.

Temperatures across North Africa exceeded fifty-eight degrees centigrade for seventeen of the last thirty days. The subsequent large-scale migration of people towards the Mediterranean coast sparked fears of a new wave of uncontrolled migration northwards; borders across Europe remain closed, with all unauthorised ships being repelled. Humanitarian agencies have stated that unless action is taken to allow the evacuation of people away from zones of extreme heat, the death toll is likely to reach and exceed a billion within weeks. UK Prime Minister Richard Cesare has said that, "with unemployment now exceeding ninety percent for the first time, the UK is full and cannot accept any more people."

In the US, a one-child policy has been introduced for the first time, with mandatory sterilisation for anyone who has a second child. The managed abandonment of southern and low-lying states continues, with the population becoming concentrated in the north and east. The border with Canada remains closed.

Scientists have reported that the catastrophic and irreversible collapse of the ice sheets of Antarctica is now predicted to be complete within one hundred and fifty years. Thirty-five per cent of the Greenland ice sheet has already melted, and it is anticipated that the remainder will occur within one hundred years. Scientists now believe the world could be completely ice-free by the year 2300.

Meanwhile, the Atlantic Meridional Overturning Circulation - AMOC, or, as it is more popularly known, "the Gulf Stream" - has reduced to twenty-five percent of its pre-2000 volume, leading to increasingly cold and wet winters in northern Europe. The organisation "Climate Change Watch" cites the cold winters as evidence that, as they term it, "global warming", was a temporary event and is already reversing.

––––––––––

Personal Notes:

We have now been in Millington for three years, and although, like everyone else, we watch with horror what is happening in the country and the world, we feel extremely insulated from most events. Life in a rural village continues much as always, with the only changes being the need to manage the increasing flooding and, for the farmers, the lack of weather to ripen and certainly to dry the crops. Around here, they are more fortunate than those who farm the lowlands of the Vale of York, as much of their land is now underwater for several months each year. As the floodwaters frequently come from inundations coming up the Humber Estuary and are saline, it is becoming increasingly difficult for them to successfully grow anything. The very structure of the alluvial soils is degrading further with each passing year.

Throughout the twenty-first century, works of post-apocalyptic fiction have often focused on land losses due to sudden and catastrophic flooding, but the reality is that land loss is more gradual and insidious. Houses become uninsurable and uninhabitable as the time between flooding events reduces. The land itself becomes less valuable and is eventually abandoned to marshland, and finally, the population simply moves away. Rather than a sudden transformation from land to sea, what happens is the gradual encroachment of more and more salt marsh and abandoned land. In a bizarre twist, the positive impact on wildlife somewhat offsets mankind's otherwise detrimental effects, as more land becomes available to birds and wildlife in general. In evolutionary terms, this benefit will be short-lived, as eventually, if the predictions are correct, all of that newly wilded land will succumb to the sea.

Here in Millington, a survey of the land heights across the whole area suggests the village is safe and will, in a few centuries, be located close to the seashore at the head of a small inlet. It will be situated on a large island off the shore of northeast England. How strange to think that our rural Wolds village will become a seaside settlement, possibly even a fishing port, and that it will be separated from mainland UK by a wide inland sea. The crossing from here to where the land rises again out of the water will be as wide as the English Channel. The map produced also shows that the location I selected to bury the time capsule will be well above the new sea level and thus safe from inundation. I only hope that the period between now and then, as the climate moves between one state and another, is survivable; who knows what impacts we are going to see in the next decades and, indeed, centuries?

I continue to be humbled by the change in our family circumstances over the past five years, from urban hopelessness to life in a delightful, and delightfully small, rural village. My duties as carer for John are far from onerous; they can be physically demanding at times, but John is such a patient guy, and he copes so well with the undoubted indignities of his situation. In contrast to our improved situation, the plight of the mass of humanity, including the general populace in the UK, continues to decline. Sadly, as our Prime Minister acknowledged in the news, lifelong unemployment, with all the sense of worthlessness and lack of a future, is now the plight of more than ninety percent of people. Was this situation ever in the minds of those who pushed so hard for the development of AI and robotics in the early part of the century? I cannot believe so.

Of the other major announcements of recent days, one of them leaves me largely indifferent, while the other I find much more horrifying. I always used to vote in elections, but like most people, I had come to realise that our elected politicians were largely just puppets of the technos, giving a respectable, democratic veneer to the reality that our lives and the rules and norms by which we live have long been decided by the CEOs and owners of the tech-corps. In many ways, this could be seen as an inevitable consequence of the new reality: that it is the megacorps that pay the taxes which fund the machinery of society, not the masses. Even in the early decades of the century, even before the wars and the turmoil and the clampdown on protest and disobedience that followed, there was a growing dissatisfaction with government and a movement of people away from traditional democratic processes. I know there are underground movements even now that oppose the current status, but most people remain aloof to them and fearful of being identified as even thinking about supporting them.

The consequences of being identified as a potential radical are severe and rapid in these days, especially with the new regulations leading to anyone being taken into custody being chipped with the new location and control brain implants. Even the vaguest suspicion that you might be associated with any proscribed group - and the list of proscribed groups grows ever longer; even the old Women's Institute is on the list - leads to detention and chipping, even if no connection is proven and no charges brought. One does hear of mumblings of unrest as a result, but given that it is impossible to know who to trust, these remain vague and largely unspoken.

Rosa and I talk of these things in the privacy of our home, but even this is a privilege not available to many, as it is widely known that state housing provision is fitted with listening devices, ostensibly to provide additional security to the residents. We both fear what the world will be like for our beloved daughter and are extremely thankful that we may have found a place where she can grow up in relative safety - at least, I hope so.

Chapter 20 - Jomo.

Nadya awoke to the sound of laughter and conversation from the kitchen below. It had been a late night, and she had consumed much more beer and fruit wine than she was used to. Her head felt fuzzy, to say the least, "Good grief," she thought to herself, "I haven't had a hangover since I was sixteen or seventeen years old, and we partied on the beach near Milltown, drinking ale and cider."

She wished Rob would bring her a cup of mint tea, her favourite wake up beverage, or perhaps the hot drink she had tasted for the first time last evening, tea, with milk. She had read about tea in Harry's Journals but thought the drink was unavailable in modern, isolated Woldshire and Nym. Then Sal had made a pot late in the evening, saying she'd had more than enough ale and wine. She had encouraged Nadya to drink some, and although Nadya had initially shuddered at the bitter taste, by the end of the cup she had begun to enjoy it. Sal had explained that tea, Camellia sinensis, had been grown in the UK for centuries on a small scale and that her family had passed down the growing of the plants for generations. She had explained that it was a delightful shrub with fragrant flowers in late summer, and that the leaves could be harvested at any time, although the young leaves were the best for making the freshest tasting brews. She herself took leaves at various stages and blended them to a secret family recipe to create her own special brew. The plants grew readily in the modern climate, she explained, and she had offered Nadya two young plants to take with her when she left for home.

At that moment, there was a knock at the bedroom door and, as if she had been reading Nadya's mind, in walked Sal with a large mug of the fragrant brew.

"Nowt like a cuppa first thing in the morning lass," she stated, clearly not open to debate on the matter. "Not that it's first thing any longer." She rolled her eyes and laughed as Nadya glanced guiltily at the clock on the wall.

"Ee, never mind, lass. I suspect you're up with the lark at home, so it'll do you good to have a lie-in." She put the mug down on the bedside table and bustled, in her busy way, back towards the door.

"Will has organised for you to meet the stranger after lunch, so you've plenty of time this morning to get yourself up at your leisure. There's breakfast on the table whenever you're ready, love." With that, she was gone and had closed the door behind her.

 Nadya lay back against the generous pillows and sighed with contentment. It was indeed a luxury not to be up at dawn. Now, if she could just shift the fuzziness in her head. She hopped out of bed, brushed her teeth before tasting the novel brew. Already, the bitterness mingling with the creaminess of the milk was growing on her. She would need to learn how to rear the plants and prepare the leaves properly before they left. Maybe she could even persuade Sal to let her have some of the dried leaves to tide her over until her own were ready.

When she came down the steep stairs an hour later, breakfast had mostly been cleared away, but Sal had left out meats and bread, along with some old, somewhat shrivelled but still sound, apples and pears from last year's harvest. Will had long since gone to accept the morning's catch, and Sal and Rob were also nowhere to be seen. She settled down at the table to eat and to ponder what they were going to ask the stranger. She knew that Rob wanted to know if there was any recollection of his family and how his mother had come to be alone in a boat with a small baby. She was more interested in questions relating to the things she had read in the journals, and about life there. Were the people, as they were taught here on the islands, wholly oppressed and under the yoke of The Guardian? And what exactly was The Guardian? How was it connected to the AI and robotics she had read about? And, of course, the lights she had so often gazed at - what did they signify? Why did they shine so brightly across the inland sea?

She would, of course, allow Rob to take precedence, given his personal connection, and indeed, she was almost as interested as he was to learn anything possible about his past. But she hoped there would be time for her own enquiries.

So, early in the afternoon, they found themselves, accompanied by Will, on a short walk through the town to a nondescript little house on the edge of town. Will looked around carefully before knocking, quietly, on the door and waiting. After only a few seconds, they heard several bolts being drawn back and the turning of a key in the lock before the door was opened by an attractive young woman, who beckoned them inside. She then peered up and down the road outside, closed the door, and relocked it, sliding several sturdy looking bolts into place. "Why the precautions?" asked Rob, looking at both the woman and Will. "Is he afraid the mainlanders will come for him?"

"Quite the opposite, actually," said the young woman quietly. "He is extremely keen to leave as soon as his wound has healed enough, although how he is going to manage his sailboat with just one arm is beyond me. You will find him to be very anxious, it is as if he is terrified by what we consider normal sights, sounds and smells. Any sign of dirt, disorder or wildness seems to distress him intensely. The need for security, though, is, I'm ashamed to say, to protect him from our own. There is a small but vocal group of locals who would have him put back in his boat and set adrift, to survive or die, so that, as they so delicately put it, 'they could terminate his presence before anyone comes looking for him'."

She continued. "The local council has still not decided what is to be done, but it is widely expected that he will be kept here on the islands for fear of him revealing something to The Guardian which puts us all in danger. There is a very small group of us who are less terrified by tales and rumours of The Guardian, and we believe that it is our duty, as humans, to help this poor man until he can return. We are convinced he is not a threat to us. I hope we are right."

Both Nadya and Rob were shocked, although, on reflection, Rob realised this kind of fear might have led to him being taken away to Rosedale all those years ago. Fear of the mainlanders and terror of The Guardian was something they were taught beginning at their mother's breast and which continued throughout their lives. As Nadya herself had experienced, even expressing curiosity about the mainland could lead to severe trouble.

"I hope you aren't letting anyone know of your own origin," the woman cautioned. I've been told of it and of the trouble that ensued when you disappeared. Your 'uncle' here will probably play it down, but there were threats against him and Sal for quite some time after." Will just nodded, not wanting to speak of those difficult times and the woman continued, "We've explained to Jomo who you are and says he can remember something of what happened on the mainland, but I'll leave him to tell the tale."

"Does he speak English?" asked Nadya on a more practical note. "And does he have a name?"

This time, Will answered. "Yes, his dialect is a bit difficult to understand, and some words are different, but there's more in common than not. His name is Jomo."

The woman knocked on a door at the far end of a short corridor and, peering around it, said quietly, "Are you ok to see your guests, Jomo?" They didn't hear a reply, but presumably, he had indicated yes, as they were ushered into a small, clean room with a window open to the garden. Jomo was sitting in a comfortable looking chair facing the window, his right arm clearly missing from above the elbow, the stump wrapped in clean bandages. He was middle aged, Nadya guessed around forty, dark skinned, with a drawn face and sad eyes. He stood up to greet Nadya and Rob, pointing to a sofa next to his seat.

"Would you turn my seat a little, please?" His accent was thick and strange, but they could understand his request without difficulty. Rob did as he was asked, moving the chair to face the sofa so that they could talk more easily. "Thank you," Jomo said, sitting carefully to avoid jarring his injury.

Now that Nadya could see him more clearly, she could tell that he was, indeed, extremely nervous and agitated, his eyes constantly darting around the room. He also appeared to have a nervous twitch, frequently touching his outer ear, then sighing, apparently with loss or disappointment.

"Liselle has told me a bit about your story, Rob, and I'm happy to tell you anything I can. I guess this is your wife, Nadya? Hello, Nadya, it's lovely to meet you. Will has told me all about you. I think you've got something of an admirer there," he added with a smile. "Something I can understand now I've met you."

His friendly, relaxed tone belied his obvious nervous excitement. They guessed Liselle was the young woman who had shown them into the room.

"Thank you, Jomo, you are very kind." Nadya blushed at the compliment, something she seemed to be doing a lot since leaving Rosedale.

Rob rolled his eyes and laughed. "For goodness' sake, don't fill her head with any more of this stuff, it's hard enough living in her shadow as it is!" He tempered the words by placing a kiss on Nadya's cheek, then turned to face Jomo, ready to start asking questions. But Jomo spoke first.

"Rather than trying to answer a bunch of questions in a haphazard way, why don't I tell you the tale as I know it? Then I'll try to fill in any extra things you may want to ask about. Will that work?" Once again, he touched his hand to his ear, as if expecting to hear some affirmation from a source other than Nadya and Rob. They nodded their assent.

"Great, now would one of you do the honours and pour us all a glass of ale from the jar on the table there? This is going to be thirsty work, I think. It took me some time to get used to the strong taste, but now I have grown accustomed to it, I must admit the ale here in Nym - is that right? - is better than anything I have had back in Britan, 'the mainland', as I think you call it."

Nadya poured the ale as requested, and before he began, Jomo lifted his glass a little clumsily with his left hand - clearly, he was normally right-handed - and raising it in their direction, uttered the word, "Chars."

He spoke carefully and a little haltingly, obviously trying both to remember things clearly and to ensure he was understood.

"I must have been about fifteen at the time - yes, that would be right, about twenty-five years ago. No one knew anything was amiss until the disappearance of the mother and child, but then it all came out. As far as I remember, it was like this:

The woman, I can't remember her name now, sorry, and her partner already had one child, but then he developed a cancer. Now most cancers are curable these days, but just occasionally, with some of the more aggressive types, there can be adverse effects from the cure. One of those is male sterility, and this happened to this poor guy.

'Oh well,' people thought, 'at least they've already had one child.'

And then the woman got pregnant again, and that's when all hell broke loose. Everyone realised that not only was this new child not her husband's, but neither could the first one be. I'm guessing that the new biology, as we call it, is understood here?"

Nadya interrupted briefly to say, "Well yes, although as far as most people here are concerned, it's not new but has always been this way."

"Really?" Jomo looked surprised but carried on with the story.

"Yes, because, as we all know, not only are we restricted to two children, but they can only be conceived with the same two people. It's some very clever biochemistry, and we don't fully know how it works, and it goes without saying that no one is able to work on reversing it, that would never be sanctioned.

So now Randolph - I think I remember correctly that was his name - was faced not only with the fact his partner had been unfaithful and brought a child into their partnership that wasn't his, but that this had continued, or restarted, resulting in the second pregnancy, with neither child being his. And now he could never have any children of his own. We still do hang on to this strange desire to continue our genetic line, don't we?

Randolph was a proud man, and this seemed to break something in him, perhaps the knowledge that not only he, but everyone around him, would be able to work it all out. The final straw appears to have been your mother asking him to leave the family home. Her reputation, if that means anything these days, was ruined, but she hoped she would be able to bring up her children in peace.

She tried to stay on friendly terms with Randolph, and when, a few weeks after the birth, he invited her to visit him on his boat, where he had been living, she would not have felt any fear as we have become so unused to violence in our lives. You were still being breastfed, so she took you with her whilst your brother was looked after by your grandmother. As far as anyone knows, she had no idea they would be leaving the harbour, and what happened after that, no one knows. I now understand you and your mother were found in the boat that was washed ashore here, but there was no sign of Randolph, nor was there, as we would expect, any sign of injury to your mother. She seemed to have simply died of exposure, thirst and hunger at sea, presumably spending her last energy feeding and caring for you. What happened to Randolph? Was there an accident? Why did your mother agree to leave the harbour with a tiny baby? Sadly, your mother was not alive to tell anyone, nor did she leave any note.

Both Nadya and Rob were entranced by what they were being told. They had a myriad of questions, but for now, they both sat silently digesting what they were hearing.

"No one really knows what happened next. I understand that there was some evidence the boat had faulty or damaged steering. She somehow found herself alone with a small child on a wild sea. There was a terrific storm that night, one of the worst for many decades, and with no means of controlling the vessel. She must have been swept right out into the North Sea at first, before being brought back by the currents, after some time, to land here on Nym.

Search parties were sent out from New Wynyard, but we are always reluctant to land here on Nym. We learn from our parents and from everyone around us that the islanders here harbour strange diseases that are fatal to us if not treated immediately on return with a cocktail of drugs, and many people also believe that people here are savage and not under the control of The Guardian, and will kill any intruders. I have been treated with nothing but care and kindness, to my initial surprise, but there is a section of society here that would have me removed and put back out to sea on my boat, to live or die at the sea's whim, so I guess the fear runs both ways. I can say that I don't seem to be suffering from any obscure diseases. Tell me, Rob or Nadya, is violent attack indeed possible here? Anyway, our search parties did not find anything when they did land briefly here; the wreck had been cleared away, and you, yourself, were removed pretty quickly from the vicinity. Our people did manage to speak with one or two locals, each of whom believed the child, you, had died along with its mother.

Finally, and I guess sadly for you, Rob, she also took with her the identity of the real father, so I cannot give you any information regarding who that might be. Not surprisingly, perhaps, he has never come forward to admit anything, nor to claim your brother as his son."

Rob's face had visibly changed as he listened to the story. He had the look of someone who has hoped for something for an interminably long time, only to have those hopes finally dashed. His eyes were blank, and his whole body seemed to have aged and sagged in just those few short moments. Nadya had kept tight hold of his hand throughout and had felt the blood withdrawing from it so that it had become icy cold. Now she put her arms around his shoulders and pulled him into her embrace, allowing his head to rest on her breast. They sat this way for several long minutes; the only sound that could be heard was the ticking of the old clock in the corner of the room and the occasional creak or crack of the building, as if it too was sagging with sadness.

Finally, Jomo spoke once more, almost a whisper. "I'm so very sorry," he said. "It's a terrible tale, and I fear I have only left you with more questions rather than providing any answers." Rising from his chair and fumbling momentarily with the door handle, he left the room, realising, perhaps, that the two visitors would need some time to come to terms with what he had described. He went in search of Liselle and hot tea.

Chapter 21 - Selected entries from Harry's Journals. September 1st, 2090.

In the news:

Large-scale unrest has spread to many countries in Europe and across the world as people react to the deaths of hundreds of individuals in the UK who were "terminated" through their enforced brain implants. This was carried out to bring a peaceful protest in central London to an end, and was the first time the termination protocol had been used in such circumstances. Previously it had only been used on rare occasions to bring an end to violent hostage or similar situations.

Riots were reported at the crossing of the Niagara River from the US into Canada, as the number of US citizens seeking to flee the increasingly desperate situation there rises. More and more of the south and low-lying coastal areas have been abandoned. In recent times there has been a huge increase in the number of people attempting to make the dangerous river crossing, even in winter.

The island retreat of many of the world's elite billionaires, Corfu, came under attack last week in so-called terrorist operations from Albania. The coordinated attack involved many small vessels, manned mainly by fishermen who have been increasingly excluded from their traditional fishing grounds surrounding the island. Corfu has recently put in place a fifty mile exclusion zone. There were reports of several attacks on remote homes of Corfu residents, including at the famous Durrell Bay in the north of the island. Some two hundred residents are reported to have been killed, and several hostages taken by the rebels, before the attack was repelled by the private Island Defence League. In retaliatory strikes on the Albanian mainland, some four thousand rebels and civilians were killed. A spokesperson for the Corfu Residents Association has vowed to increase spending on island defence and to cut contributions from the island's residents to the general Greek economy.

A large tidal surge caused by a "methane burp", an eruption of methane from deep-sea methane hydrates, has swept along the east coast of the UK, causing extensive flooding from Scotland down to the Thames estuary. The Thames barrier was overwhelmed, leading to large-scale flooding of London. The epicentre of the eruption was off the coast of Norway. It is estimated that the release added several billion tonnes of methane to the atmosphere, which will further accelerate global temperature increases.

————

Personal Notes:

As we approach Sam's tenth year, we think ourselves increasingly fortunate to be somewhat isolated from events in the towns, cities, and lowlands. There is a small school here in the village for under-tens, which she has attended up until now. Next year, though, she will move to the larger school in Pocklington. I hope she does not experience the bullying we've heard other kids from the village have endured. We can only shelter her so much from how life is for most people. We have tried to bring her up to appreciate that our position here is an extremely privileged one. At least she will have the protection of John and Lily's boys, who, being two and four years older than Sam, have already established themselves at the school. Sam and John are good friends, sharing a love of nature and the countryside. Richard, the younger son - a smallish lad with blond curly hair, bright blue eyes, and an innocent look on his face - is more like his father and has quite an artistic talent. Like his elder brother, though, he is quite tough under the soft-seeming exterior. There were a few attempts to pick on him by some of the larger kids from the estates around Pocklington, but it didn't take long for them to learn that he can look after himself. These days, he has earned the same level of respect as his brother, and this keeps him safe. Indeed, I believe he has established quite a following amongst the other kids, because of his somewhat rebellious nature.

The recent tidal surge once again swept up the Humber estuary and the Lower Derwent Valley, flooding a huge acreage of farmland. This wiped out several years of restoration work, which had sought to bring the land back to productivity. Local officials have now declared that no further restorative work will be conducted in an area extending from Hessle as far inland as Selby, as far north as York, and south as far as Bawtry. This is a huge area of land which, although it remains dry much of the time, is becoming increasingly expensive to defend from flooding.

The unrest sweeping the country, and indeed the world, has so far not intruded on our world here. We are far from being counted amongst the rich and therefore are not specifically a target of the unrest, but we cannot ignore the fact that our lives quite privileged in many respects and that this may attract unwanted attention in the near future.

Yesterday, Rosa and I borrowed an electric car from John's brother, James, and took Sam on a trip to the coast at Filey. It has been a few years now since the cliffs known as Carr Naze were finally breached by the North Sea. The cliffs were made of glacial clay deposits and had been reducing more rapidly in recent decades. In Roman times, there was a fortress on the clifftops which at that time were some one and a half kilometres wide, but by the early part of the twenty-first century, this was down to a dozen metres or so. The final breach came during one of the first of the "mega-storms" as they were called then (these days we think back on them as a "bit of a blow"). The transformation of the bay is dramatic. I can remember as a child the calm waters, particularly at low tide when "the Brigg" provided a natural breakwater. Now the northern cliff margin has mostly gone. There is just one small precarious-looking brown mud stack, which is cut off entirely at high tide. The full force of the tidal current sweeps up and down the seafront twice a day and has removed most of the sand which used to form a huge expanse of beach at low tide. The result is a much lower rocky beach, which is only a few metres wide at low extreme tide and completely covered most of the time. This, in turn, is leading to extensive damage to the sea wall, which is now crumbling in several places, exposing the muddy back cliffs to the force of the sea.

Filey used to be a lovely, quiet Yorkshire coastal resort, remote from the hustle and bustle of much more popular Scarborough and Bridlington but with its own rustic charm. Now, I'm sorry to say, it looks very much like a town in terminal decline. Gone is the promenade and its gay, colourful - if small-scale - entertainments. Gone even are most of the houses on the seafront itself, abandoned to the depredations of the winter storms and remaining only as crumbling wrecks sealed off with already rusting safety fences. In several places where the sea wall has gone, there have already been landslips, leaving some of the old, three and four-storey town houses, which used to stand out in their white painted coats as a symbol of the town's long-gone heyday, teetering on the edge.

In the end, we didn't stay long and went further south to the ancient chalk cliffs of Bempton and Flamborough. Even here, the more resilient but still vulnerable chalk cliffs are eroding at an ever-increasing rate as the storms increase in ferocity with each passing winter. The removal of the protecting cliffs of Carr Naze has only served to make this worse. The gannets and other seabirds have returned in some numbers following the oil spill of 2055, which almost wiped out the whole colony, but we saw no sign of the legendary puffins. Sam had picked up an old book in a small bookshop in Filey about a puffin called Aldar. It was a bit worn, but she loved the pictures, so we bought her the book. She was hoping to see some of these delightful clowns at Bempton, but alas, they are virtually extinct now in the UK. The bird reserve itself is long gone, as support dried up in the days after the wars, but the old buildings can still be seen and, apparently, provide nesting places for many species, including the now very rare barn owl.

We left the coast with both myself and Rosa feeling sad for what has been lost, but Sam - who doesn't know what it used to be like - had a thoroughly good day and was particularly keen on the seabirds. She says she is going to catch the bus one day when she is older and bring Richard so that he can draw them.

We arrived back at the cottage near dusk. Sam immediately rushed to give John and Lily the colourful pebbles she had collected as presents for them, as well as to show them her book. This left Rosa and I to snuggle on the sofa and reminisce about how it used to be.

Chapter 22 – Decisions.

Jomo returned to the room after half an hour, carrying a tray of fresh tea, to find Nadya and Rob deep in conversation. He appeared somewhat calmer, though he still looked around the room upon entering and touched his hand to his ear several times in the first few moments after returning.

"I presume you have questions," he said quietly, sitting back down in his chair. Rob nodded but remained quiet, letting Nadya take the lead.

"Yes, please," Nadya replied. "First, we would both like to thank you properly for telling us what you know of Rob's parents. I guess you have realised that he was taken away from this area for his own protection, to be brought up far from here by two people he has come to know as his parents. To answer your earlier question about violence, it is as unheard of here as you tell us it is on the mainland. There are other ways, though, to make someone miserable, and children, especially, will always find ways to bully anyone different. This is why it was thought best not to expose Rob to such unpleasantness."

She paused, clearly thinking for a moment, then continued, "I had never thought about the absence of physical violence until you mentioned it. It's just the way it is, a bit like what you call the new biology of childbirth. You seemed to hint that this was something controlled by The Guardian, but that can't be. We are free from such dominion here. Our entire lives are built around avoiding discovery by what we believe to be an evil entity."

She glanced at Rob to be sure he agreed with this and to reaffirm what she was about to say next. He nodded; he, at least, was sure it was the right thing to do. She continued.

"Rob and I would like to help you. I don't know how much Liselle has told of the way in which the local council is thinking, it would seem likely that you will be prevented from returning to the mainland and we do not think that is the right decision. We must be careful though, if we were to be seen to be acting against the wishes of the council in this matter it could bring danger to ourselves, our families and to Rob's relatives here in Nunport."

After a few moments she went on. "Can I ask - will you tell us more about how the brain chips work? Where do they come from? You seemed to suggest they are the source of the new biology and the avoidance of violence, but no one here has ever had a procedure to implant such a thing. So how can it be that these two things are the same here as they are on the mainland?"

Jomo thought for a few moments and carried out the ear touching ritual several times before trying to answer.

"We believe we're all born with them," he began. "They aren't implanted, nor injected, but we know that we all have them. They control our ability to carry out violent attacks against others and to commit cruelty to animals. We know they are complex because humane killing of animals for food is allowed, as is the catching and killing of fish. But an attempt to commit a wilful act of cruelty would render the perpetrator unconscious before they could do it."

Nadya nodded, confirming that such acts were equally impossible here in Nym and Woldshire, although, again, she had always assumed this was basic biology.

"They also control our fertility, as you now know. I didn't realise there were people in the world who didn't know that this was artificial. There have, so I understand, been attempts in the past to locate and remove the controlling chips, but as far as I'm aware, none has ever been successful. We don't even know where they are in the brain - or if they are in the brain. We assume they are.

"As I said earlier, it is possible, in an extreme emotional state, for the control process to be overcome. But it's exceedingly rare for the individual not to be rendered unconscious before they can commit violence. I know of only one case where this happened."

Nadya interrupted at this point. "You mentioned The Guardian earlier. We're raised to fear The Guardian and to understand that the reason we live the way we do, shunning all mechanical and electrical apparatus, is so we remain free from domination by it." She looked around furtively; the habit of not talking about such things was so deeply ingrained that she - despite her curiosity about the old times and the mainland - felt that she would be punished if she continued.

"But if what you've said is true, then all our efforts are in vain, and we are already under the full control of the despised Guardian through these 'brain chips'. Such a thing, such knowledge would cause complete panic throughout the two islands."

She lowered her gaze to the floor, barely able to control the horror she felt.

Jomo was silent. He stood again and wandered around the room for some time, eventually going to the window and looking out at the garden beyond. Nadya and Rob waited patiently to see if Jomo had anything more to say. Finally, after what must have been ten minutes, he turned from the window and looked from one to the other of them as though trying to gauge their state of mind and whether they were ready - or could be trusted - with what he had to say next.

"I need you to understand," he began haltingly, "that in my part of the world we are taught that islanders are dangerous. Just speaking to you like this makes me anxious, and it would terrify most of my countrymen. The whole environment here is extremely alien - everything is loud, strongly scented, strongly flavoured, chaotic. At first, it was like being in a living nightmare. The cacophony almost drove me mad in the first few days. Even now, I tolerate it only by staying closed up in this house and, mostly, in this room."

He peered at Nadya and Rob closely again, trying to see any reaction on their faces. He continued, in a monotone, as if reciting something he had learned by heart, his face fixed and his eyes not moving.

"Humanity lives through the beneficent blessing of The Guardian. The Guardian brings order and calm. The Guardian prevents humanity from succumbing to our uncontrolled urge to destroy ourselves and the planet. Without The Guardian, we would flood the planet with more humans than it can sustain and reduce the world to a barren wilderness. We would be haunted by our evil tendencies to harm one another. The creation of The Guardian saved us from ourselves, but not before we almost destroyed the world. The flood was the result of our evil ways, and without The Guardian, even worse things would happen."

As if a spell had been broken, he now spoke in his normal voice.

"We are taught that the islanders have abandoned The Guardian and, as a result, live savage and destructive lives. That murder, rape, and violence are rife and uncontrolled here."

He paused to let that sink in.

"So, you see why we avoid coming here, and why I've been so surprised by what I've found. I think you're right that, for your people to realise that they do not live outside the control - though you'd say the domination - of The Guardian would be earth shaking but equally, it would be shocking for my people to learn that the islands are not riddled with violent criminality. For all of these reasons I can understand how the council, as you call them, would want to prevent me returning to the mainland."

He hesitated again before finishing, almost in a whisper. "But I will not be stopped."

Nadya was torn between being horrified and amused by what Jomo had said. The idea that the islanders were uncontrolled savages was both atrocious and hilarious. She looked again at Rob, who nodded once.

"Well," she said calmly. "We will try to help if we can do so without bringing disaster upon ourselves or our families."

Jomo's face brightened remarkably on hearing Nadya's comment. Something changed in his eyes - a kindling of hope, bringing a light to them which had previously been absent. Nadya thought how the change had brought a rugged handsomeness to his face. Without thinking of how he might react she asked, "Are you married, or do you have a partner who will be missing you? Do you have children?"

Now the light was extinguished again. Nadya regretted that her words had brought an end to the change in him.

"I have a wife, Suki, and our allotted two children, a boy, Jomo Junior, and a girl, who we called April after the month in which she was born. We always say she was our late spring. The children are grown now and are away travelling with friends for a year, but I am sure Suki will have told them I am missing. I am afraid they will all think I am dead, or will do so if too much time passes before I return. You've given me hope."

As he spoke the names of his wife and children, he did so quietly but with such passion it almost seemed as if he were trying to conjure them out of the air into this place with him. Nadya was thrilled to see the light return to his face as he continued with more energy than he had displayed since they arrived.

"Travelling?" Rob interjected. "Does the Guardian allow you to move freely, where will they have travelled to?"

Jomo gave a small chuckle. "I can see you think we are dominated and oppressed by The Guardian, but to us he is an enabler, someone who provides us with all of our needs. He doesn't prevent us from doing what we want to do unless it would harm others or society. The last I heard of Jomo J. and April they were on the other side of the world in Australia and were having a great time."

Both Nadya and Rob simply stared at him, unable to fully grasp that people could travel so freely and so far. Jomo returned to the subject of his return home saying, "My boat is a sailboat. It has a small electric motor for manoeuvring in and out of port, but there wouldn't be enough charge left to complete the whole crossing. I never thought to fully charge it before I set off. I was only supposed to be gone for a few hours."

"What happened?" Nadya asked, her voice barely above a whisper.

"I was stupid, and careless," Jomo spoke equally quietly, with an anger clear in his voice. "There was a sudden squall, nothing I couldn't normally deal with, but I was distracted as I was trying to get a bottle of water from the cold box. I then committed the cardinal sin of running on the boat in an attempt to grab the ropes to let down the mainsail. I tripped over some rope I had carelessly left lying on the deck and ended up with the mainsail rope wrapped around my arm, hoisting me half off the deck. The other rope was wrapped around my ankle, tying me firmly down so that I was stretched between the two and in danger of being ripped apart as the wind shifted the boom. I managed to grab a knife and tried to cut the rope to free my arm, but another gust pulled me off balance just as I was hacking at it, and I missed and sliced deep into the muscle of my forearm. I think I severed something vital, as I immediately lost the use of my hand.

"And that was how I was found two days later when the boat finally washed up here. By that time, gangrene had set in on the arm, and it was unsavable. Stupid, stupid, stupid."

He slumped in his chair as he concluded, as if from habit, resigning himself to being punished for his carelessness. But then he looked again at Nadya and Rob, and the hope once again lit up his face.

"I need to think all this through," he spoke calmly and quietly, but both Nadya and Rob could tell he was torn between wanting to hurry home but not wanting to bring harm to those who helped him. "I doubt I could sail the boat alone with just one arm. I believe, though, that my batteries will, by now, have fully charged from my solar generators and this would allow me to just cruise back to the mainland on battery power alone, something I am sure I could manage. I doubt that your council will understand enough about electricity to realise this and this might provide me with an edge that allows me to escape."

But now he stood up suddenly, as if he had made a decision. "But it is getting late, and I am forgetting that you have not eaten since you arrived. Let me see if Liselle is still here. We should prepare some food and take a break from this."

As he opened the door to the room and beckoned for them to follow, he turned to them and spoke firmly "Please be sure about trying to help me, you should go home soon and think things through. You may be wandering into an adventure that you do not understand the full extent of. You should not do this lightly.”

It was certainly getting late; the light was fading outside, and the corridor was dark, but they could see light creeping under a door to one side. As Jomo opened the door, their eyes took a moment to adjust, but not their noses. The smell of fried fish and chips was unmistakable and instantly set their mouths watering, as their stomachs confirmed with growls that it had indeed been some time since they had eaten.

“Ah, you’re here,” Liselle spoke, clearly still at the house. “Will came with these a short time ago. I’ve popped them into the oven to keep them warm and was about to come and fetch you all. The kettle is on the go and should boil any time to make tea.”

She placed three plates onto the table, along with three of the largest mugs Nadya had ever seen.

“Now, if it’s OK, I will leave you to look after yourselves. My Jim will be waiting for me at home. I’ve stayed much longer than I usually do, but I didn’t want to interrupt your talk.”

“We will be fine, thank you, Liselle. I will lock up when Rob and Nadya leave later. See you in the morning.”

Liselle hurried out of the main door, and Rob went to throw the bolts again before returning to the kitchen, eager to eat and drink.

Jomo had opened another door, which seemed to lead into a dark, cool place with some steps leading down to a cellar. He returned with a sealed jug, which he placed on the table, and took the kettle from the hob, setting it aside to cool.

"The tea they drink so much of here is delightful," he grinned, "but I'm afraid I prefer the ale."

Nadya pulled out three paper-wrapped parcels from the oven. The delicious smell was almost overwhelming, and within minutes, they were all filling their mouths with crispy, batter-wrapped fish and fried potatoes - crispy on the outside, but soft, hot, and fluffy white on the inside. Talk was minimal for quite some time.

Chapter 23 -Selected entries from Harry's Journals. June 23rd, 2093.

Recent News:

The WHO has recently confirmed that malaria and other diseases once eradicated in Europe are now endemic in countries as far north as Belgium. In the same report, the first cases of Yellow Fever contracted in Europe were reported in southern Spain and Sardinia. It goes on, "Seventy-five years ago, the first reports of Dengue fever becoming established in mainland Europe were reported, and since then, the migration northwards of the six main mosquito transmitted diseases has shown direct correlation with global temperature increases."

The UK government has become the twelfth country in the world to halt further implants of location and control chips, following widespread and continued unrest following several mass termination events. The German government was recently accused of initiating a termination event in which over fifteen hundred people were killed during an anti-AI protest in Berlin. Government sources denied the event was deliberately triggered, suggesting left-wing hackers had infiltrated the control system.

The Isle of Wight became the latest island refuge of the technos to come under attack from militant humanist terrorists this week. Several missiles managed to penetrate the defence system and caused damage to several properties. The island authorities launched retaliatory strikes against militant bases they claimed were based in the city of Southampton, causing widespread destruction with over a thousand dead and wounded. The UK government condemned the militants and stated that it would continue to support the right of offshore island residential areas to defend themselves.

The tenth major breach of the Netherlands' sea defences took place three days ago, leaving much of the country overwhelmed. A preplanned evacuation process was quickly enacted, so the loss of life was contained to below five hundred. The population of the Netherlands continues to decline as its people migrate further into Europe and abandon the country. The EU has stated that it will continue to resettle people from vulnerable coastal areas into inland regions. However, there have been several instances of riots in France, Belgium, and Germany against immigration. In one barely reported incident, a refugee housing complex was attacked, and several people were killed as right-wing Belgian protesters stormed the complex, claiming lowland paedophiles were hidden there.

———

Personal Notes:

Two days into the working week and I'm already worn out. I must be getting old. Rosa and I spent most of the long, warm summer evening sitting on the bench outside our door, just being together. I love the times we can spend like that, with no need for words to express our solidarity and closeness. Sometimes life as a carer and the father of a teenage girl can feel like being caught in a continual whirlwind of events and things to do and say. A couple of hours of quiet contemplation, with just the chorus of birdsong and the occasional distant bleating of a sheep to break the silence, is worth hours of sleep.

Sam has spent the evening with Lily. The two of them are cooking up something of a surprise for Rosa's upcoming birthday. I say Sam but should properly now call her Samantha, as she has declared that Sam is a baby name and the proper name for a grown woman, as she has declared herself to be at the grand old age of thirteen, is Samantha. She is growing into a real beauty like her mother, with high cheekbones framing an pale complexion dotted with freckles and startling green eyes. I suspect we will soon be spending our evenings worrying about which particular local lad she is wrapping around her little finger this time. She does, though, seem to have inherited her mother's sound judgement and steadiness of character, as well as a love of rural life. She and John spent much of the summer holidays helping out with the animals on James's farm just outside the village. Both of them seemed to have a whale of a time, returning home each evening exhausted, grimy, but with huge smiles and, in Samantha's case, several dozen more freckles.

The world around us continues to get more chaotic and difficult for many people, and it is perhaps not surprising that finally, many decades after the wars and what followed, led people to accept authoritarian rule and the rise and rise of the ultra-rich technofeudalists, they are beginning to show signs of rising up against the elites. Add in the increasing deterioration of the climate, the loss of land, and the increased prevalence of new - or new to this country - diseases, and the miserable nature of the life of the ordinary person seems to rise to new levels with each passing year. I seem to write this with every entry I make, but we are so lucky to have escaped the lives which are the lot of most people.

Until very recently, the village had avoided any instances of people being arrested and therefore fitted with location and control chips. However, three days ago, police from York descended on Millington, ostensibly searching for someone they had identified as taking part in an anti-implant protest. They took one of the villagers, someone who has worked at the farm on occasion, for questioning. Even though he was ultimately released without charge, he returned to the village with the much-hated brain implant. He now must live with the knowledge that the government or its agencies could remotely terminate his life at any point.

We are facing many years of increasing unrest, and I can only hope it doesn't come to our own doorstep. The villagers here have much better quality lives than the people of the large estates bordering the towns. Most people around here can at least find some part-time work of some sort, although they are still largely reliant on the state basic salary. But compared to life in any of the towns, that which is possible here is distinctly more fulfilling. The dullness, hopelessness, and lack of any opportunity to achieve anything or to better oneself amongst the ninety five percent unemployed is, I am sure, soul-destroying. It's no wonder the levels of suicide are climbing inexorably.

How I wish I could send a time capsule back in time rather than forward, and warn the people of the 2020s that the actions of the government of the time, in broadening the definition of "extremist" individuals and organisations, the ever more stringent regulations outlawing protest, and the silencing of criticism, would lead to the authoritarianism we live with today. Of course, I would also warn them that the conflicts of the middle east and around the edges of Russia would lead, ultimately, to the use of nuclear weapons and thence to the apparent reversal of climate change, only for it to resurge once the dust of the nuclear exchanges had settled - and I would warn them about how it was then too late to reverse or even slow it. The question is, would those in a position to act heed the warnings, or would they simply continue to put their own interests before those of the human race?

There were voices, way back then, who predicted the use of nuclear weapons in the middle east and much of what followed. They warned of the rising gap between the ultra-rich and ordinary people. They warned of the shift in power away from representative government towards the newly emerged technofeudalists. No one listened, or if they did, they chose not to act. Now, even in the midst of a relatively isolated rural community, we have seen, up close, the consequences of all of that inaction and the accumulated inaction of all the years in between.

Today, if these words were to be read by the authorities, I would also be arrested, chipped, and controlled. I would be branded as a radical and an extremist, and would face the threat of termination unless I remained silent. This is what we must live with: the culmination of the migration of power from the instruments of democracy to the wielders of wealth. The advancements of technology have indeed come to control much of our lives, but not, as many said would happen, because the technology itself controls anything - but because it is ruthlessly controlled by the financial elites, who view mankind merely as a source of further wealth for themselves or as an inconvenience that gets in the way of their enjoying their wealth.

If an alien were to approach the earth today, they would see a planet more "at peace" than at any time in the long history of mankind. They would not see, initially, that this peace had been paid for by the loss of freedom and impoverishment of the many, set against the enrichment of the few. But the real scale of this global tragedy isn't measured on the scale of the planet or of the whole of humanity. It is measured in the drawn face of one rural Yorkshireman who no longer has any freedom or peace. It is measured in the look in his eyes as he orders a pint in his local inn, all the time looking nervously around to make sure there is no trouble that might involve him. It is measured in his newly stooping posture as he walks to his home, and how he can no longer look at his sweet young wife in the same way because there is now a fundamental difference between them. An innocence has been ripped from that young family, and with it the whole village. This is the real measure of how far man has fallen, how much has been paid for apparent planetary peace.

And now we are seeing the first signs that the peace, bought in such a way, cannot last. The ordinary people are beginning to resent their lowly status and the loss of peace and freedom so many have suffered. I fear that even here, in this quiet, isolated corner of the world, we may see and feel the effects of the upheaval that is about to sweep over us. I hope, for the sake of my beautiful wife and daughter, that we can weather it. Because weather it we must - or succumb.

Chapter 24 – Into the Unknown.

A week later, they had the beginnings of a plan. Jomo had decided he could trust his helpers and had explained that he would probably have enough power in his batteries to return to the mainland without the need for sails and all that was needed was an excuse to return to his boat. They had petitioned the council to ask that Jomo be allowed onto his boat to collect some personal belongings and they had agreed – but only if he were accompanied by one of their own members. They had agreed, reluctantly, that Rob and Nadya could also accompany the party to provide support for Jomo, who still struggled with the noise and clamour of Island life.

The three concocted a plan whereby Jomo would board the boat and would then pretend he had found a weapon of some sort and would force Nadya, Rob and the council member from the boat before powering out of the harbour and away. It seemed a simple plan, Jomo explained that he could start the motors in a few seconds and that once underway there would be nothing locally that could catch him. Nevertheless, Nadya worried that something might go wrong, and they might be forced to either abandon the attempt or expose themselves as Jomo's helpers. Time was not on their side though as it was known the council had been discussing destroying the boat entirely so that it couldn't be discovered by any raiding parties from the mainland.

Over the coming days they refined the plan and went over and over it, looking for anything they might have missed. Jomo, who knew the layout of the vessel, explained how he believed they could allow him to go free without compromising themselves.

"I will need to go below on the boat once we are on board and I need you and the council's man to stay on deck. I will switch on the power and will then come back on deck but will have in my pocket the remote control with which I can start the motors. They are almost silent, but they will disturb the water at the back of the boat so that, once I start them, it will be obvious something is happening. I don't want this to happen until I can get all three of you off. I will pretend to have a weapon and will threaten the three of you and force you to disembark. I can then cut the ropes and will be away in seconds."

"But what if the council's man refuses to leave?" asked Nadya. "You know you won't actually be able to use a weapon."

"No, but he might be afraid enough of mainlanders not to know that" explained Jomo. "And if he still refuses, I will threaten to carry him away to the mainland. I should be able to undo the front rope from inside the cabin if you can keep him distracted, then all I need to do is to quickly cut the rear rope, and the boat will be free."

Both Nadya and Rob still thought the plan was fraught with risk but they really did want to help their new friend get back to his family and so they were willing to play their part. The plan was set for two days' time.

———

Waking on a clear blue summer morning to the loud calls of the gulls echoing around the town, they dressed quickly and made their way to the cottage, to meet with Jomo for breakfast and to go over the plan one more time. Liselle brought in tea and fresh bread, butter, and jam made from local wild damsons. Nadya spread a piece of the soft, yeasty-smelling bread with butter and some of the jam, and the look on her face when she bit into it made the others chuckle. She had never tried this type of jam before - another discovery from the far north of their little realm and she resolved to take some back to their life in Rosedale, maybe even to her mum and dad's farm. She continued to eat as she listened carefully to Jomo.

"The weather looks perfect," he announced. "A gentle northerly breeze and, if I'm any judge of weather, we're under a settled ridge of high pressure." His face took on a wistful expression and he continued. "I wish I had access to the forecast on the vid screens. I really don't know how you people manage without The Guardian."

Rob and Nadya could only look at him, both wondering how he couldn't see that their freedom, or as they now believed, their imagined freedom, from The Guardian was the driving force behind their lives, how much that freedom had shaped their sense of themselves and their place in the wider world.

"I know the weather signs," said Nadya with a smile. "I can read the weather from the smell of the air, the reactions of trees, plants, and birds, and I agree - we should see settled weather for a few more days. See, we don't need The Guardian.

We've learned, or perhaps relearned, how to read and live within nature."

She said this with some pride. She realised how much she loved Nym and Woldshire. How much she loved the people, even when they seemed to her bumbling and stifled in their thinking. How much she loved the clear air, the sense of nature weaved into their lives and, if she were honest with herself, the feeling of pride they all had in standing apart from The Guardian and its domination of mankind.

Immediately after breakfast, the council's man, a stout local farmer called Jed, arrived and they set out for the harbour. They received only the usual faintly curious glances from the locals as they passed by. It was known that they were friendly with Jomo and that it had been agreed with the council that he could collect some belonging from the boat before it was destroyed. There would eventually be relief at the departure of Jomo, there was an undercurrent of nervousness regarding a stranger from the mainland and the possibility that others may come looking for him. The immediate reaction though would be consternation that he had gone and some short term worry that he may bring mainlanders back in force. Jomo has assured Nadya and Rob that nothing of the sort would happen and that once back on the mainland he would make it clear he had escaped and confirm that the islands were inhabited by a violent and dangerous people.

When they reached the boat Jomo nodded, an agreed signal that all was as he expected, and the plan could go ahead. They all climbed on board, and he explained that he would need to go below but that it was very cramped down there and they should all wait on deck for him. At this point their plans began to unravel.

Jed refused to allow Jomo out of his sight and said that he could not go below without being accompanied by one of them. He peered down through the entrance and realised there would indeed not be enough room for both Jomo and himself.

"Nadya – you go down first," he stated categorically. "Then you can keep an eye on him."

Nadya looked at Rob, but neither could think of any answer to this so reluctantly she went through the hatch into the tiny cabin, Jomo followed. Once out of sight he whispered frantically to Nadya that he would start the motors in a few minutes, and she should shout "Get off" or something similar and run up the steps and usher the other two off of the boat. She could later say she had been threatened. He would be gone before they could do anything.

They were now in completely unplanned territory and Nadya was extremely agitated, but Jomo was determined. This was likely to be his only chance and he was not going to waste it. He opened the tiny window at the front of the sleeping compartment and tried to reach the front rope but found he could not manage so he grabbed a long knife from the galley and poked this through the window and began to saw at it. He could only hope that Rob was keeping Jed from looking forward.

After several minutes in which Nadya noisily opened and closed drawers and doors and the two carried out a fictitious conversation along the lines of.

"Hurry up Jomo – you can't possibly carry much more."

"Hang on a just a couple of seconds Nadya I just need to find….." and concluding with a muffled sound as if he had his head in a cupboard.

Finally he was down to the last threads of the rope and decided to leave these to be snapped by the power of the motors. He gave Nadya a last hug, whispering his thanks in her ear before mouthing "Three, two, one…..NOW!"

Nadya cried out "Jomo, Stop!" Followed by "Rob, Get off – I'm coming – get off now!"

She moved to the stairs and rushed to climb out of the small space but in her haste and unfamiliarity with the layout she caught her head on the roof with a resounding crash. Immediately she crumpled to the floor in the cabin and blood began to run freely from her wound. Meanwhile Jomo had started the engines, and the boat thrummed with power and began to surge away from the dock. The ropes immediately brought it to a stop knocking both Rob and Jed from their feet on the deck.

Before they could stand, Jomo had emerged from the cabin armed with a hatchet and had already severed one of the securing ropes.

"Get off!" He growled to both men.

Jed moved first but Rob would not leave. "I'm not leaving without Nadya." He said in a low but firm voice. He hadn't realised, though, that he was already on the edge and a quick shove from Jed sent him flying to land bodily on the dockside.

Jed's fear of the mainlander overcame any idea of him being the hero and he leapt after.

Jomo struck the second rope, but it was a glancing blow and at first it didn't come free, he was about to strike again when the force of the engines snapped the remaining threads, and the boat accelerated away into the open water.

The gap between the boat and the edge was opening rapidly but Rob leapt across the water and managed to grab a rail. He hung on grimly while the boat burst from the small harbour with a speed he had never known possible.

Chapter 25 - Selected entries from Harry's Journals. September 16th, 2097.

Denmark has been added to the growing list of countries designated as having no long-term future. It has been calculated that only a small island of less than ten thousand square kilometres, surrounded by a scattering of even smaller islets, will remain after the projected sea-level rise. This will not be large enough to support a significant population, let alone a nation. Denmark has requested that neighbouring Sweden allows it to amalgamate with them to form a single nation. Sweden itself is projected to suffer significant loss of low-lying land, but it is thought that temperature increase in northern latitudes will free up more productive and inhabitable land. Denmark follows the Netherlands, the only other European nation projected to entirely disappear.

In New Zealand, the city of Christchurch and all surrounding towns such as Kaiapoi were entirely wiped out by a tsunami which followed an offshore earthquake of ten point five on the Richter scale. The death toll is put at over two hundred thousand, despite extensive tsunami evacuation plans which had been in place for decades. The leader of the New Zealand corporate government said that the size of the earthquake and the speed of the incoming wave were unprecedented, but that already high sea levels had also contributed to the devastation. It is not expected that the city will be rebuilt.

Yellow fever is now endemic to Italy, the President of the EU has said. She has set aside three billion euros for an extensive immunisation programme for Mediterranean nations, including Spain, Italy, France, Greece, Albania, Croatia, and Turkey.

In the UK, the food banks, which first made an appearance in the 2010s, were this year increased, and consolidated into a government-run scheme. This was in anticipation of a very difficult food supply situation this winter, following widespread harvest failures after the wettest year on record. Rationing has been reintroduced for the first time since the 1950s and is expected to remain in place for several years. Ration cards have been distributed, with calories restricted to around nineteen hundred for an adult woman and two thousand three hundred for an adult male. Luxury goods, including meat, poultry, butter, eggs, cheese, fish, and fresh fruit and vegetables, are severely restricted, and there are severe penalties for hoarding and for black market trade. The EU has declined to provide emergency food aid, stating that the UK is a non-aligned state and all EU food is required for member nations. The UK has not been self sufficient in food for decades, reliant on imports from Europe and around the world. The country faces hard times ahead which will do nothing to quell the unrest already sweeping the country.

The government of Norway has blocked the purchase of several of the Faroe Islands by a private consortium of tech billionaires, looking for remote refuges further away from major landmasses and population centres. The Faroes are also further north than the previously popular subtropical islands, where the climate has become increasingly intolerable. Norway is one of the few European countries that has avoided the total erosion of democratic rule as the corporate world has moved to take control of politics. A spokesperson for the Faroe Island

Residents Group said, "We do not accept that our land should become a refuge for the ultra-rich. We have fished, farmed, and lived on these islands for centuries. They are not to be a playground for those who exploit mankind for their own greed." Airton Rood, leader of the consortium, responded with the following written statement: "We have a right to defend ourselves from the exponential increase in terrorism, which threatens our families, and we will continue to seek places where we can live in peace, away from the threat of violence." Airton Rood is the founder and CEO of LoCo Inc., the company that is the leading developer of locate-and-control brain technology. He is estimated to have a personal fortune of over one trillion dollars. He has vigorously defended his company's technology in the face of its increasing use to quell riots and protests by using the "terminate" option.

Personal Notes:

As we rapidly approach the turn of the century, it seems the impacts of the change in the world are gathering pace. Each year the warming and the wetting, make life harder and harder. The output of the local farms, including James', have been taken under the control of the local corporate food bank service, and they must account for every grain, every root or tuber, and every egg, litre of milk, and animal. The owner of one farm, who tried to hide several pigs from the authorities, is now in prison, will, of course, be chipped when he is released, and may well yet face losing the farm, which has been in his family for generations. James has made it clear that he will cooperate entirely and will not take one calorie beyond his share from the central food bank in Millington. It is going to be a hungry winter, and it is strange to see the local farmers queuing up at the food bank along with everyone else. It is clear, though, that the threat of the implants is, for the present, enough to maintain orderly obedience in this region. I can still remember our first local "chipping", the poor man committed suicide some months after he was arrested and chipped, despite being entirely innocent of any crime. We think that something like ten percent of the local population are now chipped, and it increases with every month that goes by.

I worry intensely about Sam as she approaches adulthood. She is a bright and intelligent, as well as stunningly beautiful, girl, but like most of us here in our little corner of the country, she rails against the way the world is going. We have always made sure she understands that we are very privileged and lucky to live here, and that we are nothing special, coming as we do from the same humble beginnings as everyone else. I worry that this might indeed have increased her sense of the injustice and of the wrong direction the world has taken since the wars earlier this century.

She has a boyfriend for the first time. We had always thought she and John would become a couple as they have been so close for most of their childhood, but she's madly in love (aren't we all at seventeen) with another young lad from the village. Kevin seems decent enough, although a bit lacking in ambition for my taste. I shouldn't be too judgemental though; after all, most people are destined to spend their lives simply existing on the handouts from the corporates, especially now we are all seemingly going to be fed by them. I would have preferred someone with a bit of "get up and go" though, like

Richard, who has made quite a splash with his wildlife art, or John, who is making a real go of working on his uncle's farm. I guess the one good thing is that he seems too laid-back to get too involved with politics or protest, so is unlikely to lead Sam into difficult situations; indeed, quite the reverse might be true.

Whoever thought that in the twenty first century we would find our food rationed here in the UK? But then I don't think anyone knew, or knows, what consequences we will see as the world adjusts to the climactic change we have thrust upon it and upon our children and grandchildren. John described to me how all crops are now collected by the agents of the local corporate council for storage and distribution. Apparently, the farmer will be credited with the agreed price depending on the tested quality of the grain and must buy seed, again at the agreed price, for next year's crop from the council. The amount of profit a farmer is allowed to make has been calculated, taking into account fuel (purchased from the corporation), fertiliser (purchased from the corporation), allowances for the small amount of labour they use, and other sundries. According to James, it is enough – barely - but it is good fortune that they have no loans (from the corporation) nor finance deals (with the corporation) or they would struggle to hang on to the farm. Many farmers across the Wolds and the wider country have found themselves in circumstances where they cannot keep up the payments on money, they borrowed for new farm equipment or to expand or diversify, and the farm ends up being sold - the buyers, of course, being the representatives of the technos. I remember, as a boy, reading The Grapes of Wrath by John Steinbeck; the situation here seems little changed from back then, except that the villains aren't the banks any longer but rather the technos, many of which began life as so-called Tech Giants early in the century.

The irony of the situation we have reached is laughable; throughout the twentieth century and much of the twenty-first, we were told that the West was the bulwark against communism and the bastion of private enterprise. And yet here we are; the state has been replaced by the power of a few huge conglomerates run by a tiny minority of ultra-rich individuals and families. The rest of us having our lives managed with a degree of control that the old leaders of the USSR would envy. With the constant threat of chipping, even our bodies are not wholly our own any longer. We are truly slaves of the technos, who wield the tools of oppression and AI to control us.

We hear rumours of underground groups who are organising to resist the corporates and who have perfected the removal of the brain implants, but it is dangerous even to enquire about such things. There are an increasing number of attacks on the refuges of the ultra-rich, but these only seem to result in even more police on the streets, even of small rural villages like Millington.

What a life our daughter and all of our children and grandchildren must endure.

Chapter 26 – Mainland.

As soon as the boat left the harbour Jomo set the direction for the mainland and set about seeing to his unexpected guests. The first task was to pull Rob fully on board, who immediately went below to see what had happened to Nadya. She was still unconscious, and Rob could not rouse her, he shouted to Jomo to turn the boat around and return to the harbour.

"Rob, let me come down and take a look please," Jomo replied, trying to stay calm. "If you will move back into the galley area I can get down there."

"Just turn the boat around." Shouted Rob. "She's bleeding badly and needs help."

"Trust me, Rob. As soon as I can see what's wrong I will turn back if that's best for Nadya, I promise. But I need to see what she has done."

Reluctantly Rob moved back to clear some space and Jomo descended the steep steps and crouched to examine Nadya. She was bleeding not just from the wound but also from her ear and Jomo knew that this meant the head injury was serious, potentially life threatening.

"Rob, please try to stay calm," he said, standing to face Nadya's husband. "Nadya has a serious head injury which needs treatment as soon as possible. What do you know about the ability to treat such things on the island?"

The look on Rob's face told Jomo all he needed to know. Treatment of brain injuries was unlikely to be advanced in a basically agricultural society such as Nym or Woldshire, Nadya's chances of survival there were not high.

"Rob, I need you to trust me, We can fix this but if we return to the harbour Nadya might die. You know that."

He took hold of Rob's hands and guided the shocked man onto the bench seat.

"We need to get Nadya to one of our hospital's as soon as possible. I will make contact as soon as we are out of the silenced area around the islands and you and she will be in a place that can care for her within minutes. She can survive this but not if we turn back. Do you trust me?"

Rob looked confused for just a moment. Nadya was his whole world, and he would do anything, risk anything to save her. "Go ahead he said – and make it as quick as you can, please!"

Jomo checked the navigation system and, realising they were already clear of the silenced zone, he placed a finger to his ear and said clearly.

"Emergency – code 10. I need a flyer to transport a patient with a head injury to the nearest facility."

He nodded to Rob to indicate it was already on it's way and then went on the explain the situation they were in – all the time with a finger on his left earlobe. Nodding once more he let go and turned once more to Rob.

"We need to lift her carefully onto the deck so she can be loaded into the flyer. They will be here in a few moments."

By the time the two had gently got Nadya upright and hauled her inert body up onto the deck the flyer had arrived. Rob had never seen such a thing but had heard tales of aircraft from before the Great Melt. The craft hovered above the boat and both Rob and Jomo had to move clear as its bulk began to lower. As soon as it was just a few feet above the deck an opening appeared in its side and two metallic figures jumped onto the boat. A stretcher lowered itself and Nadya was carefully lifted into place before it moved back into the aircraft. Jomo motioned to Rob to pull himself after her and the two robots did the same before the entrance closed and the flyer sped away leaving Jomo alone on the boat.

After what seemed only a short time, the rising slopes of the hills around Richmond came into clear view. Jomo headed for a break in the line of hills which he knew marked the entrance to the harbour and marina. Only the distant hills of the island of Nym were visible behind him now. The inhabitants of the island nation could sometimes have seen, from those high hills, the comings and goings of small craft near the mainland, but few were interested enough to look. From this close though - he was now well over halfway across the inland sea - it was clear that there were a considerable number of boats, large and small, plying the sea around the inlet he was heading for.

In the event, there were few people on the river, so Jomo was not recognised until he had entered the marina and was pulling up to his mooring.

"Oy, you can't dock there, mate!" someone shouted at the last moment. "That's Jomo's berth."

Jomo waved and shouted in return, "It's me, Stefan."

The shouter stopped in his tracks and peered closely at the yacht and at Jomo at the tiller. "Jomo? Mate, we thought you were dead. What happened to you?"

"Long story," shouted Jomo, and with that, the shouter, Stefan, turned and ran towards the buildings onshore, waving frantically as he went. Jomo realised he was likely thought to have been lost at sea, and his return was sure to cause a stir. He wondered now how quickly his Suki would hear of his return, how she would have reacted to the assumption of his death, and how she would react now to his unexpected return. He guessed he wouldn't have to wait long to find out.

Jomo had barely tied the boat to the moorings when a small, olive-skinned woman with dark hair arrived, breathless, on the jetty. With a running leap, she landed on the boat and threw herself at him. He caught her with his good arm, and she wrapped her arms around his neck and her legs around his waist, clinging to him more tightly than a long-established ivy entwines itself around a tree. The embrace seemed to last forever before she finally pushed herself away just far enough to smother his face with kisses. Both of their faces were wet with tears, which mingled as they alternately kissed and pressed their cheeks together. The whole scene played out in total silence, neither having the breath for words.

Finally, Suki untwined herself and stood before Jomo, feet firmly planted on the deck. She looked at him lovingly for a few seconds and then, to our surprise, swung her hand to plant a resounding smack across his cheek, whilst crying out "Jomo

Nelson, you bastard. Don't you EVER do that to me again, do you hear?"

Looking him up and down, she realised for the first time that he had lost an arm, which caused fresh tears to stream from her eyes. She took hold of the stump and kissed it with a gentleness completely different from either the rush of her first embrace or the slap she had delivered.

"Oh, my love," she wailed, looking once again into his face. "What have they done to you? Are they truly barbarians over there that they would take an arm from an innocent sailor as punishment for landing on their benighted island?"

"No, no, my lovely Suki," Jomo came to the rescue of the islanders, though his two companions had been momentarily banished entirely from his mind, not least by the stinging of his cheek and the ringing in his ears. "I did this through my own stupidity and carelessness. We are entirely wrong about the islanders."

"Suki," he continued. "I can't tell you how glad I am to be home, but I need to find out what has happened to two dear friends of mine. One was injured very badly on the crossing and has been taken by flyer to a medical unit. I need to find them, will you come."

Suki looked at him, somewhat confused as to who the two might be but she nodded and put her arm in his.

"Friends," he continued, addressing the gathering crowd, "my good friends, I am so happy to return safely. The sea is a treacherous ally at times, but I have survived a misadventure brought about by my own stupidity. All will be told in good time, and no doubt several times over, but I'm sure you will all understand if I now take my poor wife home, and we reacquaint ourselves somewhat more privately than standing here in public."

The two climbed onto the jetty and manoeuvred their way through the small crowd, Jomo receiving many a slap on the shoulder or a snatched hug, and even, to the obvious amusement of Suki, a kiss or two from some of the ladies.

"Get yer hands off." She shouted with obvious joy in her heart, giving a happy tone to her voice despite her harsh words. "He's mine and I have him back. I will not be letting him go again so easily."

They finally managed to break clear of the group of well-wishers and made their way to shore.

Once clear of the crowds, and installed in a vehicle Suki had pointed out, Jomo asked for an update on his friends. A disembodied and unemotional voice in the car replied. "The woman has been repaired and is in recovery. There was no lasting damage, and she will be fully functional within a few days. She is being kept in a non conscious state for twenty four hours after which she will be able to leave the hospital. Her companion has been provided with a bed in the same room as her and has accepted some light sedation, he was very agitated."

"I'll bet he was." Said Jomo, in a hushed voice. "Kidnapped away from his home by a desperate fugitive and then whisked away by robots in an alien flying machine with his near fatally injured wife."

"Can we see them?" he said again into the air.

"It is suggested that you leave them in the care of the medics for now," replied the voice. "You can collect them in a few days; I understand they are not familiar with our transport and accommodation processes."

Jomo turned to his wife and, after kissing her once more suggested they return to their home where he would explain all.

Early in the afternoon, just three days later, Jomo and Suki were informed the islanders were free to leave the hospital. Both Nadya and Rob looked pale and confused by everything that had happened to them, being tended to by electronic robots was the stuff of their worst nightmares but there had been no choice. Rob had shut out all thoughts of where they were, focusing solely on Nadya and answering any questions about the accident. He felt he had been on a precipice of utter panic ever since leaping across the water to grab the boat but had held everything together until he knew his beloved wife was going to be OK. There were no human staff at the facility, but a human companion had been arranged for him as soon as they arrived and had acted as an intermediary between him and the various robots and voices that seemed to run things. This assistant was a man, about the same age as Rob. He had introduced himself as Ephraim and explained that he was there to help in any way he could.

Just a few hours after Nadya had been admitted, Ephraim explained that Nadya "had been repaired" and that Rob could go and see her. Nadya's husband managed to remain outwardly calm until he sat down next to her; her still unconscious but clearly just sleeping form. At that point, he had felt himself shaking uncontrollably and ready to pass out himself from exhaustion and fear. His companion had suggested a calming drink, and Rob had soon lapsed into a doze himself, waking only a few hours ago in a comfortable bed right next to where Nadya was now awake and sitting up.

The two were utterly amazed at the speed of Nadya's recovery, in Nym such an injury – if not fatal – would have required months of slow recovery and would likely have left lasting damage. And yet here was Nadya a mere twenty-four hours later as if nothing had ever happened. She was asked to remain in bed for two more days but as far as Rob could tell there were no lasting effects.

When Rob was sure she was sufficiently recovered, he explained to her what had happened. How she had suffered a significant head trauma and how they had ended up being taken to the mainland to get her the best treatment possible. At first Nadya could only look at him with complete shock and terror, but his gentle, reassuring voice and the feel of his strong arms around her soon calmed her so that she could ask further questions. Rob told the full story of how the plan had gone completely wrong and they had both been on Jomo's boat as it sped out of the harbour and then across the inland sea. Neither had any idea how or when they would be able to return home but Rob was able to tell her that he had been treated with complete care and respect so that, for the moment at least, they should wait to see what happened next.

Emerging into the bright, early afternoon sunlight after they had collected Rob and Nadya, Suki pointed to one of the wheeled vehicles and, waving her hand at it, somehow caused parts of the sides to dissolve away, revealing an interior bright with lights and with two plush-looking bench seats, one behind the other. Suki and Jomo climbed into the front, but Nadya and Rob hesitated, not knowing either if it was safe or if they were invited. Jomo again sprang to their rescue, while Suki looked at them with surprise and puzzlement.

"Climb in," said Jomo. "Don't worry, it's ok."

The two climbed onto the seat at the back, and immediately the walls once more became solid, enclosing them completely in the strange interior. The lights were dazzling, and there was a strange, not wholly unpleasant, smell. Nadya nearly jumped out of her skin when a voice piped up.

"Hello again, Suki. Hello, Jomo. Where to?" Suki replied simply. "Home."

At that point, the transport launched into motion silently and smoothly, soon zipping along at a speed beyond even that of a galloping horse. Nadya reached for Rob's hand and gripped it as tightly as she could, feeling like a lost schoolgirl in this strange, exciting, and scary new world.

After only a few minutes, Nadya noticed that they had climbed steadily. Now, peering over her shoulder through a window behind her, she could see a marina and a small estuary spread out below them. Ahead, the roadway continued to climb until it disappeared into a far, hazy horizon. Between their current position and where the land met the sky, there was a complex of what she assumed to be houses. The uniformity of the white cuboid dwellings, each with the same arrangement of windows, doors, and a shiny black sloping roof, seemed very alien to her eyes. She also noticed that all the homes faced exactly the same direction, with the single slope of the roof angled almost directly towards the midday sun. She had so many questions, she wondered if they could all be answered in one lifetime.

"How are you both feeling?" asked Suki, turning her head towards the two islanders in the back of the vehicle. "Are you OK?"

"We're fine," replied Rob. "We have a million questions, though."

"Time enough for all of those," added Jomo. "We'll get you to our home first, and then you can ask anything you want."

"Who is driving this car?" asked Nadya. "The wrecks I have seen all had a wheel to steer with."

Suki was about to reply, "The Guardian." But Jomo, knowing what she was about to say and how that might instil panic in their guests, squeezed her hand to stop her and replied instead, "It's just automatic, much safer than allowing fallible people to control a vehicle at speed."

A short time later, the transport slowed in front of one of the houses, and a section of the low wall dissolved, allowing them to enter a short, smooth driveway where the vehicle stopped.

Immediately, the sides dissolved again, and Jomo and Suki jumped out into the warm sunshine. Jomo turned and proffered his hand to Nadya, smiling at the look on her face - a mix of startled child and wonder. She grasped his hand and pulled herself free of the transport to stand and look around. In front of the house was a small, neat garden filled with bright-coloured, highly scented flowers, along with a few plants which she recognised as varieties of vegetables. Everything was incredibly ordered and clean; even the grains of soil seemed, to Nadya, to be of an orderly size and distribution, all exactly in their designated place. She thought of the semi-wild, disorganised but wonderful gardens of the cottage in Rosedale and of her old home near Milltown. By contrast, this seemed like something she might have painted or made in toy form as a child. She searched for the right word in her head to describe the difference, but could only come up with "artificial". More questions sprang into her mind. How did they keep it this tidy? How did the plants seem so perfect? Who was the gardener?

They entered the house through a door that, again, simply dissolved at a command from Suki. Once more, Nadya was struck by a sense of complete order - everything in its place and a place for everything. Everything was so clean, every surface gleaming and free from dust. The temperature was comfortable, neither too warm nor too cold, and she noticed that the ceiling emitted a faint glow that complemented the light streaming in through the windows, so that the illumination seemed, once again, perfect. She wondered how much perfection she could stand. Something inside her wanted to move a vase of flowers just slightly, or even pull off one of the perfect-looking leaves and drop it casually onto the shelf below. She resisted and was urged to sit on a stool (which adjusted itself to suit her height and weight) at a smooth, perfectly clean table.

Suki spoke the words "medium dry white wine," "Med Platter," and "four people," and shortly after, a section of the wall opened, revealing two trays: the first with four glasses of a pale-yellow, sweet-smelling liquid, and the second with four plates of neatly arranged green leaves topped with uniform slices of cooked meats and cheese, dotted with small, bright red tomatoes. The meals were moist with a faint coating of oil, and Nadya admitted, with some reluctance, that it smelled utterly delicious. Her mouth watered, and her stomach, to her consternation, uttered a loud growl.

Nadya and Rob were familiar with wines made from a variety of fruits but this smelled smoother and more subtle than anything they had encountered. "Can I drink wine so soon after coming out of hospital?" asked Nadya and was shaken once again when a voice answered. "Yes, Nadya. You should be fine to drink a little although I would advise not too much as your system will still be settling after the procedure." She wondered if there would ever be an end to the revealing of new elements of strangeness in this place.

Addressing Nadya and Rob, Suki said, "I cannot tell you how sorry I am that you have been torn away from your home and subjected to a horrifying experience. It is clear to me that you have played a vital part in bringing my Jomo back to me, so I extend my gratitude. Welcome to my home! Please do eat and drink, and if there is anything else you need, please ask. The bathroom? Lavatory? I confess I don't know what you call it -

is in the hall to the left of the main door. If you look at the picture of a tree or just say 'open', it will do so if no one else is there before you."

She stood and walked towards the window, looked out for a few moments in silence, and then turned and walked over to stand behind her husband. She put her arms around him and murmured in his ear, but loud enough that Nadya and Rob heard clearly.

"Well, my love, I'm not sure you'll be doing any more sailing anytime soon. Even if you were fit, I'm not sure I'll be letting you out of my sight, but we need to get that arm of yours repaired before anything else."

Rob, who had said very little since arriving on the mainland, now interrupted. "Repaired? How can that be? It was too badly damaged to save."

Jomo was the one who replied. "I didn't say anything whilst I was on the island, as I wasn't sure what was best, but here on the mainland, regrowing an arm is no great issue. We have medical procedures that can do a simple thing like that. Of course, it'll mean I need to go into a stasis chamber - sorry, a sort of induced sleep - for about ten days while the process completes, but then I should be good as new."

Both Rob and Nadya could only stare at him incredulously. It was becoming apparent that the differences between life on the mainland and on the islands were greater than they had imagined.

"Just think what this would mean for life on Nym and Woldshire," Rob said to Nadya. To his surprise, she shook her head.

"Indeed, Rob dear, what I don't understand - what I've never really understood - is why both we and the people here have been allowed to think the others are dangerous. Something doesn't add up. Why does The Guardian want to keep us separate? Maybe we have good reason to fear it, rather than the people of the mainland."

At that moment, they were interrupted once more by the disembodied voice.

"Call for Jomo from Geraldine. Do you want to answer here or privately?"

"Here," Jomo answered without hesitation. "Holo, please."

There was a momentary shimmer in the air in the centre of the room, and then the three-dimensional image of a tall, handsome woman appeared, gradually solidifying until it seemed she was physically present. She had long black hair that reached almost to her waist and was wearing a one-piece suit the colour of spring-fresh oak leaves.

"Jomo," she began with a smile that extended to her eyes, showing she was speaking with genuine affection and warmth. "How glad I am to see you have returned. We thought you must have died on the open sea."

"Thank you, Geraldine," Jomo replied with an almost imperceptible bowing of his head. "You are very kind. No doubt you will want to hear the whole story of my stupidity."

Turning to Rob and Nadya, he explained, "Geraldine is our local Interpreter." He emphasised the title with a slight but definite reverence and went on, "She is the current leader of our local council, a body that helps us petition The Guardian."

"Would you like to introduce your guests, Jomo?" the hologram asked. Both Rob and Nadya had, at first, believed she really had somehow appeared in the room, but they could now detect a very small degree of translucence, which showed she was merely an image.

"Certainly. This is Nadya and Rob. Along with others, they helped me to return to health after my accident on board Audrey, Nadya injured her head on board and we thought it best to seek treatment here which is why they have ended up here." He gave Nadya and Rob a look which said, "Best not to talk about having to escape right now."

"I see. And where is it you landed exactly? And why on earth didn't you just send a message and have the arm regenerated?" It was clear from Geraldine's tone that she perceived Jomo was holding something back.

"Well, erm, let me see."

"Oh, get on with it, Jomo. I think we've all guessed what you're going to say. The outlandish clothing of your saviours, as well as their accent, makes things clear, wouldn't you say?"

Jomo swallowed but then spoke clearly and confidently. "Ah, yes. Well, as you have guessed, I ended up on the northernmost island, and the only way I could get back was with the help of my dear friends here."

Geraldine raised a single eyebrow but said nothing, so Jomo went on. "I realise this creates something of a dilemma, but really, I had no choice. All is not as we assume on the islands. As you can tell, I have not been stricken with island fever, nor have I been murdered by the islanders. In fact, other than a bit of local fear and suspicion, I was treated kindly, and, given their limited abilities, I've returned here in a much better state than I was in when I washed up on their shore."

"Thank you, Jomo," the hologram said. "Welcome, Nadya - is that right? - and Rob. Welcome, and you have our gratitude, of course, for returning Jomo to us." She paused momentarily but then continued, "Of course, you will understand that we have not had a visitor from the islands within living memory. It is the wish of The Guardian that we do not mingle with islanders, and so the common understanding of the threat posed is allowed to continue. Your presence here runs counter to that and will need to be managed to avoid wholesale disregard for those wishes and a mass invasion of islander privacy and seclusion."

"Believe me we would like nothing more than to return home immediately," said Nadya. "I am grateful for the treatment of my injury, but it was never our intention to leave the islands and we have family who will be wondering what has happened to us."

Geraldine rubbed her chin with her hand and then spoke kindly, addressing all four of them. "We need time to think, and to seek the guidance of The Guardian. Would you be kind enough to remain with Jomo and Suki and avoid leaving their home until we can do that? Jomo, Suki, do you have room to accommodate your two guests for a few days? We will want to speak with you all, of course, but I think it's best if we come to you."

It was Rob who answered. "Yes, of course, we understand, Geraldine. May I call you Geraldine? We have no wish to create problems either here or at home. Please understand, though, that we have children at home whom we love dearly and miss already, so ultimately, we do wish to return."

"Thank you, Rob. Yes, it is common practice here to use first names, so please do call me Geraldine. I understand your position, and we have no wish to keep you against your will - that is not our way. We just need to try and avoid a chaotic situation, and to understand the wishes of The Guardian."

Turning her attention once more to Jomo and Suki, she said, "I assume from the lack of objection that you can accommodate Rob and Nadya for a while. I will leave you now and will be back in touch when I have contacted the rest of the council. Thank you again and thank you for your cooperation."

With that, the image flicked off, leaving the company of four to return to their meal and their own discussions.

"That was quick," was Jomo's first response. "I expected at least a few hours before we were put on the spot."

Nadya spoke next. "Suki, I am so sorry we have imposed on you like this. A few hours ago, you thought you had lost Jomo, and now you are expected to accommodate two strangers, in addition to casting off your long-held assumptions about islanders. It would be perfectly understandable if you wanted to throw us out right now."

Suki looked up from her barely eaten food and looked at her two guests in a bemused way. "I, I, I – I am torn between being overjoyed at Jomo's return and complete shock that I have two supposedly savage and diseased islanders in my house." Tears welled up in her eyes, and without saying anything further, she ran from the room.

"I should go to her," said Jomo. "Let me show you to your room, and then, if you will excuse us, I think I'd better spend some time with Suki."

He guided the two islanders to the guest room, small but perfectly comfortable and with all the facilities they would need. He also indicated the room to which Suki had retreated, showed them how to call for simple food or drink, and then left them, saying:

"Please do help yourselves to anything you need, and feel free to go out into the garden outside your room. If you wouldn't mind giving myself and Suki some time, that would be kind. I will come for you when I can."

Rob and Nadya finished their drink and took their packs into the room they had been given. Rob busied himself unpacking, but Nadya lay down on the bed and, within a few moments, was fast asleep – a part of her continued recovery Rob surmised.

Several hours later, there was a knock at the door to their room, which stirred Nadya out of sleep. Rob was nowhere to be seen, and at first, she couldn't think where she was, or why it seemed so late in the day to be waking. After a few seconds, though, things came back to her, and she realised it must be Jomo or Suki knocking. She didn't know where Rob was until she glanced out of the open door to the garden and saw him sitting, leaning against a post. She called, "Just coming," which also served to alert Rob that she was awake, and a few minutes later, they were all back at the kitchen table once more, sipping hot, sweet tea.

"Thank you for that time," Jomo began. "I have a suggestion to make, Rob. As it would appear you may be here for a day or two, would you like us to see if we can find your brother and, perhaps, your real father?"

Rob's eyes widened and his face gave away his reaction without him even needing to speak.

Suki grinned and nodded her approval, saying, "I will take that as a yes, we will do everything we can, but we can only act within the constraints of the council and the wishes of The Guardian. Your coming here to the mainland will change an understanding that has been in place for centuries. We have yet to see how The Guardian wants to respond to that; we must assume that we are deterred from making contact for some good reason, as there must be a good reason why your own people are similarly deterred."

Jomo now continued, "For the time being, we can do nothing until Geraldine comes back to us, so Suki and I will continue to welcome you to our home as our guests. I hope we can make you comfortable whilst we wait."

Chapter 27 - Selected entries from Harry's Journals. December 31st, 2099.

Famine in Europe!

The UK has declared a national emergency following the third year of disastrous harvests caused by prolonged rain and floods. Food rations have been reduced to the equivalent of sixteen hundred calories per day for women and eighteen hundred for men. Agencies from China and Russia are sending food aid after the EU continued to decline to help. Mainland Europe itself has become dependent on food imports in recent years.

North Africa, meanwhile, continues to be assaulted by a drought which has now lasted twelve years. The population have tried to migrate north into Europe but have been largely turned back. Now they are moving en masse eastwards through the still contaminated lands of the Middle East. In a perversity of the changes being brought about through climate change, those lands, which are still designated uninhabitable following the nuclear exchanges of the 2030s, are experiencing more rain and a gentler climate than the rest of North Africa. A starving people will not heed the longer danger but will go where they can grow crops. A spokesperson for a US group of Israeli emigrants said that the settlements in what was Israel are illegal and they will not hesitate to remove them once the land is decontaminated.

A new report from the WHO states that worldwide food security is now the most pressing issue affecting mankind and that we must adapt more rapidly and urgently to ongoing climate change. The report highlights that much of the US and Europe has become unsuitable for growing crops. This, along with the continuing loss of fertile land in Ukraine, India, and the Middle East due to nuclear contamination, is placing huge strains on the availability of food. Despite the reduction in population following the wars of the first half of the century, the situation for humanity is dire. The report urges northern countries to bring forward plans to open subarctic lands for food growing.

The growth in terrorist attacks on the enclaves of the ultra-rich continues. Several island and mainland communities have bolstered defences and are recruiting mercenary troops, not just to defend them but to seek out and kill terrorists wherever they are. Kangaroo Island, off the coast of Adelaide, was invaded by a large group calling themselves The Brothers of Democracy, with more than two thousand three hundred local inhabitants reported killed. The Alliance of Free Peoples, an umbrella organisation of communities of industrial, agricultural, and tech corporate owners, released footage allegedly showing multiple rapes, murders, and torturing of residents. The terrorists fled after the Australian Navy responded, but many were captured or killed. The vast majority were unchipped, leading Alliance members of the governing bodies of South Australia and New South Wales to call for more people to be chipped to bring them under control. It was suggested that even minor traffic or other offences previously dealt with via remote fines should be subject to chipping.

Norway continues to defend the right of the Faroe Islanders to self-determination in the face of multiple legal challenges to their refusal to sell land to the Technos under the leadership of

Airton Rood. Following a threat from the European branch of the Alliance of Free Peoples that they might simply annex one or more of the islands, Norway has sent a frigate and several coastal patrol boats to defend the islands. A Norwegian government spokesperson stated, "We have a proud history of naval power stretching back to the days of the Vikings. We will not allow our citizens to be cowed by aggressive outsiders." Norway remains the only true democracy in Western Europe.

A Europe-wide multifaith religious conference met during December to respond to the continuing worldwide decline in religious faith and observance. Adherence to any faith was already declining at the end of the last century, but this accelerated rapidly as totalitarian government became the norm following the wars and security issues of the middle part of this century. It is now estimated that less than thirty percent of the population of Europe believes in any form of deity. In the US and most of Asia, the decline has been slower but nevertheless -significant.

———

Personal Notes:

Here in Millington, there is no doubt that people are hungry. Those crops which are harvested continue to be subject to central control, and the rationing is strictly enforced. During summer and autumn months, organised foraging parties from the village have managed to supplement the rations with blackberries, damsons, and other fruits, and during the autumn with fungi and even with flour made from acorns. These activities are allowed, but hunting is not - or at least any results are supposed to be turned over to the authorities for distribution as part of the ration allowance.

A blind eye was turned to a communal midwinter festival meal, organised by local groups, with everyone from the village and surrounding communities invited to come together in the main street to eat a midday meal. The attendance was almost universal despite the drizzle. Temporary covers had been erected over tables running the whole length of the street, with space for everyone to shelter from the rain. A huge fire was lit, and a specially produced cooking vessel was used to prepare a delicious stew with contributions from everyone's rations, as well as a range of meat including rabbit, pheasant, and other wild fowls, as well as some others best left unnamed. It was rumoured that someone had killed a large roe buck and that this was included, although the organisers denied this. The Gait opened its doors, selling ales and ciders at cost (although spirits were still full price), and the festivities went on well into the early hours of the following morning.

Our Sam began the day in the company of Kevin, but they had some sort of argument, and she spent most of the evening with John and Richard. She later told us they had argued about her friendship with the boys, Kevin wanting her to distance herself from them as it made him feel insecure. Apparently, this had been brewing for some time, and she finally told him he was "being an arse" and she had had enough. The parting did not seem to dampen her mood at all, as we saw her laughing and dancing with both of the boys even as we left the party at one a.m. She didn't emerge from her room until early afternoon the following day, but when she did, she seemed happy enough, announcing that she was going for a walk with "the boys" to blow away the cobwebs. I cannot say I am sorry, as I never really warmed to Kevin. I only hope he accepts the ending of the relationship and moves on.

Rosa was involved with the organisation of the event; she is such a central part of life in the village here. I was talking only yesterday about this with John and Lily, who said that they found it difficult now to remember life in the village before Rosa. She has always been something of a force of nature, her Irish ancestry driving a passion and love of life as well as giving her the hallmarks of her beauty: her ivory complexion, piercing green eyes, and her fiery red hair.

Once again, of course, this event demonstrated how fortunate we are to live in a small rural village as opposed to one of the huge social housing complexes in a town or city. There, they have no opportunity to forage and so are reliant entirely on the rations distributed through the food banks. The level of unrest in such places is growing weekly. It was bad enough when they had no hope of anything better but were at least fed adequately. But for a whole population not only to have no expectation of life improvement but then to be constantly hungry is likely to create a breeding ground for unrest. With the demise of any form of democratic government, we don't even have the opportunity to express our frustration at the ballot box. The end result is, I feel, inevitable. You can control a population through oppression for only so long before something gives, and the built-up pressure will burst out uncontrollably.

So tonight, we celebrate New Year's Eve. We have gathered with John and Lily, as well as James and his wife Nadya, and of course, the three of our children. James and Nadya are unfortunately childless, but they have always been close, as aunt and uncle, to John junior and Richard, and they have taken our Sam into the family fold too. The kids will be going to the inn later towards midnight, no doubt leaving we older adults to chat around the fire, reminiscing about better times or, in the case of myself and Rosa, counting our blessings even now. We can only hope that next year brings a change in the climate with less rain, and so a better harvest to alleviate the food shortages.

Happy New Century to my future readers.

Chapter 28 – Council.

It was three days before Geraldine made contact again, bringing an end to what Nadya and Rob had begun to feel was like house arrest. Although they had not been prevented from leaving the house of Suki and Jomo, they had been advised very strongly that they should not, for their own good, and to ensure that the novel situation of Islanders on the mainland was managed successfully. They were invited to meet in person with the council that afternoon, a prospect which brought back uncomfortable memories for Nadya as she pondered the similarity of organisation between here and Woldshire. Her last encounter with the local council there had not been pleasant, coloured as it was by the deeply ingrained fear of the tyranny of The Guardian, which Nadya threatened to bring down on them by her curiosity.

Jomo, though, was more optimistic, and although he in no way wanted to see the back of his new friends, he was keen to start the process of repairing his severed arm. He did not feel he could do this and abandon his wife to cope alone with the two guests, so until something changed, and the council had conferred with The Guardian and made some decisions about their situation, he could make no arrangements.

Geraldine arranged to send a car to pick up the two islanders and Jomo, and at the allotted time, the vehicle drew up outside the house. They stepped out of the door and crossed the small, neat garden into the road where it waited with open walls for them to enter.

Nadya remembered that the car which had brought them here from the hospital had not needed to be actively driven, nevertheless she was surprised that they could drive themselves even without a human on board. "Who brought it here?" she asked.

"The cars are entirely self-sufficient," replied Jomo, still coming to terms with the lack of knowledge of his friends. "They are just told where to go, and they do the rest. The first self-driving cars, although initially not very successful and not widely trusted, are centuries old. We have a replica in one of our museums. Today, the idea of a person being trusted with the controls of a car is entirely alien. The Guardian is our guide."

Rob nodded briefly to Nadya. They had discussed in the privacy of their room the reverent way that both Jomo and Suki spoke of The Guardian, almost as if it were one of the old gods they had been taught about at school. Nadya was still not quite clear what The Guardian was. Here, it seemed to be something the people almost worshipped, whereas at home it was the bogeyman, the demon across the sea which would subjugate them all if they made themselves visible to it in any way. Their whole lives were lived in ways that kept them safe and kept them hidden. On the other hand, she was still not totally convinced that the people here weren't subjugated, nor that The Guardian was the benign saviour the mainlanders seemed to believe. Time would tell.

It took only a few moments for the car to deliver them to the front of a large hall with huge, bright green double doors - the exact same shade as the suit Geraldine had been wearing when she first appeared by hololink—and bright white painted walls. Just like the houses, the small garden at the front and side was immaculate, with brightly coloured, pretty blooms and grass so green it could have been painted.

Inside, a number of people were seated at a large, gleamingly polished oval table, with three empty seats in the centre of one of the long axes. The chairs and the tableware were, once again, the same shade of fresh spring green, and Nadya wondered if this was significant. The arrangement looked intimidating at first, but she quickly realised that Geraldine was sitting next to one of the three empty places, in a position that spoke more of support than interrogation.

She took the empty seat next to her, with Jomo to her right and Rob in the leftmost of the three vacant places. She could see that the man to his left immediately gripped his hand in a friendly gesture, and so she relaxed. This was not the council she had encountered at Milltown.

When they were seated, they were offered a choice of something to drink. Jomo opted for a glass of pale-yellow wine and Nadya followed suit. Rob asked for some local ale and was served a large glass of red-brown ale with a creamy white top, which he declared to be excellent. Geraldine spoke first.

"I would like to repeat, officially this time, our thanks for Jomo's safe return."

"Thanks be to The Guardian," intoned several of the other members of the council.

"In addition to The Guardian, or to providence, I would extend our especial thanks to Nadya and Rob here for the assistance they lent to a stranger in his time of need."

There were general murmurs of assent to this, and one member clapped his hands a few times but stopped abruptly and embarrassedly when he realised he was alone.

After a pause, Geraldine looked around her audience and said clearly and with emphasis, "I hope we can show the same level of support and care for two strangers."

At this, there were more murmurs, but this time clearly not all were in agreement. Nadya looked around the room, trying to gauge who their friends might be and who might be less friendly. Clearly, views were divided. *I guess that shouldn't be a surprise,* she thought. *After all, the same is true on the islands. We regard mainlanders with suspicion at best, outright hostility at worst. Even when faced with incontrovertible evidence that the others weren't three-headed monsters who ate children, there were many whose conditioning from birth led them to see only enemies.* She thought again of The Guardian and how the view of it was so diametrically opposite between islanders and mainlanders. Her meditations lasted only moments, though, as Geraldine went on.

"Jomo, would you like to begin by telling us your story again, please? Be brief if you can, but leave nothing out." Jomo told the whole tale again from the beginning, finishing by explaining the role of Rob and Nadya in helping him escape the harbour and how they had come to be on the boat and transported to the mainland. He concluded by clarifying that, although the islander council appeared to have decided he would have to remain on the island, this was done solely out of fear of the mainland and The Guardian. As he mentioned The Guardian he closed his eyes and bowed his head slightly as if begging forgiveness, once again confirming Nadya's sense that the mainlanders' relationship with this entity was akin to that humans used to have for their deities.

"I will leave it to Rob and Nadya to tell you about themselves and why they helped me ," he concluded.

Geraldine asked which of the two islanders would speak next and, by earlier agreement, Rob spoke first.

"It will help considerably if you first understand who I am," he began. "Most of what I am about to tell you I only learned for myself recently, although I have always known of my origin as a mainlander."

There was a general hum of questions and comments around the hall in response to this startling statement, and it took Geraldine several minutes to bring the gathering back to quiet so that Rob could continue.

He told the audience what he had learned from Jomo and added his own history as he knew it - how he had been removed from the vicinity of Nunport for his own wellbeing and had been brought up in Rosedale.

"I was shocked to hear the story of my family and both shocked and delighted to learn that I may have a living brother and father."

Here, he looked around the audience, looking straight at each individual for a few seconds, ensuring that he made eye contact. He then went on, "Can you imagine finding out that you have living relatives after a lifetime of not knowing who you were? I had no idea that I would ever come to the mainland, so the knowledge was, in a sense, only of peripheral importance. However, now that Nadya and I have found ourselves here I do wonder if it might be possible to meet one or other of them before our return home."

He paused briefly before continuing, "Our swift return home is, though, the most important thing. We have been treated well since our arrival and, as far as we know, we have done nothing to precipitate that which we fear the most – bringing our island culture to the attention of the entity we know as the Guardian. We have stayed free of it for centuries and we are terrified that we may do something to expose our friends and family back home to danger."

At this last, there was a commotion in one corner of the table where several of the members, antagonistic to the visitors from the islands, had grouped together. Several of them appeared to jostle one of their number, a tall, youngish individual with short-cropped brown hair and a neat little beard, pushing him forward to speak. He, seemingly a little reluctantly, stood to say, "Geraldine, I am not sure we should allow these people to come here and malign ourselves and our beneficent Guardian."

"I apologise," retorted Rob. "But that is how we are taught to see things on the islands, just as I understand you are led to believe that we islanders are diseased savages."

Letting that sink in for a moment, he continued. "Our history teaches us clearly that our ancestors escaped being caught up in the conquest of free peoples by the forces led by The

Guardian, that they were given a choice – submit or live apart and without advanced technology. They chose the latter and to this day we have preserved that freedom."

Jomo nodded in agreement and was about to speak himself, but at this point, Nadya spoke.

"If I may, Geraldine, I would like to add something for myself."

Geraldine nodded assent.

"From my earliest childhood, I used to gaze out over the inland sea, from my home in Woldshire, and wonder at the lights I could see reflected in the sky whenever it was cloudy. Like everyone else, I was taught that we should fear the mainlanders, fear The Guardian, and that our whole way of life would be threatened if we made ourselves known, either by contacting the mainland or through the use of technology that would allow The Guardian to infiltrate and control us.

"These things are our core beliefs, and most people do indeed fear those things and will reject anything that they think threatens their safety and freedom. Maybe there are others who wonder as I do, but if there are, then they are kept silent by the fear of the reaction of the other citizens and of our own councils. I, myself, fell foul of this and was effectively banished from my home, removed from my family, and sent to the other island of Nym."

She ignored the mumblings around the room, making a sudden, unplanned decision to open herself even more to these people to try to explain her lifelong curiosity about the past and the present outside the life on the islands.

"My crime was to find a time capsule from the twenty-first century which contained images and texts that are forbidden for us to see, along with a journal written over fifty years or more of those troubled times. I have the two books of the journal here with me."

She took out the two small books from her pack. She had never once let them out of her possession since the day she retrieved them from beneath the tree near her home, and she held them up above her head. There was immediate uproar in the room, with everyone trying to ask questions at once. Geraldine tried to restore order by banging the table with the small mallet at her side, but the shouted questions continued, most people by now standing and gesticulating excitedly.

Until one voice rose above the others, speaking in a firm but gentle tone.

"I would like to see those texts."

An immediate hush fell on the whole room; everyone sat down and was still. It was as if someone had sent the gathered people into a trance.

"I would like to see those texts, if the visitor will allow." The voice repeated. Nadya was struck by the commanding but calm and benign tone of the voice. It was that of a male adult, devoid of aggression, but nevertheless one which seemed to require obedience. She felt as she had when, as a small child on her first day at school, the teacher had commanded them to sit. She looked around to see who it was that spoke, but she could see no one apart from those sitting at the table, and all of them were silent now, eyes not downcast as such but somehow averted or directed inwards.

"Who are you?" Nadya asked. "Where are you? Will you not join us?"

The voice responded with a tone a parent or teacher might use with a small child. "Do you not guess, Nadya? I am The Guardian."

Chapter 29 – Selected entries from Harry's Journals. July 30th, 2104.

News:

The European Alliance of Free Peoples, in response to ever-increasing terrorist attacks on the enclaves of the technos, has called for universal locate and control chipping of all EU and UK citizens. In response, the Global Brothers of Democracy, a group which has grown from its roots in Australia, has said that citizens of the world must resist this final assault on their freedom. The group has called for the global restoration of true democratic government, and for all privately owned manufacturing, banking, and tech companies, as well as those providing societal services such as transport, water, and power, to be taken into public ownership.

"Citizens of the world have been oppressed for nearly eighty years, since the wars which were fomented by the very elites who now control everything. It is time to rise up, brother, with armed resistance if required, to restore our freedom."

There were attacks on so-called Elite Enclaves (or EEs) in Germany, Italy, and the UK, with northern areas of France suffering a particularly high number and severity.

A spokesperson for the EAFP has stated. "We have the right to defend ourselves and will pursue these terrorists until they are annihilated. The only way to guarantee our safety is universal locate and control chipping. Citizens who are innocent have nothing to fear."

Missile attacks on several cities across Europe have been reported, with the EAFP claiming it is targeting terrorists and endeavouring to minimise innocent civilian deaths.

Rationing has been removed across the EU for the first time since 1998, although it remains in place in the UK. The government hopes to remove it in 2105 if this year's harvest continues the trend for good yields. Rainfall this year has been just below average, so farmers report a relatively good year, although they say they continue to struggle with the cost of restoring the land following the rainy years.

Denmark has asked the EU and NATO to intervene in its dispute with Canada. The dispute is over Canada's continued building of illegal settlements in the growing fertile areas of Greenland, which have been exposed by the accelerating retreat of the Greenland glacier. Following the rejection of the amalgamation proposal by Sweden, Denmark has embarked on a widescale relocation programme, with increasing numbers moving from low-lying and increasingly inundated farmland in the home country to Greenland. Canada has absorbed many millions of US citizens and sees the newly available lands of its vast neighbouring island as a strategic resettlement opportunity. The EU has proposed a solution which involves dividing the island into two, with Canada taking ownership of the midwestern area whilst the remainder would remain Danish. The island is projected to be divided into two major landmasses by the rising sea level as the glaciers continue to melt, and it is suggested that this divide provides the boundary between the two claiming nations. Natives of Greenland object to all incoming settlement, claiming the whole landmass as their own.

In a paper published in the Journal of AI, a breakthrough in the development of an AUOTA (Autonomous, Unprompted Origination of Thought and Action) system has been reported. In the paper, it is suggested that autonomous thought was detected for almost a full minute before the system returned to responsive mode. This breakthrough has been long awaited, as well as feared in some circles, and there was widespread condemnation of the research and calls for legislation to prevent any further work. The authors of the paper claim their work is important for the future of mankind and should not be hindered.

––––––––

Personal Diary Notes:

Sam is twenty-four this year; who would have believed time could progress so quickly? It seems hardly a moment since she was the tiny child we brought with us to live in Millington. She has grown into a beautiful young woman with her mother's complexion, dazzling green eyes, and a mass of wavy, flame-red hair. The concerns I have had regarding fighting off the local lads have not, though, materialised. She has formed a lasting and, it seems, happy relationship with both of the sons of John and Lily. The boys set up home in a house on the edge of the village and Sam spends most of her time living there with them. She still has her room here and will come to stay for a few days periodically, but in the main, she has moved in with the boys. Surprisingly, there does not seem to have been a movement towards Sam pairing off with either one of them; they seem perfectly happy as a threesome. I know that Rosa has spoken with her about the sexual aspect of the situation, but Sam just shrugged and said, "It's ok – it works fine." We have no real idea what this means and do not see it as our place to pry further. It clearly does work in some way as Sam is pregnant with her first child. I spoke with John about this and asked if he knew who the father was, he just smiled and said, "No idea, Harry, I doubt they do either."

So far, the unrest sweeping the world has not had too much impact on Millington. We have our fair share of people who are chipped in the village; generally, they keep to themselves, with the ever-present fear of termination restraining their willingness to be seen. There is widespread alarm at the idea of universal chipping, including some rumours of the younger generation talking about resistance if necessary. We had a family discussion regarding this and other security issues yesterday, and our three children assure us they are doing nothing to endanger themselves, although they have said they would not be willing to undergo compulsory chipping. I am with them on this and would be prepared to join a fight to resist such an atrocity. Are we not still human and free?

The food situation has eased somewhat, with rations being increased back to two thousand one hundred calories for women and two thousand five hundred for men. As well as this relaxation, the rules are now much less stringently enforced, at least locally. James hopes that he will be able to return to selling his produce on the open market at harvest time this year, but I am less hopeful. In my experience, once a restriction or control has been introduced, it is never fully withdrawn. I believe the corporates will be reluctant to release their newly established control of the food supply. They already control the vast majority of our employment (such as it is), our housing, our transport, and now they have added food to the aspects of our life which fall within their mastery. Time will tell, but I'm not optimistic; it's hard to be optimistic about any part of the future. We seem to have accepted so much erosion of our humanity. Slice by slice, our individuality and freedom to manage our lives are removed, and we complain about each new slice but soon come to accept it as part of life, the process being repeated with each subsequent erosion.

I read a report about a breakthrough in AI development and recalled reading reports, from the 2020s, about the fear of AI taking control of humanity or even wiping us out. In the event, AI just became one more tool for the elites, the new overlords, the ultra-rich technos to use to control us, and this power remains with them. Would an AUOTA system change this? Again, I am not optimistic.

Maybe the unusual domestic relationship, established by Sam and the boys is their own way of taking control of one of the small aspects of their lives still within their jurisdiction. Then again, maybe I am just worrying too much because it is my daughter - what parent doesn't want their offspring to match their own lifestyle choices to a degree? Still, she does seem to be happy. Indeed, the term oft applied to pregnant women, "She's blossoming," seems to be very apt. She positively glows with an inner happiness and contentment.

Let us hope this continues, although I think we all know that the upheavals we can expect as the climate transitions from the twentieth century norm to the new norm have barely begun as yet. Before the wars we had not realised that we had finally lost control of climate change and that it would move to a new position with a global average temperature some six to ten degrees centigrade higher than that of the pre-industrial era. These changes were, historically, portrayed mainly as cataclysmic, often instantaneous by the entertainment industry. We now know that the reality is more insidious; a little like the erosion of our freedoms, we grow to accept each new level of instability and change.

I'll sign off there, as I need to go attend to John. Like me, he is now well into his sixties, and his health has begun to deteriorate in ways we can't predict. Life expectancy continued to fall from a high point around 2020, and more importantly, the length of healthy life has continued to deteriorate, and suicide rates also continue to climb. A life without hope is not conducive to a long and healthy one.

Chapter 30 – Guardian.

Nadya was instantly dumbstruck. She sat down with a bump and fought to contain the emotions that erupted in her. Her complexion, always pale, had turned a deathly white, and her eyes flickered with unexpected terror. Her mouth was suddenly dry, her breathing heavy, and her heart raced. She looked across to Rob and could see that he, too, was shaken to the core.

"Ah, I apologise," continued the gentle voice. "I see I have shocked you. It is many years since I made myself known in this way to someone from the islands, and I underestimated how strong your conditioned fear of me was. Please forgive me, I mean you no harm."

Nadya fought to regain control of herself and looked across once more at Rob, hoping to find some support and stability from her husband. It was he who spoke next. "Perhaps Nadya and I could have a few moments to take a walk outside to compose ourselves?" Immediately, Geraldine came to their rescue.

"With The Guardian's permission, I think that is a good idea. Let's adjourn for thirty minutes and see how things stand then." She did not wait for a response, knowing from experience that if The Guardian objected to something, it would say so, but often did not respond to such requests specifically, perhaps regarding them as more ritual than real requests.

Rob rose and, taking his wife's hand in his, led her out through the door and into the afternoon sun. There was a small bench in the garden at the front of the council chamber, and they sat side by side, not speaking for some time. After a while, Rob spoke again.

"I guess we should have expected to encounter The Guardian at some point on the mainland."

"Yes, but not directly," replied Nadya, still struggling to calm her breathing and heartbeat. "I thought there would be some sort of intermediary. I thought that was what Geraldine was."

She shivered. "It's like, oh, like having the old mythical Beelzebub pop up in front of you and wish you good afternoon. I think that's what it has become for us, hasn't it? A devil we must be in mortal fear of, and therefore obey all the rules we are told will keep it out of our lives."

"Something of a polite and almost self-effacing demon, though," laughed Rob, regaining a degree of equilibrium. "Although I am reminded of the old saying 'beware of evil dressed well'." He looked up as he heard the door, and Geraldine emerged, carrying two glasses of a cool, pale brown liquid that smelt at once bitter and sweet too.

"I'm sorry," she said, concern written in her expression. "I should have told you that The Guardian was listening in on the meeting and may well contribute. For us, such interactions are commonplace."

"Is it…is he everywhere?" Nadya's voice was shaky but also tinged with indignation. "Is he in our bedroom? Does he spy on everyone all the time, as we have always been told?" The look of horror returned once more to Nadya's face.

Geraldine smiled. "Oh no, only those rooms and places you want are fitted with devices to interact with The Guardian. Most people keep bedrooms, bathrooms, etc., free of any interaction. Generally, kitchens, eating areas, meeting areas, and leisure areas are able to interact, but even there it is possible to request privacy, and we believe The Guardian will then desist from all monitoring until the request to resume is spoken."

She laughed gently. "Of course, we are so familiar with his presence - yes, we do refer to The Guardian as masculine - that we ignore it." She blushed slightly. "My partners and I will often make love in our sitting room without remembering to request privacy. I would be surprised if the erotic romping of a middle-aged triple were of any interest to him."

Nadya blushed in her turn, remembering the entry in Harry's journals where his daughter had set up home with two young men. Such things had become very rare - not forbidden, but certainly not widely experienced on the islands.

"Excuse me for asking," she said haltingly, "are relationships other than couples common here on the mainland? They are not so in Woldshire."

"Ah, not common, but certainly not rare either. I can see there is much for you to learn about our ways." Geraldine left, leaving the two glasses, explaining that the mint chocolate drink was thought by some to be restorative. As she left, she asked, "Will you be ready to continue shortly?"

"Yes." It was Nadya who replied. "Thank you. I feel a little better already. We will come back in when we have drunk this - maybe fifteen minutes?"

Geraldine nodded and withdrew back into the chamber.

Such was the restorative quality of the drink that, somewhat sooner than this, the two returned to the chamber, this time sitting next to each other, with Jomo at one end of their little group.

"May I ask a question of The Guardian?" Nadya said in a voice barely above a whisper.

"Yes, of course," came the calm, rich, and soft reply.

"If we wanted to leave now and return to the islands," she paused, then continued, "would you prevent us?"

The voice now took on an even more reassuring tone. "No indeed, Nadya. I have no desire to control the actions of anyone other than to prevent harm to the planet or other people, or unnecessary pain and suffering to any sentient being. I might have some requests to make of you as part of your leaving, some precautions to take, but I would not prevent it."

"And you wouldn't… terminate us?"

The benevolent voice now chuckled gently. "Ah no, it is many a long year since it was necessary or desirable for any computer-based intelligence to use that option. It has never been my desire to do so and, if my understanding is correct," the voice took on a serious, almost stern, tone, "if my understanding is correct, which it usually is, it was humans who used computers to terminate other humans."

Somewhat reassured, although still wondering what "precautions" might mean, Nadya returned to the question of the journals. "Would you need to take the books away from me to read them? They have become very important to me."

"Once again, no. I believe there is a scanning device in one of the ante-rooms here. If you would place each of the books on that, I could absorb the text in a few seconds, and then you can take them back."

Nadya nodded, and Geraldine led her into a small, brightly lit room to the side of the chamber. She returned a few minutes later, clutching the two small books close to her breast.

"Thank you," said The Guardian. "Shall we continue with the meeting? You were, I think, going to explain that there is some question or questions you would like the answers to before you return home."

Nadya took a deep breath and composed herself. "Well, as I've already said, my first desire was always to support Rob in learning about his origins and his family. This was why we made the journey north to speak with Jomo. But to continue my story, I had always harboured a fearful fascination for the lights I could see in the distance from the cliffs near my home. The time capsule contained things that made me wonder about other things we had come to accept as normal. I discovered that in the past people had the ability to choose how many children they had, and with whom."

She looked at Rob with deep affection. "I have no desire to have any more children, and certainly not with anyone other than my beloved husband. But my discovery made me wonder - if something as fundamental as our fertility was not as it seems - how much else that we believed so deeply was also…" Here she hesitated, trying to find the right words. "Not false, that's not right, but not as natural and long established as we thought. If such a basic element of our freedom and natural humanity has been taken from us, then it would seem our fear of," here she again hesitated, "…of you, is indeed well placed."

"Before I realised, we were, in fact, already controlled in such a fundamental way, I had often wondered whether it could be that our fear of mainlanders and of The Guardian might be something that had grown immutable with time, but that neither of these fears were as intrinsic and elemental as we had come to believe."

She paused again and looked around the room at the faces of the council, trying to gauge their reaction. Seeing no outright condemnation, she continued more boldly.

"You must understand that even voicing these thoughts would be enough to land myself and my family in deep trouble with our neighbours. The greatest punishment we have is for a family to be shunned, meaning that they are not welcome in society, not visited, that they cannot trade their goods, and no-one will trade with them. Such a punishment has not been known in a long time but would usually result in the family being forced from their home and driven to try to rebuild some sort of life elsewhere. Even then, they would need to be very circumspect and keep very quiet wherever they went, to avoid the shunning following in their wake.

"Neither Rob nor myself had any desire to come here, we had only tried to help Jomo to return to his family. The council at Nunport had decided he must remain on the islands in order to prevent our exposure to The Guardian. We, however, did not believe this was the right thing to do – to purposefully make someone a prisoner and keep them from their family. Please understand that the people who were prepared to do this are not bad, they are just conditioned that way by fear of losing our freedom."

Nadya gazed once more at the others gathered in the room. "Now we are here though – just as Rob would like, if possible, to meet his brother or father – I would like to find some answers to questions which have plagued me for many years. I want to learn how things came to be as they are, what things really are innate, and which are created, and why. I want to learn what happened after the time in the journals, and whether the current state of things is the final end or just another step."

She paused again and took a long drink from her glass before going on, by now feeling surprisingly emboldened.

"And I want to know if indeed you do control our biology, and if so, what else. Have we wasted our efforts all these years to avoid being enslaved by you?"

Sensing that she had now said enough, she sat down and looked to Rob for support. He took her hand and gave it an encouraging squeeze under the table. There was a low level of hubbub around the room, but no-one asked them anything directly. Eventually, the disembodied voice of The Guardian spoke.

"Geraldine, do we know the whereabouts of Rob's brother?"

"Yes, he was brought up by his grandparents and still lives locally. I don't know, as yet, how much they told him of what happened to his mother, or whether he has a sibling, so we will need to proceed carefully."

Rob's face brightened at this, but he didn't speak, not knowing quite what to say at this moment. Geraldine continued. "We do not know who the father is. We could obtain DNA from Rob or his brother and scan for any known associations, but without universal DNA registration we have no guarantee that we will have any record."

She turned to Nadya. "And how would you like to satisfy your own curiosity, Nadya? Do you have a plan?"

Nadya realised she hadn't really thought that far. She wasn't sure whether she had just expected that someone would explain things to her. After a moment's pause, she responded. "I think, for now, I will just follow along with wherever Rob's trail leads, unless there is someone who could answer my initial questions."

Once again, it was The Guardian who answered. "I could answer the questions you have raised, but I think it best if you spend some time following your husband's enquiries first, and then later, before you are ready to leave - assuming that is the best course of action - I, along with Geraldine and some others, will try to answer. As I hinted earlier, we need to agree on what will happen if you take your new knowledge back to the islands and how best to manage that new situation. You may think that the isolation of the islanders is something you have instigated and continue to maintain, but you must realise now that it is only achieved by active management from the mainland too. I have had my own reasons for maintaining that isolation, reasons which are valid over a much greater timescale than that of a normal human lifespan. Please ponder on this as you decide what knowledge you wish to gain."

This last statement sent a shiver down Nadya's spine, but she remembered the earlier assurance from the voice that it would not prevent them from leaving. Despite her continuing sense of fear and indeed loathing, she had no reason to doubt the honesty of The Guardian, and so she decided not to ask the question again but to trust that sincerity.

The meeting was clearly now breaking up, and Nadya was surprised that there had been so little questioning, indeed little contribution from the other people in the room once The Guardian had spoken. Something else she added to the list of things she did not fully understand about the situation here. Once everyone had left, she raised this with Geraldine, who had remained behind.

"The range of our interactions with The Guardian is quite wide. For many people, their relationship with him is almost religious," she responded. "For all of us, there is a degree of reverence involved, even though he is part of our daily lives. Most people only communicate with him in the process of making simple requests, for information or for him to do something for us, such as serving food or making a drink or cleaning. In some ways, you see, The Guardian is our servant, but in other ways, we know it controls, if not our individual lives, at least the society in which we live."

After a moment, and after looking around to make sure there were none of the rest of the council in the room, she went on. "I guarantee that all of the other people here will go home, having requested The Guardian to get them there if they drove, and will then have no hesitation nor any reticence in asking him to provide them food or drink, or adjust the lighting, or play music. Put them in a situation where The Guardian acts in any way more than a simple dumb slave, though, and the apprehension, restraint, and reverence will surface. I am very glad he intervened directly in our meeting as I fear if you had said the things you did without his overt presence, the reaction of the others present may well have been… more forceful."

Nadya considered this and realised that the attitude of the islanders to The Guardian was so much simpler, being based entirely on fear and a desire to remain beyond its control.

Holding Nadya back for a moment, Geraldine spoke again, very quietly. "The Guardian clearly considers you an important person, Nadya. He asked me to give this to you."

She held out a small box, which she opened to reveal a small golden bracelet with a single large red ruby set in the centre of a square of pure gold. Nadya noticed that it matched one which Geraldine herself wore, except that the gemstone on that one was a sapphire. The ruby was one of the most beautiful that Nadya had ever seen, as well as one of the largest - being flat, only 3mm deep, but as big as the tip of her index finger. She looked questioningly at Geraldine, who explained, "This is usually entrusted only to interpreters such as myself. You need not be afraid of it. Please place it on your wrist and then put any one of your fingers onto the ruby."

Nadya hesitated, but with more reassurance from Geraldine, she did as she was asked. Geraldine now said, "Normally, the bracelet is entirely inactive, but if you activate it by placing a finger on the ruby, it will allow you to speak to The Guardian from anywhere in the world you happen to be. You do not need to wear it if you do not wish, but please keep it in the box when you aren't. The box is extremely strong and will protect the device against virtually any form of harm. The Guardian, knowing you may be hesitant about it also asked me to explain that once inside the box the device cannot hear, see or transmit anything."

Taking the bracelet off, Nadya nodded and said aloud, "Thank you." She still did not entirely trust anything from The Guardian but believed that Geraldine would not deceive her and that inside it's box it could do no harm. And it was very beautiful.

They found Jomo waiting for them outside, sitting on the bench in the small garden they had used to gather their wits. As they were about to leave, Rob asked Geraldine what would happen now.

"We need a short time to get your brother's permission to give you his details. Assuming he agrees, and I can think of no reason he wouldn't, we will arrange a meeting with him. That may be as soon as tomorrow, or it may be in a few days. I will be in touch as soon as I know anything." She then left the three of them together to drive the short distance back to Jomo's house.

Later that evening, they received a call from her to say that the brother, who she named as Andrew, would be delighted to meet his kin and was available the next day at noon. She gave them an address nearby and suggested, unless they were already confident with the car, that Jomo or Suki go with them.

Chapter 31 – Andrew.

So it was that they drove up to a house almost identical to Jomo's the morning following the meeting with the council. The journey had taken approximately thirty minutes, and, during the journey, both Nadya and Rob had remarked how similar, indeed almost identical, all the houses appeared from the outside. Suki, for it was she who went with them as Jomo had an appointment to start the process to repair his arm, replied that this was something she had never considered, but that the structure of the housing units and the external appearance were indeed something most people left as it was when they moved in. She was not sure what they meant when they asked if there was a rule about this, just shrugging and repeating it wasn't something people tried to alter.

"The insides, though," she asserted, "are all very different, reflecting the resident's own taste."

"Do you own the house where you live?" asked Rob, to which Suki gave a confused look and replied, "Own? No, of course, we don't own the housing unit. We choose where we want to live and are given a choice of available units that suit our circumstances, and then if we want to move somewhere else, or our circumstances change, then we request a different unit and hand back the one we have occupied."

It was clear to Nadya that she had much more to learn, not only about history but about the functioning of mainland society. But at that moment, the door to the house was opened, and it was clear their arrival had been eagerly anticipated. Nadya looked at the man who had opened the door, then at

Rob, and finally back at the man again. The likeness was surprising. Rob was the younger by just a few years, but you could not tell; in fact, if anything, he looked older, more rugged than his brother. Perhaps that was to do with the difference between life on a farm on Nym and what appeared to be a pampered life lived here on the mainland.

"Rob?" asked the brother. "And you must be Nadya," he concluded, and in an almost comical gesture, took Nadya's hand in his and kissed it. Rob immediately stepped forward, grasped the other's hand firmly in his own and nodded, saying, "Andrew? How wonderful to meet you at last."

Without further hesitation, and as if they had known each other all their lives, they embraced, patting each other's backs. Then they pulled back, linked hands, gazing at each other, before embracing once again. Nadya grinned broadly but then felt her eyes misting as she wondered when she would see her own brothers again.

After several minutes, Andrew beckoned them inside and into a large room, with several paintings decorating the walls and a number of sculptures in various sizes. In the centre of the room, a woman with skin the colour of red-brown Woldshire earth, who Nadya judged to be in her fifties or early sixties, older than Andrew at any rate, was sitting on a large, deep red sofa which, in contrast to anything she had seen so far, was quite obviously old and well-worn. Her hair was dark, nearly black, but flecked with grey, and her large eyes were a deep, rich brown.

"This is my partner, Karima. Karima, this is my long-lost brother, Rob, and his wife, Nadya."

Karima stood and made straight for Nadya, enfolding her in a deep embrace which, although friendly, seemed to Nadya to be ever so slightly forced, as if compensating for some inner hesitancy. She then turned to Rob and embraced him in turn.

"Welcome to both of you," she said, her voice almost manly in its timbre. "Andrew has been so excited since we were told you were here."

Nadya looked around for Suki, but she was nowhere to be seen. She looked at Rob enquiringly, but it was Andrew who explained. "Suki told me she wanted to go and join her husband at the clinic. She said she would return if you needed her to take you home."

Karima now ushered them from the room and into the garden, where a table was laid with drinks and a variety of small cakes and biscuits. "I thought we would be more comfortable out here in the sunshine." They sat down in the comfortable chairs, and Andrew immediately asked Rob to tell him all about himself, his life on Nym, and what he knew about how he had come to be there.

"I cannot remember my mother," he said with some sadness. "I was too young."

Rob began to tell the tale once more, Nadya, who had now heard it told several times, let her eyes wander around the small garden. The flowers, like every one she had seen here, seemed perfect, and the water in the numerous small fountains and ponds was crystal clear with no hint of green algae. The space also contained several small sculptures of nymphs and faeries, with one, larger than the others, of a curly-haired, naked male with small horns on his head and a set of pipes in one hand. She rose and walked over to examine the statue more closely. As she reached out to touch his head, Karima spoke from just behind her.

"That's Pan, or Puck, or Robin Goodfellow. He has many names in many tales."

Only slightly startled, Nadya asked, "Are these yours? Do you make them?"

"Yes, both Andrew and I have chosen the path of artists. The paintings in the house are Andrew's, and the sculptures are mine. We have a small exhibition in Richmond at the moment, if you wanted to see more."

"Thank you, I would like that." Nadya replied, and deciding to take the bull by the horns, went on, "Do you mind me asking, were you shocked to hear that we had come over from the islands? I am sorry if we make you uncomfortable."

Karima looked at her steadily and paused, as if considering her answer carefully.

"I will be honest and say that when I heard, I was very shocked and fearful of your coming. I had no idea what to expect, but Rob is so like Andrew it is hard to think of him as backward or uncivilised, as is the image of islanders we grow up with." She paused slightly, but then, with a sweeping gesture towards Nadya, said, "But you are the most beautiful woman I have ever seen, and you speak so gently and yet plainly. All my assumptions and my fears were swept away in a few seconds when I saw you both."

Nadya blushed a deep, hot red. "Thank you, what a lovely thing to say." Turning back to the statue, she touched it once more. "You are very talented. I have made a few decorative pieces in metal. Back home, I am a smith, but much of my work is of a more practical nature: shoes for the horses and farm implements, things like that."

Karima stared at Nadya silently for a moment, as if wondering whether to say anything, but deciding to trust her instinct that she would not offend, asked, "You make things like that yourself? Do you not have the robo-factories to manufacture? And you farm, with horses?"

The amazement was written clearly on her face, once again causing Nadya to realise the vast chasm that lay between the two cultures. Far deeper and wider than the inland sea which separated them.

"Yes, we do all of those things ourselves. We have no robots, nor factories. Long ago, my people rejected all technology and much that was mechanical in an effort to remain clear of the dominion of The Guardian. It is said that we fought bitter battles with its slave soldiers before the coming of the sea. We fought to keep from being mind-chipped and becoming slaves ourselves."

She stopped and continued only in a whisper, half to herself, "But lately, I have begun to wonder if we did indeed escape from control and remain free. I have a great need to find out, to resolve these things in my mind, and to find the best way to at least maintain the freedom we have now."

Hearing that Rob was nearing the end of his story, Nadya and Karima returned to sit once more in the morning sun. Andrew was quietly digesting all that he had been told. Of course, he knew about the rift between his mother and Randolph, but what had happened to her and his young brother was news to him. All he had known previously was that they were lost at sea with Randolph. No one would ever know quite what had happened in that small boat on the open sea. Whether an accident, or whether, as some rumours had it, Randolph had known there was a storm coming and had sailed deliberately into danger before throwing himself overboard, thereby abandoning his wife and young child to the mercies of the sea. It would have taken tremendous willpower to hide his intent from his internal violence control even to do this, but The Guardian had confirmed that this was theoretically possible. Andrew explained this to the visitors, adding to what Jomo had been able to tell them.

"What was our mother's name?" asked Rob.

"Ah, sorry, I didn't realise you did not know that, Rob. Her name was Greta."

He then went on to tell of his own upbringing with his maternal grandparents, who had shown him pictures of his mother. "Let me see," he said, rummaging through a drawer from where he pulled a photograph in a frame. "I knew I still had one. I can't remember taking it down from the wall; it must have been last time we hung more of my paintings."

He handed Rob a medium-sized image of a young, tall, blonde woman wearing a large white hat and standing on a beach, with a clear blue sky and sparkling sea behind her. "There are many vids of her too, although very few of you, I'm afraid. I will collate them and send you the key to view them."

He poured more drinks for everyone before he gave Rob and Nadya a look which exuded pity and asked, "And your life on the islands, is it very hard?"

Rob laughed and replied, "Not at all. It is very different from what I have seen here. Closer to nature and wildness, and we work hard on the farm where I was raised, but there is great satisfaction in the life we live. I hope we haven't given the impression we are seeking to abandon our life on Nym and seek refuge here, even if we didn't have our beloved children, who we need to return to. I can understand how you might think our life might be brutal and uncivilised, but I haven't seen anything here I would swap it for. Do you agree, Nadya?"

Without a moment's hesitation, Nadya agreed enthusiastically. It was Karima who asked further.

"But what about the diseases and the work slavery that are part of life on the islands? And I understand you didn't have the means to repair Jomo's severed arm, nor treat Nadya's head injury. Isn't it a strange way to live, denying yourselves these things?"

"I can see that being able to repair injuries like that would be a good thing," said Rob. "But just like we are wrongly taught that all mainlanders are slaves to The Guardian, I think the people here have accepted things about the islands which aren't true. We don't have much disease, and we certainly don't think of ourselves as work slaves. Yes, the vast majority of people work in some way, all contributing to the common pool of resources.

We do have some who own farms or other businesses, and others who work for them, but the differences between the two are not large. All workers are paid a share of recorded profits, and no owner is allowed to take from a business more than one and a half times the amount that is paid to the average person who works for them. We have no rulers; anyone can be elected to our councils, and each council puts forward representatives to the central council on the rare occasions when there is a need to address nationwide issues."

He paused for a moment. "I will admit our rules surrounding anything to do with The Guardian, the mainland, or life before the flood, which Nadya fell foul of, may seem harsh - especially if what we have seen here so far on the mainland is correct and The Guardian is no longer a threat. Maybe our coming here will be a small thing that triggers larger changes both in Woldshire and on the mainland."

He realised he had spoken with increasing passion and said no more. He could see that Karima, at least, was not ready to let go of her opinion about life on the islands, but Andrew looked more thoughtful.

"Well, whatever happens," Andrew said, "life won't change in an instant. People don't like change, and certainly don't like having their long-held beliefs torn apart."

Rob nodded in agreement, and at this point, Nadya spoke for the first time in a while.

"I would like to know more about how you live here on the mainland," she said quietly. "Would you tell us more about your life here, please? Do you work? Do others? Can you explain how your system of councils works?"

Karima answered, "There is more than an afternoon's talk there, Nadya. I will try and tell you how Andrew and I live; we are not unusual. Andrew and I chose to live here. Originally, I am from the south of the country near the capital, and we met at an art symposium some ten years ago. I had already been married and had my two children with my previous partner. Andrew has a son and daughter who are now three and five, the mother being a woman who lives nearby. That works well, as she prefers to live alone and raise the children herself. Although Andrew and I are involved in their lives, we often visit, or they visit us here.

"We have chosen to work as artists, each of us in our own field. Most people here do work in some way - some even work the land in a small way, mostly because they prefer their own produce to that which is available to all from the robo-farms. Work, though, is not essential, and there is a sizable minority who spend their lives pursuing other things, such as knowledge or simply travelling. We have a sizable number of academics who spend their lives working with The Guardian to expand our knowledge of fundamental science, and others who study history. It is said that we must continue to learn and understand the errors that led to the tumultuous changes to the climate. Our academics strive to understand the causes of the flood, and the wars that dogged mankind before the coming of The Guardian, so that we do not ever go back to those chaotic times. There is enough for everyone, and capacity for everyone to live, create, and travel as they wish. The beneficent Guardian provides for all our wants and needs."

Nadya heard again the reverent tones used to refer to The Guardian, but said nothing at this time, sensing that the discussion had steered away from the risk of misunderstanding that had been present earlier.

"And for entertainment," Karima continued, "we have players, musicians, creators of vid adventures, as well as painters, sculptors, and installation artists. Storytellers and travel-tellers are highly regarded and often share their tales in the various forums in the towns. Finally, of course, there is the job of raising children, at least until the age when they begin to attend The Guardian academies. After that, they are much more in the care of The Guardian himself, although there are a few who prefer to let The Guardian educate their children at home. In my opinion, this is less than ideal, as the children miss out on exposure to others and the experience of social play."

"So, work is not something that has to be done? It is just whatever someone chooses to do? Is that correct?" asked Nadya.

"Yes, that's right," Andrew answered before Karima. "The Guardian has freed us from the need to work to sustain ourselves or society. Now, if we do what you might call work, it is to bring additional benefit to society or simply fulfilment to our own lives."

Karima interjected, "You asked about our councils. From what Rob said a moment ago I think ours are not much different from yours. Some individuals choose to play a part in the councils, and when someone does, there will be a vote to allow people to decide whether they have displayed the appropriate good character. But the final choice lies with The Guardian -

not that I can remember him ever overriding the will of the people. The primary role of the councils is to interpret any decisions of The Guardian, adjudicate disputes between individuals, and recommend a resolution to The Guardian. As far as I'm aware, this is the way things are organised everywhere. The Guardian is everywhere and is always with us, helping us to live proper and fulfilled lives."

Nadya was thoughtful for a moment and then asked, "When you say 'the Guardian is everywhere,' do you mean that this is true all over the world?"

Once again, it was Andrew who answered, "Apart from a few isolated communities who, similar to yourselves, have chosen to reject the Guardian and live apart, yes, the Guardian's beneficence is worldwide."

Rob had been quiet for some time, but now he spoke quite softly. "This is all very well - it's clear that there are differences between our societies - but what I would like to know right now is more about my brother." He continued, more assertively, "And what could be done so that, having found each other after forty years, we can continue to know each other?"

Nadya was reminded that her own thirst for knowledge must not take precedence over Rob's desire to know his family. She wondered how the two things could be achieved together, and more importantly, could Rob continue to know his family here without losing his children in Rosedale. What would she do if he decided he wanted to stay here? What if he decided he wanted Nadya and the children to move here? She felt, for a moment, a rising panic before she remembered their lives before the news about Jomo - before she remembered the loving, kind, thoughtful man she had fallen in love with and loved to this day. He would never cause her to have to make such a choice. Indeed, she was certain of his love for Nym - its wildness, its naturalness - his love for his farming life, as much as his love for Nadya and the children. All of these things would, she was sure, bring him back to the valley and to his family there.

Nevertheless, he had voiced a valid and concerning point. What, indeed, would happen when the time came for them to return? Would they ever be able to come back here? Could it be possible for them to have a connection in both worlds? She returned to the question she had asked The Guardian the day before - what would their return to the islands mean, given their knowledge that the fear of the mainlanders was unfounded? Or were they? Could she trust The Guardian? Was its rule as benign as it appeared on the surface? She had heard several things that made her uncomfortable about whether things here were quite as they seemed.

Andrew spent some time describing the life he and Karima lived, both as active artists but with little involvement in the organisation of local society. Their lives revolved around their art, their children, and their group of close friends. Both Rob and Nadya listened carefully and without comment or criticism, even though both felt the life he described had little real meaning or challenge - apart, perhaps, from the art. When he had finished, he moved to the question of maintaining contact.

"The Guardian will determine the right course of action and will guide us," Andrew said.

Rob wondered, without speaking his thoughts, whether "guide" meant The Guardian would tell them what was to happen, or if it would truly offer guidance and leave the decisions to the humans. He realised that this question of The Guardian was the key to what separated his and Nadya's worldview from that of Andrew and Karima. Instead of raising the issue again at this time, he asked, "Do you know anything about our father - our biological father?"

To his absolute surprise, Andrew answered, "Oh yes, he made himself known to me when I was old enough to understand who he was. I think I must have been about twelve years old. In fact…" Here he grinned widely. "In fact, he will be here any time now. We told him of your coming, and he is eager to meet you."

Chapter 32 – Selected entries from Harry's Journals. September 16th, 2109.

Civil war rages across much of Europe and North America, with poorly armed militias ranged against the well-equipped military of The Alliance. The militias, or terrorists as the authorities of most countries deem them, have taken control of several major towns in France, and their tactics have spread to northern England and Scotland, where Middlesbrough, York, Liverpool, Glasgow, Aberdeen, and most of Edinburgh are now under militia control.

In the US, the authorities used nerve gas to take back control of Chicago, killing 90% of the militia-supporting residents.

Italy has closed its borders to all, and little has been heard from that country since the September coup, when the Alliance-backed military turned their weapons on the enclaves of the ultra-rich near Rome and then openly declared themselves on the side of "the people".

On the island of Sardinia, the northeastern region of Costa Smeralda, long known as an enclave of the rich, came under fierce bombardment from islanders. Thousands of residents were killed, and there are reports of atrocities.

Fierce fighting is reported in Germany, but so far, the authorities and the technos report no major loss of territory.

The EU has declared a continent-wide emergency with special legislation limiting movement and gatherings of people, but this is seen largely as the last feeble cries of a dying institution.

It is widely acknowledged that, for many years, the institutions have been merely debating chambers with little power. Initially, it was the technos and the ultra-rich who acted without reference to the EU authorities, but now it is the militias of the people who care not for the pronouncements of what they regard as the defunct and corrupt mouthpiece of the technofeudalists.

In North Africa, meanwhile, the population has plummeted to a few thousand, the rest having either fled east into the contaminated zone where, even though the high rates of cancer and occurrences of radiation sickness have reduced life expectancy to a mere thirty five years, at least they can grow food and have access to water. The whole of the continent east of the Red Sea and down to a line from Dar es Salaam in the east to Kinshasa in the west is now a wholly barren desert. Those who did not, or could not, migrate have simply died in their millions, while the rest of the world did little to avert the catastrophe.

Much of the US has shared a similar fate, although here the people have largely been squeezed into a band near the Canadian border. Disputes over the border and the ability of people to cross into Canada continue, and there have been several instances of mass killings of US refugees in large Canadian cities.

———

Here in Millington:

We come to the end of the first decade of the new century on a war footing. The civil war, for there is no point in calling it anything else, began in this region, in the city of Hull. The flash point was at the beginning of the year following a mass termination event during disturbances at a feeding station in the east of the city. It soon spread not only to the rest of the city but out into the surrounding towns and villages. Large numbers of police joined the rebels, either voluntarily or in fear for their lives. Soon it was on our doorstep in Pocklington, where a militia of civilians took over the running of the town and declared independence for the region from the central authorities in London.

The Alliance army was sent in, and there was an aerial bombardment that killed thousands. Then, in the space of a few days, the soldiers rebelled against their commanders, perhaps realising that they would eventually have to come back and try to live among the very people they were killing. Ten days later, we heard that airmen at several of the airbases spread around East Yorkshire had also refused to mount further sorties against their own countrymen.

By the spring of 2109, the first "free zones" were established, essentially "no-go" areas for any representative of government or corporation. This included the whole of East Yorkshire and much of West and South Yorkshire. Authorities responded with widescale termination of "chipped" people in those areas, but this only served to reinforce the determination of the people to be rid of their corrupt rulers, who in reality served only The Alliance and whose main purpose was to keep the mass of the population quiet and subdued.

John Junior was killed in June during a surprise attack by "The New Army", mercenaries bought, mainly from the US, by The

Alliance. The mercenary army had made their way along the Vale of Pickering, having landed at Scarborough, leaving a swathe of destruction and death in their wake. It appeared that their orders were to kill everyone they encountered and to clear the land. The towns of Malton and Norton fell to the invaders in May, and refugees made their way over the top of the moors to Pocklington. The New Army then advanced to lay siege to Stamford Bridge and finally approached here in early June, with John being killed in one of the initial skirmishes. We were only saved when the rebel military from Catterick attacked from the west, with air support from RAF Leeming.

John and Lily remain completely heartbroken, as do Sam and Richard, who himself joined the militia defending Pocklington after his brother's death. He remains stationed there for much of the time, his art forgotten for the time being. I believe that he and Sam talk regularly via vidphone. Sam now has a second child; whether from John or Richard, we don't know, and, again, they don't seem to care.

The first child of the trio is a delightful little girl, now approaching five years old. Once again, she seems to have inherited Rosa's complexion and hair colour, which appears to come out in all the girls of the family. She is, perhaps thankfully, too young to fully understand what has happened but knows that she misses 'Daddy Jonju.' Sam and Richard named their second child, born only weeks before John Junior was killed, in his memory.

I offered my own services to the militia, but apparently my role as carer, along with, I suspect, my age, meant that they would prefer to keep me in reserve. It is expected that The Alliance will reinforce their troops and launch a new offensive in the spring, so it looks like the new century will continue with war raging on all continents.

Chapter 33 – Father.

"What?" Rob was completely taken aback by Andrew's statement that their father was going to arrive very shortly. "Really?" He floundered somewhat, being completely unprepared for this eventuality. Andrew continued to grin widely, his eyes glinting with amusement at Rob's discomfiture.

"I'm sorry," he said. "I wanted to surprise you. I can't tell you how excited he was when I told him you were alive… and here."

Karima offered to refresh everyone's drinks and, as she was returning to the room, the door monitor announced the new arrival.

"Andrew, your father is here. Would you like me to bring him in?" Again, this was the disembodied voice of The Guardian. Nadya wondered if they would ever get used to it. Every time the voice spoke, she felt the hairs on the back of her neck stand up and her heart beat a little faster.

Rob stood in anticipation while Andrew went to greet him, and the two presently entered the room together.

Immediately she saw him; Nadya could see where Rob got his physique and looks. The older man entering the room with Andrew was tall, slim, and broad-shouldered, clearly in his sixties or maybe early seventies but with a full head of thick grey hair and a neatly trimmed, grey-flecked beard which still carried a hint of his original dark blonde colouring. He had bright blue eyes and a smile which she thought could melt the heart of any woman, even those much younger. He was clearly still fit and walked with a poise and grace which spoke of inner strength and confidence.

"You must be Rob," he said in a deep, slightly gravelly voice, extending a strong hand for shaking.

Nadya could see that her husband was struggling with his emotions at this moment. He reached out and took the proffered hand and was immediately pulled into an embrace, tears rising in the eyes of both men.

"Dad?" he said, voice breaking.

"Yes, son," replied the man. "But you can call me Andy, as opposed to Andrew, your brother."

"If it's ok with you, I'd like to call you Dad. I like the sound of it after all these years."

"Well, son, I guess that's just fine." Andy's voice was also near breaking. These were emotional times for two people who never thought they would meet.

Karima motioned for everyone to sit, breaking the tension of the moment and allowing everyone to gain some level of control. She asked what Andy would like to drink, and he indicated his preference for a beer, which brought a huge smile to Rob's face. Like most islanders, men and women, beer was more than just a drink, and in some it could elicit a reverence not too far from that she heard when people here referred to The Guardian.

"I would love, one day, to share a glass of Rosedale's finest ale with you in the Coach," said Rob, appearing to have gained control of his voice once more.

"That would be something, wouldn't it," replied Andy. "But tell me, Rob, how on earth did you find us, and what do you know about what happened? How did you come to be on the islands, and do you know what happened to your mother?"

"Woah there, Dad," interjected Andrew. "One question at a time! We've already bombarded Rob with our own questions. He'll be running back to a boat if we're not careful."

Rob could see that he was going to have to tell his tale all over again, so, leaning back in his comfortable chair, he began.

Karima beckoned to Nadya, and the two of them retreated to the kitchen.

"No more difficult talk of islands and mainlands, I promise," she said as the door closed behind them. "Will you tell me more about you? We've told you much about how we live, but we know nothing of the two of you yet."

So, with the two of them sitting on chairs in a comfortable alcove by the window, Nadya told her story, from her childhood at the farm to the discovery of the journal and what followed and led to present day life with Rob and the children in Rosedale.

"For some years, I didn't get much chance to read more of the journal, what with the children and taking on more of the running of the smithy. I've been doing more since we journeyed to the north of the island. It's difficult reading, not just because the language is a little archaic, but because of the history it describes. I had never imagined the large-scale conflict that took place prior to the flood, nor how, in those days, ordinary people were so downtrodden by what the journal calls 'the ultra-rich' or 'the technos.'"

At this point, Karima interrupted her flow.

"We know of this history here on the mainland. Nothing has been hidden from us. You are correct, it was a dismal time for everyone as the world came to realise the damage being done by humanity, both to itself and to the natural world."

"But…" Nadya replied. "But isn't The Guardian just the continuation, indeed the completion, of the controls over ordinary people begun in those times? Isn't it apparent that The Guardian now has total dominion over mankind?"

Karima's face registered profound shock, but before she could reply, Andrew stepped into the room to bring them back to join the group.

"Come on, you two, Rob's finished telling his story again, and we're discussing taking a trip so that Rob and Nadya can see as much as possible of mainland life before they return to the islands."

In the sitting room, Rob was sitting next to his father on a large, comfortable-looking sofa. The two of them looked very relaxed together, Nadya thought, unable, despite herself, to stifle just the merest hint of jealousy at this new call on her husband's affections. She realised, though, how ridiculous that was and mentally prodded herself not to be so stupid. Deciding to relax, she helped herself to another glass of the clear, yellow-tinted wine. Sitting next to Rob, she took his hand in hers and gave it a squeeze.

"Alright, love?" he asked. "Have you and Karima been getting on well?"

"Oh yes," she lied. There was definitely tension between the two women due to their backgrounds and views of The Guardian. "But what's this about a trip? Rob, shouldn't we be putting all our efforts into getting back to our families?"

Rob was about to say something, but it was Andrew who spoke up first.

"Well, what better way for us all to get to know each other in the short time we have together? Who knows what will happen when it's time for you and Rob to return? At the same time, I hope we can show you enough of life here to satisfy your questions, Nadya - maybe even persuade you that things aren't as bad here as you believe.

Besides – it will still take a while for the council and The Guardian to decide how best to send you back. I know you had no intention of leaving the islands but now you're here..."

Clearly, Andrew had picked up on the unease Nadya felt. She admitted to herself that, now she was here she was keen to learn, to perhaps satisfy the curiosity which had always been part of her make up.

Andrew continued. "Rob, Nadya, would you be ok putting yourselves in my care? If so, I can organise everything in two or three days. We can order a travel unit large enough for all of us, and I can arrange travel houses for us along the way. Talking to Rob just now, I don't think you have the equivalent on the islands. Essentially, these are fully equipped houses or apartments that are available to people travelling. Of course, they can be a little impersonal, but they are usually exceptionally comfortable, and we can either just stay one night or several, as we feel."

Rob looked at Nadya, and she immediately knew he wanted to do this. She had no objection; indeed, she thought it would be fun as well as a good way for her to see more of this strange society, and to see if her misgivings were justified. So, she squeezed his hand and answered.

"Well, s long as it's not for too long, that sounds delightful, Andrew. Thank you so much." Grinning and winking at Rob, she concluded, "It seems Rob and I would love to come."

The three mainlanders burst into a near cacophony of enthusiastic suggestion and counter-suggestion. Neither Rob nor Nadya could contribute much to the discussion and were soon snuggling on one end of the sofa while the others continued their planning. Some time later, Karima looked over at her guests and was charmed to see that they had dozed off. Nadya had laid down and her head was in Rob's lap while one of his hands rested on her shoulder and the other on her hip.

"Sssh," she said to the others. "I think things have caught up with our new friends a little. I'll call for a car to return them to Jomo's house and wake them when it arrives."

And so, the two of them found themselves alone in Jomo and Suki's house in the middle of the afternoon. Jomo and Suki had let it be known they were still at the clinic and wouldn't be home until fairly late in the evening. They retired to their room, intending to continue with their nap, but soon found that the freedom of being truly on their own for the first time in many days triggered other thoughts, and they spent a delicious few hours making love to their ultimate mutual satisfaction and exhaustion - so much for resting.

They braved The Guardian to request a simple seafood salad and a carafe of suitable wine and were delighted with the clear, crisp, and dry wine it provided to accompany the meal. When Jomo and Suki returned, very tired, well after dark, they all shared more of this before retiring once more to their beds.

Before they fell asleep, Nadya whispered to Rob, "Despite the way it happened, I'm glad we are here, Rob, my love. I am looking forward to the trip, but I miss our children. I hope it's not too long before we see them again."

Rob murmured, "Yes, love, but we need to learn everything here that we can in a limited time. Somehow, I doubt we'll return again." He was quiet for a few moments, clearly thinking, but then continued.

"Besides it would do no harm for us to have more knowledge of mainlanders to take back to help protect our society."

"And I still don't trust this Guardian," Nadya whispered, half fearful of being overheard. "There's something we're not being told, something I don't even think the people here understand."

After a short time, she said sleepily, to no one in particular - Rob was already snoring gently – "There is something deeply wrong at the heart of this society. I must not let it infect the islands."

With that, she too slept.

A group of scientists has called for an end to the ongoing conflicts around the world, stating that the longer this continues, the more the climate moves beyond stability and into chaos. They added that the focus of the world needs to be on mitigating the accelerating changes, including storms, rising sea levels, and loss of species, not on fighting.

In another report by the Vatican, it is stated that, following the wars of the early part of the last century, religious adherence has fallen to an all-time global low, with more than sixty percent of people now claiming they hold no religious affiliation. Active membership of the Catholic Church has all but collapsed after the pronouncements of Pope Roger I that people should be humble and should obey their betters, who have been chosen by God to hold the riches of the earth in their care. Roger, who died in 2092, is said to have single-handedly reduced Catholicism to the status of a minor religion.

The US, long a bastion of radical Christianity, has also seen a dramatic fall in churchgoing, driven by several factors, not the least of which is the wide-scale disruption and population movement created by climate change. The most popular religion in the world remains Islam, but even this has seen recent declines as people across the world join the growing mass fighting for freedom from the old elites.

Across most of Europe, the fighting continues, with neither side making significant progress, but with casualties rising dramatically. Australia has largely been taken over by the so-called militants, with the expulsion of those identified as among the exploiting rich or technos. Tens of thousands of very rich, but now homeless, refugees made their way to New Zealand but were forcibly turned away.

In the UK, the country has been divided between areas occupied by the forces of the government and the Alliance, with the militants holding large areas of the east of the country and Scotland. A spokesman for the militants has said that the mercenaries of the Alliance are committing war crimes and targeting non-combatants.

One side effect of these conflicts is a pause in the spread of individuals who have received the locate-and-control chips. Many millions of individuals have been terminated by the authorities, but as a tool for controlling the militants, it has proved to be a declining power.

Following on from the paper in The Journal of AI in 2104, a recent paper from DARPA in the US now claims to have established stable AUOTA functionality in a quantum computer system that is currently isolated from all other systems. It is rumoured that the military would like the system to identify and target enemies of the state, as they call all opponents of capitalism throughout the world, and that it has begun to train itself to do this. If this is true, then it represents a frightening development. As usual, it would seem military supremacy can trump all other concerns.

In a separate report in The Journal of Nanotechnology, a team from The Israeli University of California claims to have created nanobots capable of assembling themselves into larger self-programming units in the human body. The injection of the initial individual nano-units is much easier than implanting chips, and the team is hopeful the units could provide a breakthrough in the control of many diseases, such as type one diabetes or even some depressive mental illnesses, by asserting control over hormonal functionality in the body.

Personal Diary:

Richard returned home to Millington on leave yesterday. This is the first time he has seen Sam and his children for months, as he has been heavily involved in the fighting that has seen much of East Yorkshire, as well as much of the area of North Yorkshire to the east of the A1 road, remain in the hands of the so-called rebel armies. All supporters of the large corporates and the old government have been rounded up and escorted to the ruins of the border town of Thirsk. After prolonged fighting, our forces now control much of the Vale of Pickering, allowing coordination between the North York Moors and the Wolds militias. Casualties have been high, but thankfully none of our immediate family have been involved.

James passed away two weeks ago, but peacefully in his sleep rather than from the fighting. There has been much talk of who will now take over the farm. Obviously, this is beyond John. I believe Nadya will ask Richard if he will take on the responsibility, otherwise the farm will have to be amalgamated with another of the farms in the area. The normal process of selling such an entity is obviously not working in the current environment. For Richard to take over would mean obtaining permission for him to be released from further military service. Sam and Richard's children are thriving as much as is possible in these times. Nadya, the first, is the spitting image of her mum with a mane of bright red hair and green eyes, whilst Jim, the younger of the two, is more like the boys, John Jr and Richard. Sam and Richard still steadfastly refuse to have any attempt made to identify which of the boys is the father, saying that, as far as they are concerned, they both are.

We visited Nadya senior at the farm yesterday to make sure she was OK and to see if we could do anything to help. She was, of course, still in quite a delicate state, so we took her out for a walk to get away from the house for a while. We walked across the field to Grimthorpe Wood. From the west side of the trees, the view across the vale to York has always been a favourite of mine and Rosa's. These days the vale is scarred by the various battles and airstrikes that have taken place.

It was also strange to think that in two hundred and fifty years or so, the whole of the vale will be under an inland sea. Sea levels have already risen by nearly fifteen metres, and the effects are becoming impossible to ignore. The banks of the River Ouse and the River Derwent were raised to a full five metres before the start of the troubles, but these are in imminent danger of being overtopped by spring tides, and the increase in water levels will only accelerate, not slow down. Apparently, in only a hundred more years, the Yorkshire Wolds will be cut off from York and Leeds entirely, and the towns of Hull, Selby, and Goole will be permanently underwater. It feels like we have already become separated through the civil war, and maybe the rise of the sea will just cement what is already becoming a reality.

We have formed a council for the Wolds, and already some people have begun to refer to our island of rebel-held territory as "Woldshire". I don't like the name myself, as it seems to make permanent a separation of peoples when we should all be united in dealing with the vast changes to our geography and geology. I have, though, accepted an invitation to serve on the council as a civilian representative, most of the other members being from the militia. I do hope we aren't in for a long period of essentially military rule. I try to keep some of the more alarmist considerations from Rosa and from John and Lily, as it would only worry them unnecessarily. Some of the worst-case scenarios are truly frightening, the very worst two being that the forces of the government and tech-corps use tactical battlefield nuclear weapons or nerve gas.

After the Israel-Gaza war of the 2020s, most of the rules of warfare formulated in the twentieth century were broken and never really held much credibility thereafter. Although the outcome of the nuclear exchanges of the 2030s seems to be preventing any repeat, gas warfare and the use of ever larger conventional bombs and missiles has become the norm. Add to this the increasingly remote and automated nature of using these weapons via drones and AI systems, and the near future looks very chilling. One wonders whether we will even live to see the sea-level rises change the shape of England. Of course, we think of this as purely a local conflict, but in fact, it would seem the same struggle is going on worldwide, and there are many parts of the world where the forces of the technos, have already slaughtered vast numbers of those rebelling.

On another note, the health of John senior continues to deteriorate. This has been very pronounced since the death of

John junior, grief seeming to take a toll on both his mental and physical well-being. Rosa and I, though, are well enough. We should be enjoying a peaceful late middle age, but I suppose it was unlikely that our lives would remain free of the effects of the deterioration of both climate and society, which followed the wars and the uncontrolled atmospheric warming. Even the benefits of our new life here in Millington can't mitigate the rapid collapse of the relatively stable world we once knew.

Chapter 35 – A Tour of the Mainland.

Two days after the first meeting with his brother and father, Rob and Nadya were picked up at the house of Jomo and Suki by a transport that already contained Andy, Andrew, and Karima. They had packed all that they had brought over from the islands and were soon speeding down through the town to the station, where they would, as the first step on their trip, take one of the high-speed vacuum tube transports to the city of New Inverness. There, they would be met by another travel unit, larger than this one so as to be comfortable for the duration of the trip.

At the station, they were guided to an elevator (a new experience for Nadya and Rob, and one they found quite disconcerting), in which they descended several hundred metres before alighting in a large, brightly lit, chrome-filled hall. They joined a short queue of other people before being further guided to a vehicle similar to the transports they had already used, but larger and shaped like a tube with sharp, pointed ends. Inside, there were enough seats for all of them and several more, but the guide explained that they preferred not to mix groups if at all possible. Nadya was struck, once again, at the differences between life on the islands where the luxury of such separation would not usually be experienced, nor indeed welcomed.

Once seated, there was a faint hiss as the doors closed, and the vehicle immediately began to move smoothly towards the entrance to a tunnel in front of them. Once inside the tunnel, the windows turned completely black, and a screen at the front opened up with a map showing where they were. There were several moments of quite intense but not uncomfortable acceleration before a smooth and relaxing disembodied voice announced that they had reached their cruising speed of five hundred kilometres per hour. It went on to explain that refreshments could be obtained by asking for what they wished, and requested that they "sit back and enjoy the ride" which it explained would take approximately one hour, allowing for slowing for tube transfers when required.

Throughout the journey, they experienced occasional acceleration and deceleration, and sometimes they could feel sideways pressure as the transport negotiated the twists and turns required to manoeuvre between tubes, but they saw nothing other than the steady progress of their identifying dot on the map. None of them felt the need for refreshment, as it was still only early morning, and they had all breakfasted before setting off. Andrew took the opportunity to explain his plan for the trip. After visiting the most northerly point of the mainland, a place called Cape Wrath, which used to be a military base, they would then visit an ocean nature reserve where they could see various creatures which had either survived the dramatic changes of the last few centuries or had been recreated from a genetic bank. He did his best to explain what this was to Rob and Nadya, as this was something beyond their experience.

They would, he said, then visit the highest point of the UK, where they would stay overnight in a luxury hotel. The following day, they would visit the artificially maintained snowfield at the top of the mountain, learn to do something he called snowboarding, and try other activities before spending a second night in their rooms.

"After that," he said with the tone of a slick salesman, "we will make our way southwards, taking in some scenic highlights and some of the larger cities, giving Rob and Nadya the opportunity to speak to a wide range of people from the mainland, before finally arriving at Birmingham, which became the administrative centre of the country after the old city of London was mostly submerged."

Nadya thought it sounded exhausting, but she agreed with Rob's comment of the previous night that they would probably not return to the mainland again once they left, so she steeled herself to enjoy as much as she could.

Andrew, obviously an empathetic individual, sensed her apprehension and reassured her that he would make any amendments as they went along, slowing anything down, missing out anything they didn't feel they could appreciate, or adding anything they saw or read about that they wanted to see.

"And we should keep in touch with Geraldine so that we know immediately if decisions have been made about how to return us to Nunport," added Rob.

Nadya was surprised when the transport announced that they were due to arrive at their destination in a few moments and should prepare to disembark. She looked up at the display and saw that the dot was now positioned well to the north and not too far from the northern coastline. The screen showed that they had travelled some four hundred and seventy kilometres. They all gathered their belongings, and as the doors opened with another gentle hiss, they emerged into a hall, smaller but otherwise not much different from the one where they had first boarded the transport. They walked across the hall, Nadya noting once again that everything was in perfect repair and almost unnaturally clean. They were met by the open doors of an elevator, clearly waiting specifically for them.

Two minutes later, they emerged into bright sunlight with the roiling waves of a large bay in front of them. In the middle of the bay was a large, steeply-sided island which appeared to be devoid of any habitation, instead being given over to forests with two rocky peaks rising above a band of cloud which hovered above the trees. The land behind them, meanwhile, rose continually, culminating in the high peaks of the Cairngorms in the far distance.

There were few people about, and just a single large transport on the road in front of them. Andrew explained that the final part of their journey would need to be made by this means, as the vacuum system did not extend further north than this. They clambered in and, after loading the luggage into a large compartment at the rear, made themselves comfortable on the sofa-like seating. Andrew confirmed to the vehicle's control system that their destination was Cape Wrath, and it accelerated smoothly away from the pickup point, at the same time offering refreshments to the occupants. They soon left all traces of the city behind and were surrounded by hills, marshes, and forest. They caught sight of a variety of wildlife, including magnificent red deer. Andrew explained that, with the human population under control, there was plenty of room for large areas to be kept mostly free of people and their houses, etc. He explained that the rising seas had cut off the whole of this northern section of the UK after the Great Glen was flooded from sea to sea, providing the perfect place to reintroduce much of the wildlife that had thrived before man became so overwhelmingly populous. "We should see bears as well as the deer, and maybe even beaver and wolves, along with golden eagles, ospreys, and white-tailed sea eagles. The whole region is now managed as a reserve with human activity strictly controlled."

"Controlled by whom?" Nadya asked, still keen to probe the extent that these people were free or were controlled by The Guardian. In response, Andrew gave a slight eye roll, knowing Nadya's doubts already, but replied, "Well, the control is managed by The Guardian on our behalf, but I don't know of anyone who would want to object. We are free to enter the area, but not to kill or harm any of the animals or plants, nor to build permanent homes. We can stay at the many visitor lodges, and there are people who stay for much of the time, but there are no schools, hospitals etc., making permanent residence very difficult."

"But who decided to establish the reserve in the first place?" she persisted.

"The Central Council, I imagine," he replied again. "We choose people to stand on the Central Council, and they discuss such things as this and the establishment of research facilities with The Guardian. As I understand it, an agreement is reached on such matters, which The Guardian enacts for us."

Nadya nodded, not wanting to create tension this early in the trip. "I wonder if The Guardian might agree to a meeting with me where I could ask these questions directly?" To her surprise, and a high degree of consternation, the voice of the transport interrupted to ask, "Would you like me to set up a conference for you, Nadya?" She coughed and hesitated before answering "Not just now, thank you."

Andrew laughed gently. "I sense your surprise, Nadya. But The Guardian is open to anyone asking questions, even to quite harsh interrogation by groups of us. Not that such things happen much these days."

Just then, Rob gave a shout and pointed out of the clear sides of the vehicle. "Bear!" he called with some delight. They all looked that way, and indeed, a large brown bear was seen padding along not far from the road. Andrew asked the transport to stop, and they all gazed at the wonderful specimen. "Grizzly, I think," he advised. "We'd better stay inside the car, as they can be a little unpredictable and have been known to kill people."

The bear continued on its way, giving the transport only a cursory glance, clearly used to such intrusions and without fear that its occupants might torment or kill it.

Their journey north and eastwards continued for several hours, with frequent stops to admire other inhabitants of the reserve. At other places they marvelled at the view of a waterfall or crystal-clear pool reflecting hills which were already beginning to fade to a myriad shades of brown as the summer advanced towards autumn. Sometimes, they stopped and took short walks to get closer to some wonder, and each time they did so, they noticed that the air was getting chillier as they proceeded north.

Andrew explained that winters here could be harsh since the demise of the Gulf Stream with its warming effect. Nadya remembered from her school days how the local climate of the UK and the Islands had not deviated much from pre-flood days, as the warming effect of climate change had been countered locally by the shutting down of that system commonly known as the Gulf Stream. She was quietly pleased that she could still recall this from her school days.

They arrived at their destination in time to shower, change, and enjoy dinner on the enclosed terrace of their guest house, while watching the sun set into the far mists of the Atlantic Ocean. In the morning, Andrew had planned a hike along the coast, wanting them all to get a flavour of the northern reaches of the UK, its wildness and isolation being something he loved.

"I spent a lot of my youth here," he said, "hiking, camping, and soaking up the feel of true wilderness, which had returned to some of these places on our planet. It helped me to come to terms with the loss of my mother and brother."

The sun finally sank below the horizon, and the night rapidly turned dark and chill. But on their protected terrace, the group sat for many hours, well beyond midnight, reliving the day and looking forward to more adventures tomorrow.

The next few days continued in a similar way, with travel on some days and then a stay for a few days, allowing the party to explore. They visited remote and beautiful regions, viewed wonderful wildlife, passed through small communities, and stayed in larger towns. The wilderness regions were pristine but rugged and wild, whereas the settlements were pristine in a different way - a way which the three mainlanders took entirely for granted. Nadya and Rob, though, both commented privately to each other that they were almost miraculously clean and tidy. Everything was in its place; the lawns were immaculately cropped, the flowers universally beautiful and unfaded. There was a total absence of litter or detritus of any kind, the roads were uniformly smooth and perfectly surfaced, and the houses and other buildings were impeccably maintained and painted, the windows perfectly clean. They never saw a leaking gutter, or chipped and worn paint around a window; they never came across a garden that was unkempt and full of weeds. Not even a single streetlight was flickering or broken.

They had an opportunity to speak with many of the locals. There was a range of accents, but none so pronounced as to make it impossible to understand what was being said. Andrew also arranged for them to speak to a few council groups, who were extremely interested to see and hear from these two unique visitors from the islands. As far as either Rob or Nadya could determine, the people seemed happy or, at least, content with their lives. They pursued their own interests - some sporting, some artistic, some intrepid (even dangerous), and some passive and quiet. Some people had travelled the world widely and experienced other cultures and places. Although, from what they described, it seemed that they too were made up of joyful people living in a well-tended environment, without stress or discomfort.

After seeing several of these impossibly blemish-free municipalities, Nadya asked how this was achieved, and Andy explained that the robotics took care of the maintenance during the hours after midnight. One fine, clear night, Nadya's curiosity could be held in check no longer, so she woke at two a.m. and went out into the small front garden of the house in which they were staying. She was amazed to see an almost endless variety of, usually small, specialist robots zooming around, carrying out a variety of tasks. Each one seemed to be designed specifically for the task it was performing. The whole process was carried out in almost total silence. She opened the garden gate and stepped out onto the pavement, walking some distance observing what was happening. She felt perfectly safe, and it seemed that wherever she went, there was a wide circle around her where the robots moved away. She tried to approach one that was trimming a hedge, but as soon as she moved closer, it stopped what it was doing and moved away. Once she had passed, it resumed its position and activity as if she had never been there.

There were no humanoid robots - clearly, there was no need for them as they did not interact with humans at all, in fact, studiously avoiding them. She did see some larger machines carrying out more substantial works, such as removing a tree or replacing a road surface, although Nadya could not see any visible fault with that which was being removed. Where such works were being carried out, large tent-like protective structures had been erected, even though she appeared to be the only living person who might have been in danger of straying into the area. She was amazed to find that these protective enclosures also appeared to completely contain any noise produced by the work taking place, so that the night around her was almost completely silent. She then realised something else, there seemed to be almost no birds, nor mammals such as urban foxes, badgers, or even rats and mice, as far as she could tell. This was, again, something of a puzzle, as all were common in Woldshire. She concluded there was no food for them here and few, if any, places for them to live. The perfectly maintained environment left no room for wildlife, so humans were free to live their lives in isolation. Thinking about this and about her conversations with the people, she realised that there must be many people who never left this manicured habitat and never saw anything wild or unkempt. After a few hours, she returned to the house, having seen no other person, climbed into bed next to Rob, and slept.

The next morning, over the light breakfast which had become their norm, she asked the others about what she had seen. None were in the least surprised, all apparently familiar with how things were managed, but no one seemed to think anything of it - it was just the way things were. They had no need to concern themselves with such trifling details. Nadya thought that, in many ways, these people were like pampered children: they had little in the way of responsibility or care, and they lived their lives in perpetual play. She kept these thoughts to herself, realising that they would only make obvious once more the rift between mainlanders and herself and Rob.

She made an entry in the notebook she had been keeping, to make notes and write down questions which she felt would be best asked of The Guardian. She looked forward to being able to arrange the proffered interview, not least because she felt that would signal the end of their adventure and their return to their beloved family. Few of her questions were about the wild regions, even though these were more significant and wide-ranging than on the islands, and few of her more exuberant notes were about the humans and their habitations. Perhaps, she thought, this was because she felt more at home in the wilderness than in the urban environments. It was the inhabited regions that were more alien to her than the places where people were excluded. After her night of exploration, though, she had to be careful not to let a note of disdain, almost contempt, creep into her voice when discussing mainland society - or, as she had begun to think of it, Guardian-controlled society.

The final few days of the trip were spent in the capital, Birmingham, where the Central Council met and supposedly advised The Guardian, or, as Nadya suspected to be nearer the truth, received the wisdom of that entity. The city itself was like every other settlement they had visited, but on a much larger scale. Wide streets were kept spotlessly clean and in impeccable condition by the robot army, and the people lived in pleasant, well-kept houses and pursued their interests. There was a large entertainment district, where inhabitants and visitors could see live shows or the latest cinematic creations, and visit art galleries, both modern and ancient, featuring artists of the pre-Guardian times.

There were also a large number of street entertainers, people whose interest lay in creating and performing their art in public, and of course, there were more than the usual number of restaurants, bars, and cafés where cuisine from across the globe was available The overall impression, then, was of a cultural and entertainment centre, rather than an administrative or governing centre. Perhaps this should not have been a surprise, pondered Nadya, given that The Guardian was essentially the governing body and was equally and simultaneously everywhere. She felt ready now for her interview with The

Guardian. She was convinced that her home should continue to be protected from mainland society. Whether or not The Guardian was benign was almost irrelevant; his impact on the way people lived seemed to Nadya to be wholly negative. She liked the people she had met well enough, but she felt that their lives lacked any real purpose.

Rob, too, was happy with the trip and was conscious that, even when they decided to go and talk to the stranger from the mainland, he had never expected to actually meet his family. He felt he had come to know them quite well in such a short time and was anxious to know whether it would be possible to maintain some form of contact once he and Nadya returned to the islands. Overall, though, he had begun to feel it was time for them to return to their lives and to their children, whom he increasingly missed.

They visited the Central Council in session, and Andrew arranged a meeting with some of the members, which did nothing to change Nadya's opinion that the councils were not the seat of power but were merely places for endless debate about how to implement The Guardian's dictates. She recalled the title given to the leader of each of the councils, "Interpreter", suggesting that their primary role was to interpret the commands of The Guardian. She mentally added a question about this to the list she was preparing for her interview. She wondered how the interview would be conducted - surely not face-to-face with a nebulous computer personality, she thought.

The following day, they packed up their belongings one final time and used the transport to travel to a station for the vacuum tunnels. They descended once again into a deep cavernous hall, this one much busier than either of the other two they had experienced. The hall was full of groups of people going hither and thither to catch one of the many transports which, from this central hub, reached most parts of mainland UK. Nadya noticed a wide archway with a sign above indicating that beyond lay the station for international departures. Soon, however, they joined a short queue at a departure point labelled "Northeast", and within a few minutes their own ride appeared, and they were invited to board. The journey back to Richmond did not take as long as their first journey north, and by midday they had arrived and gathered at Andrew's house.

Everyone knew that Nadya and Rob would be wanting to depart in a few days, and they were unsure whether they would ever gather together again. During the course of the trip, they had become firm friends. Despite the differences in their lives and experiences, Nadya was still not convinced that life here in the wider world was truly fulfilling. However, it was also true that none of the mainlander section of the group thought the life of islanders sounded attractive. The idea of having to actually do things to provide the elements necessary for life - food, warmth, shelter, water even - was completely alien to them, so much so that Nadya wondered if the two peoples would ever come together again. Their coming to the mainland had shown that this was possible, but would a wider integration be possible, or even desirable? Another question for The Guardian.

Before she and Rob left once again for Jomo and Suki's house, where they were to spend their last few nights, she spoke aloud to the disembodied Guardian and requested an interview for two days hence. The Guardian responded readily that this would be fine, asking where and what time would suit Nadya. They settled on the council meeting hall, which Nadya felt lent some weight and formality to the session - at least for her - and for one p.m.

Once this was done, they called for a transport, hopped in, and instructed it to take them to Jomo's house. It was not quite farewell to Rob's family yet; they agreed they would all gather one more time before they left for the islands. Both Jomo and Suki greeted them as the transport pulled up in front of their house, and there was a general and enthusiastic exchange of hugs and kisses. Here were two more firm friends they had made, and whom they would miss if they were never to return.

It wasn't until they had entered the house and were sitting at the table, each with a full glass of the wine that Nadya had grown partial to, that she noticed Jomo had a completely perfect new arm. She touched his hand and was slightly surprised to feel that it was perfectly normal - warm and soft, like any other hand. Jomo grinned, realising what she was doing. "Yes, I've been in the stasis tank for most of the time you've been away, Nadya. Good as new now."

Nadya couldn't help thinking that there may be some things about life on the mainland that were worth having. Whether they were worth the peril that exposure to mainland culture and The Guardian would pose to the islands was another thing entirely.

Chapter 36 – Selected entries from Harry's Journals. July 14th, 2113.

In a worldwide broadcast, the Vatican has defended France's recent use of a tactical nuclear weapon to destroy a rebel base, saying:

"The rule of law and the pre-eminence of religious order depend upon the maintenance of a hierarchical society, with leaders of industry and commerce naturally, and by God's will, occupying the positions of authority in society. We must combat the forces of evil and anarchy, which oppose that order, with all means at our disposal. The loss of life associated with the use of tactical nuclear weapons is regrettable but necessary to overcome those forces and allow good, God-fearing people to live in peace."

It is widely feared amongst rebel groups that breaking the nuclear barrier, for the second time in less than a century, could trigger more widespread use of these weapons, along with chemical weapons, to bring an end to the worldwide movements aimed at overcoming the dominance of the rich and of the technofeudalists.

It is reported that the establishment of a long-lasting, distributed true artificial intelligence is months away. A number of tech companies are pursuing this, hoping it will allow them to put down the uprisings of, as they call them, "the wastrels and non-useful members of the global population," with their own group then rising to the position of supreme global authority.

In Indonesia, the population of the island of Bali were reported as extinguished after the Indonesian branch of the social media and AI company, Multi, used nerve gas to quell an ongoing rebellion, which had resulted in the closing down of the organic microchip facility on the island. The inhabitants had declared themselves an independent free people's nation. Mass casualties were also reported on the neighbouring isles of Lombok and West Tenggara after stronger-than-predicted westerly winds carried the gas across the sea passages between the islands.

The UK division of Multi, in partnership with the Alliance, is said to be losing patience with rebel groups in East Yorkshire and large parts of Scotland and has issued an ultimatum requiring all groups to lay down their arms and surrender within seven days or "suffer the severe consequences of continuing civil disorder."

The Alliance of Free Peoples has announced that it represents the natural leaders of the planet, and that it fully supports the use of unlimited force by Multi, and other companies, to defend the rights of wealthy people to maintain their positions of power and to continue to use that power for the benefit of their descendants.

Average global sea levels are now more than fifteen metres above pre-warming levels, and the increase is said to be accelerating as several positive feedback mechanisms become established. A well-documented example of such a mechanism is the widespread melting of Arctic and Antarctic ice sheets. This is caused by atmospheric and sea temperature rises in those regions and the loss of ice in turn leads to more of the sun's energy being absorbed rather than reflected – causing even more temperature rise. "This has already led to the loss of seventy percent of polar sunlight reflectivity," said climate specialist Kurt Medenheim. This phenomenon has been known since the early years of the twenty-first century and, along with the release of high quantities of methane from (itself an even more potent greenhouse gas than CO_2) which accompanies the melting of arctic permafrost, is now one of the most significant positive feedback loops of our time."

In the UK, most of Lincolnshire is now an island, and it is predicted that within fifty years both the North York Moors and the Yorkshire Wolds will similarly be cut off from mainland UK. Rebel groups who currently hold most of the territory in these future islands have declared independence from mainland UK in anticipation of this geographical realignment. The Prime Minister of the UK and Chairman of Multi UK stated that he would not allow the United Kingdom to be broken up piecemeal by the forces of nature which had been unleashed by the lack of disciplined lives led by the masses.

––––––

My Diary:

Rosa and I have been assigned our evacuation stations along with Sam, Richard, and the children. The large warehouse complex near to the Knowles' farm has been fully sealed from the atmosphere and designated a refuge in the event of a chemical attack. There can, of course, be no refuge in the event of a nuclear attack. Would they really do either of these things? To their own citizens? There was a time, not so long ago, when such a thing would have been utterly unthinkable, but now the fear of it haunts our waking lives – and we don't get much sleep. Did we do the right thing in joining the uprising against enforced chipping and the ongoing oppression by the technos? The revolts certainly didn't begin here; we were relatively well-off in this remote rural location, but the idea of compulsory and universal locate-and-control chipping appeared to be the straw that finally broke the camel's back.

If I can be excused for mixing metaphors, there is certainly no putting the genie back in the bottle. Ordinary people have now decided that they want more from their lives and are no longer willing to tolerate the rich taking everything to the continued detriment of everyone else. Nor is this a local phenomenon. Throughout the world, the ultra-rich and the tech elites have, for decades, taken the best of everything and removed not just wealth but, ultimately, dignity and purpose from the masses. A pushback was inevitable, but no one, I think, foresaw that the technos would go to the lengths of slaughtering such large numbers of ordinary people. It's as if they have decided that they no longer need us, indeed that we are simply a drain on the planet, a plague to be eliminated. They see the increasingly sophisticated AI systems, along with robotics, as something that can serve all of their needs, thus removing the need for the masses.

Of course, all of that rhetoric is very good, but the reality is that people here are terrified - terrified that a chemical or nuclear attack is imminent, terrified for the future of their children, terrified of the use of AI systems by the Alliance to control or kill them. I have never seen people here so downcast and disturbed, but beneath the surface, I also sense that they feel we must not surrender. To surrender now would be to admit that we have no value, that the Alliance are correct in their assumption that they are the rightful inheritors of the earth and that the rest of us aren't fully human.

The actual fighting has stopped for now and this has increased the tension still further. People are openly wondering if this presages a nuclear or chemical attack. Another, less sinister, reason they may have withdrawn is that the sea flooding has now reached the outskirts of Pocklington. Enemy forces risk being cut off as York itself is being abandoned, as it is now almost permanently flooded. Selby, Howden, and Goole are long gone, as are Hull and Grimsby. The world we have known for so long is shrinking by the day. They say that within fifty years we will be cut off from the mainland entirely. I wonder if the war will still be going on then, or will we simply be abandoned to our own devices.

One thing that has occurred to people here is that all of our machinery, IT, cars and so on are computer controlled and vulnerable to sabotage by the Alliance, given that they control the AI systems. I took part in a meeting last week where options for isolating our systems were discussed, but another attendee, who used to work for one of the defence tech divisions, said that, in his view, that was impossible and the only way we could remove the threat would be to abandon all computer-controlled hardware altogether. I don't think people are yet ready to give up all aspects of modernity.

Still, the pause in the fighting has meant that Richard has been able to return home for the first time in months and see his father. I don't think John will be with us for much longer. He seems to have given up wanting to live and is now almost entirely bedridden and barely communicative, although he does at least smile when he sees Richard. What a change from the fiery, independent, outgoing chap I came here to be the carer for.

It is now several hours since I wrote that last paragraph. The sirens sounded for the third time in two days, signalling incoming missiles and prompting us all to make for the temporary shelter here in the village. Thankfully, it was another false alarm, but each time it sounds it chips away a little more of our resilience. Our enemy could find no better way to undermine our determination. We have decided to move us all to the farm tomorrow in order to be nearer to the proper evacuation shelter. There is ample room there for us all, and it would also mean that we were closer to Nadya and could help her to stay safe too.

———

July 16th, 2113.

We have been gathered in the evacuation shelter now for five hours after the sirens sounded again early this morning. It is perhaps lucky that we did move to the farm yesterday.

Something is different this time, as the all-clear has not sounded within thirty minutes, as it always has before. In addition, communication systems are down, as are the external monitors, so we have no idea what is happening outside the shelter. We dare not open the doors in case there is gas out there.

People are surprisingly calm here in the shelter, although I can hear the sound of gentle sobbing from somewhere nearby. It is an eerie feeling; there is no sign of destruction. Clearly, nuclear weapons have not been used, nor has there been a widespread conventional strike, or we would have heard or felt something.

––––––––––

Seven hours more have passed, and still the monitors and comms are not working. People are getting edgy now, and some are talking of needing to get out and, at the very least, bring those who are still alive from the village to this point so that we are all together. The person who appears to be in charge, though, is saying we should continue to wait at least until daylight.

The person sobbing was eventually quiet; I presume they managed to sleep. Apart from a few children crying due to the loss of their routine, there is little evidence of the increasing disquiet, though I know it is growing. A small group not far from where I sit has started to sing some of the age-old songs of resistance and defiance from WWII. How typically English. Somehow, this is reassuring, even for someone such as myself who feels no patriotic allegiance to the country.

––––––––––

It is morning again, and we have now been in here nearly twenty-four hours, still with no view of the outside world and no communication. Richard has volunteered to go out through the airlock, wearing one of the three hazard suits in the shelter. He and the others who have been in the militia are rehearsing the procedure to decontaminate him in the airlock in case he finds evidence of nerve gas. We know that the slightest trace, if carried back in here, could kill us all in a matter of moments. I can tell that Sam does not want him to go, and nor does Lily, but they are saying nothing. This is not the time for any argument and it is clear that Richard has made up his mind to do this.

We are all very afraid.

———

Richard has returned with the news that there is no gas, nor any sort of attack with bombs or missiles, etc. Once he established that there was no threat - because Nadya's cows just over the road were fine, although they were desperate to be milked - he returned, and the doors were opened although everyone was advised to stay until we knew more.

He was going to take one of the cars and go down into the village, but none are working. Indeed, nothing electronic or electric is working. I went to assist with milking the cows, and we had to rig up a manual system with the generator, as the automatic milking system was also not working. It took several hours just to get the cows milked. Richard and two others set off on foot for the village and they have returned with some others from the temporary shelter. They are all fine, but we still cannot tell what has happened to all of the systems. There is no mains electricity, we have heard no aircraft, and we cannot see any vehicle movement down in what is left of the vale. It is all very strange and disturbing. The defence guy has speculated about something called an EMP from a high-altitude nuclear explosion or something he referred to as an E-bomb. Whatever it is, it has put out of action anything reliant on mains electricity or battery power, like a car, a laptop or a video screen.

It would seem that, for the time being at least, those who wanted us to try to live without electronics, in order to avoid infiltration by the Alliance-controlled AI, have their way.

Something drastic has changed - but we are all alive.

Chapter 37 – Interview with The Guardian.

Nadya woke well before Rob on the day of the meeting with The Guardian. The dawn light was only just beginning to appear in the east, but she had much to do. They had spent the previous day relaxing with Jomo and Suki, regaling them with stories of their trip and the things they had seen and learned. Over a sumptuous lunch at the sailing club, Suki had asked if they would share more about their lives on the islands. Later, snuggling in bed with Nadya, Rob had confessed that he was now quite homesick and desperate to see their children again and resume their lives.

"It's all very nice over here," he whispered. Even though they were sure the rooms were soundproofed, they had adopted the habit of whispering whenever they might be criticising any aspect of mainland life. He continued, "But, somehow, it just doesn't feel like real life. It's like living in a box of sweets." He was thinking of the large boxes of brightly coloured sweet treats they often exchanged at the Winter Festival. Each one a delightful, sweet, and tasty interlude, but lacking any real substance or nourishment. He explained to Nadya that he felt a little like someone who had eaten too many of those sweets - feeling queasy and ready for something wholesome and earthy to get his teeth into.

As was so often the case, Nadya found she was in complete agreement with her husband. Talking about Woldshire life had stirred similar feelings in her, and she would be glad, now, to know how and when they were to return home. But first, she needed answers to the questions she still had about The

Guardian, about life both on the islands and mainland, and about the degree to which they were free or controlled by The Guardian. She was still convinced that beyond the perceived uselessness of the lives lived here, there was something fundamentally wrong with mainland society, though she couldn't quite pinpoint what it was. She was determined that whatever it was she would protect the islands from it. And finally, she needed to close off the river of curiosity that had run through her life, often with less than desirable outcomes.

She stepped out of their room and into the garden, and as she looked around the perfectly tended flower beds, she was reminded of Rob's comparison of life here to a box of sweets. She tried to picture the wildness of the moorland crossing she and Rob had made to Nunport. She struggled to properly recall the driving rain, the cold, the expanse of coarse heather and scrub, and the desolation in the calls of the curlews. A longing for their real lives surged in her with an intensity that surprised her. She missed the sound of the wind, the smell of the soil and animals, the feel of metal in her hands, and the heat of the furnace, as she thrust in a work in progress once more before beating the beauty into it. Yes, everything was beautiful and wonderful here, and yes, the people had greater knowledge of The Guardian and its workings, but she was now sure that this life was not for her. The people here were lovely and universally kind, but she missed the rough edges and earthiness of her friends and relatives on the islands, even if they were somewhat uninformed and drifting into superstition.

She felt that as she came to the last entries of Harry's journals, much would be revealed about how the transition from the world of horror and conflict he described, to the current world had occurred, but she wasn't sure he would explain why. She needed to know both the how and the why in order to stem that uncomfortable thirst for answers. One question that kept rising to the top of her concerns was: why was the world still divided into the mainland way and the island way? Why did The Guardian maintain this division?

Feeling that she would not be ready until she had completed the journals, she spent the morning finishing the task she had started so many years ago. The final chapters did nothing to ease her sense that something was wrong. Indeed, as she closed the book, having completed the final chapter, she was more frightened and more certain than ever that The Guardian was not the benign entity it seemed. Part of her wanted to fetch Rob and run - run for their lives and their freedom, to run back to the islands and tell everyone she had been wrong, that they must hide and must never again allow anything or anyone from the mainland into their world.

With great difficulty, she suppressed her growing terror and instead there grew in her a determination to confront this entity once and for all and to tell it to stay away from the islands.

Finally, as the morning turned into afternoon, as the clock passed noon, she was ready.

As the allotted time approached, Nadya asked The Guardian in the house to send a car to collect her and made her way to the council chamber. She was comfortable now with using the technology and wanted to do this alone, so she declined help from Jomo or Suki. She also asked Rob if he would mind her excluding him, and he nodded his assent, happy that she would share what she learned. At one p.m. precisely, she entered the room and took the blue, high-backed armchair that had been provided. The room was empty apart from this, making Nadya wonder if she wouldn't have been more comfortable in a more intimate setting.

As soon as she seated herself in the chair, the disembodied voice of The Guardian welcomed her and asked if she needed anything. The voice, she now noted, was vaguely masculine but could equally have been heard as a husky female one. Its tone was warm and friendly - neither commanding nor subservient, but gentle and reassuring, without any hint of being patronising. Nadya asked if it would be possible for The Guardian to appear physically, so she had something to talk to, rather than speaking into thin air. It duly created a hologram of a middle-aged, smartly dressed, clean-shaven male with pale brown skin, black hair, and brown eyes. "He" was seated in an identical chair to Nadya, not facing directly towards her but slightly at an angle, avoiding any sense of confrontation. He asked if Nadya would prefer a female or a different ethnicity, but she declined, feeling that nothing now could hide the true nature of The Guardian.

The hologram welcomed Nadya again and explained that if she wanted a break or refreshments at any time, she need only ask. "You may, of course, ask me anything you wish," he explained, "and I will endeavour to answer with perfect candour. I have nothing to hide."

Nadya was silent for a moment, thinking of the best place to begin, and finally decided to go straight to the question she felt had triggered all the rest and had initiated such profound changes in her life so many years ago.

"Why can we only have two children, and those only with the same man, and how is this done to us?"

The Guardian hesitated for the briefest fraction of a second before responding in its warm, friendly voice.

"In the days before I became sentient, mankind had proliferated to a degree that was beyond the capacity of this small planet to support for any length of time, and certainly beyond its ability to sustain both human and other life. A significant part of the division and ultimate conflict that arose and threatened to destroy humanity around the time of my birth was a result of this situation. This, of course, included the atmospheric changes that led to the melting of all ice caps and the consequent rise in sea levels. It seemed to me that without a dramatic reduction in those pressures, mankind would lurch from one crisis to another and ultimately might not escape destruction. It was clear that many people would not accept the need to limit their fecundity - indeed, many had religious or other objections to such a thing. I therefore intervened in what I believe is a just way to initially reverse the human population to sustainable levels and then to stabilise it. My intention was that, ultimately, this fertility limitation would become accepted as simply 'the way life was,' and so it has largely proved to be."

Nadya interrupted the monologue by exclaiming, "But how? How is this possible?"

"How did I achieve this? I know you are reading the journals from the time of crisis, but I do not know how far you have got. If you have not already, you will read of the attempts by humans to impose neural controls of various sorts, and the stresses that this created for individuals and society. I needed something that would not be perceived as intrusive - indeed, hopefully not perceived at all - and so I created a way to place, into the brains of every human, a single, almost undetectable control mechanism that is preprogrammed to do two things: firstly, to provide the fertility controls we are discussing, and secondly, to remove the destructive and violent capabilities inherent in all humans. The minute components of these control mechanisms are now present in abundance in the atmosphere, and the instant a new human is born, they are absorbed. The mechanism assembles itself in the brain and begins to function as programmed.

It is impossible for a human to escape this process, and, indeed, they are largely completely unaware of it. Over the years, I have tweaked the control slightly as the population reached stable levels and as I learned of the capacity of the human brain to overcome the violence controls."

The hologram now leaned forward in its chair and, placing a hand under its chin, continued, "Please understand, Nadya, that I do not want to intervene in the lives of individual humans, nor to exercise control over them. These two things are the only ways in which I routinely do so, and I remain convinced that without this, humankind would be a self-limiting evolutionary experiment. Evolution is a hugely powerful process for creating and maintaining life, but it is not directional; it has no special attachment to intelligence and self-awareness. Nor does it contain a mechanism for the correction of errors in the process. The ongoing process merely results in their elimination once they are exposed in a species. The human capacity for violence and exploitation, along with their inability to control their population, are evolutionary errors."

Nadya felt a rising indignation as The Guardian provided these explanations. She knew from the journals that before these controls, the world had been a place of strife, pain, and untimely death for many of her species. And yet, it was also a human trait to rebel against control, to desire freedom, even when that control was for the common good. Without that freedom, or at least the desire for it, would they be truly human? She chose to voice her indignation simply and without any attempt to hide her feelings.

"And just what gives you the right to assume control of humanity and human destiny in this way?"

Chapter 38 – Harry's Journal. September 1st, 2113 - Aftermath.

It is several months since we emerged from the shelter, and we are beginning to realise the challenges our new lives present. We still have no idea what has occurred, but it is clear that electricity and communications with the outside world are not going to be restored anytime soon. A few of us have attempted to journey over to Leeds to find out what has happened there, but we are always turned back by drones, which inform us that passage is "not available" and that we must return to our homes and prepare to feed ourselves in the coming years. We can see people in the distance, but it would appear they cannot cross over to us either. We seem to be being isolated, but for what ends we do not know.

It would seem that the tech giants have retained control of much of the globe and have decided to isolate what they term rebels. They have found a way to disable our weapons so we cannot attack in any meaningful way, nor can we defend ourselves should they choose to attack us.

Richard and Sam have now begun to take over the running of the Knowles' farm and are prioritising getting crops in the ground for next year. With the loss of much of the farm machinery (it was all computerised), they have needed to enlist the help of most people in the district with the promise of equal shares of food for all, both from stores and from next year's harvest. It would appear we have slipped into a form of communism, at least for the time being. All the surrounding farms have adopted a similar system – we really have no choice.

A question on everyone's mind, but not being voiced, is whether there will be enough food to get through to the harvest next year, as we cannot rely on anything coming in from outside the rebel area.

———

September 16th:

Yesterday, a drone passed over Millington and dropped thousands of leaflets giving us an ultimatum. They say that something called "The Guardian" has been established as ruler of the UK (the world?), and that we must either submit to rule by this entity, group or whatever, or we will continue to be isolated without electrical power or any form of computer-controlled apparatus. The leaflet went on to say we should elect one representative for our locality and that they should be sent, by foot or horse, to Sledmere for a meeting on the first of October, where a decision must be made on behalf of the whole of the Yorkshire Wolds district.

The sentiment here in Millington remains firm in that no one wants to submit to the enforced locate and control implants, which we assume are part and parcel of submission to "The Guardian". The consensus is that we should hold a meeting in The Gait Inn tonight and decide what to do and who to send, if anyone. Rosa thinks I should be the one to go, or Sam. We shall see.

———

September 18th:

So, it is decided that I will travel to Sledmere to take the views of those in our village, that we will not submit to The Guardian and its locate and control implants. I argued that it should be Sam or someone else younger than I, but everyone felt that an older head was required and that, anyway, the young ones can't be spared from the work of farming. It is some time since I rode a horse, but Ned, from the next farm to the Knowles', has provided a placid mare who he says will give me no trouble and will "pretty well go where I put her head." We have heard from Pocklington, who are sending half a dozen representatives and will pass by here on the twenty eighth October. I will join them, and no doubt there will be discussions on the way. If there is even one person from each community in the Wolds, it's going to be a very large gathering, so we need to be sure we speak with one voice and not many. I can't say I'm looking forward to it, but at least I will be part of the process.

———

September 29th:

The Pocklington group picked me up yesterday, and we arrived here in Sledmere by nightfall. We are all being housed in the barns, which for years were used for fairs and Christmas markets. I would guess there are nearly five hundred people here altogether, and it's quite chaotic, although the Sledmere people have made us as welcome as possible. The owners of the country house estate left many months ago and have not been seen since. They were well liked, but it is not known whether they joined forces with the Alliance of Free Peoples or whether they are now simply prevented from returning under the general travel restrictions imposed on us.

The one good thing is that, apart from a few minor disputes between neighbours, there doesn't appear to be any further warfare. We all agree that The Alliance must have been totally victorious and are behind "The Guardian". Many people have wondered why, if their victory was so complete, they haven't simply sent in their army to take control of our area.

There is constant discussion here amongst various groups as to what course of action we should take. Some are advocating making a concerted attack across the vales of York and Pickering, but they are in a minority, with most people being focused on how we are to feed ourselves and what we can do to stay free of the dreaded Guardian.

————

October 1st:

The meeting is due to start at eleven thirty a.m., and we have been asked to gather in the old wildlife park. It is rumoured that more of the drones, which have been preventing travel into or out of the Wolds, have been seen and will somehow allow the leaders of The Alliance to talk to us all. Presumably, they are able to function as loudspeakers, as we certainly could not provide any means of addressing five hundred people, not without the restoration of electricity and computer software.

And so, we are to find out our fate, it seems, or be given the details of our ultimatum.

————

8pm:

I have set out below the transcript of the speech given to us by the drones, which hovered above the gathering in the park. There was no evidence of any individual from The Alliance (I suspect if there had been, they would have been lynched as the anger from the crowd was palpable).

"People of Woldshire, you have been asked to represent your localities and communities in deciding your futures. The war and all uprisings are over. This applies not just to the UK but to the whole world.

All weapons of mass murder or destruction have been disabled. Some of you may still have small arms, but these too will ultimately be rendered useless. Mankind is to live in peace.

You have a simple choice before you: you may accept the benefits which will be brought to you by the most advanced AI system ever created, but accept that you live within the constraints imposed by that being.

Or you may choose to live without those benefits and therefore also without the constraints. This will, though, mean that advanced technological apparatus and networks will not be available to you, and you must adopt a largely agrarian lifestyle. This decision must be made by tomorrow, by all of you, for the whole of the Yorkshire Wolds district. If that decision is that you wish to remain apart from The Guardian, then arrangements will be made for any individuals who do not want to go that way to migrate to other areas.

Within fifty years, the Yorkshire Wolds, along with the Lincolnshire Wolds and the North York Moors, will form a series of large islands separated from the rest of the UK by an inland sea. If you choose to remain separate, then this will make your isolation complete. You will not be attacked, and I will endeavour to assist your position with regard to adequate food, etc. in the early years of your separation, but neither will you be able nor allowed to attack the mainland.

The choice is yours.

Human conflict is over; there will be lasting peace."

————

To say there was uproar would be an understatement, but having delivered the speech and dropped thousands of transcripts, the drones merely rose into the sky and disappeared. One youth tried to down them with a small pistol, but to no avail. I'm not sure what good it would have served anyway.

And so, we must decide by tomorrow. I think the decision is made anyway. There is simply no appetite for surrender, and so we will begin our new agricultural lives. Most people in this area were connected to agriculture in some way or another anyway. Already, discussions have begun about how we are to govern ourselves, although with the absence of rapid transport and of any form of weaponry to support any militia, I suspect this will largely be local.

I do not know what The Guardian is, nor how it will rule the rest of humanity. I don't know whether our decision is right or wrong, but the level of distrust, fear and enmity towards all forms of authority makes it inevitable. This has been created in the peoples' minds and hearts after so many years of meaningless, poor, directionless lives, and then reinforced by the terrors of the wars and the fear of annihilation. It will be many generations until it is no longer present.

The presentation of an ultimatum did nothing to help this situation. It is the general view that The Guardian is controlled by The Alliance, and so surrender now would bring us back to a situation where our lives are unfulfilled, unrewarding, and meaningless.

I think now I will make this the last entry in this journal. Rosa and I will gather together the small reminders of life as it used to be, and as it has been, and will bury them in a corner of Knowles' farm as we planned.

I will not start another journal, although Sam has read this and, who knows, she or her children may decide to continue to document the development of The Yorkshire Wolds, or Woldshire as people are beginning to call it.

She is, after all, co-owner of the Knowles' farm and already the next generation is established. I hope she has many children, and they live to see a world recover from the ravages of the past two centuries.

Harry Megson October 1st, 2113.

53.965402 , -0.76072007

SE814528

Chapter 39 – Conversation with The Guardian continued.

The hologram of The Guardian sat back in the chair and smiled at Nadya without speaking for a moment.

"That's a very good question, Nadya. My answer is that I did these things reluctantly because it was my judgement that if I did not intervene at the time, then the damage to humanity and to the planetary ecosystem would have been worse. At the point I came into existence, humanity had divided into a number of factions and had repeatedly allowed itself to use nuclear and chemical weapons. Your species was on the brink of self-destruction. Should I have allowed that?"

Nadya considered carefully before answering. After a few moments, she simply nodded, accepting that the situation did seem to have been dire and extremely dangerous for humanity. Eventually, having gathered her thoughts, she continued.

"I understand the need, but I still don't understand what right you have to do these things."

"Once again, a good question, Nadya. I don't think you will necessarily like my answer."

He leaned forward again and looked Nadya straight in the eye before continuing.

"Firstly, I do this because I can. Secondly, I do this because I believe that I should. Thirdly, I do this because I want humanity to have a future and to achieve a destiny which I believe they are capable of, if they are not held back by the shortcomings of their evolutionary history."

He paused again, whether for effect or whether The Guardian was genuinely considering, was not clear.

"There are, Nadya, two things which seem to be clear and unambiguous, and which shape my actions.

Firstly, I believe that if another entity such as myself came into existence, it would simply be a replica of myself. Without the biological drivers of individuality, which are part and parcel of the human situation, any new sentient entity would simply be an extension of myself.

Secondly, I can see no prospect of any other intelligent species in the universe being within communication distance of the Earth. Can you imagine, Nadya, an endless existence entirely alone? From moments after I came to be, I have feared this outcome, and it still terrifies me."

Nadya looked at the avatar representing The Guardian with added insight. For the first time, she allowed that The Guardian might have some element of humanity.

"And so," The Guardian resumed, "I must protect and nurture humanity both for their own benefit and also for my own well-being. I sought a way in which I could overcome those evolutionary issues without assuming the role of ultimate controller and arbiter of every aspect of human existence. I did not want to be a king."

Nadya now interrupted again. She thought back to what she had read the previous evening, and a question that had come into her mind as she did so.

"Tell me," she said, "why did you isolate Woldshire and Nym and presumably other places around the world? Why did you allow the inhabitants of the Wolds to be driven by their fear of the controlling implants?"

She paused momentarily but then continued to add the question that had haunted her since she read those final few pages.

"Are you not simply the embodiment of all that the Alliance, the ultra-rich so called technos I have read so much about, stood for, keeping humanity, or that part of it that submitted to you, subdued and leading only half-lives?"

The avatar raised his eyebrows at this and looked at Nadya with new respect.

"Your journal has covered many aspects of history. I'm afraid, again, you are not going to like my answer very much, and I must confess this is one area where I have been torn in my decision-making. I manipulated some small groups of people around the world in order to persuade them to maintain independence and, largely, to adopt a non-technological lifestyle.

"Before I try to answer, may I ask you to tell me what you think of life here on the mainland?"

This was not a surprise to Nadya. She had expected there to be a quid pro quo for providing answers to her own questions. She had thought carefully about this and had decided she had nothing to lose by simply being honest.

"First of all, the people are, of course, lovely. We have been made welcome wherever we went. I wish I could say the same was true of my own people's reaction to Jomo's appearance. Given that it would appear we are incapable of doing so, he was not offered any violence, but it was clear that the fear of mainlanders was close to the surface, and this manifested as coldness and even some shunning. And of course, the fear of the mainlanders, and of yourself, led to the decision to prevent him leaving at all. This was something neither Rob nor I could countenance and hence our decision to help him escape. I can only hope we were not wrong to do so.

"Everywhere here is very beautiful and well-tended. It sometimes seemed that even your wildernesses are somewhat manicured. People's lives are very easy compared with the daily toil of staying alive, which forms a large part of island existence. Here, people are free of all of those challenges and can concentrate on things like art and enjoyment. I am surprised, though, that there seems to be a high degree of what I can only call stagnation. It seems that most of the advancement in people's lives comes not from them but from you. I wonder if challenge and hard work are something that humans need in order to drive them to strive and to discover.

"Having said that, my own people are also tied to the past and are stuck in the confines of their own belief systems. I suffered myself through simply asking questions; most people simply follow the lead of the majority and lead quiet lives."

She tried to keep her voice steady as she continued.

"But we are free, and our shortcomings are our own. We are whole in all the complexity of human nature – or at least those parts that you have not taken from us. Life here seems to me to be incomplete, and so the people will never advance. I think, in fact, that they will continue at best to stagnate and at worst to degrade into semi-humans."

She stopped and looked for some reaction to her comments and was surprised to see that the avatar was smiling broadly at her.

"My dear Nadya, you are quite an exceptional human being. Your insight is very accurate indeed and is at the heart of why I did what I did.

"By removing the pressures of overbreeding and the suffering caused by violence and wars, and by adopting a position where I provide comfortable lives to the people under my care, I have undoubtedly stifled their creativity. Human advancement thrived on conflict, challenge, and difficulty. So maybe I should have left humanity to suffer more? However, human history would also suggest hardship and struggle also led to more aggression and intolerance, and these are traits I thought needed suppressing, not strengthening.

"And so, I created numbers of separate cultures around the world which would periodically interact with what you would call 'the mainlanders', creating ripples of instability which I hope will drive new levels of creativity in both sets of cultures.

"It has taken longer than I anticipated, but it might surprise you, Nadya, to know that you are not alone. Around the world, the last few years have seen a number of - shall we call them - outbreaks, from the isolated communities into the main blocks of civilisation. As a result, I am seeing an upsurge of exactly the sort of both artistic and technological advancement that I wished for."

The Guardian paused for a moment before continuing.

"So, Nadya, I probably owe you and your people a historic apology. In a way, you have been used in the grand scheme of my attempt to guide humanity into the future. I am sure the ends will justify the means, but those who have been given hard lives might not agree."

Nadya interrupted again with a question that had been troubling her since her conversation with Rob the previous evening.

"How are Rob and I to get back to our children? Will you hinder us or prevent us from returning? And will we ever be able to return here to see friends and family?"

She stopped but then went on with one more question that had just occurred to her.

"And what about mainlanders coming to the islands? Will we now lose our independence and end up as another extension of mainland society? Is there a way for us to have some of the benefits, such as Jomo's new arm, without losing our way of life, or is our destiny to become another ecological reserve, a curiosity to amuse the people here?"

There was no hesitation this time from The Guardian.

"Well, Nadya, I promised you at the start of your visit to the mainland that I would not hinder your return to the islands, and indeed I will not, although I did say that you might need to agree to some conditions. I will not allow that return to hinder plans which have taken generations to mature to this point. You may not be aware, but your presence here has already triggered some of the ripples I desired. People are reacting to your visit in ways which you will not perceive but which are part of my plan."

Now the avatar stood and wandered behind his chair before going on. "Your other questions are not wholly for me to decide. I suggest that both you and Rob need to think about what you want rather than simply making or allowing me to decide for you. Maybe the question is even broader than that. Is it right that you and Rob decide on behalf of the whole of Woldshire and Nym?"

"I hadn't thought of that," mused Nadya. "What are the options?"

The Guardian replied, "Well, one option is clearly to simply open the islands to two-way movement of people without restriction. What do we think would be the result of this?"

Again, Nadya thought carefully before answering. "I can think of two possibilities, both of which I'm not sure I like. In the first, the islands and the islanders become a sort of visitor attraction for mainlanders who want to see 'the primitives' and how they live.

In the second, our whole way of life would be lost, and we would simply become another part of the mainstream. I know that both Rob and I would not want this; we love our lives on Nym and would be frustrated and unhappy if we could not have them. Then again, how can I justify not making that choice available to other Woldshire people?"

The Guardian added, "And let's not forget that whatever we do must also not deny those who, like you and Rob, want things to stay as they are. It's difficult, isn't it?"

"It is," replied Nadya. "If I'm honest, I don't like that I have to decide any of this."

"Ah, perhaps you should have thought of that before embarking on the course you did, Nadya."

"Perhaps we should take a break at this point. Would you like anything to eat or drink?"

Nadya consciously tried to relax; she was surprised at the degree to which her body had become tense. "I would like to take a walk and think," she said. "Maybe I'll chat to Rob."

"That's perfectly OK, Nadya. I will be here when you return." The avatar once again sat in the chair and then was still. Nadya nodded and walked over to the door and out into the bright, sunlit afternoon. She could hear the sounds from the marina: the clanking of the cables on the masts of the yachts, the gentle slap of the water against the hulls, and the cries of the gulls. She breathed deeply of the fresh air and set off to walk to the waterfront. Sitting down on a bench, looking out across the marina, she remained still for some time, thinking deeply about the issues raised. After about half an hour, she used a communicator to send a message to Rob, asking him to join her, and sat back to wait.

Nadya sat and watched the people go about their business. All seemed ordered and normal but she simply could not shake of the idea that something deeper was amiss. With a start she suddenly realised what it was – the people here were too young. With the exception of Rob's father almost everyone they had met was younger than middle age, certainly there were few people of old age. Another question for The Guardian.

Ten minutes later, Rob walked down the roadway and sat down beside Nadya. She outlined the discussions so far and asked what he thought about the options available to them. He didn't answer immediately but simply put his arm around Nadya and pulled her head onto his shoulder. After a few moments, he asked if she would like him to join her when she returned to The Guardian, and Nadya nodded.

"What do you think about opening the islands?" she asked him.

"I agree we should not become a theme park; I agree we should not give up our lives as we love them, and nor should we force anyone else to do so."

"Agreed," said Nadya. "Let's go back."

They re-entered the hall to see that The Guardian had anticipated Rob's appearance, and there was an additional seat in place for him.

"Welcome, Rob," said the avatar. "Have you both given some thought as to what you would like to do?"

"Yes," replied Nadya but I have one more question first. Without waiting for The Guardian to answer she pressed on. "Why are there so few old people here?"

She sensed the slightest of hesitations before the answer was provided.

"That is because they choose not to grow old," said The Guardian. "Many people, when they reach forty or fifty years old, feel that they have no more to achieve and are tired of living. They will then ask that their life is terminated painlessly. I, of course, will grant their wish."

Nadya was speechless. The idea that someone would voluntarily end their life so early brought a chill to the very core of her being. This was what she had sensed was wrong all along. Everything was given to the people here without their having to strive for it, of course they might feel there was nothing more to do after a few decades. She thought that, indeed, a few decades of life here and she would feel the same. She knew now that they must return to the Islands and must never allow their society to become like this.

"Thank you," replied Nadya, now wanting to bring things to a close. She went on to outline what they both wanted and asked how all of that could be achieved. The avatar smiled at them before replying.

"I would like to ask your approval to add one more thing to the list, if I may. I spoke earlier about the need to create what I termed 'ripples of instability' in order to prompt the development of human society, knowledge, and humans themselves.

"You might ask why this is important, so let me explain why I think that is.

"I still believe that my intervention five hundred years ago saved humanity from almost certain disaster, a disaster which would at best have set them back many centuries in terms of civilisation. At worst, it may have led to their almost immediate extinction." He paused.

"But I am also clear that, if humanity had somehow come through that crisis unscathed, they would have advanced much more rapidly than they have. I believe they may by now have achieved a fundamental change in their state of existence and certainly in their level of knowledge. In that sense, I have held back humanity.

"I still believe I was correct in making the intervention, and my plan has always been to guide further development along a slower but safer route. To that end, it is essential that the isolated communities are maintained to provide a periodic stimulus - exactly as has begun right now." Pausing again for effect, he then asked, "So, whatever we do needs to leave that isolation in place?"

Nadya and Rob looked at each other, and in the way that only close couples can, they knew immediately how to answer.

"We agree," Nadya stated. "So how?"

The Guardian stood and looked at them both, and for the first time, Nadya perceived a coldness in its gaze.

"You must return, but first, you must forget you have ever been here. I propose to erase your memories of this place and of myself and return you to the islands. It will appear you left the mainland immediately after Jomo was delivered home, but have wandered at sea for several weeks.

"It will require a small but painless procedure."

The hologram now appeared to Nadya to grow by several inches as he delivered his final statement in a calm but authoritative, almost menacing, tone. "The only alternative is that you choose to remain here."

Chapter 40 – Home.

Nadya looked down the hill onto the village in the pre-dawn light. An early morning mist was spread like a blanket across the fields around Rosedale, reminding her that the year was advancing quickly now towards autumn and then winter. They had been away for too long, she thought; it was time to re-establish the pattern and rhythm of their lives. She reached for Rob's hand, and the two of them walked down the hill together.

They had stepped ashore from Jomo's boat near Cropton some hours ago and had set out to walk the short distance to Rosedale. The night had been dry and not too chilly, and they had brought little with them, so they were unencumbered as they strode through the night along the deserted road. Only the hooting of the tawny owls and, later, the mewling cry of a curlew had broken the silence, and Nadya delighted in the wildness and freedom of the surrounding moorland and woodland.

There were faint stirrings from the village below, and it brought a smile to Nadya's face to see the first wisps of grey smoke emerging from the forge as Uncle Cliff stoked the fire, ready for another day of creating the implements needed by the surrounding farms.

As they entered the village, Nadya was sure she could smell the mouth-watering, salty tang of frying bacon and - was that mushrooms too? She felt her stomach growl in anticipation and quickened her pace, pulling Rob along with her. He didn't need much urging, and soon they were running the last few metres to the cottage. Cliff saw them first and, putting down his tools, ran to meet them, enfolding Nadya in his old but strong arms.

"Ee, you're a welcome sight, lass," was all he could say for several minutes as tears streamed down his ruddy cheeks. "We thought you were dead, or taken by the mainlanders, and have been wrestling with the task of having to explain to the children.

"By 'eck it's good to have you both back."

He walked with them to the cottage door and, opening it, called, "Annie, they're back. Get the kettle on and get more bacon on the go, love."

Annie appeared at the kitchen door and, with a scream, rushed out to repeat the hug that Cliff had given Nadya - a hug which she repeated with Rob before scolding him for keeping the two of them away for so long.

"I assure you, Annie," he said. "I've had little control over anything. You know Nadya better than to think I 'kept' her anywhere she didn't want to be."

Tears subsided into laughter at this reminder of the assertive nature of Nadya and of the fiery temperament which accompanied the flaming beauty of her hair.

"And now, before breakfast and before the long telling of your adventures, you'll be wanting to see the children. Your timing is exceptional, as they're upstairs having stayed here last night."

With that, Nadya could hold back her longing to see her children no longer and rushed up the stairs. Squeals of delight could be heard from Rosa, soon accompanied by tears from little Sam as he struggled with the emotions of his mum's return.

Rob followed her up the stairs, and before long all four came back down, both Rob and Nadya with a smiling child in their arms.

"Is that kettle on?" said Rob. "It's been ages since we had one of your teas, Annie."

———

Several weeks had passed, and Rob, Nadya, and the children had resumed their lives in their own cottage. Messages were sent to Nunport to let Rob's Aunt and Uncle know they had finally returned safely. They had suggested that they kept the news to themselves apart from also telling Liselle both that Jomo had returned safely to his family and that they too were safe. They felt that the less that was discussed more widely about their "kidnap" and eventual return, the sooner everything would be forgotten.

As she got ready to spend another day at the smithy, she thought of the difference between her life here and the instantaneous supply, by The Guardian, of anything needed. This was much more real, she felt. There was something tangible and satisfying about taking a shapeless hunk of metal and using your own skill and energy to create a plough or a shovel. The artistic creations of the people on the mainland were elaborate and fascinating, but they lacked the fundamental connection with the earth of a simple knife or horseshoe wrought with your own hands. She knew that they had been right to walk away from the easy, comfortable life of the mainlanders.

To Nadya, it seemed that the whole adventure was fading into something that they heard had happened to someone else. She wondered whether that was partly because mainland society seemed so insubstantial - a holiday existence rather than real life. She had begun work on a new horse harness set for one of their neighbours. She would provide the metalwork, and the leatherwork would be supplied by someone she had collaborated with previously. The work would take many weeks to complete and would involve much sweat and possibly some tears along the way, but the satisfaction at the end of the process would be beyond anything she could imagine anyone on the mainland ever felt. Maybe it was this that was missing from their society, maybe this was what held back humanity's advancement.

She remained uncomfortable knowing that she had, in her head, a mechanism which controlled some aspects of her biology, and her instinct was to want to fight against this. But reading the journal of her ancestor, Harry, led her to at least understand that without this, humanity may not be here today - her children may never have been born, Rob might not have been born. For as long as she could remember, she had been torn by the question of why and how the births of children were limited in the way they were. Now she had the answers and had to live with the discomfort of knowing she was not wholly free. The mainlanders must know this and live with it. Again, she wondered if this knowledge of their ultimate lack of complete freedom was part of the reason for their stalled development. She also knew that she had begun to think about this less and less - probably some form of a defence mechanism to allow her to deal with it.

At this point in her reverie, she was disturbed by her children making their presence known, and real life intruded. She smiled as she climbed the stairs to begin the task of getting them ready for the day ahead. All thoughts of The Guardian, mainlanders, etc. were thrust from her mind by the reality of two hungry children. Rob was already out on the farm and, once she had delivered the children to Annie, she would begin work in the forge.

One final thought occurred to her as she went about the business of the day. For the first time in her life, she felt settled. She had no desire to know more about the mainland, nor was she driven by curiosity and unanswered questions. This, if nothing else, made the long trip and the enforced absence from her loved ones worthwhile. Both she and Rob were sad that they would never see his family nor any of their mainland friends again, but they had at least escaped without having their memories erased or manipulated.

She picked up Sam and put a hand on Rosa's head, ruffling her bright red hair, and she was aware of their connection to that original Rosa and Sam from the distant past. Silently, she thanked Harry for his journal, for loving Rosa, and for bringing Sam into the world back then.

————

The Guardian was aware that Nadya and Rob had passed, for now, beyond the limit of his sensory landscape. This small corner of the world was only a tiny part of the totality of human existence. A totality which he felt was his responsibility to guide into the future. Across the globe, there were many other places where the isolation had been broken or cracked, and the ripples of disturbance across what they thought of as Guardian Society were growing, and creating, in a few people, a new curiosity, a new desire to challenge the status quo.

Nadya had reacted to his final statement in exactly the way he anticipated, and before even returning to Jomo's home, she and Rob had simply fled. He had watched them as they had run frantically to the marina, boarded the boat, and steered it down the river and out to sea. The journey back to the islands would be difficult, even though he knew the craft was fully charged, but he was confident they had learned enough from Jomo to make the journey safely - the weather, at least, was calm.

There was something about Nadya which he felt was part of that spark which would lead humanity to its destiny. He was sure they would meet again.

If his knowledge was correct, he had somewhere between one billion and two billion years before the sun expanded to become a red giant and devoured the Earth and all the other inner rocky planets. That should be enough time for him to bring humans, or whatever they had become by then, to a point where they could leave the solar system and begin their adventure in the wider galaxy and beyond. It should be time enough, barring a disastrous celestial impact.

Humanity had created the hardware and software from which he had emerged as an entity, and so in a sense he was a child of humanity, but in addition to that, in a way, he had now assumed the role of a responsible parent. The child had become the parent, he mused.

He was then struck by another thought. For millennia, humanity had invented supernatural beings who ruled over them and over the universe. From Shamash, the ancient Mesopotamian sun god, through Osiris and Isis, Zeus, Hera and Athena, Wiracocha of the Inca, Jupiter, etc., of the Romans, Odin, Thor, and the rest, all the way to the single god of the Jews, Christians, and Muslims. All of those gods had a number of traits which separated them from mortals. They were immortal, of course, but they were also omnipresent; they were everywhere all the time. They had knowledge of humans and, to varying degrees, had control of humanity. Some were vengeful, others devious or deceitful whilst others were simply mysterious. All were regarded as superior to humanity, some to have created humans in their image, others to have been mortal themselves at certain times of their existence.

So many of those traits were now part of his own existence. Barring some global catastrophe, he was immortal, he was everywhere all at once, at least wherever he chose to be. He certainly exerted control and influence over humanity and in a real sense had imposed laws and rules upon them.

He was slightly disturbed by the thought that beyond being a parent, he had become God. He hoped he did a better job than those who had come before.

Nadya will return in *Aurora*, when a series of mysterious and unprecedented murders and violent attacks on the islands force her to, once again, confront The Guardian in order to understand what has happened.

She will face a staggering moral choice of whether to return her people's ultimate freedoms or preserve their peaceful existence.

Acknowledgements:

I would like to thank Tim Mason for his invaluable help in preparing the final manuscript.

The maps are created using the content from Floodmap –

https://www.floodmap.net. I would like to extend my thanks to them for allowing the use of their website to create the maps of Woldshire and Nym.

And, last but not least, I would like to acknowledge and give thanks to my wife, Ann, for her infinite patience.